a
CIRCLE
on the
SURFACE

ADVANCE PRAISE FOR

a CIRCLE *on the* SURFACE

"Reminiscent of Kate Chopin's *The Awakening* in both style and approach, Carol Bruneau's *A Circle On the Surface* captures the complexities, right up through to its tragic, memorable ending, of a woman's role in 1940s Nova Scotia."

–Donna Morrissey, award-winning author of *The Fortunate Brother*

"A compelling, unforgettable story of how World War II came to Nova Scotia, *A Circle on the Surface* reveals the sea changes for Enman and Una, a couple about to start a family. Delving into the depths of their lives, Bruneau gives us a powerfully haunting novel."

–Anne Simpson, Griffin Poetry Prize-winning author of *Is*

"Carol Bruneau's latest novel holds your heart right to the last, devastating sentence. In the tender lives of Enman and Una, naïve love and profound loneliness are infused with universal questions: peril and mortality, how and why we love, and the unknowable mystery of a human soul. A compassionate and beautiful read."

–Carole Giangrande, author of *All That Is Solid Melts Into Air*

"*A Circle on the Surface* is a vivid, sensitive, often aching, imagining of a small Nova Scotia community looking fearfully out to sea during the Second World War. The sense of period and place is impressive but the characters and situations are timeless. Bruneau mines each minute, observing in exquisite detail. The book is an unsparing but nonjudgmental portrait of a community and of a marriage facing threats from without and within. Bruneau creates memorable characters, presented in all their complexity and contradictions in a clear-eyed way, and then she goes that important extra step of truly inhabiting them."
–Mark Blagrave, author of Commonwealth Award–shortlisted novel *Silver Salts*

"Carol Bruneau's novel *A Circle on the Surface* brilliantly explores the complexities of family dynamics with well-crafted characters and a most engaging story. She deftly portrays the lives of Maritimers affected by World War II and after as they emerge from a time of darkness into an ever-changing modern world. Once again, Carol Bruneau proves herself to be one of Atlantic Canada's finest novelists."
–Lesley Choyce, award-winning novelist and poet, and author of *The Unlikely Redemption of John Alexander MacNeil*

"*A Circle on the Surface* is an amazingly good read that will only go towards elevating [Bruneau] in the eyes of her longtime fans and the Canadian literary world at large."
–The Miramichi Reader

a
CIRCLE
on the
SURFACE

CAROL
BRUNEAU

Vagrant
PRESS

Copyright © 2018, Carol Bruneau

Vagrant Press is an imprint of
Nimbus Publishing Limited
3660 Strawberry Hill Street, Halifax, NS, B3K 5A9
(902) 455-4286 nimbus.ca

Printed and bound in Canada
NB1349

Cover image: *Open Harbour*, 24"x48", oil on canvas, 2017, Lynn Misner
Design: Jenn Embree

This story is a work of fiction. Names, characters, incidents, and places, including organizations and institutions, either are the product of the author's imagination or are used fictitiously.

Library and Archives Canada Cataloguing in Publication

Bruneau, Carol, 1956-, author
A circle on the surface / Carol Bruneau.
  Issued in print and electronic formats.
  ISBN 978-1-77108-592-2 (softcover).
  —ISBN 978-1-77108-629-5 (HTML)
I. Title.

PS8553.R854C57 2018   C813'.54   C2018-902853-X
                                        C2018-902854-8

Nimbus Publishing acknowledges the financial support for its publishing activities from the Government of Canada, the Canada Council for the Arts, and from the Province of Nova Scotia. We are pleased to work in partnership with the Province of Nova Scotia to develop and promote our creative industries for the benefit of all Nova Scotians.

For my beautiful men: Bruce and our sons.

He has marked out a circle on the surface of the deep
as the boundary of light and darkness.

–Job 26:10

1

SOME DAY SHE WILL LEAVE HIM TOO, AS OTHERS HAVE LEFT HIM. IN THE blink of an eye, before he even realizes his daughter is ready to leave the nest, she'll be gone—as sure as buds become leaves and sounds become notes. Life has this much logic, thinks Enman Greene. He shifts in his scuffed wooden seat, one of a few mismatched chairs in the otherwise empty space. You would expect, given its fancy new digs, the conservatory would be better furnished, he thinks. Piano scales spill through the waiting room's walls, the bleats of a trumpet, some honking clarinet. Couldn't they make this grand, echoey house a bit more comfortable for pupils and parents? At least the light is good, spring sunshine pours in through lofty leaded windows.

More random notes rise and fall, a broken chord. It's Penny's playing he's listening to. He hopes his dear girl's maturing will follow the pattern of a nicely timed melody, though he knows it will have its share of discord, like everybody's. It's how life goes, he thinks, adjusting his cane. Tapping it like a walking stick, as if it's an accessory not an aide. Though some people like to believe life goes according to plan, it's foolish to think it will, and foolish to baby your loved ones. There will be something seriously out of whack if Penny *doesn't* leave. If she finds a man, Enman thinks, may the marriage fare better than his. Though it's jarring to think of Pen married. She's not even a teenager yet. Imagine that baby face becoming a woman's. He can't, not really.

Yet it *is* happening, Pen's growing up. His recognizing it is no epiphany. The odd thing is that until today, her twelfth birthday, he barely entertained the notion. The notion itself is a slap upside the head, as his neighbours in Barrein used to say. They also said, *Enman, you crazy-arsed fool, what paradise have you been living in?* If everything then had been paradise, he thinks, I would hate to see hell.

The sudden blast of a trumpet shakes dust from the chandelier. How are these students supposed to hear their mistakes over the din?

From behind her little window the receptionist points to the clock. Other parents don't wait like this. Twenty minutes left. Does he seem on edge? He should have tucked the money for Penny's lesson into her hand, waited in the car as he did before the conservatory's move from more temporary quarters downtown. But he wanted to see its new surroundings, this turreted, supposedly refurbished pile as grand, once, as the house his wife, his dead wife, grew up in, not that he had ever been inside it. With the Second World War eleven years in the past, the conservatory, like the rest of Halifax, wants to be on the up and up. It's scrambling to catch up with the rest of the world. God forbid another war will come and set the province back a further fifty years.

But here's progress: when he was Pen's age he'd have killed to take lessons in the city. The most his mother had managed for him was some accordion lessons in the room behind the village store. The accordion itself had wound up in a snowbank, heaved there by his father. The conservatory is the last place Enman imagined being, let alone as a parent waiting for his child. It seems only yesterday Pen was toddling around, peanut butter fingers grabbing his fiddle when he finally worked up the nerve to haul it out. Pen had that knack for getting into things he thought were out of her reach. It was especially acute before the sad, saddest, part of their past got put behind them.

Now, squealing violin joins the racket. The noise dips, swells, dips, swells. Like ocean waves, money markets, a panic attack. At least he's not the panicky type, Enman thinks—luckily, given the scrapes he's found himself in. One thing he is certain of: he's never made an instrument shriek like *this*. A symphony of the harbour's horns, groaners, and bell buoys would sound more musical. Yet the receptionist doesn't flinch. Stifling a laugh, Enman clenches. A stiffness moves from his jaw to his shins, to his war wounds, nerve damage. He reaches for his handkerchief, then inside his sportsjacket for the thin little envelope. Finding it safe there, he adjusts his tie, though it's Saturday. It's not every day your daughter turns twelve. Today is the day he has chosen to tell Pen about her mother.

"Steady on, man, think harmony," his old bachelor buddy Hubley used to say. Once he got over some of the guilt he lugged around, Enman had lived for music—other people's music, not his own—as well as for Penny. The same friend would strum a beat-up Les Paul guitar, hoping to entice Enman into accompanying him on violin. They even performed together a couple of times back in Barrein before Una, his wife, disappeared. But he quit playing even before moving to town. There's no one here to play with anyway, and practicing is problematic with neighbours so close, living cheek by jowl. In Barrein there was space.

Penny's rendition of the G major scale drifts in as if breaking through fog. Through the door behind which she disappeared, someone coaxes, "Pretend you're holding an orange. You think Hanon was invented for someone *else*, Penelope?" The Hanon exercises, devised in 1873, says the dung-coloured book untouched atop Pen's rented Willis. This is *1956*, Enman wants to shout, can't you people jazz things up a little? Next, he hears Pen stump through an arpeggio, childish fingers forced into a fruit-hold.

"Penelope, dear, this helps the *attack*."

Since when was playing a military maneuver? No wonder Pen hates practicing. Don't most kids? Yet he insists to her that music is a joy to carry you through sorrow. And playing it keeps idle hands busy, a distraction and a safeguard against less wholesome activities. She's only been taking lessons for nine months. "Music soothes the savage beast," Hubley used to say. Enman never bothered correcting him. "'Breast', you mean." Though playing violin hasn't always been the balm or the distraction Enman needed, he sometimes wonders whether, if Una had had more of an ear for it, music might have eased what ailed her. As for Penny, he doubts that nagging is worthwhile. But how do you teach a child that few gains are made without some degree of pain? "If life was all cherries, you'd wind up with wicked gas," his mother used to say.

Then, abruptly, Pen's playing stops. "Jesus turns our sorrow into dancing," his ma also said, quoting her priest, then chuckling, "Not quite." Seconds later, Penny bursts through the doorway, clutching her books. Her body is like a foal's, he thinks, all elbows and knees, shins bluish below the pedal pushers she *had* to wear though there are still patches of snow on the ground. Her scowl reluctantly shifts to a grin. He pats her shoulder. "Give it a few more weeks. Don't give up. Your birthday gift might help change your tune."

"I'm starving." Her eyes flash an adolescent's impatience. "Are we going to lunch, like you said?" Her plastic barettes refuse to stay put; her straight, fair hair frames cheeks of baby fat. Just yesterday he found her rubbing red stuff on them, lipstick, probably, that Hannah got somewhere cheap. Hannah, who keeps house for them, no doubt encouraged her. It's what Hannah does, however she can, being the closest Pen comes to having a sister. Not that either he or Pen can afford to be choosey, he realizes. It's hard for Penny, not having a mother. If they had stayed in Barrein somebody might have filled in, the woman next door or the one down the hill, either would have helped. He tries his best to look after her. Though not long ago, when prompted by Hannah, Pen asked, "How come you never got married?"

"But I did. You know that."

"Again, I mean." She paused. "Why not to Win Goodrow?"

"Your mother was much better looking."

On the way to the car Penny flutters and flaps her books in the air. They're filled with composers he has never heard of. Their covers are as stiff and glossy as when he purchased them at Phinney's, the music notation book with its leaves of blank staves barely opened.

In the pure April sunshine Pen's eyes have the liquid sheen Una's did, their irises the same cool transparency. Her hair, nothing at all like her mom's, has his ma's ever-so-faint reddish tinge, so he often tells himself.

"Still up for Camille's? Fish 'n' chips still the plan?"

Hannah will be beside herself with excitement, waiting at home with the cake and presents. Someone needed to be there for the deliverymen. If he'd scheduled things differently, if he hadn't planned to speak privately to Pen, Hannah might have come along, except she hates fish.

"You could just get chips," Penny advised, ever thoughtful.

"I still hates the smell."

Acting grown-up, Pen acquiesced: "Suit yourself, Han."

AT THE OTHER END OF the city, Camille's is practically underneath the brand new suspension bridge. You have to wonder at the towering girders, cables holding up not just the roadway but streams of cars and trolleybuses. During the war the harbour was so crammed with convoy traffic that ships would have struck its piers.

Pulling in to the curb, Enman tugs on Pen's hair. "Cod or haddock—or go for the halibut?"

"For the helluvit."

"All right, enough with the language."

"Hannah says it."

"Hannah says lots of things. She can get away with it."

Pen smiles. She looks sheepish, almost indulgent.

Moving up the harbour, a solid bank of fog blots out the Dartmouth side, hides the far end of the bridge. It swirls in tumbleweeds along the asphalt. Penny takes a giant whiff. The air's salty riff is easily Enman's favourite smell in the world, reminding him sharply, as it does, of Barrein. The Gulf Stream mixing with the Labrador Current, they were taught in school.

The fish 'n' chip shop is the same inside as when they started coming here, he and Penny, just after they moved to Halifax. Arborite, stools, a couple of tables with dispensers for ketchup, vinegar, salt. He may be a *tad* overdressed, but who cares? The smell hits them straight away, chip fat and the sweet tang of tartar sauce. Deep-fried everything; just the thought gives him heartburn. But it's Penny's favourite. Except for two fellows at the counter, they have the place to themselves.

"I bet Hannah wishes she came."

He feels for the envelope inside his jacket, and something else, tucked inside the hankie, a tiny token of Una.

"It's just as well she didn't. There's something I'd like to talk about, just you and me—"

"About my present?" Pen looks confused, her curiosity dulled by dismay. "It's not a doll, is it?" Enman smiles, thinking of last year's gift, the walking doll she'd requested, a doll the size of a large child. Pen's look brightens. "I know! It's a puppy! It is, isn't it? Daaad, tell me. I can't wait!"

Neither can he. The gift, the special one, should soon be in place. There's already a record waiting for her, Elvis's new 45, *Heartbreak Hotel*, with "I Was The One" on the flipside. Both songs are much too old for her, he thinks; she asked for the record at Hannah's urging. Then he remembers the tiny present inside the car's glove compartment, the one item Pen coveted, a new charm for the silver bracelet he surprised her with at Christmas. Every girl wants one of these, the clerk at Birks had said, the bracelet adorned with a teeny-tiny cat and a wishing well complete with a windlass. Penny was tinkled pink by the well. He hopes she will like the miniature roller skate he has chosen, which Hannah had wanted to wrap in waxed paper and hide inside the cake she baked. He could limp out to the car and get it, but the charm will keep.

Enman scrapes together all the things he's summoned up about Una, anticipating this day. A day that's been coming since before Penny could talk. Now, as the waitress sidles over, he wonders if his girl is mature enough to hear them.

"Get whatever you want, Pen. A one-piece? Two-piece? Halibut?"

"Just don't say my eyes are bigger than my belly."

"Go on, go crazy." Briefly, he wishes there was chowder on the menu. The first time he played his violin for Una was the first time she cooked for him, clam chowder. Orange-tinted margarine melted atop watery canned milk. Now fear steals his appetite. "Nothing for me, thanks—just water." How to pull together what he remembers and spit it out, without making Una sound awful? He has avoided talking about it for this long. "Fill your hollow leg, little girl—what doesn't get eaten can come home with us. It's your day."

He takes a deep sip of water, a deeper, buoying breath. Pen deserves to know. He's sure about his half of the story, but can only guess at Una's. Guessing is all you're left with, speaking for the dead. Filling in as much as anyone can.

"Sweetpea? Has Hannah told you—?"

"What? About my mother?"

This throws him off. People talk. He has been so careful to filter what she hears, to shield her from gossip. Perhaps after he's told her the hardest part, how her mom died, he'll feel lighter, relieved not just of this duty but of the guilt which led him to put away his violin for good. Maybe he will feel inspired to pick it up again, which he hasn't tried to do since Pen was a toddler. Though its strings may well be dust by now. The way we'll all be, someday, our bodies anyhow, he thinks. Who knows but souls don't become like sounds that other species like dogs can hear but humans cannot, that exist beyond our hearing range? Spirits of the dead lounging in an airy realm where all sounds create harmony.

Just thinking it makes his water go down the wrong way. If Una was in such a place, he hoped it *was* peaceful.

Una had no patience for the idea of an afterlife of any sort. His ma, however, believed in purgatory, a netherworld between heaven and hell. For Ma, limbo was no ethereal place. She had visualized it as a theatre crammed with everyone who had ever lived, each person forced to re-enact all their earthly errors before the audience while simultaneously watching themselves on the theatre's gigantic stage or screen. A play or a movie that ran continuously until God decided it could stop. Possibly this was an idea Ma's priest had fed her.

"Your gran had some funny notions. She didn't mind sharing them, especially with your mom. Your mom was looking after her when Ma died, see. We'd only been married a few months. It probably wasn't the best arrangement."

Listening to such ideas, no wonder Una had felt cooped up. No wonder she left Ma alone when she should not have. It was a small error in judgement; he has long forgiven her for it.

"Notions like what?"

"Oh, about places, imaginary places, where the action runs non-stop. Movies and such."

Pen peers at him, the bridge of her nose wrinkles. "What's bad about that?"

"Well. Just think of the performers, how they'd feel. Think if everybody had to go onstage. Not just actors. Pianists, practising their Hanons with no break." He winks.

He's stalling, of course. She shakes her head, perplexed. It's a good thing she can't see inside his. He's thinking about himself and Una, how if they wound up in Ma's purgatory, facing some eternal judge or audience, in their scenes they might appear separately. And it would not be on a screen, but on a stage of bald granite. He pictured himself standing on a whaleback surrounded by crow- and blueberry bushes, scouring a high barrens for some sign of her, and Una slipping from a rock by the sea.

"Sweetpea?" He takes a smaller sip, it goes down just fine. For all he knows, that's where Una's life ended, near a rock. He walks his fingers along the arborite, along the tabletop's metal edging, playing an octave he pretends to hear.

"She liked to swim." The words float on the lip of his glass.

"You're going to tell me how I was born? I know babies, real babies, don't hatch." She blushes, and he guesses she's thinking of the "baby" in Elvis's "Hotel." God almighty, what he would give to save Pen from the grief behind a song like that!

"I'll tell you what I can." *No one can know the heart of another person*, his neighbour, Win Goodrow, had said. "Hatched. You mean like a duck. A turtle. What's that joke I heard Hannah tell you? About tadpoles. A dirty one, wasn't it?"

He beams at her then and a warmth floods his face, a strange, uncomfortable warmth, the recognition of love, old love, a love he thought was well behind him. He leaves the envelope where it is, and his hankie, too, with its little treasure inside, though he might need to pull the hankie out and blow his nose.

"Do the math," he has always told her and Hannah. When something appears to make no sense, try doing the math. And when Pen asks if he really is her father, that's what he'll say.

If only words could be shaped with the logic of numbers in the way that music was, and could only convey harmony. If only the dead, like stray notes, spoke for themselves.

2

JUNE 1943

IN THE WORLD WHERE UNA GREENE LIKED TO THINK THINGS MADE SENSE, it would be reasonable to say she spied the man first, high above her in the dunes, and well before the man spotted her. She was desperate for fresh air. Not quite summer, the breeze had a nip but a welcome one. It reminded her of being in school. She was glad to be away from the sickroom.

The man had something in his hands and, bringing the object to his face, aimed it at the sea and its infinite blue. Una was too far away to see, at first, that the object was field glasses. Youthful, tallish, bare-chested, the fellow wasn't much more than a stick figure against the cloudless sky. His face was shadowed by glare. Focused though he was on the surf, his presence felt intrusive. This was *her* spot, this sandy pocket above the beach, where Una came every chance she could, to collect herself. A small, secret spot in the dunes, away from the stuffy little cape house in the village, with its knick-knacks and medicinal smells and her mother-in-law. Tending the sick was not what Una had imagined signing a marriage license would mean. She was a teacher, *not* a nurse.

God forbid she and Enman would be stuck in this place much longer. But, should things drag into July, this was a good spot to sunbathe. She had thrown on her suit before fleeing the house, pushing summer a bit. A couple of days shy of the solstice, the sun was almost its strongest—her favourite season, even though she loved teaching. What devoted teacher didn't relish the summer break? Being far removed from the classroom complicated this summer's anticipation, made it bittersweet. Una missed the kids, even their runny noses.

Lying on her stomach, she smoothed out Mrs. Greene's blanket. Easing down her bathing suit bodice, anxious to start a strapless tan, she flattened herself to the blanket's moth-eaten wool. It smelled of Beecham's licorice cough drops, or worse. She longed to relax into its warmth, but something prevented her. It was as if the marram were a field of antennae around her, each blade of grass picking up her every move. Being housebound made her anxious, wary. No, looking after Mrs. Greene only sealed the fact of being marooned somewhere. This place was so small and backward that its residents shunned anyone not born here. As if anyone who wasn't a native should just scuttle for cover under a rock.

"Don't be silly." This was Enman's take on her feelings, her husband given to such comments. Barrein-born and bred, of course, he had been quick to marry her, and she was the better for it. "It's your imagination in high gear, sweetie. Why do you think everyone's watching you?"

Perhaps not *everyone*. Not this particular man, anyway. He had briefly turned his lenses her way before training them again on the water. Perhaps he mistook the waves breaking over shoals as the spume from a pod of whales sounding. She had mistaken this phenomenon for whales until Enman had pointed out and named various undersea hazards, one of which had the colourful name Mad Rock. To the naked eye these rocks and shoals looked like lines of white froth just before the horizon, and not far from the low, rocky island out there with its very old lighthouse. Its revolving beam, which Enman said had aided seamen since the 1700s, was imperceptible now, extinguished or absorbed by the sun. Maybe she just imagined the absence of its revolving flash? The man was, however, as real as the neighbours' whispers and snarky glances. She was pretty sure he didn't "belong," as they said around here, though wouldn't this observation coming from her amount to the pot calling the kettle black?

The males around here were either seniors or infant boys. In the middle of a war or not, there was nothing in Barrein to keep hold of a young man with brains—which Enman had been once, she was certain—and nothing, alas, to prevent one's returning. Blood was thicker than water, apparently. She and Enman had only been married three and a half months when Mrs. Greene took ill, and he had resigned from his banker's position in the city to move them in with his mother. Packing up everything in their flat, he promised it would only be for a little while. Una supposed in a way it was a good thing she hadn't been working. Even in wartime the school board enforced the rule that no married women could teach classes.

For all she knew the man with binoculars "belonged" as much as her husband did. Why else would he be here, even for an afternoon? A weekday afternoon at that, when even in Barrein most men, including Enman, were at work. Enman had managed to take a stopgap job doing the books at the tiny boatyard down the hill from his mother's. An office job, he called it. Working in a dank little building by the wharf, totting up accounts received and payable, to the smells and sounds of a welder, a riveter, and a machinist at work. This, when he had been in the running for assistant manager at the bank's main branch on Hollis Street. And look at her, after twelve years of teaching, left to sponge-bathe an eighty-year-old when she wasn't fetching the old lady's smelling salts or watching her doze. It was not where Una had hoped to be in her thirty-seventh year, not after dedicating herself to the classroom. If she got slightly impatient sometimes and her imagination was overactive, it was out of boredom. Boredom that, she was sorry to think, was largely Enman's fault.

Whoever the man was, he had yet to move off or show signs of noticing her. Her stomach to the blanket, she took advantage of his preoccupation with the scenery to arch herself up enough to pull up the top of her suit. Its stiff cotton and a touch of grit inside the material felt bothersome. Was her body unusually sensitive? Such tenderness meant either that her period was coming or that—perhaps—it wasn't. Which either way meant suffering, as her friend Kit would say. While still giving her all to teaching, Una had been inclined to agree, thinking children were better enjoyed at a distance. But, getting married, Una had soon opened herself to the idea of getting pregnant, having a child of her own to dote on. By Valentine's Day, two months before landing in Barrein, she had thought, Why not? The only problem was Enman didn't seem terribly keen.

A vague hopefulness flexed itself as she rolled over and sat up.

Lowering the glasses, the man saw her then—and only then, she felt sure, as he raised his hand in a startled wave. A stranger certainly, most likely a local who had left a long while ago and had, until now, the sense to stay away. A true local would have pretended she wasn't there. So—a youthful visitor, from town or further afield?

She sat straighter, shoulders back, which had the effect of emphasizing her chest. Posture, said her inner voice, her teacher's voice, the way she had reminded her students: shoulders tucked, head held high, chin lifted. She was no Betty Grable, but now that the man had truly noticed her, he kept looking. Shaking out her striped towel, she draped it over her thighs. Coming home briefly for lunch, hearing of her planned jaunt to the beach, Enman had cautioned her about sunburn, "especially with your complexion." She was fair for having such dark hair. "I've got nothing against freckles, my darling, but if I wanted a lobster I'd cook one." Her husband said things like that, being funny.

When she looked up again the man was gone, his absence highlighted by the forlorn zigzagging line of spruce backing the dune—no sign of him or anybody against a swath of woods or the length of the beach.

A mirage, was he? Mrs. Greene was always nattering about ghosts, the ghosts that inhabited this stretch of shore. Shag's Cove was where the old woman's people had lived briefly, arriving from Massachusetts too many years ago to count, before they had pulled up stakes and moved all of two miles to the narrow, sheltered harbour in Barrein. This was one of Mrs. Greene's favourite memories. Sitting at her bedside, Una had heard it umpteen times. Enman, being at work, was spared these stories. Now, a certain disappointment darkened Una's view of the shoreline before her.

"Come back, whoever you are," she wanted to call out, flexing her toes slowly. Sparkly white sand sifted between them. The sad stirring in her throat echoed the sand's fine drifting. She could have used someone to talk to—and there it was: we all could use someone to talk to. The sense took hold, as it too often did, that, like the beam of light out on the island, she was invisible. Invisible the way women became at a certain age. And following that sense was the thought that life, her life, was swimming by like some finned creature out there in the deeps.

Already it was time to go back, to give Mrs. Greene the pills the doctor from O'Leery prescribed. No one seemed to know what exactly ailed Enman's mother, besides age, although the doctor had mentioned pleurisy, heart trouble, a slew of other possibilities, Mrs. Greene's body simply, inevitably, shutting down.

On impulse, Una made a brief stop on her way back to captivity. She would be back soon enough, taking up position in that upstairs room. It was the bigger of two airless bedrooms in the one-and-a-half-storey house, their space diminished by low, sloping ceilings. If she hurried she would make it to the schoolhouse before the teacher left for the day. The one-room school occupied a shabby building not far from Barrein's only store. The yard outside lacked a tree, let alone a swing. Miss Rooney, fresh out of Normal School, had pupils from grades primary through twelve, although most children around here quit before grade eight or nine. With the school year soon ending, Una thought Carmel Rooney might appreciate help. Una could do some marking, pack up textbooks, order bookplates from The Book Room in town as prizes for Miss Rooney's top students. At least these small tasks would help her keep a finger in the pie, provide some relief from what felt like house arrest. The novice teacher needn't mention a thing to the school board people.

Una arrived at dismissal, ten or twelve children of various heights and ages flying like birds from the coop. She smiled at them as they passed her. Miss Rooney was already outside, beating a blackboard brush against the school's paintless shingles. Looking harried and suspicious, as if Una was angling to steal her job, the teacher thanked Una for her interest but said she had managed this far and any help would be too little too late. Then Miss Rooney disappeared inside, barely murmuring goodbye.

Letting herself into Mrs. Greene's kitchen, Una poured some lemonade and gulped it down, then put a glass of water on a tray with saltines. She should have baked something, tea biscuits maybe, or tried to. She hated baking and the taste of anything made of flour was bound to elicit some tale about the merits of Purity over Red Rose brand, and how Mrs. Greene and Iris Finck, the widow shopkeeper, had a long-running debate concerning these. Stifling a sigh, Una started upstairs. She waited for the old woman to call out, "Is that you, dear?" As if it could or would be anyone else. Age and sickness had not hurt her hearing.

When Una crossed the threshold, she knew things weren't right. Mrs. Greene's breathing was laboured and harsh. The old woman was lying under her quilt in the dimness, the window blind as Una had left it, drawn down to block the sun. Mrs. Greene's eyes were wide and frightened, her hands appeared blue. Una took them in hers and rubbed them. They felt awfully cold. She held the water to Mrs. Greene's lips, but it trickled down her chin onto the neckline of her nightie.

"Help!" Una cried out. She hurried downstairs to call the doctor. His office in O'Leery was fourteen miles away, the nearest hospital, in the city, five or six miles beyond that. Doctor Brunt was presently on a house call, his secretary said. Una hung up and called the boatyard. Enman answered. It would have wasted precious minutes explaining things to his boss, another octegenarian, a relic really. Grizzled and half-deaf, Isaac Inkpen was as old as dirt, Mrs. Greene had once said. It sounded funny then but didn't seem so funny now.

Una spoke slowly and clearly, as if it were a long-distance call.

"I think, dear, it's happening. I think you'd better come home."

3

HOLDING HIS MOTHER'S WAKE IN THE PARISH HALL WOULD HAVE BEEN convenient. But Enman thought it more fitting to use the front room of the house his ma had grown up in and resisted leaving. The house Ma's grandfather had moved there by barge when the mackerel and herring grew more plentiful in Barrein's harbour than in Shag's Cove.

Most of Ma's neighbours came to pay their respects. They filled the small room, its plank floorboards groaning underfoot. Una handed out cups of tea, passed a plate of scorched cookies. The smell of burnt food drifted from the kitchen—she wasn't yet used to the oil-fired range. Most people stood, but a few sat in chairs arranged around Ma's casket, chairs the Goodrows had been kind enough to bring over. All four of the kitchen's pressed-back ones were used to rest the coffin upon, leaving only an easy chair and a rickety ladderback from upstairs.

Father Heaney, Barrein's elderly, hollow-cheeked priest, prayed the rosary over Ma, starting with the Creed. "'…The communion of saints, the forgiveness of sins, the resurrection of the body.…'" Greeley Inkpen's wife, Isla, prayed along. Isla's daughter, miserably pregnant, slouched on the horsehair sofa, hiding her eyes. The priest and Isla fixed theirs on the statuette on the corner shelf, Ma's Beautiful Mother. A porcelain figurine of the Virgin Mary, symbol of mothering's joys and sorrows, it had been found by a lighthouse keeper after a shipwreck, so the story went. A ship that had foundered off the nearby island, all hands lost, the keepsake passed down through Ma's family. A miracle of survival, Ma had called it, wanting Una to have it.

"Long day for you, buddy." Isaac, the Inkpen family patriach in his suit shiny with wear, thumped Enman's shoulder.

Enman glanced at Ma's face, sharp-featured and sunken in death. "The longest."

The first day of summer, a hard time to leave. Ma had loved the heat, he thought. Wouldn't go near the beach, though, until mid-August, convinced that any sooner than that, swimming was a death wish, the water so cold.

Una's friend from town came and stayed only long enough to drop off flowers. Hubley Hill gave Enman a curious look at that. Enman returned his look. "Should have brought your guitar along, Hill."

Una put the flowers in a vase on Enman's desk, next to a big bunch of pink and purple lupines Isla had picked from the hillside near their house.

"'Salve, Regina, mater misericordiae: vita, dulcedo, et spes nostra....'" Father made the sign of the cross over Ma, then he and Isla sang two verses of "Saint Patrick's Breastplate," her favourite hymn. Isla's voice reminded Enman of the furnace whirring as it started up in the apartment house where he and Una had lived in Halifax. Isla's daughter rolled her eyes.

Isaac nudged Enman's arm. "Marge was a good woman, a smart woman. She thought the sun shone out your arse." The old man rubbed his stubbled jaw. "You wouldn't have survived if you'd been left to your old man." Enman had known Isaac all his life and mostly feared him. But since coming back to Barrein as an adult he was getting to know Isaac better, Isaac's sons too, Greeley and Robart. Greeley was the boatyard's machinist and mechanic, Robart its riveter and sheet-metal worker, and young Edgar Lohnes, who lurked in the hallway smoking, was Inkpens' all-purpose labourer.

Robart elbowed Isaac, pulled a flask from his pocket.

"What are you thinking, boy? Not in Marge's house, put it away." Isaac's raspy voice turned almost unctuous as he raised his teacup to Enman. "Your ma could be a battleaxe, no question. But that was a good thing." Then Isaac told the story of Enman's father finding Enman in Lester Finck's living room behind the store, Lester demonstrating how to play "Jack was Every Inch a Sailor" and how, overhearing this while buying cigarettes, Cleary Greene got so irked, jealous about Lester one-upping him over his son, that he'd barged in, ripped the accordion from Lester's hands, and, well, everyone knew about the snow damage to its bellows and how Cleary ended up replacing it.

"Your mother didn't brook fools easily. Used to see her in her garden. Missed her lately. Can't believe she's gone, can you?" Sylvester Meade, the neighbour between Ma's house and the boatyard, stared at his shoes as he spoke. One of Sylvester's sons and his wife wolfed down cookies as their two little boys played tag around the mahogany coffin. "Stop, now." Win's voice was sharp.

"It's good to have you back, Greene"—Isaac stuck his foot out to trip the bigger kid—"You've got your job as long as you want it. Remember that."

Una set the plate of cookies down on top of the desk. Enman knew she was listening.

"Well, now you've got the house, plenty of room for you and the Missus. Room to fill it with kids. Now that you're here you're here to stay, I guess."

"That's the plan?" Enman voiced it as a question not a statement. Una came close and pressed her little high heel into his foot. Then she slipped out of the room with a tray of Ma's cups and saucers. He heard her working in the kitchen. Heard the back door opening, the squawk of seagulls outside. Burnt offerings, someone observed.

"Call the fire department." Clinton Goodrow laughed and Win shot Clint a look. "They'll be here soon enough, don't joke. Those civil defence folks. They'll be busy tonight, I heard. They said on the radio." Everyone turned to look at Enman's wireless, as if trained to do so, and in the process admired it. The latest thing, it shared its mahogany cabinet with a phonograph. Planning the funeral, Enman had been too busy to tune in. Isla trilled the famous code words meant to prepare them all for a blackout. "'B is for butter.'"

Una reappeared. "Yes, and I'd like to know what they'd do in the event of an air raid, with their little air pumps and hoses. Those ARP people." She let out a dismissive *tsk*. "In school, you know, we taught boys and girls how to recognize a Messerschmitt."

"Is that right." Isaac smiled. "Imagine that, little kids identifying enemy planes. Suffer the little children, eh, Father?"

The priest tightened his grip on his missal. "You miss the classroom, Mrs. Greene?" Enman gave Una an encouraging smile. It hurt to smile, the strain of Ma's death catching up with him. The shocking strangeness of it. Una did not smile back, only nodded. There was a small silence.

"Have you had Una out to the island yet?" Clinton could be trusted to lighten awkward occasions, except he forgot how Enman hated boats.

"What's out there, anyway?" Una sounded half interested.

"Oh well. A lot more than a lighthouse, don't you know. It's got the devil's staircase."

Una looked mildly intrigued. Clinton regaled her with the tall tale everybody knew, about a straight black crack in the granite out there, with steps in it leading into the sea.

"An intrusion dike." Enman knew the geological term. "Like the boulders around here are 'erratics.'" But Una wasn't listening to him. Clint had launched into foolish lore, how at a dance one night a handsome, finely dressed stranger charmed the prettiest girls, hogging them all to himself. Chasing the stranger from the hall, their husbands and boy-friends saw he was wearing only one boot, his other foot being a hoof. "A cloven one." Enman winked.

Una's expression was half smile, half smirk. "Oh, go on."

Clint continued. In his wake, the smoking trail the stranger blazed straight into the ocean hardened into a perfectly formed staircase of black stone.

"Magma." Enman stroked his wife's arm, let his hand linger at her elbow. Its sharpness through her sleeve was a comfort, it anchored him. She reached for his hand and squeezed it.

Then Win remarked how nice it was having the long bright evening, sparing them a little longer than usual the rigamarole of blackout blinds and candles. She brushed crumbs from her dress, watched Isla go to help Una wash up. Clint lifted two of the chairs they brought. "Darn those air raid people and their precautions, anyway. Surely they'd make allowances for a wake."

Isaac put on his cap and leaned in to Enman. "Take all the time you need, boy. But don't forget, we've got that meetin' in a few weeks. I'm counting on you to ace it."

Greeley and Robart stayed where they were. Greeley eyed Enman. "Come on outside, we'll raise a toast. What's a wake without a tot?"

Enman hesitated. He thought better of doing so. But as the room emptied, he couldn't stand the thought of being in the house with the body and only Una nearby, God love her efforts to feed people, at least she tried. Ma's death had come as no surprise, but the neighbours' camaraderie did. Just their presence helped him—though some had not shown up: Lester Finck's widow, Iris, and Barton Twomey, but that was fine. And Clint's crazy tale about the devil added levity to things, until Enman imagined Ma picking up where the priest left off: "Oh blessed mother of God, to thee we raise our cries, mourning and weeping in this valley of tears."

Life was a vale but there were plenty of things to help you through it.

"Sure, just a little shot, fellas. Nothing wrong with one, one would be all right."

The sun had just set, and the three of them stood out back in the treeless yard, passing Robart's flask of rum. The house was on a low knoll overlooking Barrein's tiny harbour and the shoreline's rocky fingers of land. They reached into the sea as far as you could make out, and further along near Ma's old birthplace a headland rose, spiky with spruce. It had made Enman think of a porcupine when he was a boy, and still did. From up here you could see most of the village, even in the deepening dark, ten or so houses scattered along the shores and head of the inlet, small wooden capes like Ma's, like his, now. Five rooms, including the bathroom that had been created by one bedroom being halved, a tiny hall and staircase, a cellar not much deeper than a crawl space, an outdoor privy.

At least two people from each house had been present this evening, a few Enman hadn't seen in years. Across the harbour, just opposite, he could see the arched gable window of the Fincks' house, the tall, forbidding place which had always housed the store and post office, and would continue to, he expected, until Iris, like Ma, expired. There was something soothing, restorative, about the view. He supposed it was because it contrasted so sharply with the city, where you were hard-pressed to find a quiet spot away from servicemen roaming the streets. He had known this day was coming, that the house would end up being his, and he had dreaded it. But now thinking of the contrast made him calm.

Greeley passed Enman the flask and he took a good long haul from it. It had been some time since he had allowed himself a drink. Robart talked business, so much repair work coming to the smaller yards since the major shipyards couldn't keep up. "Well, all that loss out there"— Greeley waved the flask, gesturing towards the sea—"someone should benefit. Better us, I guess."

Enman thought, maybe not for the first time but with a bit of a shock, how it mightn't be so bad staying. He could do a lot worse. Robart talked about the meeting coming up in July, the meeting at the bank where Enman had recently worked. At the far end of the village, in the opposite direction from where the beach lay, past the church and the cemetery, a dull light twinkled at Barton Twomey's place. Not everyone worried about a visit from the defence warden, a volunteer based in O'Leery, or about being fined.

"How are you doing, anyways?" Greeley's voice had turned tentative. He wasn't asking about losing Ma, Enman knew. Robart and Greeley were eight and ten years younger than he was, respectively. Perhaps being younger made them curious, in a vaguely eager way, about what had happened to him. More curious than their father was, Isaac already knowing how it felt, maybe, being slightly hobbled.

"Oh, you know. I've still got pain. But my old legs, they work fine. Fine enough. Can't complain." Still, he wished Greeley hadn't brought it up. The moon had risen, a full, bright moon, which cast an explosion of light over the sea's blackness. Enman watched the horizon uneasily. The low, dark outline of the island was barely visible, its lighthouse in full darkness. The Devil's Staircase, indeed. "They don't always black out the beam, though, do they?"

Both men shrugged. "Sometimes yes, sometimes no. It's just routine, this blackout business." Robart took a drink, wiped his mouth, set the rum atop the huge rock shielding Ma's flowerbed, a formation she had likened to a rhinoceros. Greeley lit a cigarette. Enman lit one too.

"Must've been hell on wheels out there, buddy." Robart held his cigarette out for a light.

"One way of putting it." Enman tried to laugh, but his breath felt locked in his chest. There it was, alive in his imagination: the night almost a year and a half ago when he had been out on that same sea and his ship got hit. He could still almost hear the whine of the torpedo aimed towards them, its shearing blast hitting the tanker he had signed himself onto.

"What were you doin', joining the navy, of all things?" Greeley must have heard Isaac's stories about Cleary Greene throwing his son off the wharf. "Sink or swim," Enman's father had said. Enman was only three or four years old. He'd grown up hating the water, hating the sea. Sink or swim, though. His former manager at the bank, who had become a good friend, almost like a brother, had joined the merchant marine. George Archibald had planted the idea: the best way to overcome fear is to face it.

"Why the hell not the army, though?" Robart looked mystified.

Enman shrugged, picked up the flask, shook it. "Who knows. I thought I was being brave. I hated walking. Never saw myself marching." He laughed again. He hoped neither of them heard his voice quaver. "Don't suppose you've got more of that stuff tucked away somewhere? That barely wet my whistle." Remembering that fiery February night at sea, the last time he had seen George alive, made him want to drink.

"Could always pay a visit to Twomey."

"Not a thirst strong enough to send me to that bastard."

Una came out and stood on the doorstep. She looked a bit at a loss, waving to him. "You're not leaving me alone in there." Her face and the bits of grey in her curls picked up touches of moonlight, the same silver light outlining the flowerpots in the mudroom window. Ma is the one who's left alone, he thought. Turning, nodding to both brothers, he stubbed out his cigarette, followed Una inside. The kitchen was tidy, Ma's dishes were neatly stacked on the little shelves, the baking things salvaged with a good quick scrubbing, and put away.

"I've put fresh sheets on, cleared out the last of the medicines and that." She had stripped Ma's bed after Doull's, the undertaker, had come from O'Leery and taken the body to prepare it. She had washed all the bedding and dried it on the clothesline where the old man's rosary still hung, placed there by Ma to ward off bad weather, a precaution.

"I'm not sure I'm ready to sleep in her bed." Or share the bed his parents had all through their long rocky marriage.

"I know. But it's only for a little while, isn't it. And it'll be more comfy." A step up from sharing his boyhood bed, Una meant, the spool one in the room divided to make space for the bathroom.

She took his hand, drew him past the front room, dark as a cave through the open doorway, led him up the stairs as steep and narrow as a ship's ladder. After Enman and Una had moved in, Ma had not descended them again.

Una had done a good job of clearing out his mother's effects, packing them into cardboard boxes, sliding the boxes into the cupboard under the eaves in his old bedroom. Una is nothing if not efficient, he thought. When they met six months ago she'd told him how she could control with ease a room of forty or fifty ten-year-olds. He had told this to Ma to impress her.

Ma, however, had not been as impressed as he hoped. "I don't approve of wartime marriages, son."

"But this one, you'll see, is different."

"There's a war on, last time I heard." She hadn't attempted to hide her dismay. "You married someone you knew for three weeks."

Two weeks, actually. But, fudging it slightly, he had corrected her: "A month, Ma."

"That quick on your feet, you could've married Win before that Clinton came along."

The room had been stripped of Ma's presence. But now her absence was palpable, it was a presence in itself which Enman felt as a numbness that hovered about his ears and shoulders, a sensation that was neither chilly nor warm but *there*. He balked, undressing, folding his clothes over the ladderback chair his father had used for that purpose. Then he slid under the sheet beside his wife. Turning to him, Una pressed herself against him in the mattress's sag. Her nightie had ridden up a little, her legs warmed his. The soft warmth of her skin helped drive the numbness away.

"About this baby business." She curled closer. "You know, after *forming* so many kids in the classroom, I wouldn't mind forming one of my own. It would be fun, wouldn't it?"

"One of your own? Takes two, I thought." Then he kissed her hair, glad just to have the wake and its prayers behind him. First thing in the morning would be the funeral mass, followed by Ma's burial. Though the moment struck Enman as being an odd time to discuss babies, he chose to take comfort in it. "If that's what you'd like, as I told you before, I suppose then I'm up for it."

4

SNUGGLED NEXT TO ENMAN, UNA LISTENED TO HIM DRIFTING OFF. EVEN with her talcum powders and colognes replacing Mrs. Greene's dried-up potions arranged on the dresser, it was dismaying to lie in the old woman's spot. When her own mother died, Una had the cleaning lady help sort, then bundle everything off to charity. Even with assistance, dismantling the trappings of her mother's life had taken many months. An inverse of *Rome wasn't built in a day,* a saying both Una's parents favoured when advising patience all through her growing up. Her mother only stopped saying it when Una began looking after her, while figuring out what to do with her own life. "Where would I be without you?" her mother often said, along with something Una remembered just as vividly. "A child is a comfort, you know—unlike a husband. Sadly, you can't have one without the other." A tacit recommendation against marriage, it seemed rather dead-end. It wasn't until after her mother died that Una enrolled in teacher's college.

Una had never thought she would marry, nor had she thought she wouldn't. She had felt the same way about having children. Having wed

Enman without hesitation, she suspected that the saying about building Rome—as well as the saying about doing as people did when in Rome—applied to marriage as much as it applied to having children. Her doctor in the city, Dr. Snow, not the quack in O'Leery, had said as much during her appointment in February, just after Valentine's Day and before her birthday. After a two-day honeymoon at the start of January, she and Enman had celebrated their first month of marriage by dining out most evenings at the Green Lantern or Diana Sweet's restaurant, much to her relief.

Seeing Dr. Snow, she had simply wanted to ensure that all was well, all was normal.

"Timing is important, if you're thinking of starting a family." Snow had inspected her with his warm brown eyes. "You might begin doing some exercises. Tighten up the pelvic floor." He even recommended that she take her temperature first thing each morning, and afterwards she had rushed to the drugstore to purchase a thermometer.

"Each fraction of a degree can help you determine," the doctor's voice came back to her now, as Enman shifted slightly in his sleep, "when you and your husband should be most successful."

"We're both good with numbers." She'd said it to ward off any embarrassment. "Enman a little better than I, though."

"Now, remember, you're an active participant. How old is hubby, again?"

Hearing that Enman was forty-five, Dr. Snow had made a few more recommendations. "Don't forget to write down your readings—it's important to keep track." He also suggested having a pillow under her bottom to help with the angle of penetration, a recommendation that made her blush. "Oh, and stay still afterwards. Don't be jumping up to have a cigarette."

This would hardly be an issue, she said, since she didn't smoke.

Unaware of her troubles, however, Snow hadn't raised the issue of what effect stress could have on the whole enterprise—the stress of an occasionally surprised, hungry, or balky husband. Or of her nerves and nighttime worries, occasional insomnia over what had happened, the reason she had been let go from her job. It had taken place just before Christmastime, the days leading up to the holidays.

And no one could have predicted Mrs. Greene's illness.

Especially on the eve of the funeral, sleep might have offered respite and would have, if not for Enman's snore, his bearish heat trapped in the mattress's sag. His poor mother's olfactory ghost infused there, the memory of her wheezing from its springs. It was almost enough to make Una want to creep back in to his childhood bed and sleep alone.

After some quick, perfunctory lovemaking—more a comfort, a distraction to him in his grief, than any move toward passion—the wetness down there had dried to a chalky feel, the way salt would after a swim.

His snoring, God help them both, was like a party noisemaker unfurling in and out. And given the mattress's softness, Una thought, no wonder Mrs. Greene had suffered a dowager's hump. The thought of her own hands massaging it made saliva thicken in her throat. Looking after her mother had not meant such intimate care, this had been left to a nurse. The things that age, illness, and childbearing inflicted on women's bodies, not to mention the work piled on by tending children, cooking, and housekeeping! Somehow Una had expected to avoid most of this. Too much work had not been her mother's problem nor had it led to her demise. She died of isolation while keeping up appearances—cocktails before and after dinner, sherry before bed—while Una's father had entertained his business friends, when he wasn't overseeing the refinery. His position in Imperoyal had kept Una and her dying mother more than comfortable, until his death brought to light debts no family could recover from. When *her* mother died, the doctors had largely blamed the Change. Hot flashes and other symptoms of bodily flux exacerbated by gin.

One of the things Una liked about Enman, that had appealed to her from the start, was how he mostly shied away from liquor and his remarks that you didn't need it to have a good time while mixing and mingling. She supposed a drink or two after the wake was more than excusable, understandable.

Now she contemplated mixing and mingling, but of a different sort, the mixing and mingling of cells, although she preferred to fancy it being more than simply biological. Romantic. Cells smitten with each other, embracing in a hotel's luxurious bed.

"Despite all my tips, the point is, it should still feel effortless, enjoyable," Dr. Snow had said.

Una's imagination skipped ahead to an infant sleeping peacefully in a nursery, and not in a cramped, untidy room like the one next door. There was barely room in there for her textbooks and teaching notes after adding Mrs. Greene's things to the clutter. What Una visualized was a perfectly formed, impeccably behaved baby in a freshly painted white crib, ten perfect little fingers, ten perfect little toes. Waking, smiling, reaching out to be picked up, held. An abiding comfort in her old age, a compensation for the children whose smiling faces she was missing.

Would it be cheating just now to get up? She had lain quite still for a while. She would have liked tea. A warm drink in the middle of the night had often helped her sleep, after the dressing-down she'd received in the principal's office.

The downstairs clock chimed twice, as unreliable, though, as when Mrs. Greene wound it. Then Una remembered the corpse lying downstairs, the poor woman. So much for tea. And so much for sleep, as elusive as civilization and the city presently seemed.

Perhaps by now those cells had turned in, were rolling over. Soon she and Enman would pick up where they had left off, but with a child. Enman would want it to be raised somewhere with paved streets, municipal water, decent schools.

A nursery in a spacious, solid house in the city.

Meanwhile, the man could sleep through Armageddon.

A DULL SENSE OF OCCASION filled the house next morning as Enman went downstairs, leaving Una to wash and dress. In the kitchen, he had pulled up the dark green blind, and sunlight passing through the lace curtains made patterns on the walls. As he lit the stove she listened to the oil glugging from its carboy. In town, a place with such a stove would rent as a cold-water flat. As he filled the kettle the electric pump in the cellar whirred. Mrs. Greene's cat scratched to come in, rubbed around Enman's shins.

"Maybe our Tippy's all the ankle-biter we need, Una, what do you think? He's easier to mind than a baby would be."

She couldn't tell if he was joking and kept mum. Opening some sardines, Enman flicked one into the cat's dish.

"A good day to go in the ground, I guess. Father Heaney said he'll meet us at the church."

If not for the body, which Doull's would soon come to transport, Una would have slipped into the front room and put on the radio, just to add some life to things. Instead, she boiled eggs. It felt strange eating from the teaspoons she had so recently used to feed Mrs. Greene small servings of broth.

Somewhere nearby, the Meades' mongrel bayed and seagulls squawked. Una peeked outside through the kitchen window. On the ground there wasn't a single cookie left. Not a leaf stirred in the wild rose bushes or on the plant snaking up the trellis Enman had set against the boulder, overkill if ever there was, given the garden's fledgling state.

She had never seen him so quiet. She spoke to fill the silence: "Do you know what one of my pupils asked once? Right in the middle of doing times tables." She paused. "'Where do birds sleep, anyway?' It was the cutest thing."

He drew what seemed a patient breath. "And what did you say, Una?"

"'Well. I have no idea.' Was I supposed to lie? It was a good question. I still don't know the answer, do you? The whole class looked at me, stunned."

"At least you were honest." He smiled wanly. "I guess that'll be Doull's I hear now?"

At last, it was the undertaker, remarkable for his pale, well-groomed hands and creased black suit, waiting at the door.

5

MID-JULY 1943

DEATH HAS A WAY OF SLOWING THE DAYS SURROUNDING IT, SLOWING IF
not stopping you in your tracks, Enman felt the need to explain to Una.
Even as the rest of the world continued to spin like the rides at Bill Lynch's
fair.

"I get it." She almost seemed to brush him off. But it was his way
of explaining his distraction and any lapse in his attentions, whether
real or imagined. At least the numbness around Ma's absence had
lifted, evaporating into what felt like an airier emptiness. Going back
to Inkpens' had helped, but he would feel better once today's meeting
was behind him.

"The meeting that's to your credit, you mean." Una was quick to
bolster his spirits. "Take advantage of it. You are going to speak to them,
aren't you, about getting your job back?"

It wasn't enough that Una was eager for him to do this, Isaac and his
sons expected him to secure funds needed to cover operating expenses

until a certain customer paid up. The customer was the navy, the bill for repairs Inkpens' had made to a badly damaged cutter. The pressure Enman felt had led him to have a drink or two the night before with Isaac's sons, from the forty-ouncer Robart kept in the safe. But there was more to his nerves than business. The meeting he had with the Inkpens at the bank meant travelling to the city by water. Enman had offered to drive, but all three Inkpens, Isaac, Greeley, and Robart, as well as that youngster, Edgar Lohnes, only laughed. "We want to get there, man. And what if you can't drive back?" Because the trip to town was supposed to be for pleasure, too.

It was true, the Chev wasn't the most reliable. "Beulah," George's widow called the car she gave to Enman after the sinking. "I don't believe in naming cars after girls," Una had pointed out the first time he'd taken her on a real date just before New Year's, a mere block from their place, to see a movie at the Oxford Theatre.

"Do you feel the same about boats?"

"No." She had laughed. For a month or two he had quit calling the car "Beulah" to please her, before lapsing back into a habit that stuck. He knew not to mention the book at Inkpens' that compared a ship to a woman, about no two ships behaving alike, nor any one ship performing the same way twice in the same fashion. *She is as capricious as a woman in fair weather, and as patient in foul.*

HE WOKE WITH HIS TONGUE glued to the roof of his mouth. The sun coming into the bedroom hurt his head, and he tried not to think too much about the trip ahead, the five of them motoring out in the *BlueBelle*, Inkpens' thirty-foot cape islander. His parts shrivelled just thinking about it, far less about the meeting than the getting there and back.

Una was still sleeping, a mixed blessing, as having breakfast with her would have made him want to linger over tea, as they had on Quinpool Road. A slurry of foolish excuses for staying ranged through him. But humming his favourite bit of Dvořák's *New World* symphony, he dressed in his best suit. He nudged the cat aside with his shoe, then, feeling guilty, stooped to scratch its chin. Ma had named it because of its missing hind leg, a casualty of a dog's attentions. If Sylvester Meade and his sprawling clan fed their Chubby properly, the creature might not have attacked, he thought, following Tippy outdoors.

The sea mirrored the pale, uncluttered sky. It was a gift of a morning, at least it was with his feet on terra firma. His fears were hardly ancient ones, about the sea's teeming with monsters like giant squid and octopi. His worries had to do with how deceptively calm and empty the sea appeared, how fickle he knew it was.

Losing sight of Tip, he crossed smooth granite to Ma's cosmos and marigolds and a few scraggly nasturtiums and sweet peas flagging in their bed. He had planted them when Ma couldn't, an effort that seemed important at the time. If not for kelp shielding their roots, the sun would have done them in. Already the day promised to be unusually warm, a scorcher.

Funny, how all the elbow grease in the world often yielded nothing, and sometimes barely lifting a finger wrought magic. He wondered how hard or how easy it would be for Una to get pregnant.

Careful not to muss his clothes, Enman unrolled the hose. The last thing he needed was the kid behind his teller's wicket noting mud on his pants, the kid who'd joined the bank when Enman enlisted and no doubt had his sights on being the assistant manager. But the rain barrel jerry-rigged to the downspout on the sea-facing side of the house was bone-dry. Go figure, when rain and fog were the rule, nine summers out of ten. Yet, along Sylvester's side of the fence the knotweed thrived, impervious to dryness. Ma had complained about its spread. Fetching bleach, seeing that the Meade's dog was tied, he doused the weeds, guarding his suit.

Then he hurried to peel an orange and leave it on the table for Una, their custom since the first nights they spent together, which seemed ages ago, suddenly. Stuffing the ledgers into his satchel, he inspected himself in the mirror. Decent enough.

The run to town would take a few hours. But the sweet peas by the front stoop needed mulching and there was no need to rush. Isaac and the others knew the bars didn't open till noon.

He found Ma's trowel, hoping Una wasn't up and looking out—she'd be liable to call down and invite him to share the orange, as in the days before Ma's illness. The routines of Ma's care had put an end to the cosy little rituals they had settled into earlier in the marriage. Routines of care he had happily delegated to Una, though he avoided saying so, and cosy rituals he hoped would return. Digging in a bit of seaweed, he struck metal; more than rocks grew from the soil. The remains of a toy truck glinted, transporting him back to being seven: he was kneeling in the grass, Ma shouting from the doorway, "Have you seen your father any-wheres?" Cleary staggering up after some altercation with Lester over their wives, stumbling inside. "Like oil and water, those two," Ma used to say, flushing when people hinted that Lester would have made a better husband.

The Chev was parked, bald tires and all, at the top of the lane. Why hadn't he said he would meet the others in town? Because, driving back inebriated was not something he would do nor would he want known. They teased him enough at Inkpens', though their razzing was good-natured: Enman Greene in his pinstripes, thinks his shit don't stink. He always had been different, Ma had ensured it. There was comfort in knowing he wasn't—entirely—a chip off the old man's block.

The night before, Isaac had told him to be good and sure he wore his best suit.

"Where's the fire, bud?" Clint yelled from his sunporch when Enman passed. Win, who was standing next to him, called, "How does your garden grow, hon? Nothing new with Una?" Win would talk the shirt off you. But such talk was her friendly way of showing that life after a loss went on, that life would return to normal. "Seen her heading off to Shag's again. Not swimming, is she?"

Everyone, including the Mounties, knew Shag's Cove was where people went to comb for "treasure," supplies that washed ashore from ships, or to watch the non-existent "submarine races," as young people joked, before anyone thought of the present U-boats or wolf packs, forgetting those of the First World War. Then Win started in about some pair being caught in the dunes—so-and-so with another so-and-so's wife, pants to his knees, and Barton Twomey, out duck hunting, stumbling upon them—and Enman felt warm under his collar. It was a hot day to be wearing wool, not to mention a tie. "Poor bugger, lucky he didn't shoot." Clint laughed. "Imagine, thinking they wouldn't get caught."

Enman couldn't help wondering if Una had not gone to Shag's Cove the afternoon Ma died, she might have reached the doctor sooner. She had apologized, of course. It still bothered him a little, but he saw no point in rubbing her nose in it.

Being in Barrein made it easier to let go of things that seemed pointless. Another example of pointlessness was wearing ties, a city formality. Aside from at Ma's funeral, he had pretty much stopped wearing them.

"Poor, poor Twomey." Enman rubbed his jaw. "That model of good behaviour." Then, wishing he could take it back, he grinned, as if all that awaited was a simple day of making out invoices.

All three Inkpens and Lohnes were waiting at the wharf, also dressed in their funeral clothes. The *BlueBelle*'s hull had recently been scraped of barnacles, caulked, and freshly painted. "Have something better to do, or what?" Greeley slapped his back. Famous for hoisting barehanded a swordfish out of water, he looked a little odd wearing a suit Isla had no doubt picked out.

Isaac hiked up his shiny-kneed trousers. "Well, I wouldn't blame you, Greene, with Foxy up the house there. Slept late, did you? She finally had to kick you out? Just wait till she's got a bun in the oven. Then it will change." White-haired, freshly shaven, the old man was a formidable sight despite his stoop and the drag of his pants, a sign of his shrinkage. Isaac had been a pal of his father's, always the taller of the two, Isaac and Cleary. Funny to think they had been friends, Enman decided, and that most of his own life he had feared Isaac, along with admiring the man. Isaac's diminished height had not reduced his stature. "What're we waiting for, gentlemen? Hallowe'en?"

The tide was low. Isaac's sons climbed down and into the boat, Robart taking position in the wheelhouse. Greeley helped his father on the ladder. Edgar Lohnes leapt around, a scrawny monkey untying ropes. Enman peered down at Greeley's prematurely thinning hair and the ruddiness of Isaac's ears poking out from under his cap. "What?" Isaac looked up. "You've got the figures? Don't stand there froze. We're gonna have ourselves a time."

Enman gripped the satchel. Of course he had the figures, no great thanks to Isaac's accounting. The boat's engine burbled. Robart gazed up impatiently.

"You do have an in with that banker, right?" Isaac sucked his teeth.

"No need to be chicken, old buddy. Anyone hear the 'B as in butter' message? Listen. Nothing's going to happen."

Keeping his gaze on the pilings—their greeny black slime under nets of reflected sunlight—Enman descended as quickly as possible, the satchel a lifebuoy. Taking a seat in the stern, he avoided looking at the creatures clinging to the pilings below the tidemark—mussels, barnacles, purple starfish—and at the kelp waving from the bottom. All that life made him think of floating bodies, bodies drifting, then consumed by fire. He tried to focus on the fact that, even at ebb tide, the water was the same green as Tippy's eyes and Una's favourite dress.

Her words came to him, jarring if true: Look at the cat, *he* manages all right without a leg. As if a ship getting torpedoed was in any way, shape, or form comparable to a feline being mangled by a dog. You mustn't let a tragedy spoil your life forever, Una had said when they first met. "Really," she had reminded him, "you've had *amazing* luck." Her words hammered home what he knew plainly. Meeting her had helped him put much of the sinking and his hideous memories of it behind him.

Still, he wondered, is it true that lightning never strikes the same spot twice? At least with the tide out it won't be as deep, he thought ridiculously, as if a fathom or two made any difference out past the ledges and the island with its flashing light.

Isaac waved his cap. "Grand day for a toot, fellas. You can see for goddamn miles." But fog would have made a buffer, Enman thought, a blindfold—though whatever were to happen would happen anyway, whether or not he saw it coming. He supposed it made a difference, the quirky fact that, despite living all their lives on or near the water, none of the Inkpens had joined the navy or merchant marine, let alone gone overseas. Each of them had been exempted for some reason or another.

"Eh, Greene? What's the matter, missing the Fox already, are you? Oh hell's acre—I'm sorry, it's about your mother, isn't it. Poor old Marge. Listen, we're glad to have you aboard." Isaac sank a bony elbow into him as they hove out towards the island.

When George Archibald had quit his manager's post to sign up it was the noblest thing Enman could think of doing, to follow suit.

They made it past the first three bell buoys in silence, gaining on the island and the nearby Mad Rock, then cutting sharply towards the channel far to the left of both before anybody spoke. Then Greeley piped up. "Right about here's where that sub was, Iris Finck says. Germans bold as day sunning themselves on deck, charging their goddamn batteries."

"Iris Finck sees lots of things. How long since Lester died, and he's in her bed every night?" Isaac spat over the side, careful not to wet his tie.

Iris Finck could be a snake, Enman guessed, but she'd never done him or Ma any harm. "Ah, but she's old. Who at that age isn't a bit touched?"

"Being old doesn't exempt you from being an arsehole." Robart's shout travelled from the wheelhouse, and Isaac spat again. "Plenty of old arseholes."

Even Enman laughed, despite the sourness filling his throat.

Isaac sucked his teeth. "Poor Iris. Quite a looker, once. Cleary thought so, till he got snapped up by your ma." Isaac's wife, Lucinda, had gone to her grave too long ago to remember.

"As long as Iris gives the right change, I ain't complaining." Greeley uncapped a mickey of something and passed it to his father. Pursing his lips, Isaac took a genteel sip. "You got that off Twomey, I suppose—wha'd he charge you, an arm and a leg and your brother's wife? Scuzzy bastard."

This time no one laughed. They were near the place where the British tanker *Kars* had gone down less than three weeks after Enman's ship got hit, which had happened farther out to sea but still within sight of Halifax Harbour. Unlike with Enman's ship, the *Kars* lost its full crew: forty-four men, one of whom died after rescue. The explosion happened around eleven at night. Greeley and Robart and most of Barrein had seen it from the shore. Una said if her father were still around, he'd have been very distressed not only at the loss of life but of thirteen thousand tons of aviation fuel.

The tightness in Enman's chest made it a little hard to breathe. Greeley handed him the mickey. "Have a good big slug, bud. As much as you like." The liquor's burn pushed back the taste in his throat and the pulse thumping in his ears as he fought the memory of watching his shipmates trying to outswim flames, the sea around them ablaze. The blood had pounded through him, pounded hard enough to bleed itself out, he had thought, as he crouched in the lifeboat with half a dozen others, none of them able to help. He had suffered only burns to his shins, astonishingly. But it had taken months for them to heal, and the feeling in his legs was never quite right again.

He focused his eyes on where the stitching on his satchel had pulled away from the leather.

"Come on now, buddy." It was Greeley speaking again. "Those Jerries, at least they've got bigger fish to fry than five guys in a lobster boat."

As they lost sight of land, woods and barrens receding into a mauve-green distance, Enman longed to be home lighting the stove, making Una's porridge. They had both given up hope of her cooking skills improving very much. He focused on the horizon, averting his eyes from the sea breaking over the Blind Sisters shoal. The way land disappeared was too great a reminder of how easily solids became vapour.

Sunlight bounced from the surface of the sea. He let his mind drift again to Una. He had left without kissing her. He'd also forgotten to remind her to water the plants; by afternoon they'd be toasted. So dazzling it hurt, the sun forced his gaze to the wake's churning green, evidence of the fact that they had made it this far. It felt treacherous, though, to focus on its pretty froth—an invitation, a seductive dare to give up and dive in.

Maybe this was the temptation of despair that Ma's religion railed but could not guard against. Certainly it was the reason why, even before that February night, he had never trusted boats or the sea or people who favoured it. Now he had to trust it, though everything about doing so defied acting with common sense.

"Jayzus." Isaac's shout pealed above the engine's stutter. "Day like this, you can practically see France."

"Would you pass the rum this way again?" For Christ's sake, just enjoy the calm, he berated himself, and tried to picture Una eating her orange. But it came back to him afresh: the winter sea ablaze, the ship with a hole as big as a truck torn in her hull, burning from stem to stern. He made himself think of Una combing tangles from her hair. He had learned a trick, most easily performed when drinking, of clenching his jaw till the wind between his ears, the same as the roar inside a seashell, drowned out the screams that rose in his head.

The screams of men trapped aboard and of others who had made it into lifeboats only to capsize in slicks of burning oil.

A rolling field of fire, the sea had been that night. Torched bodies bobbing up, too many bodies to count.

"Greene. Pass 'er back here. When we hit the bar, first round'll be yours."

He managed another swig before Edgar seized the bottle.

The sea appeared as smooth as the quilt on Ma's—on *their*—bed after Una finished making it.

Isaac pushed some field glasses at him. "Is that Neverfail up ahead?" The aids marking the Neverfail Shoal, Isaac meant, a light and bell buoy, and just north of it the black can buoy bearing its name, where the shoal was its shallowest. "You got the best eyes of the bunch of us, man." Not true, it was only meant to encourage him.

Enman squinted through the binoculars. It wasn't a buoy rocking out there but the slick black tip of a conning tower. He swore it was, for a full thirty seconds. But as he blinked and stared it arced. A pilot whale? A harbour seal? A hazard only as real as the screams for help in his imagination.

"She's a sight for sore eyes, Neverfail. We're halfway there, boys. Got your spiel ready, Greene? No reason your friends won't front us the dough, is there?"

"None I can think of, Isaac." His view of the sea was interrupted by a minesweeper that had appeared and moved back and forth across the offing. Its movement resembled a tractor's ploughing up potatoes from soil.

"Well good. Listen, you score with your banker pals and I'll buy."

Isaac's offer sounded as bright and wide open as the shimmering bay they were crossing, the vast entrance to the inner harbour. To starboard lay the low slatey-green of its eastern shore and Devil's Island as flat as a parking lot, and in the nearer distance the marker for Thrumcap Shoal. To port, steep granite cliffs rose up, the steepest topped with a lighthouse that shrank steadily as they steamed ahead.

Soon they were passing Tribune Head at the farthest end of the bay, then reaching the inner harbour, with the anti-submarine net strung from Sleepy Cove on the westerly shore to the tip of Meagher's Beach marked by its squat striped lighthouse. A red gate boat and a green one manned either side of its opening, like floating bottles of ketchup and relish. Dressings for the hamburger he would order for lunch, Enman decided, as a man to portside waved them through.

And then they were in the safe zone, the treeline of Point Pleasant was in clear view beyond buoys marking Hens and Chickens shoal. Just a squeak of a journey remained between the cargo piers and Georges Island to the downtown jetty.

A greasy rime of sewage laced the gap between the boat and the pier.

He wished he could phone Una to say they had arrived, never mind that climbing the ladder to the dock his knees still wobbled and the skin of his palms was dented from clenching his fists. Only then he realized he had forgotten her list, things she wanted him to buy. In her view, shopping was impossible in Barrein. Perhaps she was a little too picky?

More than simply missing the place, suddenly he could not wait to be back there.

6

UNA REACHED FOR THE THERMOMETER, NESTLED IN COTTON WOOL IN ITS
box at the bedside. She sat up, shook the mercury down, poked the thermometer under her tongue. She imagined Dr. Snow's mellifluous voice
saying that every fraction of a degree should be noted. On her way to the
loo she jotted the figure in a Campfire notebook. Ninety-eight point eight.
Her temperature was up a third of a degree since yesterday.

Surrounded by a balmy silence, as she ran her bath the water
coughed from the tap before reaching a steady stream. What a pleasure,
though she felt guilty for thinking it, not having to fill a basin first for
Mrs. Greene or fetch her a cup of tea. Climbing in, she felt a touch of grit,
sand from yesterday's beach-going. The water appeared slightly brown,
not at all unusual.

She would have loved to have hitched a ride in Inkpens' boat, in
spite of the Inkpens themselves. Instead she'd come up with a pretty good
list. Stockings to be picked up at Wood's, soap from Mills', writing paper
from Mahons, nothing complicated. Enman should be able to handle it,

he would have oodles of time after his meeting—if he didn't die of panic en route.

But this was mean, she shouldn't make fun, because who wouldn't get nervous after such a catastrophe? She knew he wasn't likely to take her out to the island to see the rock stairway, not in the short time they had remaining. Fortunately, she didn't share his tendency to get the jitters. Her classroom experience had taught Una the art of keeping calm.

She chose her clothes according to the weather, clothes that flattered a thin, tidy figure like hers: a sleeveless blouse, a yellow dirndl which accentuated her small waist. She wondered if it would soon become tight. Hiking it up, pushing a pillow underneath it, she eyed herself sidelong in the mirror. Her spirits flagged as the pillow slid to her thighs. Would her body feel different if she *was* pregnant, even after a few hours? Would she know? She felt a tingle of excitement. But she had more pressing concerns. For one thing, she had her letter to think about. Labouring over its wording, Una had written to the superintendent of schools, hoping the board might relax its outmoded rule about married women, and that her principal had kept her misdemeanor to himself.

She tucked the letter into her pocket, smoothed the skirt's gathers. Did it fit more snugly than the last time she had worn it?

Downstairs, the cat pestered to be fed. After its mishap, some would have put it in a bag and dropped it into the sea. But, a credit to Mrs. Greene, it didn't appear to be suffering. Then she spotted it. Under the sugar bowl, exactly where she had left it, her list. Enman was generally good at remembering and liked to surprise her with presents, so perhaps he would bring a few things. Souvenirs, Enman called them. If she could have taken herself shopping, to real stores—not Finck's, where you were lucky to have your pick of tinned goods—she would have. If they had a decent car. Then she noticed Enman's note, next to her orange: *If you go out, dear, don't forget to lock up.* God, as if this were Halifax or New York City. No one in Barrein locked their doors. No one had things to steal, and stealing would be too much work for a local. *Brain,* the villagers called the place, as if saying the name properly took undue effort, which, for such things as knowing your business, they spared none.

Without Mrs. Greene to worry about, the day yawned empty before Una. Though she had relished such freedom, it felt weighted, being in the house almost as unsettling as donning the dead woman's clothes would be. Resigned to visiting Finck's, she followed Enman's instructions, locking both doors. Win Goodrow was hanging out a wash as Una attempted to steal by without being noticed. She focused on the dust underfoot. Yellow puffs of it rose from her espadrilles and coated the withered vetch along the lane. Between patches of rock, dried mud was caked like makeup.

"Dying dirt! Did you ever see the likes—no better drying weather, though, I'll give you that, Younah," Win called out. Enman had started out saying Una's name properly—Oonah—but now pronounced it the way Win and everyone else in Barrein did. "Less washing for you now, I guess, with his mother gone?"

Una had no choice but to stop.

"Ah, some day you'll have crib sheets, Missus." Even with sons grown up and moved away, Win was *Brain's* laundry queen. Her pride and joy was the new wringer-washer gleaming in the kitchen doorway. "Nothing new with youse? In the family way, I mean." As if whatever might be between Una and Enman was anybody's business. Win was relentless, shouting through a mouth plugged with clothespins. "You tell Enman he's spending time on the yard he could be spending with you. And where you off to so early? Early bird gets the worm, isn't it so." Win pegged a sock to the line, then slipped inside to feed something through the wringer. Moving on, Una was almost clear of the place when that voice trilled: "Could use some wind though—keep the linens from going stiff as a member."

Una savoured the absence of wind, the absence of crudeness. The wind ensured that trees grew no taller than children; wasn't Win the same, cutting people down to size? Halfway to the road Una heard the woman shouting again, yelling for Clinton to get his gun. What, the ARP was on the prowl, about to fine them for keeping on a light? Una thought disparagingly. A rabbit or deer had popped from the woods? Clinton just yelled back about the well running dry if Win didn't quit treating the place like a Chinese laundry.

Una felt for the letter deep in her pocket, perspiring by the time she reached the store. Mrs. Finck greeted her with a stare, flicking aside the beaded curtain that divided her parlour from the shop. Light pressed between the blinds' crooked slats. "Keep your shirt on, just a sec." The shopkeeper limped towards her, using a broom for a crutch.

Out of school, kids on bikes rattled past the open door, their shouts breezing by. The cooler kicked in. Ice settled with a clunk. "The sound of commerce, that cooler's hum. That's what my Lester calls it." The old woman wiped her nose, stuffed the hankie under her sleeve, then poked an ice cream scoop into a jar of cloudy water. "I scream, you scream, we all scream." Her eyes scoped the envelope in Una's hand. She stroked the lid of the strong box that served as a receptacle for the mail.

"Truck should be here any minute from O'Leery, just don't hold your breath. Not like the service you get in town, is it." Mrs. Finck straightened the cloth covering jars of waxy humbugs, Chicken Bones, and licorice babies. Behind her head, posters plastered the wall, a plethora of thumb-tacks and slogans. Some advertised Victory Bonds, asking people to lend money to the war effort. On another, a buff young sailor held a finger to his lips, a convoy behind him. "CARELESS words" appeared in white letters against a billowing black cloud, "cause DISASTER" in blood-red script. A couple of fresh paste-ups with old messages added to the clutter: *Loose Lips Sink Ships*; *BOLO*.

"Be On the Look Out?" Una smiled and Mrs. Finck nodded grimly.

"What do you think? Them Jerries would like nothing better than to blow us all to kingdom come."

High above the posters, a sepia photograph curled under dingy glass. It was a panoramic view of Shag's Cove, where Enman's mother and half the village had lived before resettling. Against a treeless backdrop of weather-scarred wharves and shacks, sunken-eyed men and women scowled up from gutting fish and milking cows in a rocky field above the beach.

"You know, Missus—you can hear the Jerries out there at night, charging their batteries. Lester's heard them."

Una suspected that Lester Finck, who had enjoyed some vague con-nection with Mrs. Greene, had been dead longer than the war had been on.

"I'm sure the Civil Defence people would have investigated."

"Friends of yours, are they? Bigwigs?"

"Well. No." Had Enman boasted about her city upbringing? The house in the south end, the mother who hosted charity teas, the father's position in oil? Choosing the freshest looking bar of soap, Una placed it and her letter on the counter. What people didn't realize, Enman included, was how hard she had worked to make something of herself.

By now Mrs. Finck had settled upon the cushion rubber-banded to her chair, which she drew up in thumping increments to the cash register. The bulk of her was hidden behind it as she rubbed a finger over a burn in the wooden counter, muttering about some "goddamn lush"—Barton Twomey—stubbing out a cigarette in anger when Lester refused to sell him a single smoke.

"Before I started selling them one apiece, dear," Mrs. Finck explained, for her benefit, as a commotion outside raised a strong enough draft to rattle the beaded curtain. The sound, barely discernible over shouting that reminded Una of schoolyard chaos, was like bugs clicking against a windowpane.

Prune-faced, sighing, Iris Finck inched to the window to squint through the blind. "We'll keep our eye on the prize, Missus—that goddamn truck if ever it comes." A wave of the old woman's hand released a whiff of lavender as well as the crumpled hankie. "Lo, he comes with news descending—Mr. Corney the driver—sometime in the next century, we hope." The shopkeeper loosed a chesty laugh. "'I'll always be with you, Iris,' Lester always said," and, as if suddenly inspired, she opened the box and took out the postmarked mail. "Ingoing, outgoing—some days, honest to Pete, it's Lester who keeps the balls in the air. My eyes aren't what they were." Spreading the mail over the counter, Mrs. Finck picked through it.

The ruckus continued outdoors. Una just wanted to pay for the soap, post the letter, and leave. But amid the clutter strewn before her, a few envelopes caught her eye. One was addressed to the bank in Enman's hand; one from the Goodrows was destined for Eaton's, and one from an Inkpen for a doctor in the city. Was that in payment of services for Isla Inkpen's daughter who had just given birth? You could learn all you needed to about the place by perusing addresses and addressees. A slew of envelopes were made out to "Aunt Jemima"—that contest, Mrs. Finck sniffed. Send in boxtops and you could win pancake mix and a figurine. How degrading, Enman had said. Degrading to people like the ones in Africville.

She didn't quite see why. It's *pancakes*, for Pete's sake, she'd said.

Enman could be odd like that.

There was other mail too, which Iris kept sifting through. A postcard picturing the bandstand in the city's Public Gardens was from Carmel Rooney, destined for a man in Winnipeg.

"A boyfriend, I'll bet." The old woman grimaced.

Abruptly the noise outside ceased. Iris's sourpuss grin faded. "My, my, look who it is, flashing her new teeth." Sighing, Iris addressed herself: "All right, fine then, Les—I'll be nice."

Barton Twomey's niece had come in, the slow-witted girl unfortunate enough to be related to the man known from one end of Barrein to the other as a reprobate. A stocky, hulking teen, she skulked up the aisle of tinned goods without saying a word, eyeing labels as if they contained a secret code. Even at that distance you could see her hair needed washing. Her pimply face was smudged with dirt. What's more, the girl was bosomy and slouched the way large-busted teens did. Una had seen plenty of this, subbing in grade eight.

"Yes, Hannah? What can I do for you?" Mrs. Finck's voice was almost spiteful. The poor thing cowered. God, you had to pity anyone doomed to living with a fellow best known as a bootlegger, down there in his shack below the cemetery.

Can't spell her own name, Win Goodrow had suggested.

Mrs. Finck picked through the candies, popped one into her mouth. Turned a forced smile Una's way. "That truck—what the bejeezus is keeping him, do you suppose? At least you brought the sunshine with you, Missus—that's something—wherever it is you're from." It was as if Una had only just arrived. "Isn't it uncanny?" Mrs. Finck licked back a bit of sugary drool.

"Pardon?" Una smiled at Hannah, who edged closer, clasping a tin of pears.

"The lack of fog, of course. Got something here for Uncle," Mrs. Finck spoke over Una's head, "but you got to sign for it." The shopkeeper eyed Una again, rubbing her throat, and said chummily, "Seen Enman and them putting out earlier. Off to town, are they?"

Una stepped aside to let Hannah pore over whatever had been slapped upon the counter, a bill or some other piece of mail. She couldn't help but study the dullness of the girl's hair where it parted at her nape. It looked recently trimmed, with a ruler as guide but at a slant that made her even more childlike.

"Hannah, my *darling*,"—Mrs. Finck rolled a pencil forward—"Hell western-fried, girl, I don't have all day."

You could hear spit rattle and the gritting of teeth as Hannah gathered herself. Such pretty teeth, Una might've complimented the girl, if she hadn't already heard the story of the dentist yanking out the old ones and replacing them. A story with the sorts of details you preferred to be spared.

"Now look, you're holding up Missus. It's not like I'm asking you to write me a goddamn book. No 'x', no mail."

Hannah's raw-looking hands paddled the air. A thread of saliva dangled from her lip before she could lick it away. "Uncle will be so mad, he'll he'll he'll—"

Mrs. Finck thumped the counter. "For godsake, girl."

The sounds Hannah made prompted Una to reach out and pat her arm. She thought of the girl her mother had hired once to help the cleaning lady. "It's just a piece of mail, dear." She squeezed the girl's hand, her right one. It felt sticky as a small child's mucking around with mucilage.

Somehow Una managed to angle the pencil between the correct fingers of Hannah's right hand and, clasping them in hers, traced H-A-N-N-A-H on the form. "There you go—what a pretty name. A palindrome." She eyed Mrs. Finck, who glowered.

Hannah had quit whimpering. "There you go," she echoed, and snatching the mail—notice of a fine, a summons, whatever it was—stuffed it under her shirt and fled.

"In case you forgot, it's a business I run here, not a classroom, Missus." Mrs. Finck's speckled hand seized and weighed Una's letter. Her anemic tongue licked the stamp and her bony fist thumped it into place, then, finally, on top of the pile Una's missive landed—as unceremoniously as that.

Maybe Una should have kissed it first, offered up a wish-upon-a-star.

"Truck'll be here in a jiffy. A good fella, your Enman, given all he puts up with. A good fella's hard to find, isn't that right, Missus."

Outside, Hannah knelt over the Meades' dog lolling in the dirt. Her face pressed to Chubby's mangy fur, she stroked his muzzle and with her left hand counted his whiskers.

Of course! Una should have asked if the girl was left-handed.

Chubby's eyes rolled up at her, begging her to join in. She gave his chin a perfunctory scratch.

"Out spending Enman's dough, are youse?"

Sylvester Meade leered down at her. He was with his grandson. Both acted as if Hannah wasn't there, or that the girl's petting their dog showed an awful presumption. "And where's he off to this morning?" Sylvester aimed this at Una's chest, yellowy eyes lingering there as the boy disappeared into the store.

Smoothing her skirt, she smiled coldly. You couldn't turn sideways without somebody around here taking notes.

Righting himself, Chubby proceeded to hump a tuft of weeds. Una found his doggy antics both amusing and embarrassing as Meade kept up his patter—"Gonna be another hot one, eh?"—all the while slathering her with his gaze. Eyes cast downward, Hannah backed then slunk away and started running.

With the day to kill, Una took the path around the bog and up along the barrens. The road looped below, meandering beyond the graveyard to the last house, Twomey's. A lone figure loped along it—Hannah?—and Una watched her progress until, at the edge of a thicket of wild pear, she caught a flash of movement.

A doe and its faun.

Deer had made short work of Mrs. Greene's tulips that spring. The creatures snacked on the scabby apple trees near the churchyard. Funny thing, though, they avoided the cemetery with its lofty wooden cross and carved Jesus, the graves—including Mrs. Greene's fresh one—hemmed by a spruce hedge. A person could end up in a cruder place, Una supposed. The graveyard was the first and last thing you saw coming and going from Barrein, if you drove the coastal route that hugged what seemed like an endless series of coves and bays.

Other than taking this long, meandering road or travelling by boat, the only remaining option was driving the dirt track that cut straight inland through miles of scrub forest to link the village to O'Leery, which lay near Halifax's distant outskirts. Barely wider than a path, the track crossed a wilderness pocked with lakes and bogs, a spruce-studded purgatory—or a hunter's paradise, depending. If it moved you shot it, was the attitude of a Barreiner. Her idea of game? A duck waddling around the Public Gardens' pond or served *à l'orange* in the dining room of the Lord Nelson Hotel. The thought of both made her throat tighten. Right about now Enman would be showing his books to a roomful of nicely dressed men cringing at the Inkpens' double negatives and "I seen ya's." At least Mrs. Greene had made some effort to pass down proper grammar, though how she had succeeded when Enman was surrounded by butchered language all through his childhood was a mystery.

Alcohol on Enman's breath, dust on the tips of his brogues: Una imagined these too. But she preferred to remember spotting him for the first time, his fedora bent to a November gale as they passed each other on Duke Street. He was going uphill, she was going down, bound for the shops in the streets below. It was after school, the lesson on identifying planes fresh in her mind. Rick Gregory, the science teacher, had come in to help out on details: Stuka dive-bombers with their hideous sirens, Messerschmitts and Condors. The information had been a bit overwhelming, as she had been more focused on Mr. Gregory's grin, his invitation to meet for a movie. She was off to buy a dress for their date.

Nobody had told her Gregory was married.

The heavy-set man in the fedora, a man not in uniform but imposing still in his navy-blue overcoat, had smiled and nodded. He had kind eyes and a more dignified look than Rick Gregory, who, with his shirtsleeves rolled up, had nice arms.

Who could have guessed that over the Christmas holidays the same man would glide up and introduce himself at the Egg Pond, where Una was skating to forget her troubles?

After the movie, things with Gregory had gotten cosy, escalating when she brought him home to her flat. He was funny, he was charming, so she didn't object when he put his hand under her skirt, and the rest of the evening proceded from there—why would she have objected? It was only later, in the staff room, that she learned he had a wife.

Someone, Una had never found out who, reported the affair, no more than a fling, to Mr. Sarty, the principal. One minute she was in the classroom having the kids colour in mimeographed outlines of holly and bells, the next she was in the office being given her marching orders. They took into consideration Una's years of service and her firmness in the classroom, and she was allowed to complete the final week, before

Christmas. She had hoped to take her class skating on the last day of school. But this was denied her.

Gregory got off with a reprimand. So Kit, Una's friend on staff, said.

She missed this group of kids in particular, missed in general the mustard-and-sweat smell of packed lunches, erasers, and chalkdust, missed the soft shabby feel of the textbooks—particularly the grade five geography textbook featuring exotic tribes and locales. It gave each people and their homeland a face: Juan of the Pampas; Bunga and the pygmies of the Congo, who made dugout canoes and shot game using blowguns.

The sun beating down on the road and over the barrens burned Una's shoulders. Now her work, she realized with a chilly resolve, was making Mrs. Greene's house a temporary home. Surely by the end of August Barrein would be behind them.

She wasted no time changing into the same blue bathing suit, throwing her clothes on over it. Enman had bought the suit on their last outing to the city in mid-May, more than a month before Mrs. Greene's passing. "Sweet, isn't he," the saleslady had whispered as he watched Una model several options. She was the same saleslady who had waited on them in February, and drawn Una's attention to the coat she fell in love with. Its woollen fabric was an unusual shade of blue, not quite cornflower and not quite periwinkle but somewhere in between, with buttons even more irresistible. They were jet black with tiny circles of mother-of-pearl set into their centres.

"Exquisite, aren't they?" the saleslady had cooed, positively covetous. "You don't see buttons like that every day."

"You sure don't." Fingering each one, Una had tried to resist their temptation, telling herself she didn't need the coat. "En? Honey? What do you think?" It was the first time she addressed Enman that way in public. Before she turned to him, he had his wallet out.

Venturing down the lane, Una breezed undeterred past Win and her osprey eyes, found the dirt track to Shag's. Dragonflies—darning needles, Mrs. Greene had called them—stitched the boughs of spruce in a grove where moss absorbed the sunlight. Her footsteps drummed the dry peat. The thought of Mrs. Greene's voice drummed too, a memory of the old woman musing about the possibility of grandchildren. Guessing that "even" Isla Inkpen would grow to enjoy having a grandchild, once she got over having an unwed daughter. People find worse things to fret about, Enman's mother had said.

The sun had a ways to go before being directly overhead. Towards the tip of the headland the path hugged the rocky cliff. At low tide she could have climbed down and picked her way to the sand, but now the tide was coming in. It would rise and fall again by the time Enman returned to tend his flowers and sleep off his excursion, which she supposed would involve drinking.

Mounds of kelp buzzing with flies dotted the beach. She stepped out of her espadrilles, cheap things, and followed the surf as it washed the sand. Mixed with froth, it was like cream of wheat coming to a boil. The sea itself was the colour of the Caribbean in a postcard Kit sent once. Una had never been south of Boston. The water resembled stained glass, so clear and calm you could see the drop-off. Shag's Cove was the one thing that made Barrein bearable, unless you were like Enman and could be content buried in a ledger or music. The swoony symphonies and hick tunes he played along to—the hick tunes against his will, he claimed, Wilf Carter yodelling about ponies and so forth. Records that strange old bird, Hubley Hill, had brought over just this week, trying to talk Enman into playing another dance. The first time Enman had taken his violin out in front of her, she had been forced to smile and bite her tongue. Within days of arriving at Eastertime, Enman had played with Hubley at a dance in the church hall, the duo hastily billed as the Steady Hills. Mrs. Greene had still been well enough to get in and out of bed, and Una had gone along, more to avoid being left at home than to enjoy the music. The first time Enman had played for her, he had butchered a Bach aria—her just desserts, Una supposed, for the meal she had fussed over yet still managed to ruin. They had laughed off both their failures, making a conciliatory beeline for Diana Sweet's. The dance, however, was less amusing. Una stuffed her ears with toilet paper, waiting for it to end. Since then, as far as Una could tell, Enman seemed happiest playing along to the hi-fi before nodding off to sleep to the thud of the needle bumping round and round.

As she stripped to her suit, she imagined the superintendent opening her envelope. At Mrs. Greene's wake Kit had mentioned the position in town, a high school vacancy—a long shot, but still. Perhaps when seeking someone to teach older students the board would make allowances. With any luck, Mr. Sarty the principal would continue to keep Una's firing to himself, as he had promised. Once the war ended and with it all the shortages and overcrowding, once life got back to normal, they would be crying for teachers. They would *have* to change the rules. Someday she might have a child *and* a job, and someday men like Rick Gregory might even get their wrists slapped. Enman would have his old job and they would live near Quinpool Road again, hear the Birney cars trundling back and forth under the trees' leafy canopy. So much for his distressing hints that he preferred Barrein and that if she gave it more of a chance, she would come to prefer it too. He would see, he would remember, that living in town was, as Kit said, the cat's ass.

Meanwhile, might Mrs. Finck spill the beans, asking Enman what he made of his little wife writing the school board?

September was only a month and a half away.

Sucking in her breath, she relished the tautness of cotton hugging her waist. Maybe having the perfect suit guaranteed that by summer's end it would no longer fit? This seemed the way things worked. Ask for one thing, get the opposite. Feast or famine, Mrs. Greene had said about life's blessings. In a month's time she might well have a job in the city and then what? She would figure it out. *They* would figure it out. And who knew but the new suit *and* the letter would work in tandem to make real this heart's desire—a baby.

Feeling buoyed, she entered the shallows as if stepping through glass. The water's iciness reminded her of December, just after Christmas. How Enman had skated up to her on the frozen pond and asked her name, and how she had poised the blade of her skate and etched a tiny line in the ice, the numeral one. "*Une* for Una." Obviously charmed, he'd bought her hot chocolate. He had touched her elbow gently, guiding her from the rinkside canteen to a bench.

Now she held her breath, waded to her waist, ducked. The cold slammed against her eardrums. It pinched and twisted every nerve. Might it be enough to stop the heart? In a weaker person perhaps, out deep enough. Such cold had not stopped Enman's heart after the tanker's winter sinking.

In the frigid air on the Commons, removing his skates, hiking up a pantleg, he had shown her one of his scars. He worked at the Bank of

Nova Scotia, he said. His nose dripped slightly. She said she was on a "small hiatus" from work and in describing her job, mentioned how much she enjoyed it but loathed giving the strap, blushing when he said, "That shows how sweet you are." She knew he was reasonably well off, by his clothes and his refined way of speaking.

Bobbing on a gentle swell Una fixed her gaze on the distant light-house straight ahead, its stripes red as the tiny lines and numbers on her thermometer. She had told Enman a lot of things about herself, but not about Rick Gregory or that she had been fired. She had made sure Enman knew of the school board's rules before they went to bed together that New Year's Eve, which was when he proposed. Even Kit was shocked at how quickly it all transpired.

"Marry me, Una, and you won't have to bother with bullies. No more chalk under your nails, no more giving the strap. You won't have to worry about work again." Sheer relief had drowned out any reservations she had about this, since she loved her work. But work was a moot point. When he first mentioned "going down the shore," she thought he meant Lunenburg, Liverpool, or Yarmouth, or some other picturesque town of size. Not a pile of rocks with a few houses scattered over them, twenty or more miles, as the crow flew, from Halifax.

Dr. Snow preached the benefits of exercise, but maybe such a frigid swim was not so wise? Yet the water made her weightless, carefree. She was a floating paper doll until the cold bogged her down and Snow's cau-tionary words about "hostile womb" left her feeling waterlogged. Now she was driftwood washing up, the sun and sand and the barbed cold pricking her all over.

Towelling off, she stretched out on Mrs. Greene's plaid blanket, teeth chattering, and let warmth reclaim her.

These immersions caused such numbness. Testing the body's endur-ance, they were a little like dying by degree, she thought. Perhaps the immersions even tempted fate, silencing each nerve before they slowly came back to life and returned her to the land of the living, the shore with its grit and brackish scent of marram and glinting mica, fool's gold.

Wrapped in the towel, she strolled toward a flock of terns warning her away from nests amid the rocks. The rounded boulders, fringed with seaweed, resembled people's heads, an audience of heads half submerged there. Scaling them, she made her way to the next sandy crescent and walked its length, a leisurely hike of half a mile or so, beachcombing as she went.

Not much of interest washed up here. The sea saved the good stuff for the third beach, its lagoon formed by a jut of rock as smooth as a whale's back. Once, she had found a carpet laid out there parlour-style, its fringe beaded with periwinkles. The authorities discouraged people from scavenging for items washed from ships, a decree which seemed a bit ridiculous. Currents colluded randomly with the ledges of rock in the sea's offing, as Enman called the section just before the horizon, to deposit the strangest things. The horizon itself looked like a line in a notebook drawn with Schaeffer's medium-blue ink, the colour she'd made the grade fives use.

Damned if those rocks wouldn't trick you, during a storm, into seeing icebergs or, on days like this, whales in no rush to swim away—or, as now, a foundering ship, waves breaking over its deck. A trick of the eye, certainly. But then she heard a buzzing roar; was it the hum of an invisible airplane passing by? A trick of the ear. And then—of course all this had been her imagination—the object in the sea was gone.

Too much sun and speculation, at least on the part of Iris Finck and Win Goodrow, were getting the best of her.

The ebbing sea turned the sand into a shiny-wet mirror below the tidemark. Above it, the dry sand was a scorching white. Retracing her steps, digging in her heels, she walked backwards into the sun, veering now and then into the tingling surf. Its tang smelled like something the body secreted, like the single sample Enman—poor Enman—had produced for the lab to put under a microscope. The sea puckered her toes, made them pale as an infant's; it had that power to scrub everything away, and for a moment, a few moments, she was thirty again, no, barely nineteen, before she had interrupted her life to be with her mother.

As far as the sea knew, she hadn't lost her job and her parents or acquired a husband, and had not a care in the world. With her mind stripped down to its simple, happy core, she might have stripped her body to her birthday suit, losing the pretty bathing suit, for the sheer fun of telling Enman she had done it. Who was there to see? She had walked all three beaches and seen neither hide nor hair of anyone. The only chance of being spotted was by an off-course air or sea patrol—not likely with the East Coast Port within their sights. But the sun was so scorching it almost pulsed, and how to explain having burnt nipples the next time she saw Snow?

Gathering her things, she found the trailhead, a prickle of blackberries and wild rose, and stopped to slip on her clothes. As she buttoned up, a squawking gull drew her eye to something hanging from a twig. A sock, its dingy mate dangled nearby. More than just socks—it quickly became apparent. An array of items decorated the bushes. A fellow's wardrobe: greyish shorts, woollen pants, a ragged shirt. Avoiding the clothing, Una thought of Win's tales about people doing naughty things out here. Or, like Win, someone had done a wash.

A few steps on, a jacket was hung too, right beside the path. She was close enough to inspect it. Its greyish leather was as brittle as oilskins coughed up by the sea—a grisly fact that clothing sometimes washed ashore, all that was left of people lost out there.

Out of a morbid curiosity she reached for its gored breast pocket, a saggy slit in the leather, then caught herself. If there had been money and it was now missing, who knows but she would be blamed? They were like that around here. Mind your P's and Q's, she imagined her pupils repeating, the memory of her own instructions hurrying her on, never mind the brambles snagging her skirt.

Don't twist an ankle, for God's sake, she imagined Enman's warning, his gentle if misplaced concern.

She found the shortcut along the pond. Happy little skatebugs scored its prune-coloured surface. Tadpoles clouded its yellowy edges, which reminded her of medical diagrams: beribboned balloons—cells—twisting blindly toward an egg that resembled a child's drawing of the sun.

All it took was one.

How many had it taken to breed Shag's Cove, a settlement wiped from all memory now besides Mrs. Finck's? God. The only sign a village had existed was a tumble of fieldstones in the knotweed. A tiny blue butterfly flitted by. A snapping sound rose like Iris Finck herself bundling mail with rubber bands—a bullfrog's mating call. Or were bullfrogs hermaphrodites; had the science teacher said?

Any chance to mention gonads, that odious guy.

And then she heard laughter, low, robust, and real—men's laughter, close. Lounging in a hollow a short distance away, a cleft in the bushes ringed by boulders, three or four men were gathered, fellows shooting the breeze, as Gregory had said in the staff room—"We're just shooting the breeze, Una, having a little break shooting the shit, what's wrong with that?—" before the principal walked in. The silence that had fallen around her suggested that she was the subject, perhaps of a boast?

These fellows were half-naked, stripped to their shorts. More laundry dotted the surrounding bushes. They must have been camping out, except there was no tent in sight, and their laughter sounded bored, even restless. Boy Scouts on some wilderness outing. They certainly looked young enough to be. One of them was playing a mouth organ, one hand fluttering at it like a sick bird. The tune was a jig, music everyone in Barrein loved.

She thought for a second she recognized him. Though he was closer this time, he was still at a distance, so she couldn't be sure. That narrow face, that strange intensity as he played. The others spoke over his playing, in low voices. From the path it was impossible to hear what they were saying, with the gulls and the light wind off the water, the onshore breeze pulling the surf's soft boom closer. They were doing exactly what Rick Gregory called it: shooting the shit.

Dodging a hornet, she felt depressed by their idleness: youth being wasted on the young. At their age she had stayed busy practise-teaching, learning to do lesson plans. Keeping busy had warded off self-doubt and self-pity, keeping busy had worked nicely, until now.

Oh, get over yourself, she thought, darting away before they could see her, you're not that old and washed-up. Enman certainly hadn't thought so, had he?

7

THE POMPOUS MAN WHO HAD REPLACED ENMAN'S FRIEND AS MANAGER WAS
tied up, apparently, despite his earlier promise to meet with the party from
Barrein. They were asked to wait to see the assistant manager instead.
From Citadel Hill the noon gun sounded, its concussion rattling the
bank's windows. Enman had meant to have a few words with the manager
before the meeting, about getting hired back on. But as he and the others
from Inkpens' waited on the mezzanine outside the assistant manager's
cubicle, fifteen more minutes, and then a half-hour passed. Enman clearly
wasn't going to get the opportunity to ask. He already felt insulted that
the upstart teller had replaced him, George Archibald's ambitions for
him so quickly forgotten. He had expected somebody to take note of his
experience. He had only left the bank that spring.

Passing the time, Greeley made small talk. "So when's the next dance,
bud? With Hill, I mean."

"What?" Enman smoothed the balance sheet on his lap, thinking
more about numbers. Was there anything else he had forgotten, aside
from that list? Did he have every figure that pimply juvenile would need?

"Isla and me are looking forward to it. She's always up for a dance."

"Wait a second, I never told Hubley I would—" This wasn't the place to discuss it. The problem was, he and Hill differed over musical tastes. Which was fine, except for Hubley's teasing the last time Enman had brought out his violin, a happy distraction one recent evening: "Christ, man. Give us something folks can dance to. It's fiddle they like, not a flipping symphony." Una had sighed and vanished to the kitchen.

The bustle of commerce echoed from below. "If I agree to play at the hall again, Hubley promises to split the door: all two dollars of it."

"Sounds like a plan to me, Greene." Isaac scratched and wiggled his ear, to loosen wax from it, Enman supposed. Young Lohnes dozed in his seat, and Robart leaned over the railing watching the tellers in their cages count bills.

Enman was well aware he was part of what looked like a motley crew. Yet, as a youngster—a loans officer and not the assistant manager—approached, suddenly he didn't care, not overly much. It was hard suddenly for him to believe that only four months ago he had liked working here, or thought he had. He missed George. The truth was he had found it very hard coming back the previous year, after recovering from his burns.

Una had liked him working here, though.

The junior loans officer went over his figures so brusquely that Enman very nearly demanded to see Dunphy the manager, never mind the assistant manager. But then the young fellow said he didn't see any problems with lending Inkpens' the money, and went off to get a final signature.

Enman felt a small pang of regret for leaving his former job when he noted the silver pen the kid had handed to Isaac, to sign a form, and the spiffy new adding machine atop the youngster's desk.

Outside, Isaac and his sons clapped Enman on the back, each promising to buy. Enman shouted them down. "It's a loan, remember, not a gift."

"You done good, Greene. I'll remember this." Then Isaac doffed his cap at a girl wobbling by on high heels.

It was just a few blocks uphill, a quick zigzag along staggered streets, to where the blind pig was tucked behind a tobacconist's, all in the shadow of the basilica's spire. The prospect of a good slug of navy rum, to be bought for next to nothing, soothed any vestiges of hurt pride Enman felt over his former employment, and helped put Hubley Hill's love of twang in perspective. If it was the New Brunswick Lumberjacks and not Dvořák that people wanted, why shouldn't they have them? Of course, some people hankered after hookers too, he thought, as Edgar joked about company for hire on Hollis Street at Ada MacCallum's brothel.

"Don't tell me you're that desperate, good-looking boy like you?" Enman gave the young fellow a nudge.

"Goddamn." Greeley scowled. The lineup for the bar, which was choked with sailors, straggled halfway down the block. A sailor with a black eye reeled past, almost falling into Enman. Securing the satchel's clasp, he was glad the cash loan had gone straight into the Inkpens' account.

"We can wait." The order came from Isaac, looking slightly less dapper because of the way he leaned on his stick. This was the perfect chance for Enman to duck down to Wood's to pick up something for Una, a little scarf or maybe a pair of earrings, to prove that he hadn't forgotten her. But he could hardly ask the others to hold his place in line, not a line like this. Besides, there would be plenty of time to shop, after a hamburger and a drink or two. The others were in no rush to get home. A reeling gang of men got booted out, and some of their pals in line gave up spots to cause a ruckus large enough to enable Isaac and Enman and the others to sneak inside. They even scored a table.

Only problem was, the grill was out of grub. So much for that burger with a slab of onion, its juices mixing with sweet condiments—the very thought of which had saved him earlier from seasickness.

Seasickness, yes; leave it at that.

Sliding down his gullet, the first two belts—black rum, a hundred proof—set off a lazy buzz. He had meant to stick to two. After the third and fourth he was a bee in a hive, no place finer to be, except at home in his own front room playing records and sawing along on his violin. Now that he and Una didn't have to worry about disturbing Ma's rest, he was freer to practise and blast the Dvořák. But for now the chatter around him almost matched the sibilant trumpets in Dvořák's adagio, as jubilant as the pirates' shouting in *Captain Blood*. Greeley punched his arm agreeably and in return he thumped Greeley's.

The sinewy tautness of Greeley's arm was sobering, bringing back a memory of Archibald buying coffee then challenging Enman to an arm wrestle in the staff room on lunch break. George had quit drinking in his twenties, had never touched a drop since. Once after work, in the green-tiled men's room near the vault, the basement room where they polished their shoes, Enman had offered George a drink from the flask in his locker. George had given a belly laugh. "If you think you can bribe me with that to help you climb the ladder, forget it. You're way too smart for such bullshit." Not long after, George had placed a bar of gold bullion in Enman's hand. "You think booze is your friend. Being sober is worth a million of these. More than a few times I had to be wiped off a floor, Greene, so I know what I'm talking about. You're better than that." And Enman had stopped drinking for months and months, during which George trusted him with the vault's combination and promoted Enman to securities. He had risen steadily through the ranks, following George's example. A few backbiters grumbled that if Archibald said "jump," Greene would say "how high?"

Their friendship had enabled Enman to see qualities in himself he hadn't noticed before: patience, honesty, a good head for numbers, and an unwillingness to let people get behind in their debts. The last time he and George were together was that luckless February night, horsing around, playing cards. Archibald's arm around his neck in a headlock was the last thing he remembered before coming to in the lifeboat. Archibald's body was never recovered.

"What's eating you, man?" It was Greely eyeing him.

Startled, Enman forced a laugh, then strummed an invisible guitar and said Hill wasn't a bad fellow at all, apart from having a tin ear. It was better to joke. Because, once, under the table, Archibald's hand had squeezed his knee. Feeling mildly embarrassed and nothing more, Enman had pushed it away. He felt nothing but grief at losing his friend. And he did well to forget that odd, isolated moment.

By what cosmic gaff had he made it and Archibald hadn't?

"Cheers, bud!" Isaac gave his bicep such a slap his drink slopped over the tabletop. "You're why we're here. The way you wrangled that little bastard at the bank—if I was a rich man you'd be in for a raise."

This drew a hefty laugh from Robart who sprayed liquid through his teeth, and young Edgar banged the table so hard the tattooed bruisers at the next one gawked and the barman yelled to keep it down before the cops came—came quicker than anyone could unzip to take a leak.

A burst of bravado made Enman pull out his wallet and buy doubles all around. Exactly the thing to do, being freewheeling as a fly. But the drink induced Robart to regale them with tales about his kids. He and his wife had four, and were expecting their fifth. "Don't laugh. You'll be in for it too." Robart eyed Enman. "Just remember to stop at two or three. Even if it means cutting yourself off. A pack of kids isn't all it's cracked up to be."

Isaac unleashed a sputtering cough. "Gah! If your ma and I had felt the same about you fellas…. 'Course, Lu wanted girls." Isaac gazed at Enman. "What's Foxy think of kids? Had her fill, I bet, being around them so much. Maybe she's got more important things, your missus, off on her hikes and whatnot."

It was friendly enough ribbing, lighter than their jibes about fellows "shooting blanks." Still it hit a sore spot. If Una didn't become a mother, how *was* someone like her, used to movies, shops, and restaurants being a trolley-ride away, going to fill her time? He remembered his visit to her doctor, booked at Una's urging, back in March. Talk of sperm counts and propulsion. Propulsion was for boats and airplanes, for Chrissake.

"It's not for a lack of trying." He inspected his glass. "We've only been at it six or seven months." Snow's spiel about ripened eggs conjured up a henhouse. His diagram of an ovum called to mind a child's drawing of a full-blown sunflower, Una said. Enman wasn't sure if the doctor was trying to frighten or reassure him, saying that of the more than two hundred million spermatozoa "per healthy ejaculation," all it took was one "to do the trick."

He muscled up to the bar. "Give us another round, would you. On that old fella over there. Kidding. On me."

PERHAPS HE DOZED OFF IN his chair. When he snapped to, the windowless bar appeared out of focus, as if it were under water. It was as dim as the tanker's hold that February night, where quarters had been so tight the crew slept in shifts. Except that now a sailor was leering in Enman's face for no reason, a burly kid who sounded like a Yank. Isaac was shouting: "Get your stunned arse out of here, you moron. Leave my buddy alone."

The sailor took a swing at the old man, and Greeley leapt to his feet, hooking a table leg in the process and overturning a chair. "Talk to my old man like that and you're fucking dead." The sailor raised his fist and, listing badly, clipped the right side of Enman's head. From somewhere came a hissing sound, was it rain? The sailor staggered off. At least there was no blood. But the painful bump swelled, as did the sound, which was so much like a whistle buoy's that Enman's shoulders stiffened.

Isaac thumped him. Robart gave Enman a friendly shove.

Somehow Enman found the can, urinated. He was safe and happy on dry land, never mind that the walls and ceiling spun. When he came back, the bar had emptied. Before he knew what was happening, Greeley and Robart were muscling him along by the arms. The steadiest of them all, Isaac led them through the heavy door into the tobacco shop fronting the street. Through the dying light at the window Enman took in the brawl outside, two more sailors going at it, a woman shrieking nearby. A crowd was egging them on, roaring as more men joined in. Fellows in similar uniforms punching each other out, over what? Gad! Though maybe, in spirit, it wasn't much different from collections agents and indebted customers sparring over nickels and dimes. Enman had steered clear of bad credit risks, not to mention brawls.

For no good reason, all Enman could think of was the time, years ago, when two nuns had come to Barrein and the Meades and Twomeys had driven them out—Barton and his little sister and Eddie and Archie Meade put up to firing rocks by their no-good parents, Sylvester Meade especially. The kids had started flinging gravel before taking up rocks the size of their fists. A full-fledged stoning. Mortified, absolutely mortified, Ma had been beside herself with an indignation that in the end, like his boyish shock, went nowhere.

Enman and Edgar stumbled down the sidewalk trailing Isaac, who was bookended by his sons. Edgar stopped and slumped to the curb, hung his head between his knees, and puked. Isaac glanced back. "What say we grab a bite? On me."

They waited for Edgar to stand and wipe his mouth, then they staggered downhill towards Barrington Street. They passed the Garrick Theatre where a few weeks ago somebody had found a Bosh uniform in the trash, it was said, with the stub of a matinee ticket in its pocket.

Greeley's speech was a little slurred: "I could eat a goddamn horsssh." But when they reached the Green Lantern, it was closed.

As they zigzagged towards Prince and Water Streets, passing gang after gang of rabble-rousing sailors, the walk stretched longer and longer, it seemed, despite their downhill momentum. Only Isaac seemed sober, creeping along as dignified as could be. He smacked his lips at just about every female going by.

Straight up the hill behind them the Old Town Clock said five past eight. The shops had been shut for two hours. At Mrs. Finck's, if you were desperate and banged loudly enough after hours, she might let you in. Not here, not in the big town, the East Coast Port.

Why hadn't he just excused himself, slipped out earlier and bought the jeezly scarf and earrings, or stockings? The ones Una liked, silk with seams like lines drawn down the backs of her calves. Lines that twisted winsomely on account of her hopping-bird gait. *Goddamnit.* Even if they left now he would never be back in time to stroll with her out to Cow Head, like he had mentioned doing. There was that spot where bluets dotted the grass, he could picture them. And he imagined Una and him kissing, getting the juices flowing, and, like a couple of youngsters, doing the wild thing. Right there on a grassy little knoll, and not just doing it but doing it fruitfully, tadpoles like darts. Bull's eye!

But then, passing the post office with its beehive tower and limp Union Jack, he glimpsed the harbour and remembered the trip ahead. How would he explain to Una the goose egg near his temple? Explaining this on top of how he'd forgotten her list—well, that would be another story, along with whatever he managed to come up with when she asked about the bank.

8

THE SUN STREAMING IN ONLY HIGHLIGHTED THE KITCHEN'S DINGINESS: THE big enamel sink, the calendar with its photo of dahlias, the sloping floor's linoleum. Back from her swim, Una needed to wash her hair, the salt made it a Brillo pad. She found the precious bottle of Drene and the pail Mrs. Greene had used for picking berries; it was too awkward, trying to squeeze her head under the enamel sink's dual faucets. The bathroom sink was simply too small.

Deep in the cellar the pump chugged, but all that spewed from the taps was a rusty murk. She twisted them, tried again, tried the upstairs taps too, remembering Enman's words, "If we run out we can bathe at Goodrows'. Why worry if there's no need to?"

Una would wait good and long before going next door for such a favour. "Normal School, what do they teach you there?" Win had said once. "Whatever it was didn't take?"

The lake was a hike across the barrens and through the woods. The only other option was to drive to the volunteer fire department in O'Leery, but in what? Enman could deal with the car's quirks. She couldn't. Rolling a sliver of soap in a towel—she wasn't about to waste shampoo on fish— she pinned her key to her blouse.

Twigs crackled underfoot, the woods a tinderbox. Eventually the lake's shimmer appeared, puzzle pieces of blue framed by branches. Granite boulders ringed and studded its surface, an otherwise perfect mirror. A solitary loon skimmed by; didn't loons travel in pairs?

Kneeling on a rock, she peered at her reflection, like Narcissus in some old painting. Except, unlike Narcissus, she didn't have the lake to herself. Squatting on a rock some distance away was a recognizable sight, startling all the same. It was Hannah, her faded skirt hiked to her thighs as she dipped and swished and flapped something into a basin. The flash of water was like a string of rhinestones Enman had brought home once, a cheap thing whose clasp broke when he went to fasten it at her neck, pieces flying everywhere.

Glancing up, the girl looked just as startled, mouth agape in her sunburnt face.

So much for a good cleansing skinny-dip. Luckily Una still had her suit on, and she slipped into the water. Shiza, it was like sinking into the pee sample the doctor had asked her to produce. Clutching the soap, she swam closer as Hannah slapped something against the rock, an enormous plaid shirt.

"It's for Uncle," the girl yelled out, wading ashore. Her pasty thighs glistened. "He says make his stuff smell like a rose or else." Hannah's greyish eyes fixed on Una. Not since Sarty's office or walking past the Goodrows' had Una felt so scrutinized. Yet there was something soft and disarming about those eyes, almost familiar, their grey remotely like the colour of Enman's.

Treading water, Una soaped and rinsed her hair, then waded back to the patch of coarse sand where Hannah stood tracing something with a stick. Approaching her was like stalking some rare, ungainly bird. Lo and behold, Hannah had drawn the letters of her name. Looking up at her, the girl's eyes were wary. "My other name, Missus. Can you make it?"

Taking the stick, Una formed TWOMEY. Hannah beamed, rubbing the front of her blouse—pink skin gaping between buttons—and snatched back the stick. Tongue between her teeth, she slowly copied the word, held up two fingers—"Two!"—then buried them in her bosom—"Me!" The wake of a flock of gliding ducks made the lake lap away the letters, enough to make Hannah sigh.

Finding a stick of her own, Una sketched *Two = you & me*.

Never quite losing her smirk, Hannah clapped her hands.

Pointing to the sliver of Lifebuoy on the rock, Una wrote *soap*. Rinsing her hands, she wrote *wash*. Biting her cheek, Hannah painstakingly copied each word. Una thought it was like teaching grade fives what little French she knew, or naming the Latin roots of words with Enman and his mother, a bedside game that had offered some relief from rounds of Minister's Cat—now *there* were two months of Sundays she would never get back.

Birds twittered. Horseflies buzzed over the eelgrass. From the woods squirrels nattered. Hannah couldn't hide her delight. In spite of herself, Una let her hand encircle the girl's wrist. "Mind you don't get more sunburn." It was meant as a kindness. But Hannah's glee faded, and before the girl could be stopped she kicked away what remained of the words.

Wading back to her basin, Hannah resumed her chore. A pair of nicotine-hued longjohns—two boneless legs—slapped the water.

What went through a slower mind like Hannah's? Already Una had lost her touch in dealing with a sluggish, mentally delayed student?

A movement on the opposite shore caught her eye: a boy and a girl on a rock, sunbathing. Necking.

"Hannah—" Una laughed, "Don't look."

Hannah slubbed the longjohns over granite. Gave not so much as a giggle. "Nutting new to me, Missus."

The pair wasn't close enough for Una to see their faces, but the girl made her think of Isla's daughter. She wondered who the boy was, if he might be one of the Goodrows' home from O'Leery. The Goodrows had several youngish sons; they had some sort of business selling things from a truck. Anyone but a local would have difficulty finding the lake. Seconds later they were gone.

But Hannah seemed spooked by something, irked.

"Uncle said don't take all friggin day. Got to get this stuff dry before he gives me a lickin.'"

That burning sun, would it ever cool off? A bath, *sans* suit, was out of the question, and Una's hair was almost dry. She splashed her face and offered to help. Reluctantly Hannah nodded, so Una wrung out a shirt—just the thought of Twomey's skin against it made her cringe—and laid it into the emptied basin.

Just then, Win emerged from the woods with a towel over her shoulders and a net bag filled with hair curlers. She picked her way to them.

"Got a buddy, I see, Una. Living in the stone age, are we, doing your warsh off a scuzzy old rock?" Win's laugh wasn't just mean, it had a certain scorn thrown in, as if to say Hardship? Well, I've lived it, and can I just say, you don't know squat? And then, to Hannah, "Isn't that sweet, Missus here helping. My goodness, least your uncle could do is buy himself a warshing machine, isn't that right, Una?"

Win had that knack for adding consonants that didn't belong. Other word-butcherings of hers leapt to mind—ambublance, chimbley, ashphalt—forcing Una to stifle a smile.

Win's gaze was a scouring pad, a Kurly Kate made of steel wool.

"Well that's good, the teacher being put to use."

"How's *your* water?" It was a question simply intended to keep things civil.

"Oh land, honey," Win laughed, shaking her bag of curlers, "I'm just here to cool off and set my hair while I'm at it—at it and to it."

"A bit tricky without looking in a mirror, isn't it?" Una kept her voice light.

Win's severely plucked brows had the effect of making her look shocked. "Oh, now, we can't all be in love with ourselves, can we, Una."

"More's the pity."

Win came closer then, close enough to tap her on the wrist. "Exactly right. And how nice for hubby that you and Hannah are chummy. Wouldn't his mum be tickled. Too bad she isn't here to see it." Win grinned so her gums showed. Her eyes rested on the basin. "Now, don't let me hold youse up."

Hastily gathering up her things, Una hurried after Hannah, who had already pushed her way through the bushes crowding the path. Once Win was behind them, reaching the barrens Una offered Hannah more help with her chore. It boosted Una's mood to feel useful. Maybe Hannah could be a summer project? Teaching Hannah could keep her occupied until September and life got straightened out. She had heard Iris Finck go on about Twomey's shack on the way to Cow Head and Enman mentioned it too, though he would never set foot there. Something about Hannah, something else, raised Una's concern, though she could not quite put her finger on it. Only seeing children at school, and not their conditions at home, had spared her from witnessing the less savoury aspects of pupils' lives.

When they finally reached the road, the Inkpen girl came slouching towards them. Isla's daughter was bouncing a pram over the ruts, out walking her newborn. No more than sixteen, the poor thing was the talk of Barrein, enough to curl Win Goodrow's toes and hair, how she had partied in town with sailors—"quite the orgy," as Mrs. Finck put it—and got herself into trouble.

The baby was wailing. The sound had the effect of a sharp instrument probing Una's eardrums. The girl lifted the child and thumped its back. Hannah's face lit up. "Cute little beggar." Hannah stuck a finger into its mouth and squealed as it sucked. It was all Una could do not to yank the unhygienic finger away, especially when Hannah eyed her—those eyes of hers milder than Enman's. "How come you don't got any babies, Missus?"

The Inkpen girl smirked, laying the baby down again. Squalling, it shook its tiny fists, its bonnet twisting over its face. The mother bit back tears and cursed, pushing off.

"If I *did*." The prospect felt to Una both enticing and remote as Mars. "Maybe you'd mind it for me?"

Shrugging till her neck all but disappeared, Hannah hiked up her basin of laundry, ambled a ways before speaking. "If *I* got a baby, Uncle'd beat the tar out of me." The Inkpens could not have been pleased at how their grandbaby had come about. But they were gentler by a mile than Twomey would be, she assumed, given his reputation.

Hannah hummed along with a hornet following them, imitating its drone. She dragged her feet when they reached the lane beyond the cemetery. It was past lunchtime, the sun dizzying. Having eaten nothing besides Enman's orange, Una felt lightheaded. Her brain could have been a helium balloon, her body pulled along by it.

The house stood in a swampy hollow. A keel-less dinghy rotted out front in a patch of fireweed that ringed a gigantic erratic. The boulder—which could be rocked like a cradle, Hannah said—was riven with a hook securing the clothesline to the house. One extra roll, a little extra tug to the left, and you could imagine it bringing down the structure, the whole works collapsing.

Una hung back, watched Hannah mount the sagging step and jerk open the storm door. Slipping from her grasp, the basin clanged to the ground. Wet, twisted clothes lay everywhere. Hannah's face went ruddy.

"Shitshitshitshitshit."

Retrieving things, Una shook away bits of dirt. The girl hurried inside, abandoning her there. This was just as well, judging by what Una glimpsed from outside: a room with junk heaped everywhere. Boots, rope, broken dishes, bottles, stacks of insulators from telephone poles. In the midst of it loomed a kitchen table, a bare-bellied man—Twomey—slumped in the dimness, snoring. The reek of stale beer and cooking grease wafted towards her.

Hannah shot her a warning gaze when, against better judgement, out of curiosity and an awkward sense of duty, Una stepped inside. Such a far cry, this place, from Mrs. Greene's with its prissy curtains and trinkets screaming religiosity. "Gee, thanks," she had said when the old lady "bequeathed" to her that silly figurine which even the sea hadn't wanted, apparently.

Hannah was frantically rooting around for something. Extracting a bowl of clothes pegs from under some rags, she shoved Una outside, whispered in a strangled voice, "Uncle will have a shitfit—he hates riffraff sniffing around, out to steal his stuff. He'll get pissy-mad, Missus, if—"

Una felt pure and utter relief to be out in the daylight. Yet a part of her, a small, brazen part, wanted to troop back inside and give Twomey a proper talking-to, a shaking. Pie-eyed drunk and sleeping it off, obviously, and barely past noon! What kind of guardian was he, especially for a poor child "blessed" with half a deck? she thought critically. But family is family, she remembered Mr. Sarty saying in a similar case. *A child's idea of home mightn't be yours.*

It was all she could do to shake out the creature's shorts and hand them up to Hannah, who pegged them to the line as if they were silk-and-cashmere.

Thank God home visits were not a teacher's domain. Her mother would be aghast at Una entering exactly the sort of hovel her charities assisted. Some parents deserved the strap more than their children did. And if parents would not discipline children, normal ones, not those like Hannah, someone had to. Though Una was squeamish about strapping, she had never shirked her responsibility of maintaining control, especially when punishing bullies. You couldn't let their tears eat away power that was best safeguarded, even hoarded. There'd been a grade six who had tormented whole classes, a grade five who should have lived in the dunce's corner. Those she *had* strapped deserved more than a rap on the knuckles. Even Kit said so. No one liked the whap of leather hitting small palms, but some situations called for—

A roar broke from indoors. A slurred curse, a resounding belch. It reached the yard just as Una heaved one of Twomey's shirts into Hannah's grasp. "Useless piece of shit, where the fuck are ya?"

Hannah clutched the shirt. She seemed to stop breathing, though her voice was weirdly calm. "Get going, Missus—better get your arse out of here."

Before Una could say or do anything, Hannah disappeared inside, out of sight, out of reach, too late to be thrown any sort of lifeline, the offer on the tip of her tongue: Could you, would you come for a lesson, a proper one this time? For the slimmest second Hannah's face hovered at the window, her palm pressed there, visible through the grime.

You could try and lead a horse to water, she thought. She hurried up the lane and past the cemetery, past its huge crucifix. *Suffer the little children*, read its inscription, which she had noted at Mrs. Greene's burial. She hadn't set foot since through the graveyard's sagging gates, amongst its eerily tidy plots. Why would she? Even as she had patted Enman's shoulder, that strange Catholic urge for embracing suffering had irked her: their Saviour's woodenness overseeing the only patch of ground Barrein saw fit to groom. Better, so much better, Una thought, to keep suffering contained—suffering of bodies and, yes, of minds—to keep it concealed. The way her own mother had tried to, for better or for worse, keeping to her bedroom. At least all Una had had to do was see that her mother was nicely dressed and that the nurse hired to tend her was paid from the supply of money in the bank, an ample supply until Una's father died.

She hated the idea of ashes and dust. Yet something drew her backwards and through the cemetery's rusty gates. The gates were the only opening in the low spruce hedge that enclosed it. Something made her walk between the rows of headstones, which studded the burnt, mounded grass like so many crooked teeth. It was impossible not to think of what lay beneath Mrs. Greene's polished granite stone as she gave it a wide berth. A few rows away was a stone inscribed for a Cecelia Twomey, beside it were two crude wooden crosses painted with the Twomey name, and not far off, a black marble monument for Lester Finck. A single granite marker for Enman's father, an uncle, an aunt, and his grandparents was nearby. There had been no room to plant his mother beside them.

The thought grazed her like a blade: could I end up here too? Marriage meant taking on not just one person but their clan *and* an entire place. She felt stupid for only now realizing it. Then she saw something even more sobering. There was a little marble stone for Lester Finck Jr., and another for five Inkpens who had not made it past infancy. It was cold comfort to think being childless meant being lucky.

Una's curls, meanwhile, had dried flat to her head. In her efforts to bathe, how had she neglected to bring a comb? The sun was giving her a headache. A tear snaked down—she couldn't help it. God, it took real stamina to fend off a tear fest, didn't it? The unfairness, no rhyme or reason why some had hordes of kids, kids they did not even want, while others who wanted them had none. The way some ended up as Hannahs and others Rhodes scholars. It seemed dangerous to want anything! Sometimes when Una was still teaching, a creeping sadness, like a bad cold or flu, would send her to bed, though she always rallied to face classes smiling. Still, the grief that living could generate was enough to land you in the mental, if you dwelled on it.

Just as she was passing the Goodrows' Win came running out, waving the *Herald*. Wearing a holey pair of panties on her head to keep the curlers in place, she rattled the newspaper in Una's face. Win pointed to the headline, a shadowy photo underneath it. It showed a clutch of men in some sad excuses for uniforms, wearing handcuffs. *U-Boat crew captured in the Gaspé*, the cutline said.

She could barely take in all Win's yammering. Something about a torpedo landing in some farmer's field, the man alerting the authorities, and in the nick of time.

"They could've invaded! Just like that, Una—think about it. My land, what's to stop the buggers from trying the same tricks here?" There was something almost to be pitied in Win's eagerness. Was it her need for attention?

"May I?" Patiently Una took the paper and scanned the item. It was on the *Herald's* second-last page, a bookend to the classifieds. If it was in the paper, it must be true, she guessed.

"Goddamn," Win swore breathily, her voice rising as she worked herself into a lather. "The nerve of them devils! Can you credit it, Una." This was not a question. "You know, Iris is all the time hearing them out there doing whatever they do in their boats—their subs, I mean. It's not like they stay down on the bottom all the time either."

Them and the sculpins—yes, and you're an expert in naval engineering, Una longed to say, as she saw a dustcloud billowing closer. It was a car barrelling along the road below the hill, familiar-looking but not because it belonged here. Could it possibly be Kit's? No one else in hell's acre drove in such a breezy rush. Soon enough here she was, slowing down—sunglasses, a frizz of red hair bound with a kerchief—peering above the wheel.

Win already looked miffed, any excitement she had stirred up in Una dampened by an invader. Not just any invader but a city person, and not just any city person but an ally, Una's friend. Una grinned and handed back the paper. "Gaspé's a long way away. No point getting ourselves worked up, is there."

Flagging Kit down, she turned to Win and smiled with all her teeth.

"My God, who's this now, Woody Woodpecker flying in?" Win fiddled with a curler, folded her arms.

Beaming, Kit opened her door enough to lean out. Only then did something twig in Una. Waving at Kit to wait, she tapped Win's arm, took back the paper. Aware of the car's idling rumble, she scrutinized the picture.

The men's jackets were nothing like the ones servicemen around here wore. A chill crawled down her back. They resembled the one she had spied by the beach, drying with those clothes amongst the bushes. But this was silly. Of course she was mistaken. The photo was too blurry to be sure of anything. Next she would be like Win, suspicious of anything that moved. It was a tendency Una could guard herself against, Kit had once said.

"Hop in," Kit called out. "What's the matter, Miss Oonah?" Kit asked as soon as she climbed in—the quickest possible escape from Win and having to introduce them, explain, make excuses for not lingering.

The life of Riley all right, she imagined Win crowing, can't even walk ten yards from here to her doorstep.

"The matter?" The sheer relief of seeing a kindred spirit ousted all thoughts of Win and her fearmongering. "Cripes, I can't believe you're here. If I'd known—"

"Yeah, but if I'd called, you know, you'd've been up to something—whatever it is you do out here to keep busy." Kit's eyes crinkled behind her shades.

They were barely in the house when the phone rang, that nutbar Hubley Hill wanting Enman, jabbering about some sort of plan for a dance gone awry, a change of heart. He would have kept her on there forever, with Kit waiting in the kitchen.

"Sure, sure—yes, I'll tell him. Of course he'll understand." Though something told her Enman might not, Una felt relieved. No loss to her, freed of having to sit in the church basement, ears plugged with tissue. "Yes, sure it's understandable." She said it five times if she said it once, gesturing to Kit. Kit had pushed her sunglasses up on top of the kerchief; they looked like a fly's eyes against its green chiffon. "Look in the icebox," she mouthed, remembering the water situation. At least there was lemonade.

"Sorry I couldn't stay, that day of the wake. Bodies make me squeamish." Kit grimaced into her glass when Una finally got off the phone. Kit had poured lemonade for her too. It was cloudy and tasted vaguely of onions. Shit.

"Trouble in Shangri-La-la-land?"

"Why would you ask?"

"Poor Enman. I suppose he's okay?" Kit made a face and set down her glass.

"It's kind of a relief. We couldn't have looked after his mother a day longer."

Though Una had her pride, venting helped. So she told Kit about the well, the lake, the ridiculous inconvenience—but uttering it sparked a feeling almost of panic. How was she to cope without a basic necessity?

Kit peered around, at the walls stencilled with sunlight. She looked disgusted, as if water came exclusively from pipes under paved city streets, a limitless network. "You'd never manage with a baby." Kit sounded rueful, no longer bemused the way she had been, hearing about Una's "plans" after her doctor's appointment in February.

To change the subject Una told Kit how a cousin on her father's side had been lost that spring while escorting a convoy. Not a close cousin, but a fellow Kit might know of.

"Hellish summer, all this fine weather. Crossing the ocean? Goddamn Jerries think they own the fecking thing, don't they just. Red sky at night is no sailors' delight, not for our side. How *is* hubby, anyways? No plans to enlist again, I take it."

Kit didn't wait to hear her answer, though, hopping up to get something from the car. She came back with presents. Wrapped in brown paper was a painting of tugboats, the whitewashed Irving arch in the background—a downtown scene not far from where Enman would be finishing up his day. The gift threw her off; Kit wasn't one for giving away her creations.

"You do that yourself, girl?" A staff room joke about Kit's prodigious talents that vaguely recalled and, Una hoped, deflected embarrassment about Rick Gregory, it replaced the need for gushing.

"Paid a grade six to paint it." Kit laughed, more like herself, pleased by the admiration. She nudged a cardboard box closer. Inside were a little tray of watercolour paints, two fine sable brushes, a ream of brittle manila.

"You're giving me lessons?"

"No. Just something to keep you out of trouble, out here in the back of beyond. You know what they say, lovey, idle hands are the devil's workshop—or something like that." Kit addressed Una's stomach when she spoke. It was as if she expected some visible sign of something. A grand baby bump, is that what she was looking for?

"Well, you'll be pleased to hear I've found a diversion. A pupil. For six weeks or so, I'm thinking."

Looking baffled, Kit pushed her glass away, her lemonade hardly touched.

For godsake, maybe there's water in the kettle, Una thought—enough to give her a cup of tea. "And, the posting you mentioned—the high school one." She hesitated. "I've applied."

"Oh? Better hope Sarty's got a short memory. So Enman's good with it, then?"

Una flushed, examined a fingernail. "'Wake up this side of the sod, sweetpea, and everything's good'—that's him." She forced a smile. "Beats waiting around for something to happen, a 'watched pot' and all that." Kit gave her a worried look that quickly turned indulgent.

While she boiled the dregs in the kettle, Kit's gaze fixed on the range and its carboy of stove oil. Her lip curled at the tea. "Gregory was asking about you, at the end of school. Cripes, the summer's flying, though." Kit held her cup aloft, inspecting the bottom. "Royal Albert, don'tcha know. Who was she trying to impress, your mother-outlaw, I wonder? Gawd. And when was the last time this place got painted? Enman will have to remedy that if he's planning to sell. That green is so *twenties*." Kit got up and perused the calendar's Xs and dots. "What's this now, tick-tack-toe?

"What does Enman think of making a baby? Forget I asked." Then a knowing look spread over Kit's face. "Ah! He's had a change of heart, hasn't he, about moving back?"

Kit's tone made Una go silent.

"Did I hear you say there was paint?" Before Una could stop her, Kit went beetling down into the cellar.

Kit was the type of friend intimate enough that you didn't mind her peeking inside your cupboards. Still it was unnerving having her see the cellar's dirt floor, its shelves of dusty preserves. "Mind Mrs. Greene's science experiments," Una called down, then from the bottom step watched Kit unearth the unopened paint Una herself had picked at Easter, thinking only about brightening the place. Sight unseen, Enman's mother had refused yellow, not the first of their disagreements. Laying her hands on a screwdriver to open it and a ruler for a stir-stick, Kit rooted around for a brush, one eyebrow cocked. "Wouldn't a science teacher love to see what's growing in Mrs. G's Petri dishes."

Hadn't Una insisted that Kit not mention that mess last December, promising herself to forget it had happened? As her friend lugged the paint upstairs, Una protested. "Don't be silly, you didn't come here to work. Shiza, you're my *guest*—"

"Shag it, I want to help. Maybe you need a *certain* jackass to come and persuade you—?"

"For godsake. And how do you propose we'll clean up?"

But Kit had turpentine and a little can of Varsol out in the car, her travelling art supplies. The sun and the heat made painting the last thing Una felt like doing, but she went upstairs and dug through Mrs. Greene's rag bag for clothes to work in. The old woman's blouses, dresses, and knickers were too "good" to throw away, in Enman's view, yet in Una's view, too threadbare to give to charity. Una figured he would not want people like Mrs. Finck thinking he had let his mother dress like an urchin while he went around in suits. Win Goodrow would have spread such talk, Una decided, but he had defended *her*. "Can't you give it a rest, dear? Win's not a bad person. Just ignore her."

Una tugged an elastic-less pair of bloomers over her hair to protect it, found a couple of awful shapeless blouses, put one on, and brought the other down for Kit.

Instead of smiling, Kit scowled. "Jesus, look at you. You're more cracked than I thought."

"Forget it. Let's just go to the beach." Who wanted to waste a perfectly good afternoon anyway, doing a chore more properly Enman's? Kit hated sand, though, how it got in your eyes, ears, between your toes, and in other places. Then Una remembered the jacket and the picture in the paper.

But Kit was laughing. "You've gone loopy with boredom? That green looks like fungus. One look at it and most people would turn around and leave. Shut up and let's just get 'er done."

Una touched Kit's wrist hovering there with the ruler. An oily scum had floated to the paint's surface. "Can I tell you something?"

"Well yeah—I *figured* somehow there's something not quite right. Months of looking after an old lady, ergo no chance for fun. No getting a bun in the oven. What other reason to get hitched? Poor sweetie, trouble in paradise. You and Enman, he's not—?" Damaged, incapable? said Kit's look. Flexing her wrists, Kit held out her palms, then wielded the stir-stick. "Your secret's safe with me, hon. No need to explain."

"Kit,"—she gave herself a minute to find the words, words having nothing to do with last winter's debacle at school—"at the beach. Just this morning. There were some clothes, and men, and…someone's jacket. Then, in the *Herald*—"

"*Seen* it, my darling, those Jerries up in Québec." A funny look passed over Kit's face. She had finally removed and folded her sunglasses; it was as if she'd been scared of losing them. "No. No way—those gutless wonders wouldn't have the fecking parts to do something like that here, come ashore and face us. Not with our ARP all over the place. 'Know thy enemy' and all that. Nope, no way, they wouldn't dare, that's not how those birds oper-ate." Kit was adamant; when she was right about something there was no disputing the point. "Now give us that brush. It's not a shade I'd choose, but better than what's on there now."

A FEW HOURS LATER THE kitchen was transformed. Like standing in a field of marigolds, Kit admitted. "Enman will hardly recognize it—just tell him the spirit of good taste went on a tear. Speaking of taste, I'm fecking parched."

The lemonade was all she had. They lugged two chairs outdoors to sit and cool off. Kit pulled the sweaty kerchief from her hair. Outdoors, its carroty shade looked faded, the greyness at her temples matching the lines around her eyes, still a startling green. Kit had been teaching for a decade when Una first started. Catching her looking, Kit aimed a deadpan gaze at the sea. "Would you get those goddamn things off your head before Win-Whoever sees. No better flattery than imitation."

Before Enman sees you, Kit hinted, sounding almost wistful. Perhaps, without knowing it, Kit was envious of their marriage? He would be home any minute, which meant that Mrs. Greene's paint-drib-bled undies went straight into the trash. The two of them polished off the lemonade, Kit in silence.

Although Una cared more about keeping her figure than about eat-ing, cooking, because she had to do it for Enman, had become unavoid-able. "Will you stay and have supper with us?"

"What, and squat on some rock later to help wash up? Sorry, hon." She had a date, Kit said, and as unexpectedly as she had arrived, Kit was pecking Una's cheek goodbye, waving a freshly lit cigarette from the car window."Mind your fecking P's and Q's, eh, Missus Greene. Behave, now, or I'll send the science teacher with the strap to straighten you out!"

Kit thought she was being funny—it was Kit's way of teasing, reminding Una of the bond forged between them when Una chose Kit as her exclusive confidant. The joke was poorly chosen and humiliating. Una felt stung in a way she could not have explained if she had wanted to.

"Teachers don't smoke, Miss Blackburn," she called out. "You've got a month and a half to quit that filthy habit." As the car disappeared her spirits flagged—more than the simple letdown of being left or the straightforward regret that an afternoon with company had been squandered on a chore Enman should have done.

More's the pity, Kit had not offered a word of solace or encouragement about the position *she* had suggested Una apply for. At least Enman would soon be home bearing some kind of present and in time to trek next door with a bucket.

The shadows stretched longer, and evening wore on. She fried pork steak, heated peas, ate, and set aside a plate for Enman. Across the harbour Mrs. Finck's blinds were down; she closed shop earlier and earlier, possibly due to the shortages. Even Sylvester Meade had better things to squander ration coupons on than stale sweets to bribe little girls into sitting on his lap. Still no sign of the Inkpens' boat, not that she was worried. The wolf packs, as the paper called them—if you believed they lurked this close—had bigger prey than a fishing boat. Perhaps the men had been held up by harbour traffic.

As the gloaming dimmed she occupied herself with packing more of Mrs. Greene's things. Maybe they could be left in the cellar for whoever lived here next. Listening to the radio—no blackout message tonight—she tried to read one of Mrs. Greene's books, a convoluted tale about a detective, a countess, some paintings. What kept her reading was knowing the culprits would get caught and be faced with consequences; culprits always did in books. But that was books, not life.

The clock struck eight, and still no Enman. She'd have killed for a glass of water, and not a drop to drink in the house, barring the rum hidden in Mrs. Greene's cabinet. She should go to a neighbour, except her tongue could dry up and fall out before she would go next door, and hell could freeze before she would drink from the Meades' tap. She would need to flush the toilet, wash her face.

Swinging Mrs. Greene's enamelled pail, she cut down the hill to Isla Inkpen's, where she had gone once on an errand for Mrs. Greene. By this hour, Isla's daughter would have put her baby down for the night. The last thing Una needed was to hear its wailing.

Isla invited her in. A slender, tight-lipped woman, Isla was still pretty, despite looking more worn and older than she probably was. Of course, she had more than enough to handle, being married to Greeley Inkpen. Isla heaved aside a bucketful of diapers stewing in the kitchen and pointed her to the pump at the sink. From the next room came a cooing sound, a lisping lullaby, the baby's gurgling. "A first, it'll be, if *our* well gives out." Isla crossed her fingers and legs as if she needed to pee, and laughed, sort of. "Cross my heart, hope to die. Hope for the best, Una, what else can you do? Stay for a cuppa? No point sitting up there alone. Must be hard, after what happened to Enman. You must worry about him."

But the baby started crying and Una remembered Enman's plate was at the mercy of the cat. With her pail brimming, she took the road back, since one faulty step crossing the field would make the endeavour point-less. She was already worried that one bucketful would not be enough. Then, piercing the darkness some distance from the roadside, shouts drew her attention. Some sort of hooliganism, kids being kids. Thudding foot-steps, screaming—in the darkness, out of view, some rowdy game had gotten out of hand.

Hannah Twomey came stumbling towards her, arms shielding her head. Something ricocheted from a boulder. Boys' voices cut the satiny air, echoing in the deadly stillness.

"Show us your jugs, retard! We wanna see your jugs!"

Water slopped everywhere as Una hurried to the girl, something fierce unleashed inside her. Leering faces peeked from behind a second rock, another erratic that could be levered back and forth with a stick wedged under it. God, if she could have bowled it after the brats like a gigantic marble—a doughboy, no, a wrecking ball—she would have.

Three of them hightailed it behind Meades' place as Win appeared briefly under her porch light, then vanished inside.

"Hannah, Hannah dear." Una's yard-duty voice took over. "Are you all right?" She helped the girl up the lane and her own front steps.

In the hallway she snapped on the light. Blood seeped from a gash on Hannah's head and smeared the front of her blouse. The girl made a noise like Tippy coughing up hairballs. She curled herself up as if to erase herself—a behaviour Una had seen exhibited often enough at school. She had gone out of her way to calm victims and shame aggressors. If she was lucky enough to be interviewed for the high school job she would make this known.

"I never done nothing, Missus. Swear to—I done *nothing*—God— to them f-f-fucking little christers." Hannah was crying now, a child in her teenager's body, possibly much younger than Una had imagined.

"Let's fix you up."

"Why do them fuckers hate me, Missus?" In the bright glowing kitchen, a tough smile tugged at the corners of Hannah's mouth before tears slicked it away.

"They don't *hate* you. They're just…they just—" But they did hate her, they must, just because. So what if they didn't know better? Knowing better was something Enman preached, not as grounds to condemn someone but to excuse them, which is why his consolations could feel pointless. The nastiness of children was old hat, though it never stopped being shocking.

Settling Hannah at the table, Una ladled water from the bucket into a bowl and, dipping a cloth, wiped away blood. Saliva pooled around Una's tongue. Revulsion at the boys' behaviour had got the better of her thirst. An inch or two closer and the girl would have lost an eye.

When she finished cleaning Hannah up she measured out two glass-fuls from the bucket of water. The water from Isla's had a mossy taste. Who knew such ordinary stuff could be so precious?

"There now. Take your time. When you're feeling better I'll walk you home."

Sucking water through her teeth, Hannah went small again. Under her shirt's frowzy cotton her shoulders heaved. "Uncle says them bastards just give what I got coming."

"Take a deep breath." Hannah's sobs had a nasty way of burrowing into Una.

"Uncle hates me too." Hannah's voice, so tiny just then, seemed at odds with her stocky, matronly build. The shadowy look in her eyes betrayed her other features' blandness. The small, neat chin, the smooth flatness between her nose and lips.

It was hard to resist reaching out. Una put her arm around Hannah's shoulders, reached for her stubby hand. She had seen kids who were slow, but none so slow their parents shunned them.

"Now, for pity's sake, no one hates you. Those boys—they'll be seen to, if I have any say. Don't you worry." How they would be, Una hadn't a clue, which made her feel like the mucky-mucks who boasted about beating the Germans. But Enman would take things in hand. "When Mr. Greene gets home he'll give them a talking to."

Making tea, finally, she served Hannah's in Mrs. Greene's favourite cup and saucer, placing them into her hands. The poor thing smelled a bit; the sourness of unwashed clothes and slovenly living was nothing new, of course.

She patted Hannah's arm so chummily it joggled the cup.

"Jumpin's, Missus!" But a shy smile warmed that moonscape face. "I 'preciate all you done for me. That fooking old Finck hates me too." The girl's lip curled stubbornly. "Missus, tell me...tell me again, how you spell 'Hannah.'"

Laying out a stack of Kit's paper, Una found a pencil and sharpened it with the paring knife. "It's a magical name—see? A palindrome." This time she enunciated it. Printing and naming each letter, she read them backwards. "None of those boys have a name that'll do that, I'll bet." Unless there was a Bob—there must be one, though they would take after their fathers generally, of course, with handles like Robart, Sylvester, Edgar.

Gripping the pencil like a spear, Hannah traced the letters' shapes. Her greyish eyes gleamed. "Like this, Missus? A ladder. An iron. Two hills. An iron, a ladder. A fucky-lucky name, right?" The poor thing looked so hopeful—tongue clenched between those too-perfect teeth—it was impossible to think of Hannah as anything but a little kid as she drew the letters again.

The girl's obvious delight made Una feel unexpectedly giddy. "What pretty chompers you have, dear." It seemed the opportune thing to say.

"They cost Uncle a fooking arm and a leg. Not mine though, see?" Hannah bounced both knees, flapped her arms like wings. Next came the tale about going to Hellifax in someone's truck and how the liquor Uncle gave her after her old ones got yanked "tasted like stink." Then, yes, he'd taken her to Finck's and bought her an Orange "Crushed," telling her to "Chug it an' if it comes back up, aim for that old bitch's shoes."

"And how did you like the city?"

"Well Missus, it wasn't Dee-Tee-Bee. Down. Town. Barrein. Like Uncle says."

"Of course." Una printed the letters—DTB—and in spite of her troubles, Hannah clapped her hands and laughed.

"Do you remember how to spell your other name, your last name?" Una blocked out thoughts of what *Twomey* conjured for her, something festering and malignant.

Without warning, fear clouded Hannah's face. Gulping tea, she lurched up. "I got to get Uncle's supper. He'll be real *real* mad if he don't get his supper."

"Oh?" It was almost nine o'clock. Startled, she slipped Hannah her paper. "This is yours. Take it, show him." Damned if a packet of gold stars wasn't buried somewhere upstairs.

The girl's hands paddled the air. The gash, a lurid purple, showed through her hair. Imagining whatever else Hannah had suffered made Una's skin prickle.

"I can help you, dear." Her voice felt unnaturally high. What had she let herself in for? "I can teach you to write, and read too." She thrust the stack of blank paper at Hannah. "Here, take it." But the girl let the sheets flutter to the floor. She even left behind her page of printing, lumbering as fast as her thick legs would carry her out the front door.

It was almost the new moon. Weak starlight traced Mrs. Greene's oddments in the parlour, worthless objects gathering dust on their shelves—a tiny china basket painted with rosebuds, some kitten-shaped salt and pepper shakers keeping the Virgin Mary figurine company. Despite the sorting Una had done, it would take another month to clear out the effects of a whole lifetime. The presence of such clutter was apt to creep into and overtake, become, a person's state of mind. In the thickening silence, Una set Hannah's work on the shelf beside the "beautiful," or was it "blessed," mother. She thought of the estate auction where her parents' possessions, and her inheritance, had been dispersed, the auction's proceeds and most of those from the sale of their house disbursed to creditors. Why she felt such contempt for the pitiful statuette she could not say, only that she wished a draft might catch Hannah's paper and help nudge the thing from its perch.

Settling on the sofa, she found it hard not to brood. She pictured the superintendent of schools at his desk in the red brick Academy building, reading her letter amid wafts of Dustbane and lemon oil. The principal, Mr. Sarty, had bid on her father's beautiful burled walnut desk. What if Sarty and the superintendent had words? Whether they did or did not, she couldn't make a husband, a marriage, disappear. She shifted her thoughts to babies growing into full-blown people. The idea struck her anew, that a fertilized egg carried everything needed to form a being with every quality of the human race. It said so in the book Enman had stuffed under the mattress in the little room upstairs. Reading this, he had joked, "Now I really need a drink."

What did they say at Alcoholics Anonymous, where one of her mother's doctors had suggested Una might find encouragement while staying with her, a lifetime before she laid eyes on Enman? The line that "crazy" was repeating over and over the very thing you hoped would change. The tendency in herself, which she had begun to see in Enman too, to acquiesce to things even when you meant to take charge of them.

This sobering thought led her to reach into Mrs. Greene's cabinet, where she found the bottle shoved behind sheet music, empty but for a drop or two. More surprising, the red-covered book was there too, *The Hygiene of Marriage*, which Dr. Snow had recommended and Enman had gone out and purchased. While Mrs. Greene was alive, they had both taken pains to keep it hidden: what would Marge have thought? Una paged to the section about parents. What made good ones, how mankind's future depended on weeding out the Twomeys of the world and, by implication, its Hannahs. If you believed what they said on the news, such progress came down to science. Then Una imagined Win dropping in and seeing her reading. *Those Greenes up there reading sex books—how's that for all talk and no action?*

There was still no sign of Enman. Flinging the book aside, she trooped out to the outhouse—which meant pushing aside cobwebs, plugging her nose—then, leaving the cat outside, giving up on waiting, Una trooped upstairs to bed.

9

ENMAN AWOKE, SLOUCHING IN A BLAZE OF LIGHT, TO A FLASHLIGHT BEING shone in his face. Brighter, steadier bands of light illuminated the boat's wheelhouse, flaring, dying, flaring again. He felt the boat rocking under him like a cradle. In the searchlights' beams he took in his friends, the patrolman who had boarded. They were just inside the anti-submarine net. Isaac was shouting, "What the hell would we be hiding?"

Enman straightened up, groped for his satchel. His head throbbed. The satchel was by his side.

"Routine. Got to inspect everyone coming and going." This had not happened on their trip in. The fellow passed his light over Enman again. Enman planted his feet, closed his eyes. The spins only worsened with his eyes shut.

After what felt like hours the patrolman let them through, and with Greeley at the helm they steamed off. At least motoring forward pushed back the sick, rocky feeling of sitting still. Enman pretended the dark sea was the sky upside down, a watery heaven or a very wet hell, and

Neverfail's blinking green was the pinprick light of some gaseous planet. At least all the coastal lights were running, a good sign—good enough that he went back to sleep.

When he woke up next, Robart was pointing to lights—one for The Sisters, another for the Blind Sister rock, the shoal just northeast of home named for two jealous girls who had left their sightless sibling to be swept away. So the tale went. People could be cruel, even women, thought Enman, though he had never met anyone like that.

Not soon enough, land was in sight. A solitary light twinkled from the hill. Isaac straightened his cap. "Win Goodrow on watch, boys." Robart laughed.

"Friggin' Mata Hari, that one." Edgar sounded pleased with himself.

"Now, she's not at all bad, poor Win."

Isaac snorted. "Well, you would know, wouldn't you, Greene."

At the entrance to the tiny harbour, against the dark shore—was it a dream or his liquored haze?—something loomed, pale and spectral. It looked as graceful as a ballerina primed for dancing. Dancing Dvořák's largo with movements lithe and bashful as the piece's dawning melody, the nicest of all the music in the *New World* symphony. The figure stayed still, deaf to the engine's sputter, until its shape became clear.

A great blue heron, it was as startling and as singularly at home there as only a bird could be. The sight was a comfort, as if some gentle puppeteer stood behind it, until the creature flexed its wings and took flight. For the briefest moment, Enman imagined his ma working its strings. Then it was a ghostly arrow piercing the dark. A reminder, however unsettling, that as much as things stood still they shifted too, and in shifting sometimes returned to how they had started, not always as you expected. Neither as much to the good *or* to the bad, nor as quickly as you hoped.

You did the best you could, he mused, then you died. You could belong well enough without belonging completely, which was fine too—though living in the present meant unpacking a number of emotional boxes, bags, and suitcases you were prone to lug around: a chore his Una had yet to do. Barrein was home now, he had decided, and he was determined to stay here, though he had perhaps done better for himself, earlier in life, in town. Being home didn't exclude the possibilities of other places, nor did other places exclude those of home. Look at Dvořák, who had composed his symphony a world away from his land of the Czechs, and Benjamin Britten across the ocean from England, also writing music in America.

Now Enman had music of his own to face: Una's wrath. It was midnight when the hull nudged the dock; at least he was sober. He waved to the others straggling off to their wives, all but Isaac who charged jauntily ahead. Calling goodnight to him, Enman hastened up the lane. Sleepless crows nattered from the telephone wire. Playing leapfrog, they rushed him onwards, alighting from pole to pole. One before him, one behind, another sweeping right overhead: things happened in threes. It made him think of Ma's hymn, sung by Isla and Father Heaney: *Christ behind me, Christ before me, Christ beside me.* The nuns came back to him too, the memory of the nuns, the *pock* of stones hitting bodies clothed in black. Hadn't the sisters come to help the likes of Twomey, whose father had lost a leg in a fishing accident, then lacked the wherewithal to feed his kids?

He reached the yard, stood on the patch of flat rock Ma had called "the patio." He felt the tingle of both his legs, a tingle of gratitude. A soft light burned in the upstairs window. "Pull some blinds down over yourselves, you nose-minding ARP types," he imagined Isaac saying. Not a wisp of a breeze stirred the jet-black beads glinting from the clothesline. Cleary's rosary, untouched all his lifetime, hung there by Ma, her way of hanging the old man out to dry, getting some good out of it. The beads were working overtime, Enman thought, not a lick of rain, the air uncommonly soft for mid-July. Too soon, July's arse end would be upon them. Out on the shoals, past the offing, breakers formed a thin white spit. Another month and the water would be warmed up, maybe enough to swim. He pictured the beaches at Shag's, each crescent a pearly necklace in the dark, like the one he should have had in his pocket.

The back door wasn't locked, the cat followed him in, and, leaving his shoes on the mat by the threshold, he entered the kitchen. It smelled funny, like spirits—aviation fuel? The starlight sifting in gave the walls a strange glow. He didn't bother turning on the light, better to go straight to bed. Then he recognized the odour. Turpentine? Una's friend Kit, who painted pictures, had visited, was staying over? He peered through the window. His was the only car out there. His foot caught something, the jerry can from the cellar? Gasoline. The can's lightness jerked his arm when he lifted the thing to take a whiff. Had Una tried to coax Beulah into starting? God forbid she had flooded her.

Needing to rinse his mouth, he ran the tap. Nothing but a peaty smell wheezed out, the walls around him glowing like noxious gas. It was only then he spied the bucket. On the table sat a dish of shrivelled food. On the sill above the sink, just visible, was Una's wedding ring, which she removed to do dishes.

The pain near his temple greased his guilt. The ring looked lost as a severed finger, in need of rescue before falling down the drain. Kit Blackburn had that effect, made Una scatterbrained, absent-minded, he had noticed. Leaning against a chair was something in a frame. In his hand the ring was a hard little nugget, which he placed for safekeeping in a cup.

Not a sound of Una stirring came from above, so she hadn't waited up. A bit of music would melt his worries, petty as they were. When he snapped on the light, that relic from the bank, the glow through its green glass was a poultice on his damaged pride over how dispensable he was. The *New World* was propped beside the cabinet, it slid easily from its sleeve. He placed the needle on the second track—Una would not appreciate being wakened by the first, the adagio with its swashbuckling trumpet blasts—and, soothed by the gentle folksy largo, he settled on the sofa with Tippy on his lap, the cat purring up a storm.

Then his eyes fell on a sheet of paper propped on the shelf. Manila, the type some teachers gave pupils to draw on, a child's handiwork. Not just any child's, but Hannah Twomey's, he saw, the paper with her name on it rubbing shoulders with Ma's ornament. Dear God. A clamminess came over him, that her work had crossed their threshold, Ma not fully a month dead.

He rose to whip the paper away when Tippy leapt and tripped and made him stumble, knocking the porcelain figure from its perch. He watched in dismay as it toppled to the floor, the sharp little crash ringing out above the satiny violin. The figurine's head snapped from its body.

Imagining Ma's distress, he heard Una rising and coming down-stairs. To spare himself the slightest gloat in her smile, he rolled the pieces in a doily and stuffed the works into a drawer—it was nothing some glue wouldn't fix.

If only the same could have been said for Una's humour. Her face was flushed with indignation.

"So you decided to come home, I see. Better late than never, I guess?"

"Now, now, dear, I can explain, no need to be—"

Her eyes darted around, looked past him—What, no souvenirs?—and only then he noticed the book in her hands, the smutty one. The red of its dustjacket as lurid as the advice inside it.

"Reading Everett, I see—*Professor* Millard Spencer Everett." His face felt red too. Yet a laugh escaped him. "Professor of what, I'd like to know, wouldn't you? I see you've had company. A regular rousing spelling bee with the Twomey girl, was it?"

"As if you have the right—"

"But I'm all for you having company, sweetpea—the kind that can read and write, talk intelligently, take care of itself, and—"

"Fat chance of that around here. You mean, not embarrass you."

It was like being slapped in the head, the blow coming from nowhere.

"Oh stop now. That's not fair. I'm only saying—Hannah, either of those Twomeys—they're not exactly friendship material. Not like your Kit. I suppose she was in on it, you birds playing school. What, you took it upon yourselves to go down and nab Bart's niece? Surprised he let you in. His niece, yes. But surely you know—"

"Nothing—Kit had nothing to do with it. Hannah could've been killed by a right group of savages, if you must know. I set her up in the kitchen, thanks but no thanks. Our lesson went quite nicely. More nicely than whatever you've been up to, I'll bet."

"Killed? You should've called Clint."

"I'll entertain whomever I like."

She flounced up the stairs and he went after her. It was like ascending into a boiler room it was so stuffy on the landing; no wonder she was hot under the collar. Going into their room, which was hot as Hades, he banged his head on the low part of the ceiling. He thought, for no reason, of the room where they had spent their wedding night, in the Waverley hotel where Oscar Wilde had slept—a fact which had impressed Una, him not so much. She had brought the book up here with her, and flung it on the rumpled sheet. He imagined Greeley looking at it and teasing, "Did the navy damage you that much that you need instructions?"

"Desire," as Una had called it, was, in his books, for film stars, women with million-dollar legs and men with pomaded hair, people on movie screens.

He undressed in silence, stooping to skirt the kneewall as he flung his clothes on the chair. They might have smelled a bit, he would allow that. His head had stopped hurting, but the upset of their dispute made his gut like a well with a fish inside.

He wanted to go downstairs and lie on the couch, have Tippy curl up on his chest and be done with the night. But then Una closed the book and turned to him, rubbed her fingers over the bump not quite hidden by his hair. She kissed him, her anger suddenly gone.

"Now what did you do to deserve *that*? I was worried something had happened, that you weren't coming back."

"You've got an odd way of showing your feelings. But I'm glad to hear it. I missed you too."

Then she got up and he heard her snap on the bathroom light, busy making herself pretty. Or planning a new maneouvre. The doctor had certainly given her some strange—well, Enman found them strange, strange and unnecessary—ideas. "There's no need to doll yourself up, my darling—I like you the way you are." His voice echoed unsteadily in the dimness. Right now, relieved of remorse, he would have traded a year's worth of ration coupons, even ones for gasoline, to buy her a single pair of stockings. No price was too great when it came to pleasing Una, he was lucky to have her—especially given what some men ended up with, some women like taxis without decent wheels. Una had her quirks, but who didn't?

Then he remembered Snow, whose hair matched the stuff that fell on the ground, sizing up the scars from his wounds, saying not to let himself get overheated. Overheated sperm made lousy swimmers, Enman had read someplace, maybe in that stupid book.

Was that why Una kept the thermometer by the bed? Of course it wasn't. But he worried about her temperature diving, taking those ocean dips of hers, that she'd catch hypothermia.

She came in and slid close, smelling of cold cream and White Shoulders perfume. His brain felt suddenly too big for his skull, weary, but he laced her fingers through his and brought them to his lips. Between his and Una's sticky selves and the room being so stuffy, it was hard to tell where flesh ended and the air's closeness began, the bed like a bowl of hodgepodge. Butter, cream, and boiled veg from the garden—it wasn't a difficult treat to prepare, so surely Una could try to make it, if the drought didn't stunt the summer's harvest too badly. He thought of the well, pushed it quickly from his mind. Una sighed exuberantly, working at him. He thought of a torpedo sweating in its chamber. "In all respects ready," the merchant marine's slogan drifted back. He thought how, with its spare, lean curves, Una's body had a typography like that of low, rocky land meeting the ocean's. Beautiful. It did not help that they were doing this in the bed Ma had shared with his father, where Enman had probably been conceived. He managed to get the pillow under her bottom, then felt himself wilt. A pair of maracas had started up in his head. Delerium tremens, he thought, because thinking the words helped contain them.

Una sighed, disappointed. She rolled heavily onto her side. He stroked her arm softly, apologetically. He almost said something about Olympian swimmers, wanting to joke that even they sometimes failed, missed their mark. "A deleterious effect on functioning" was how Snow labelled alcohol's interference with sex. The man had a knack for vocabulary.

Enman only meant to be funny. "I'm not a circus seal, dear, trained to balance a ball on its snout."

But Una turned and studied him. "What ball, what snout? Is that what you think, that I want you to 'perform'? So, what about your job? You asked them?"

"Just have to be patient, now. It's a matter of patience, dear Una. Everything's a matter of patience. We'll wait and see."

10

TRUDGING OUT TO THE PRIVY, UNA TOSSED ENMAN'S PORK STEAK TO THE
Meades' pooch. It was a nicer breakfast than the poor flea-bitten thing
was surely used to.

Back in the house, choosing a spot on the wall above the kitchen
table, she drove a nail and hung Kit's tugboat picture to cheer herself up.
It would only hang there for a little while, she was determined, until they
found a place in town. Meanwhile, she would show Enman she was just as
handy with a hammer as he could be, taking matters into her own hands.
She had to be, with a man who, for someone so well-meaning, wasn't
around when needed.

Grabbing the pail to go to Isla's, she spotted her ring awash in
the dregs of Hannah's cup. Wiping it off, she went to push it over her
knuckle—force of habit—but on second thought popped it into a fruit
nappy which she slid up on to the top shelf.

Would he even notice she wasn't wearing it?

Perusing the calendar, she hesitated, waiting for sounds of life—
God, was the man even alive? Her heart thumped. Calm down, calm

down right now, she told herself. Her temperature was up ever so slightly, and so if yesterday had not been, today might be prime? His job was one thing. But why squander an opportunity—to pull herself out of this present limbo—out of pride and anger, just to press a point? Last night wasn't the first time Enman had overindulged and it wouldn't be the last, she felt glumly certain. But more importantly, why should she pay the price for it?

A nice cup of tea would have tempered her feelings. But then she heard him tramping downstairs. Slipping into the hallway to meet him, she whisked Hannah's paper from where he had stuck it atop the spindly table there. In spite of everything it made her smile, Hannah's name drawn like a string of objects—bookended ladders each with one rung, clothes irons, humps like a Bactrian camel's, two hills. Shiza, *shiza*, she suddenly remembered Hubley Hill's rambling message.

Maybe Enman had already heard and been drowning some disappointment about the cancelled gig? Or had something gone amiss at the bank?

The bump on his head was the size of a child's doughboy marble. His face was the colour of raw scallops. He eyed Hannah's work. "I suppose you'll have Kit frame that too? And what's with the kitchen? If you'd waited, I'd have painted it for you."

"I'd sooner wait for Marriott's moving truck."

"Now, it's not so simple. You know in town we'd end up bunking down with a crowd. I'm not about to stick you in some fleabag rooming house, not when we've got a fine place here."

"Fine if you don't like having water, and other things. Have you, have *we* looked for a place in town? No. And you said, 'Once Ma's gone.'"

"Una. Things change. If I'd known about the water I'd have got back sooner."

"You know that's not what I mean. I agreed to come help with your mother, not to *stay*. Think what I—we—gave up!"

"Well, and you did help, a lot, more or less. I appreciate that, I appreciate *you*. But *this* is where I want to hang my hat, this is my *home*."

"And the flat wasn't *my* home?"

"It was, it *was*. But things are different now, aren't they? As I recall, New Year's Eve there was no talk of babies. None I'm aware of."

"Things *change*, you just said."

"Fine, then. Now we've got a whole house, room for *two* babies."

She looked away, glimpsed herself in the cloudy hall mirror. Through her tan, the tops of her cheeks looked almost white with anger. "A place with no amenities is no place to have *or* raise a baby."

"Well. Maybe you don't need to have one. You've got Twomey's niece you can fuss over, I see."

The smug way he said it made Una stop and catch her breath. "The sooner we get back to town, the sooner you can start at your job."

He drew a long breath and shook his head at her, as if she was simple-minded. Then he edged past her, headed for the privy. A lucky thing we didn't knock it down, she imagined him saying just as smugly. Mrs. Greene was probably somewhere grinning down, satisfied. If you believed in such tripe.

Una collected herself. Oh, but she didn't want to fight. Fighting was no way to get him to see the light.

Let him relieve himself, then she'd fry an egg, and—after he trooped next door with the bucket—they would talk, and make up.

He returned a good while later, the pail brimming. His pallor was no longer sickly, but he still smelled a bit unpleasant. He cleared his throat. "Look, I'm sorry. It's stupid, arguing, isn't it. I never mean to upset you."

"People never do." People never *meant* to. She thought now of Kit.

"But here's another thing. Not to be nasty. But, about Hannah Twomey. Poor thing hasn't the sense God gave horseflies." Enman smiled then, sort of, as if he had pulled off a fine joke. Perhaps he and Kit weren't so different, neither meant their remarks to be cruel.

Any cruelty of theirs wasn't worth the trouble it could cause, taking it up with them. Una changed tack.

"Those little devils, those boys, were complete savages, tormenting her something awful."

"I don't suppose they have names."

"Of course they do. Win could tell you."

"But you can't." He sighed, looking sheepish. It was clear he was dancing around something else. "Ah, Una. I know you mean well"—he was brushing her off, the gall!—"but next she'll be following you like a puppy."

"Excuse me?" She paused, eyeing him. "What *did* the bank tell you?"

"I know you're only trying to help—"

Forgetting, momentarily, more pressing concerns, she waved Hannah's paper at him. "They were throwing rocks! I've never seen such behaviour." Though her anger had worn itself out, her cheeks burned. "And by the way, you'll be happy to know," she let a snicker escape, "you've been shaved from Hill's roster."

He eyed her suspiciously. His face needed a shave. "You'll be pleased, spared another dance-hall bore. Can't say I blame you." His tone was infuriatingly even.

It took every ounce of energy she had not to shout. "Where *were* you, anyway?" Because she didn't want to anger him, she only wanted to know. Then they could make up, there was time before work, before he disappeared into his all-important day. Shouting only raised the blood pressure, wasn't good for anyone.

"Look, it's not the girl I'm worried about, it's Twomey. You don't want to tangle with him."

"Because she's simple, I suppose? All the more reason not to go on about *her*. What is it you're *not* saying?"

Now his cheeks turned a pasty pink. "She's as simple as the fellows at the bank. I'm telling you, that new bunch in charge—they're the ones playing with half a deck, I like to think. If you'd been there—" He raised his eyebrows, almost quizzically. Cautiously. So she had caught him out. He had not asked about the job, after all. He gave a whistling sigh. "There's more to it than that, I'm afraid." Swatting a fly, he bumped one of his mother's cups, made it dance in the saucer. "I didn't ask because I'm not going back there. They've got a new man and, well, things aren't what they were."

Tea. She needed tea. She was thirsty again, so thirsty. The pinkness had moved to his neck and he loosened his collar. His eyes and mouth looked ashen. Proper thing, she thought: he should be good and sorry, not just for last night but for lying, for leading her on, making her think—

She studied Hannah's work. There was something calming about it, enlightening. She had heard someone say that Miss Rooney deemed the girl unteachable. Hannah had shaped these letters before. People learned through repetition, despite what Al-Anon said about repeating certain behaviours. She remembered the fellowship's pleas for candour tempered with advice not against confronting but against *baiting* loved ones.

"This isn't about Hannah, is it," she waded in, "and I suppose it's not really about your job. It's about liquor. Have you always had this fondness for it?"

She gazed at him, and he blanched, and then he smiled with such a shy, beseeching weakness that she wanted to hit him. Because his look was humbling, it weakened *her*, it made her want to admit, confess, what had happened in the principal's office, how Sarty's stare had reduced her to almost nothing.

And yet he dodged her, as if he hadn't heard a word. He ran his finger over Hannah's work. "Hard to believe, isn't it, that *he's* her uncle. She's such a shy thing."

"Pardon?" Una had never confronted her mother over *her* problem. Her mother's private nature, her charitable works had made it impossible to do so. Enman's gentle words and manner softened her more. They usually did. Una forced a smile, the chance for further talk eluding her. "Hannah, shy? I'm not sure that's quite it."

As he put the water he'd fetched on to heat, she touched his arm. "There will be other jobs, won't there." Then, "Is it too much to ask, to make up? For last night, I mean. And just now."

But it was late and not exactly his fault that work started at eight.

"I'm off the booze—for good, I mean. This evening, sweetpea. After supper we'll have a cuddle. Then, we'll give'r, all right?" Now he sounded like the cretins at the boatyard, though she knew he was just teasing. Still.

"You didn't used to talk like that."

Ignoring her, he carried the water upstairs, filled the sink, and let her wash first while it was just the right warmth. Then she went and lay on top of the quilt and waited, thinking he might change his mind. But, washed and shaved, he put on his second-best suit, having hung his finer one to air.

"You're not off to town again?" Another faint hope leapt inside her.

"Thank God, no."

"Then where's the funeral? Or are you off to church, to see that crazy priest—confess to him down in his mouldy glebe? 'Lord have mercy, I never meant to get pissed.'" It wasn't a kind joke. But Enman laughed.

"The one man who never goes on a toot." His grin was like a boy's.

"Well, except for schoolteachers and such, other fellows who have to stay on their best behaviour."

"Teachers, yes. That's right." She spoke lightly. She stood on tiptoe to straighten his tie, made him bend so she could kiss his goose egg. He smelled strongly of Old Spice.

"And don't you fuss over Hannah, she's survived this long. Happy enough in her cocoon. Like a pupa." He reddened slightly, and his voice cracked as she touched his cheek—cracked with relief? She pressed herself to him, put both arms around his neck but not so tightly as to ensnare him. Because wasn't he like a butterfly that regretted spreading its wings? A bulky one in a baggy-kneed suit, though she had to admit she loved his hands—and the reliable set of his hips and waist, which helped her overlook his sloped shoulders and his limp, which others might not notice. You couldn't have everything, she realized. He kissed her cheek and, never late a day in his life, promising to look into the water situation later, left without even stopping to inspect the garden.

He wasn't gone ten minutes when Kit phoned. She offered to visit again when they had water and maybe even stay over.

Kit made Enman nervous and fumblingly accommodating. Men hardly knew what to make of Kit, the way she made fellows feel like geniuses one minute, nincompoops the next. And not just fellows. The way she would point out animal shapes in a cumulous cloud, then turn around and say your green sweater resembled snot. Kit was direct like that, pulled no punches. She had made the science teacher squirm after he mocked her ignorance of his field.

Except for his drinking, Enman was a *good boy*, so his mother had said at every opportunity. His goodness came with a price, Una realized, the price was being left to feel at his goodness's mercy. This she found mildly depressing, though not as depressing as being at life's mercy. Well, she had learned not to take things lying down, so to speak, even things beyond a person's control.

And then there were the things that were not beyond a person's control.

In the cellar, rummaging among Enman's father's rusted tools, she found a pair of wire cutters. She almost wished Mrs. Greene *was* up there somewhere looking down.

One quick snip through two tiny chainlinks—"Fight superstition with superstition!" she mouthed to herself—and the rosary slipped free of the clothesline. It was a feat Mrs. Greene's embroidery scissors might have accomplished. Landing in a clump, the beads resembled a swarm of beetles stopped in their dusty tracks.

"Let each portend a halt to cloudless days, and bring on rain!" She said this aloud, and could not help smiling. It was like casting a spell. But now what? Bad luck, perhaps, to simply toss them, so she plopped the beads into an empty flowerpot and, emboldened, remembered the silly ornament. As with the beads, Enman probably wouldn't notice it missing, not so long as she was the one charged with dusting.

But the figurine wasn't in its usual spot and, after a quick search of the house, proved nowhere to be seen. In a fit of revived taste, Enman had removed it? Then she remembered the noise that awakened her. "The Lord giveth and the Lord taketh away," Mrs. Greene had pontificated. Well, good, and so be it. Right now she had a more pressing concern: a bath. Should she troop down to Isla's, toiletries in hand? The lake would have to do, but a more secluded section of it. A bigger concern was the future, if the drought dragged on and going daily to the lake to bathe became a necessity. She would need to be here to take calls. Her letter would reach the city in a day or two, would land on the superintendent's desk by the beginning of next week.

He would see her credentials and want to discuss them. It wasn't as if she did *not* have exemplary service to emphasize. Why fret? Though the superintendent might be on vacation, or hold off phoning until he found a good time to call. The mistake with Gregory had happened eight months ago. Who hadn't acted impulsively once? In wartime a lot worse happened than adultery.

Keeping busy *was* the only antidote for worry. After visiting the lake, she would pick blueberries. There was Mrs. Greene's pail—the morning before her death, confused, the old woman had asked about going berry-picking, fingers worrying the quilt as if were a bush. How could Una forget? "Mind you don't hurt my son, he's a good boy," were among the last words Marge had spoken. Dipping a piece of cotton batting into water to dampen Mrs. Greene's lips, Una had practically bitten off her own tongue, not answering back.

And yet, nearly seven months married, she felt pressed to be more like Enman's mother at times than his wife. But if there were berries she would try to make a pie; how difficult could it be? A good way to lead a man to bed and beyond, to other things you wanted, was through his stomach—Win's words.

Something twinged in her abdomen: the release of an egg? She had read that some women could feel it. The sensation dragged her to the outhouse, which by daylight was laced with cobweb doilies. Dead flies dotted the crumbling sack of lime and its rusty scoop. It made her feel like a wildlife specimen, aiming balled-up newsprint down the hole, something galling about the deposit demonstrating that the body's basest functions succeeded while higher aspirations failed to.

How things changed.

A pie—a pie would thaw any ice between her and Enman, she decided, setting off with the pail and her bathing things. She would be nicer. Perhaps she had been a tad pressuring about his job and a flat and a baby, though, as Dr. Snow said, success in anything demanded perseverance. But Snow said lots of things, about miscarriages, damaged foetuses, and blighted ovuums, which drew from Una a shiver of revulsion at the time.

"Isn't it apples that suffer blight?" Enman had said, hearing about these.

On the barrens the berries were worse than blighted, they were wizened and scarce. A lone bee buzzing made her think, briefly, not of pollination but of spelling bees. Then Mrs. Greene's earliest remarks drifted back: *Perhaps I should've been tougher with him—or easier, who knows. If his father had been different.* It had almost come across as a warning, chased as it was by an unusually sound piece of advice regarding the wilds around them: *Never pass up anything on the beach or in the woods that's free, Una.* There. Straight from the mare's mouth. Except, these days, nature didn't seem to be delivering.

Blinking sweat from her eyes, she trekked to the lake, where there was no one to be seen. Her towel was bright enough to be spotted from the sky like some kind of signal as she spread it over a rock. Peeling off her clothes was freeing—stripping off then laying out the top and shorts that highlighted her slimness. Win Goodrow had recently asked if she was eating enough, saying once the babies started coming she would "fatten up."

Despite the blazing heat the lake's murky depths were not inviting. Stretching out in her birthday suit, she let the sun braise her, her faint muskiness mixing with the peaty scent of the water. The air and the sun were good for any blemishes. She focused on the sun warming her belly, imagined it prodding her insides. Dr. Snow had written a requisition for an x-ray, if she decided to have one, merely a precaution to rule out things like blockages, "because of your age." Yet plenty of women older than she had babies, her own mother as well as Enman's. Still, she smiled at the thought of the doctor telling Enman he had "strong swimmers, just not the largest team." She pictured cells in bathing caps. It was more pleasant than imagining physiology, the bodily tissues involved. If only babies grew the way her mother had told her they did when Una was a child, like Brussels sprouts on a stalk, miniature cabbages sporting either of the parents' faces.

Pricked and basted by the sun, she peered into the lake's bottomless brown. The green thread of an eel laced its murk. Rick Gregory had brought a similar creature into her class, preserved in a jar. A specimen of the type, apparently, that bred in a local lake, its young swimming all the way to the middle of the ocean to loll about in the Sargasso Sea.

The squiggling eel was no enticement to jump in, but when she did, the water was a tepid breeze against her midriff. Soft and near-lifeless, the water was the colour of the iodine which Barton Twomey sold when his other supplies ran low. It tinted her skin a sepia tone, like the photos she had stored under the eaves. Picturing her parents' faces, she wondered if they might have been closer, more affectionate with each other, had they married younger.

But what was age? Look at Charlie Chaplin, in his fifties marrying *his* Oona, teenaged love of his life. Age meant little when instinct and lust factored into it. Granted, Kit said all Chaplin wanted was a "baby-incubator." "Men just think with their willies, the brains in their pants. You don't know how lucky you are with Enman."

Sometimes it was hard to tell if Kit was kidding or not.

Treading water, Una ran the sliver of soap under each arm, then down below. Kit was a piece of work, other teachers had said, behind

Kit's back of course. Kit and her smokes, their clinging smell, the way it rubbed off on you. The way she kissed acquaintances like the French did, an airy graze of each cheek, the way a woman Enman had worked with briefly at the bank did when he had introduced her. With Enman Kit behaved differently, with him she stuck to handshakes. Ever since some fellow had left nail clippings on her coffee table, Kit had no time—or so she claimed—for men.

Reaching upwards with one arm, stretching it toward the sky, then plugging her nose, Una dunked herself. Something slimy glided underfoot. A boggy taste filled her mouth.

The man was sitting there on the shore, sitting on another rock, not far from hers, when she surfaced. Suds stung her eyes. The soap squirted from her grasp, sank into yellowy nothingness.

The lake licked her collarbones. Not ten yards away, he was watching. He was holding something small and shiny, lifting it to his mouth. Through the glug in her ears the sound came belatedly, the way a plane's roar lags behind its plume.

It wasn't just a noise, it was a tune, sort of, a tune being dragged through a mouth organ's teeth. The tune no more her cup of tea than one of Hubley Hill's would be.

"For godsake, put it away," Kit would have shouted and rolled her eyes.

Except, there was something rather sweet about it, winsome. The man's hand fluttering like a wing as he played, his other cupping the thing so tightly to his lips he might have been stifling a cry.

It was a tune that Enman might have tried to rescue from Hubley by making it fancier somehow, playing along. But the man played less intently, notes wandering in and out, as if he was fishing and the grating melody was a knotted line being cast out.

Should she have been alarmed? Maybe. He was no more than twenty or twenty-one, no older than Enman's youngest colleague—if an accountant could consider a labourer a "colleague."

A young fellow on a few days' leave, of course, that's what he was. Out to enjoy some fresh air and lounging under sun and stars, a break from his barracks.

Had he been there all along, seeing her undress?

He could have been decent and turned away. But he kept looking. A shivery giggle escaped her. Despite the lake's flaccid warmth she felt quite chilled.

She could not stay in here forever.

If I can't see you, you can't see me. How often had the littlest grade primaries played at this, covering their faces? She was laughing now, couldn't help it. The man would not look away.

It was a very short swim to her towel. But she was self-conscious as her knees grazed granite and she slithered onto her rock.

She thought of herself, for no good reason, of being like the little mermaid in Copenhagen that Kit talked about: if the war ever ended, Kit was going there to see it.

Smiling her best parent-teacher smile, aiming for the kind of smile she might direct at a parent when discussing a pupil's misbehaviour, Una whipped the towel around herself.

Nonplussed as could be, the man stayed put, as if lounging poolside at a resort. This close up, she saw how deeply tanned his face and hands were compared to his torso, which was fish-belly white. The ripples of muscle under that pale, hairless skin made her blush. A blessing *and* a pity he was wearing pants. She didn't like to stare, of course. Did not want to appear to be sizing him up.

The man's leanness, his muscular waist, put Enman's love handles to shame. The man stared back, all the while blowing another tune—a Lumberjacks' tune from the Steady Hills's repertoire, what she had heard blaring from the front room a couple of weeks ago.

That music all sounded the same to her.

Wrapped in the towel, she gathered her things. Couldn't help flashing him a demure smile, like Kit would have.

A young fellow cooling his heels, that's all he was. Cooling his heels at the tail end of a toot, Enman would have said.

Because Enman related everything to drinking.

The man's gaze hardly strayed. Cool and remote, his eyes were the same light blue as the sky and the lake's shimmering surface above its brown murk. His dark blond hair was wavy, longish—so he couldn't be a serviceman.

A labourer, then, a casual labourer from up O'Leery way.

She drove her feet into her espadrilles.

Oh, heavens, was he someone she had once taught? In the city she occasionally ran into former pupils.

Through the corner of her eye, she saw his hand move. His jumpy tune zigzagged after her through the bushes, where she stopped to tug on her clothes. Swinging the empty pail—not even enough berries to fill a saucer, let alone a pie—she found the path, was almost to the barrens, when, through the leaves and dappled sunlight, a flare of red appeared. Red and black, hunter's plaid. A pungent waft of sweat. Before she could veer away a barrel chest and a florid face loomed. Eyes like a bassett hound's fixed on her. Wasn't Barton Twomey a nocturnal creature? She almost shouted for help.

The path left no room to sidestep him.

His surly expression warped into a grin, a ruddy blur as she tried to squeeze past. She almost made it, when his grimy paw closed around her wrist. She might have cried out. But who was to hear, the boy at the lake?

Twomey yanked her close, his breath in her face. He gave her arm a jerk.

"Well, well, Missy-thinks-she-fucken-owns-the-place. I got a bone to pick with you."

She shoved the empty pail up by his face, grazing his chin with its brim before his fingers knocked it away. He grinned down at her. Her pulse jumped in her throat, out of fear or disgust. He ranted about Hannah: "Leave her the hell alone! You, filling her head with your old crap!"

Ignorance, ignorance—it's not to be feared but fought. A voice inside like Kit's coached her. She flailed the towel. He snatched and flung it wide, hooking a branch from which it dangled soggily out of reach. Only then he let go of her arm, though he was not yet done.

"Catch you nosing around my place again, girl, and you'll pay. Your pussy husband too. Be the last time a Greene fucks with me, you hear? You keep away from us."

His language was enough to strip paint.

But then, just like a passing squall, Twomey swaggered off, an ugly wind bending the alders.

"You *could* give Hannah half a chance!" Her shout echoed back.

Unreachable, the towel had to be left.

Hannah was waiting on the step when Una got home. The hopeful look on the girl's face was sufficient to wipe away the worst of Twomey's threat. The scab by her eye made for a pitiful sight. Her boldness was jarring:

"I want you to learn me, Missus."

Somehow Una hadn't fully expected Hannah to take her up on her offer, at least not so quickly. Like a lot of urges, a student's urge to learn could be fickle. But the afternoon was young and Una had nothing more pressing to do. She was no Carmel Rooney, so of course she invited Hannah in. If the girl proved incapable of progressing, Una would soon find out and let her down gently. Hannah would learn to persevere, or she would not.

"No time like the present, then, is there?"

It was like having a bird come down the chimney: now what? Una went upstairs to dig out her box of books from under the eaves. The photo of her parents lay tucked inside, its vague scent of furniture polish turned musty.

Should she mention the run-in with Hannah's uncle?

The grade-two reader beamed benignly at Una, dog-eared pages summoning the memory of small groping fingers. The grade-one version was nowhere to be found, so the grade two would have to do, though even Hannah would know that life was more complicated, and far less sunny, than its *Tom, Bunny, and Flip* stories let on.

As with teaching, learning required you to care. Unsure of her conviction—after all, teaching was a profession, not unpaid volunteer work—Una laid the book on the table, sharpened more pencils. The smell of the shavings was cheering, bolstering even. It got her thinking of what to say when the superintendent called. Which he might at any moment next week, possibly interrupting a pastime like this one. Which would not be a terrible thing.

Perhaps he would call on Monday or Tuesday. Certainly, he would call by the end of next week.

Hannah clutched her pencil, pawed at the first page. Fresh pimples graced her chin. Her lip quivered. The stubbornness in her eyes was almost harder to look at than Twomey's crazy, misplaced anger.

"Let's start at the very beginning, shall we?" Breathing in deeply, summoning what she could of her old patience, Una printed out the alphabet, capital letters and small ones. Upper and lower case, as they no doubt said in high school.

Tracing each with a fingertip, Hannah made a clucking sound as if approving the familiar ones.

Resigned to being patient, Una felt a calm fill her. The calm was like an old friend, or a group of friends she hadn't realized she missed, like girls she had chummed around with at Normal School, then lost touch with and hadn't seen in years. "How about a rhyming game?" She wrote a list of words.

With surprising speed, if gracelessly, Hannah was soon printing them out: *fat hat cat bat*.

"Very good." Keeping an eye on the clock, Una printed, *The man in the hat hit the fat cat with the bat*, then read it out.

Pressing her thumb under the words, its nail chewed to the quick, Hannah repeated each one, shyly at first, and ended with a shrill laugh. She shook her head in wonder. Her hair made a dull halo.

It was a touching sight, the lesson unfolding more productively than Una could have imagined. She patted Hannah's shoulder. Pleased with herself, Hannah clapped her hands. Her cheeks looked as if she had rubbed them with strawberries.

"Uncle says I's too stunned to teach nothing to."

"Nonsense." *Be practical, helpful*: that would be Kit's approach. "To *learn*, dear," she corrected. "And your uncle is wrong, dead wrong."

Gripping the pencil with fresh vigor, Hannah copied out the rhyming line with a finesse that, in spite of her reservations, made Una's chest tighten. Then the girl crowed out the words, oblivious of the screen door's *whap*.

"Shit." Out it popped before Una could help it.

"*Fit bit pit—shit!*" Dogged as a quarterback—"*snit quit SHIT*"— Hannah ran with it, her half-cocked grin cracking wide as she printed feverishly.

"I'll show them little arseholes," she yelped, either not seeing or simply ignoring Enman standing in the doorway. "I'll write them a *letter*, them bastards that hit me!"

Enman kept so quiet as to stay invisible.

"Hannah. Jesus Murphy, so here you are." He bit his lip.

The girl's eyes darted every which way. "Man in hat hit cat wit' bat." By now she had gotten up.

"Isaac let me go early, on account of—" Making a beeline around Hannah, moving like a robot, he took down a glass. "I thought we—"

"Yes?" Una's voice was hopeful as he beetled towards the front room. She heard the cabinet door squeak open. So much for his promise.

Hannah cast an anxious glance that way, eyes dodging hers. "Mister's mad. Oh, oh. Why, Missus? I never done nothing to him. How come he hates—?"

"*Anything*, Hannah." Una turned to a fresh page, smoothed it, pointed out more vocabulary. "You never did *anything*." Butt, cut, hut, mutt, slut, she thought bitterly. Mrs. Finck might have shown the girl more friendliness than Enman had. "For Pete's sake, here, hold the pencil *this* way. It's not *you* Mr. Greene doesn't like." It's your uncle he's got it in for, sat on the tip of her tongue like poison. "Did you tell your uncle I was there?" She spoke as casually, she hoped, as if asking Hannah to pass the eraser.

Hannah's sunburn deepened. "Me and you are buddies." Her eyes glistened with a strange pride, enough to lighten the effects of Enman grumbling about something from the parlour. Settling back to her printing, Hannah hummed quietly, a drone soft as a plane's passing high overhead.

If only everything, everyone, could be so straightforward.

"Why, sure we are. But does your uncle know you're here? You'd best run along now, before he worries and comes looking for you."

11

JUST WHEN ISAAC COULDN'T SEEM KINDER, HE COULD TURN STUBBORN TOO, becoming a stickler, a tyrant even, about things like work hours. Begrudgingly, an hour and a half before quitting time, he agreed to let Enman leave for the day. "Can't have poor Foxy going without water. Leave now and you'll reach O'Leery in time to fill up at the fire hall *and* see a show—that's your aim, isn't it, killing two birds wit' one stone? 'Course it will mean a small dock in pay." Even with Archibald in charge, the bank had never cut its employees any slack. If he had known Una had company he'd have stayed on till six or later, to make up for any slacking off he might be guilty of in the wake of a hangover. He could not remember a thing from their boat ride home and hoped he hadn't done anything embarrassing.

Being in Barreiners' good graces was important, all the more so now that he was staying. Part of these social graces was weighing pity for the Twomey girl against the urge some people felt to shun her. People's feelings shifted, of course, and you needed to keep them in view, acting accordingly. Even having Hannah out of sight and out of mind, Enman had hardly forgotten this. He had always dreaded having her land on Ma's doorstep.

The inch or two left in the bottle was barely sufficient: a calming, farewell sip was all. But now it was gone, this was *it*, he would stick to his guns and never take another drop. He put the empty back into the cabinet and there it would stay. Una could monitor it and see for herself. No need to belabour the point with her or anybody, he had decided. Enough, he had had enough and was resolved, the time had come, to quit for good, turn over another new leaf. The last thing either of them needed was her eyeing every cup of tea, every glass of water he took—that is, as soon as they had some—as if it might be doctored. With the darkness of the February sinking, his wounding, Ma's illness, and the fuss about his old job all behind him, he had no more need of the stuff.

Having the Twomey girl about was not something he had bargained for. But at least Una had a diversion, he consoled himself, though Hannah's presence in Ma's kitchen was not exactly restful.

His hand shook, certainly not from that smidge of rum, as he put on the Dvořák. He turned the volume loud enough to blot out their voices without disturbing the lesson; God forbid they would drag it out. When the largo finished, he replaced the needle at the beginning to savour it again, while bracing for the scherzo.

Just as he hoped, the scherzo sounded explosive enough—hallelujah!—to send their guest on her way. Hannah's leaving did not seem so much of a blessing when Una came to the doorway, arms folded. Her blouse seemed buttoned wrong, as if she'd been caught in the midst of dressing. Had she always been so touchy? How had he not noticed before?

"So?" Her voice was expectant, almost bossy. A little jarring after their morning's eventual tenderness, this expectancy was new, too. It made him feel prickly with the need to muster a force to match it.

Any effect the rum might have had was fainter than a ghostly one. Still it was strong enough to put words in his mouth whose petulant tone surprised him. "No more beating around the bush. What I'll say is for your own good." He rested his gaze on Una's top button, avoiding her eyes. "You do not want to mess with Twomey. With Ma barely gone, we don't need the complication of another needy person just yet. I know what you're thinking: well, sure Hannah's a sweet thing. You're right. Easy for teachers like Kit, say. Leaving the work behind her in the classroom, not like you. And not going through what we have, with a sick person, I mean."

"How dare you—?" She opened her mouth to say more, closed it.

"I really wish you wouldn't"—he stuffed down that rummy ghost, its wispy remnants, his longing for more of its pleasant puffing-up— "entertain the Twomey one in our house." Even as he said it he winced inwardly. It wasn't really what he meant, as if a nastiness that wasn't really his had taken over his tongue. "You know, of course, that she's a relative."

Her silence was as sharp as the silence that follows the crunch of a boot through frozen snow.

"My half-sister. Didn't Ma tell you? I figured she must've, all those hours you two talked. Surely it came up, about the old man."

Una gaped at him. Then, suddenly, it was as if he had not said anything shocking. "First off, we've been friends forever, Kit and I. Kit has never been anything but kind—"

A hollowness replaced his craving for a drink, and any trace of bravado. "For Pete's sake. This isn't to do with Kit. It's awkward, the Twomey girl coming around. I don't really want her here, simple as that." There was a buzzing in his ears, the same as when his father used to cuff them. He folded his arms too, glimpsing himself in the little hall mirror. His jaw was tight.

A silly prig is what he felt like, no less pompous than the new manager at the bank. As if having been in the city made anyone more open-minded, upright. Whether he was open-minded or not, Una knew where to stick the knife once she caught him. She protested that Hannah wouldn't hurt a fly. "What are you so scared of? You're no better than those dreadful boys."

Whatever it was in him that had stood up to her gave way. "Calm down, this is silly. It's not worth getting agitated." Nothing was, when you really wanted peace. He touched her shoulder, let his hand cap its boniness. At least she didn't shrug it off. "It's not fear. It's her uncle I don't like, you know that, and you know how people say things." He wanted to reel her closer, but she eyed him with a cool bemusement.

"No shite there, Sherlock."

Did she speak to Kit that way? Suddenly he felt like a prude.

She resisted only slightly when he drew her to him.

"There's a bit more to it than you might want to know. In case the genes run in the family."

She rolled her eyes, though not meanly. He thought of Twomey, who would have traded a healthy child for a quarter ouncer, and of his father's fondness for the bottle. Cleary, at least, had been nowhere near that bad.

"See, I feel a bit beholden, I mean guilty, about poor old Hannah. She's had a hard run of things. Everyone knows it."

"Tell that to Mrs. Finck." Una's smirk, that crooked smile of hers, did it signal her letting up?

If so, it was best seized upon without delay. Otherwise their sparring would wear him to a pulp.

"The Magnet's got that musical playing, dunno for how much longer. Might be worth seeing. Since we have to drive up there anyway. Truce?"

"Oh for heaven's sake. Fine."

In the kitchen—it was like being inside a monstrous buttercup, the yellow the walls cast over everything—she put together a picnic while he went below and fiddled with the pump. At least its motor hadn't burnt itself out, drawing on nothing. He hurried up the cellar steps to help her with the food.

"If we had water, I'd boil up some hen fruit to have with the armoured heifer." It was her goofy lingo for hardboiled eggs and Spam, lingo they had fallen into early in Ma's illness, to make the situation seem more fun than it was. Una hadn't spoken this way since spring. It seemed vaguely embarrassing now, even a bit desperate.

As he fished gherkin pickles from the jar, he glimpsed the ocean through the kitchen window. Such a steadying sight it was, viewed from dry land, despite its treachery. "Just think of it. Over there,"—on its opposite side, he meant—"those Nazi birds might string a person up for being a Hannah, or worse, even."

"You think?" An uppity note had crept back into her voice, which he chose to ignore.

Before she could turn prickly again he hurried out to the car with the jerry cans and Ma's basket packed with food. Thank God for Beulah. If they left now they could stop halfway to eat, fill the cans at the fire hall, and make the nine o'clock show. If you didn't mind driving in pitch dark, the cross-country road wasn't a bad route back, except that bubblegum and electrical tape pretty much held Beulah together. He thought of George lifting the hood when she was new, showing off the shiny engine and its pristine spark plugs. A decrepit car needed a lot more than shine to make it run properly. Sometimes, though, she'll start without the key, he liked to joke.

This evening they were in luck: the engine turned over first crack. Passing the Goodrows', Una checked her lipstick in the rear-view. It was as if their quarrelling had not happened. Maybe people weren't so different from cars, it struck him, at least in certain matters of mechanics. You could know someone intimately but have no more clue about their inner musings than about an oil leak, until the engine seized. And brains, how about brains? As Una had pondered when they first met, what makes one mind impenetrable to new ideas, another spongelike? He had supposed she was referring to students, or her people, whom she otherwise never mentioned.

Luckily Inkpens' finances and household plumbing were not so mysterious. If worse came to worst, the fire hall had a pumper truck that might come out and fill the well.

He rolled up his sleeves one by one, and as they left the village he slung his arm over the seat so his fingers just brushed his wife's arm. As they cut inland on the dirt track, the sun cast a weighty glow over the barrens, splashing rocks, spruce, and alders with a deep rose. In spite of the cheery light, everything looked withered.

You could hope for rain but hope only went so far, just as keeping something under your hat forever would not make it disappear.

Through the corner of his eye he watched Una toying with a lipstick. "I can't believe Ma didn't tell you. She had no use for the old man after that. Ma once made cookies for Father Heaney to take to her. Father Heaney likely ate them himself." His voice stayed as even as if dictating the odometer's faulty reading. "My half-sister. The whole village knew, too. Though all his life the old man denied it."

Corkscrewing her lipstick as high as it would go, Una corkscrewed it down again, then let the tube loll in her lap. "You people." She eyed him as if he were small as a woodbug. Shouldn't you be a bit bigger? her look said. Her voice was withering. "That's a bit of a snide joke about the priest. It's not very funny."

He dodged a pothole, not too successfully. Beulah's tires were beyond bald—near "roont," Clint said—and with the shortages, had little chance anytime soon of being replaced. With gas so expensive, its rationing so tight, if she hadn't been George's car he'd have parked her somewhere permanently in town.

"But, Enman—how do you know for sure, if your father said she wasn't—"

"Everyone knows. It's no secret. He made Ma's life miserable. He was that type that never grows up. Not a ladies' man, exactly, though ladies came with the territory, I guess."

"Being the life of the party." Una sighed loudly. "He looked nice in his picture." The sole picture, she meant, that Ma had saved. Enman had been surprised to find it one day propped on Ma's dresser, coming upstairs to check on things while Una prepared Ma's tray. He had been tempted to bury it too, though not, of course, with her.

Granted, his father *had* always made it to work, ensuring there was food on the table. Snarly as her illness had made her occasionally, Ma remained honest about things, as transparent as dew to the end: "Don't worry, I've got nothing that will sneak up and bite you."

"Nice is as nice does. And when Cleary worked for Isaac, he could've fixed an engine in his sleep. Ma bore the brunt of his lapses. She could never trust him. She stuck by him, though."

"Ah." Una tucked the lipstick into her purse, rubbed where it had marked her skirt.

"Teaching, you must've known of families' troubles. Cleary, if you can believe it, had a thing for Iris Finck. While just a young fella. Iris was just as crusty and cantankerous then, Isaac says. Imagine holding out a flame for her, how demented is that?"

"I guess you were waiting for the right century to fill me in. All the stuff your ma never mentioned about him, let alone Hannah."

A fresh rattle had cropped up under the left fender. He wiped his brow on his sleeve. At least she couldn't accuse *him* of not listening to Ma. "Well. It's not in the genes. Hannah's problem, I mean. I'm pretty sure. As sure as you can be. If *that*'s a worry."

"You've made your point. You don't want her in the house."

"Gad, is it my fault Cleary had it on with Twomey's sister?"

Walling the track on both sides, alders ticked the doors and rocker panels. The noise from the fender was no doubt a stick caught somewhere.

"As if I'd make it up! A dalliance." The prissy word escaped before he could find a better one. Better, though, than "screwing around" or "stepping out."

"Look, I'm not blaming Hannah!"

"Blaming her? I should hope not." Una gazed at the ruts ahead. Her face was pink with the dying sun.

"Ma didn't deserve such nonsense."

"Few women do." Una's eyes had a cool, skittish look. "Don't know about you, En, but I'm famished."

The woods were so dense and the track was so narrow there was nowhere to pull over, let alone get out and spread a blanket, so they sat in the car to eat, the windows rolled up because the mosquitoes were fierce. The meat paste sandwiches were warm and a little soggy but the pickles perked things up, even lightened their mood—enough that Una suggested a back-seat cuddle.

"Like teenagers?" And how would you propose getting the angle right? he almost teased, the venture unlikely to produce more than a stiff neck. "Later, my darling, all right? Don't want to miss the show." It was grand, Enman thought, that *Girl Crazy*'s run at the Magnet saved them the drive downtown to see it, not to mention facing mobbed streets, surly crowds. He was happy to be out on a date, though he guessed the movie might be one he could take or leave.

"The musical with Broadway flair and a western air," she repeated the radio ad dully.

Enman put his hand on her knee, and hummed "Zing Went the Strings of My Heart." His hand bounced off at every rut. The woods stretched forever. Soon the sky's deepening purple closed in, broken by the flash of a deer's tail in the bobbing headlights, the reddish blurr of a fox. The stars almost outnumbered the mosquitoes flecking the windshield. He patted her hand. "When the rest of us expire, they'll take over the Earth."

The appearance of a couple of shacks indicated that they had reached O'Leery's outskirts. In the yard outside one place a kid swung on a tire. This could be Timbuktu, said Una's expression, though compared to Barrein, O'Leery was a metropolis, with a full-service garage, a hotel behind a tidy picket fence.

Just down the hill from these was the Magnet, with its diamond-shaped marquee in near-darkness. Half the lights were burnt out and the stars' names missing letters. Una sucked her teeth. Its lack of glitter *was* a bit dispiriting after the drive. "But what would the ARP do if the Magnet went Hollywood on us?" he quipped.

There was still plenty of time to loop around to the new fire hall, which only existed because O'Leery's branch of the ARP was headquartered here. It was the one thing the place had gained as a result of the war, as far as he could see. He wheeled in next to the pumper truck. The air smelled of cars and chip fat. A fellow in overalls filled the jerry cans and helped load them into the trunk. Beulah's back end sagged under the weight, the cargo of fresh water well worth the journey.

"That'll tide us over. See? Nothing to worry about, dear." Though he didn't dare say so, he would have been just as happy to forego the movie.

Pulling out and then braking for the Magnet, he heard it again—not from the fender this time, but under the hood. A chattering sound, not likely the result of a stray stick but nothing some electrical tape couldn't fix—quite possibly, it was just his imagination. It was difficult to listen properly as Una chatted about Isla Inkpen's new granddaughter, as if the subject of Hannah had gone to seed and blown away, which suited him.

Women. Sweet as Easter chicks one minute, owly as nuns the next. A fellow at the bank had been right about that. Maybe it was no accident Enman had stayed a bachelor so long. He put Beulah into first, let the clutch breathe out, ears cocked. Maybe he was too intent on listening to truly register anything being out of the ordinary.

If there was a problem—was the steering heavy, was she pulling to one side?—Una's cussing drowned it out. "Look at this, you said it ran till Friday! How come there's no lineup? If this was the Oxford, they'd be lined up down the block."

Of course there wasn't a lineup. "Another plus of not being in town." They could have their pick of seats, instead of wrestling over one.

"Hard to think of a night being 'special' if you're the only ones out."

He babied the parking brake. A belt was about to go, or a bearing? Whatever it was, it gave him a thirst.

Despite her complaints, Una jumped out. He resisted the urge to peek under the hood, followed her down the boardwalk, past the faded posters in the window to the box office. "Well, yeah the show's on." The gal in the wicket gave Una an annoyed look. He paid for the tickets, handed Una hers. Her pretty fingernails grazed his wrist gently and he caught a delicate whiff of her perfume, masked in the car by the smell of food. The traits of a city-bred, city-fied wife, traits he had to admit he admired.

Having Una had spoiled him for women in Barrein, all of whom were taken anyway.

He could have done without her sarcasm, though, when she nudged him. "Well, knock me over with a feather, En, they have popcorn."

When he went to buy her some, Una shook her head. Watching her figure, no doubt. Timmy Flood, the manager, stood in the lobby taking tickets. Enman nodded to him and Flood grinned. Enman had given him a loan once, a favour that Flood wanted to acknowledge by providing complimentary passes.

"Too late, as you can see." Enman gave him a friendly nudge. "But next time would be nice."

Inside, the movie house was only half full. No problem at all, Enman thought; being packed in like herrings to watch a goofy musical on such a night was an experience *he* could live without. He would almost rather be in Hubley's two-room house listening to Hill's records. Out of earshot of Una, he would not have felt quite so self-conscious playing along. He had an idea that Hill was avoiding their place, having sensed that Una was not a fan of his music. While waiting for the movie to start, she squeezed his hand. "I can't wait to see what happens, can you?" Then she laughed and kissed his ear. "Oh, En. Look, sorry for being a pill, okay?"

12

BEGGARS CAN'T BE CHOOSERS, UNA SUPPOSED, SANDWICHED BETWEEN A stranger hogging the armrest on one side of her and Enman hogging the other. Settling in his seat, making it creak, he looked uncannily like his mother. Instead of watching the opening scenes he peered around, counting on his fingers. Counting heads? The place holds what, three hundred? she imagined him asking the manager, for his own edification.

Enman wasn't the biggest Mickey Rooney fan, he had admitted. Then he had wondered if perhaps, somehow, Carmel Rooney might be related to the star.

"Why would she be? Give me one reason why you'd ask that."

"Anything's possible."

Bored. Now he was *bored*. Well, let him be, Una thought. Let him have one small taste of how it feels sitting through something that's not his cup of tea. Just for once.

Except, his fidgeting was distracting. It kept pulling her eyes from the screen. She elbowed him. "Quit counting. I know that's what you're doing. It's what you do when you'd rather be someplace else. If you didn't want to come, why did you?"

It was something she asked herself these days, repeatedly, about her being in Barrein.

Someone behind them let out a sharp *shhh*. Briefly Enman's face became a moon, a bland, passive moon in a sea of such moons. A slightly smelly sea, a waft of B.O. spiced up the dark. Then he was shifting again, glancing around as if the audience was the entertainment. A couple in the seats ahead were sharing something barely concealed in a paper bag.

Una gritted her teeth. She wondered if Enman was longing for a drink, a longing she had not imagined him having, until after his mother's death. Was he wishing that Flood fellow was in the bar business? Twisting in his seat, Enman let his bare arm stick to hers. His breathing made a whistling sound, making it hard to concentrate on what Rooney and Judy Garland were saying. Una focused harder on Judy's glossy hair and Rooney's cute monkey face, his mouth a far cry from Carmel Rooney's.

People's laughter further blotted out half of what was being said. Until last winter, she would have used her schoolmarm's voice and asked them to keep it down. But getting fired had undermined her feeling of authority, and a whole term of being away from school had further eroded her confidence. It was only now that she realized this. At least the dialogue wasn't crucial. And the visuals offered a vicarious little thrill, even a brief vacation from her own love life, following Danny and Ginger's. She unstuck her arm from Enman's.

Without moving her eyes from the screen, she angled then idled her hand on his thigh. His muscles tensed. She inched it higher. God, marriage had come to this, turned her into a groper?

Enman grasped her hand and held it, tenderly. When she tried to replace it he whispered hoarsely, loud enough that everyone around them had to hear, "Please, Una."

She tried to focus on the dancers onscreen cutting the rug to Tommy Dorsey's dizzying tunes. But then the music reminded her of her old principal, who had bragged to staff about doing the Lindy hop. Stop it, she told herself. Quit thinking thoughts that drag you down. Didn't Kit have a phrase that had to do with private thoughts, a person's *jardin intérieure*. Marriage had a way of wrenching open the gates of a woman's, or trying to. God forbid, fussing and fretting beside her, Enman would be a marauding deer ready to march in and munch away at her thorns *and* blooms. And what about *his* garden? The one in his mind, not the one he tended as if his mother could see it—was his interior garden full of flowers or weeds?

Oh, damn. *Damn.* At the thought of weeds, the tangle of all she held back from him, about what had happened at work, how little by little, being in Barrein she felt herself and her world shrinking, a tear slid down her cheek. She blamed him for being too naïve to see through her idleness last Christmas, for the way his kindness made it necessary to keep the details of what had happened last December to herself. Focus on your own inner garden, for godsake. Keep it pretty. Picture roses, a crystal-blue pool. The trouble was, it occurred to her, maybe she had somehow deserved to end up in Barrein.

Mickey's lips were suction-cupped to Judy's when the lights flashed and flooded on. The movie continued playing. People stirred but stayed in their seats. But somewhere near the entrance was a rustling slightly louder than the swish of Judy's dress. People in the front rose to let someone by. The gawky man who had taken their tickets stood with his back to the screen and shielded his eyes against the film's brightness. Amid a chorus of boos, he made an announcement. Only then did Una spy the Mountie in the wings.

"There's been an incident—a suspicion of an incident, that is. No need for alarm, ladies and gents. But the ARP has asked for an evacuation of the theatre. The sergeant here requests that we leave in an orderly fashion."

The man who had helped Enman to the water at the fire hall appeared then. He was dressed in his air raid gear, his axe, gas mask, and other bomb squad apparatus strapped over his overalls.

"Reports of a sighting?" The man next to Una spoke with a lisp. "My cousin up the road runs the store there, and she said—"

"No need to get worked up, folks. We're just being cautious."

"This is just a drill? Half an hour left and you stopped the show?" The woman in front of Una demanded her money back. But everyone else was standing and people were making their way glumly towards the exit. Enman pulled Una to her feet as the rows emptied.

"If anyone sees *anything* out of the ordinary," the ARP man was saying to Mr. Flood.

"It's not like there's a bomb." Flood sounded peeved.

"A bomb?" A man shoved past Una, stepping on her foot.

She felt a burst of impatience, leaning against Enman. "I *would* like to know how it ends." She elbowed him, and tried to joke. "Are 'Danny and Ginger' going to live happily ever after?" Her voice felt high, her breath tight in her chest.

"This is a little more exciting than what we were watching." Enman tugged her through the crowd funnelling into the lobby.

She sniffed. "We paid good money for that."

Teenagers jumped the rope cordoning off another door.

Enman nodded politely to the Mountie who was now positioned outside. "What's the trouble, officer?" The policeman was taller than Enman, handsome and young, his face shiny with sweat.

"Move along," they were told. People stood in clusters on the board-walk, some chatting nervously, others griping about being gypped. "Least they can do is give us tickets for tomorrow," someone said, "I've waited all year to see this."

Overhearing, Enman raised a brow and spoke to Una under his breath. "Poor bugger." He grinned. Enman was not going to drive all this way again for the sake of thirty minutes. She felt disappointed but she also felt jittery, half-fear, half-delight. Titillation, almost, that something was *happening*. The feeling sank to nothing when she glimpsed the Goodrows standing under the streetlamp, which had not been extinguished. Its light reassured Una that the disturbance was a hoax.

"Far as I'm concerned, darkness just gives the enemy cover." Win was speaking loudly, hoping to enlist an audience? When she spied Una and Enman Win's face lit up. She spoke to Una first. "What's buzzin', cousin? Don't ask me what's going on. They should be strung up, whoever made us miss the lovey-dovey part, eh, Clinton?" Win's smiled faded as the Mountie passed. It was no secret how her boys kept O'Leery in contraband goods. Win nudged Enman. "You and Flood are buds, aren't you? Ask him what's really up."

Flood was being swarmed by people wanting refunds. But then another officer appeared, a navy man. Even in the dim light the buttons and braid on his jacket shone. If not for his grey hair he'd have given the Mountie a run for his money in the handsomeness department. Una had always liked the look of men in military uniforms. The ARP fellow, wearing a fireman's torn overalls, was cracking jokes with another man dressed the same.

"False alarm, everyone. Hooligans, that's all." The navy brass got into a shiny black car in front of the theatre, leaving the Mountie to disperse the crowd. Lying on the dirt beside the boardwalk was a book. Una stooped to retrieve it. A ratty paperback, a Webster's dictionary, half the pages falling out.

"I'll take that, ma'am." The Mountie snatched it from her. As she stood back, Win's eyes widened.

"There you go, proof of the enemy." Enman laughed.

Clinton shook his head. "Shame you and steady old Hubley won't be playing the Labour Day dance. Guess he needs a fiddler he's sure will stick around, someone he can rely on."

"That's not a problem." Enman avoided Una's eyes, cleared his throat. "Anyway, it's no big deal."

"That's not what Hubley says." Then Clinton pointed to the road. "You two walk here, or what? Don't tell me, Enman, you finally give up driving that piece of shit?"

Una looked straight at Win. "I wish."

"Now honey,"—Win gazed straight back—"if I was you I might be careful what I wish for."

"Piece of—?" Enman saw the empty space before Una did. The car should have been right there, where they had parked it. Una felt her pulse rise, linked her arm through his arm, felt his tighten. "Una?" Enman looked stunned, almost as incredulous as the first time she had unbuttoned herself and with few preliminaries pressed his hand to her chest.

"You're sure?" Clinton was saying. "You parked 'er here yourself?"

"Dying dirt. Who'd steal a jallahpee like that?" Under different circumstances, Win's mispronunciation would have piqued Una's longing to correct her: "A jalopy, you mean?" If Enman hadn't looked so unnerved, Una might have burst into nervous laughter.

Why didn't they go to the Shady Grove next door, have a bite, calm down, and figure out what to do, Clint suggested.

"We should call the police." Una tried not to speak as if telling a child to tie his shoes.

For once, Win aimed to be helpful. "It can't be far, anyway, Enman. Once whoever stole it realizes."

"You got to admit, if you were bagging a vehicle, you'd pick one," — Clint cast about for the right words — "well, like *that*," as a new-looking Ford pulled out of the Grove's lot, turning heads. Una could not imagine anyone paying more than thirty dollars for the Chev. Enman looked like he might be sick. The car *was* a memento of his friend, after all.

Despite the hour, a light burned in the hotel lobby, if you could call it a lobby, Una thought, the clerk at a desk tucked under the hallway stairs. The dining room was closed; likewise the garage across the street, which wouldn't open till morning, said the girl, hearing of their trouble. "No cop's coming all the way back out here for *this*, not this time of night." Regaining her bearing, Una mentioned the Mountie, but the others ignored her. Opening a bobby pin on her teeth, the clerk scraped back her bangs. "You *sure* you left your car there?"

Una sighed. It was late, she was tired. Now she felt rattled.

"Hooligans having a field day!" Win angled in. Even in dim light her face looked heavily powdered. "Any clue what that business at the show was, earlier? Couldn't get a solid answer out of Flood, could we, Clint."

The clerk listened raptly, then her smile turned proprietary. "*Well*, one of our guests heard—"

It was the girl's tone that provoked Una, broke her poise. Una did not even try fighting her tears, she felt so out of patience. It crossed her mind, how would she cope, being pregnant, a condition which was bound to be tiring? She felt like taking Win's head off:

"Do you honestly think we give a crap about that now?"

Enman winced. "Una."

What would he know about the moodiness doctors summed up in one word? Hormonal.

Win rocked back on her blocky heels, looking more satisfied than stung.

Enman passed Una his handkerchief. She blotted at her eyes. She must look like she'd been in a monsoon, she thought, mascara everywhere. She felt Enman loop his arm around her. It wasn't her fault, getting emotional, being stranded like this.

The clerk nattered on, meaning to be helpful. "There was a bunch drinking up the woods—up by the Run, you know, where the competition has their truck."

Win flushed. Was it by "the Run" where her and Clint's sons sold liquor, perhaps turfed out of Barrein by Twomey? Win piped up, probably to dodge some unsavoury truth. "Well, Missus, you and hubby will need a ride home."

"Not so fast, Edwina. They'll want to stick around, talk to the cops, see what's what. We'll keep you company," Clint said. "We're in no rush."

They kept talking. Of course it was queer that of all the cars to pick from, Enman's had been chosen. Clint speculated that it must be "her" rubber tires, albeit worn, while there were cabbies who drove around on wooden ones. The goddamn war, the war had everything to do with this, he griped, and Enman nodded. Win gave Una a sympathetic look, as if enjoining her to chime in. Una sniffed.

Once outdoors, Win pawed at Clint. "Oh my Dinah, I hope the boys aren't in some kind of trouble."

"Don't be silly." Clint shot Una and Enman a look. "That gaffuffle earlier? We seen some kids drinking out front before the show. Maybe they snuck in the back. Spies, Winnie—whaddya think?" he teased. "Right here in O'Leery. Or deserters, some little ship-jumpers." Clint grinned at Una. Una couldn't help but roll her eyes. She felt the prickle of impatient tears again as Win seized on something else, the way the Meades' dog seized on sticks.

"'Member, hon, when we stopped at Gannett's store—that fella asking for beer, and they sent him up to Joey's? Our young fella," she told Una, "in business for himself." Win cleared her throat. "Not that Joey condones drunk-and-disorderly. He's got a right to make a living like anybody, you know what I'm saying."

"The odd little hood, he gets. Punks," Clint corroborated, "hardly Joey's fault. Teenagers and that. Twerps. What I'd like to know is where're the bloody parents at?"

Una longed to be home in bed. "What has any of this to do with the car?"

"Rowdies, right?" Win was saying. "Figured they'd have a few, see the show. Probably got out of hand somewhere. That'd explain the RCMP paying a visit." Win's hands flew suddenly to her cheeks. "But it would have to be more than that to bring the navy out here. You saw the paper, those creatures in Gaspé. Do you think, could they be—?"

"Give it a rest. Gal in the box office would've noticed accents—"

"Exactly right!" Even Enman sounded out of patience, the chit-chat having gone from pointless to silly. "In case you forgot, my car's been swiped?"

"A regular night in O'Leery." Clint cuffed Win's arm. Win shot Una a nervous look. The whoosh of a passing car lifted the spit curls from Win's forehead

As right as Mrs. Greene had been about a few things, surely she had been dead wrong about others. Such as the idea of Win being sweet and quiet as a teenager, the girl every young fellow wanted. Win wasn't finished yet.

"Spies? Germans. I just feel it—feel it in my bones. They could be right under our nose!"

Then Una glimpsed it—and she hoped that Enman did too, even in the dark—the pitying look Win gave her. The pause, the narrowed eyes, the bitten lip. It was as if Una, for all her book-learning, could not possibly know things Win did.

"Oh my God. That's what it was. Jerries. Right here in O'Leery, possibly right under the same roof."

Una could no longer contain herself. "That's just stupid. You don't know that."

Enman shuffled restlessly. He hardly seemed to be listening. "No one was arrested."

"That Mountie didn't know his arse-ee from his pee."

Una held her breath. "I thought he was quite—Well. Anything's possible. Isn't it." She didn't care if she sounded sarcastic. Enman didn't appear to notice. Had he begun to figure out what to do, how to get the two of them home? It was a problem of some urgency.

Their truck's bed was piled with Clinton's lobster traps, the Goodrows only had room for one passenger. Enman patted Una's cheek. "Guess I owe it to George, don't I, to hang around here and try to trace the car." Then he nodded to Clint. "I owe you, buddy, for seeing Una safely home."

CLINTON CHOSE THE COASTAL ROUTE. Headlights blazing, they passed the battery from which cones of anti-aircraft light pivoted across the sky. The beams reminded Una of the spotlight in a circus's big top. Not another light blinked, the harbour and the houses along it wrapped in darkness the farther they got from things.

"Cut the lights or you'll have the ARP after us. You might slow down too, Clinton Goodrow," Win finally spoke. "Where's the fire anyway. You don't slow down, you can let us off right here, can't he Missus?"

Wedged between the two of them, Una could not imagine much worse. To his credit, Clint complied. Driving without lights had the effect of flattening the landscape into a dead zone, one stretch of rocks and trees fusing with the next.

"Dogs'll be pissing on the tires, Winnie, we go any slower."

Win yelped once more at Clint to slow down: "You're gonna give poor Una here a cardiac." Not missing a beat, she started in again, more crazy speculation, about "drinkers" at the show: "Holy dying dirt, anyone and their dog could land, walk right over us, and have a time."

Clint let out a long, noisy sigh. He snuck a wry grin at Una.

"Don't make fun. I *saw* what I saw, like Iris Finck did too." Win clicked her tongue. "I saw a few fellas trooping over the hill, up back of the beach. I was out there this morning seeing what the tide brought us." Win didn't worry about the Mounties slapping her on the wrist for salvaging "treasures" from ships that got hit. Una had picked up a can or two herself, on occasion—tinned pears, tinned peas—but it wasn't something to broadcast. "Swear to God," Win's oath joggled as they swung over a bump.

"Who were they? Tell us. See some fresh new faces from town, not just our old mugs all the time. Una would like to know." He winked, for her benefit or Win's?

"How would I know? ARP men looking for something? They were too far away. Still, like I said, I seen them."

"I hear you've taken the Twomey one under your wing. Time somebody helped her, since Enman won't. You're a better woman than most, a credit to Enman for doing it." Clint rubbed his jaw. "Hold your bladders, girls!" As he swerved around a rough patch, his elbow accidentally nudged Una's breast. Against the harbour's glint burled spruce stood in silhouette, their wafting scent recalling Christmas. She pictured kids colouring that day before the holidays. Teaching high school would be more demanding but a chance to fully exercise her gifts. Just then a screwdriver clanking across the dash rolled off and, reaching for it, Clint's hand brushed her knee. His eyes on the road ahead, he apologized.

"You think any more about going out to see the staircase? On the island, I mean. Any time you'd like to go I could run you and Enman out there. Since we're on about devils and that, eh, Win." He laughed.

"Were we?" Win sounded miffed.

THE CLOCK'S WHIRRING STIRRED THE emptiness. The house suddenly felt larger and too quiet. Since New Year's Eve, she and Enman had not spent a night apart. She lit a candle, tidied up the remnants of their picnic fixings left out in haste. His mother's basket was a hostage now, riding in the car's back seat to God knows where. God also knew what they would do if the car wasn't found; maybe God had the answer up his sleeve? Being car-less might force Enman to come to his senses, to orchestrate the move back to the world of trolleybuses and piped-in water. He must know that life meant sacrifices. Once she was working she'd buy a car—like Kit's—though it was hard to imagine Enman behind the wheel of anything new. So? She would purchase it for herself.

She slid what was left of the bread into the breadbox. Funny to think of her first sighting of Enman, braced for his climb up Duke Street's exhausting hill. Here's a man of purpose, she had imagined, a forthright man who liked his comforts, enjoyed advancement. She'd had no reason to question this until after their wedding at city hall, when he brought her to meet his mother, who disputed whether weddings that happened outside churches were legitimate. No reason to doubt his sincerity, wary as she was after Gregory's lies. All Gregory had said of her firing was "I'm sorry." He had not sounded sorry at all.

Traipsing outside to the privy, picking her way by flashlight, Una refused to let Win's ideas about strangers swell in her mind or take shape. She hoped Enman was comfortable with a decent bunk to crawl into. The

Grove was overrun with guests, the clerk had said. Officers on leave for some lake fishing—if, given the drought, the lakes still had fish.

She paused to listen to the sea's shushing and the faint, eerie moan of a buoy offshore, the groaner that marked the entrance to Barrein's harbour, Enman said. Both sounds, the surf's restless pull, the buoy's desolate groan, would be comforting if they foretold an incoming fog. But not a peep came from the island's foghorn, which had been silent for weeks. On the radio they said the Germans preferred to attack under fog. Una loved fog, the way, in town, it drew itself like a sleeve up the length of the city's peninsula, softening the outlines of buildings and trees. "Oh we get our share of fog here, don't worry," Mrs. Greene had said. Una couldn't remember the last day Barrein had been socked in, fog a sure sign of rain. Would she have to bathe in the lake all summer? Along with the fellow whom she recalled as looking vaguely like a very young Gary Cooper.

Una hurried back inside, creeping through the mudroom. God, if Win knew the half of it, that she had been caught naked by someone who could easily have been Win's son. Setting down the flashlight her hand bumped one of Enman's botanical experiments, knocked it over. Dirt and bits of clay pot lay everywhere. She tried to remember exactly how many sons the Goodrows had, four or five? Enman had told Una, and at the time she could not resist saying, "Win is quite a breeder. Don't suppose you'd have liked that."

Enman had laughed. "And, as Clint will tell you, there's nothing wrong with being childless and enjoying the rest of your life."

But life was a slippery thing, Una knew, as was time. In ten years where would she be? In four or five, if she conceived, would she have the energy to chase one preschooler, possibly two? And this didn't touch on the risks that multiplied with age: giving birth to someone like Hannah. Ten more years and without question she would be in the grips of The Change. Was it crazy to even want a child, or, as Enman mused, to bring one into the world as it was?

A dullness overcame her as she paused in the front room. Under the feeling's spell, she imagined her uterus as a pear snapped from a twig, her spirits sinking the way the car had earlier in ruts of dried mud. In her imagination Enman whistled a country tune he claimed to hate. Who knew what Enman really thought, what he truly felt? His true feelings surfaced about as often as a whale did: a flash of fin, a bit of spray, appearing mostly to be a vague, random nothing.

Yet his absence cornered her. Collapsed on the sofa, she was a bundle of nerves, a set of empty arms. The upholstery smelled of his hair tonic. Then she imagined the garlicky-sweetness of his breath. Was he lying awake now, at the Grove Hotel? Did he miss her? Not likely, with Beulah on his mind. Men were one-tracked that way, she decided: unable to spot a single bush for the forest it grew in.

Caring for them, for him, was what complicated everything—making plans, acting on wishes about where she could be, what she might be doing.

Keep busy, Kit would say. Moving by candlelight, Una rose and dug out the paintbox and brushes her friend had left, remembering too late the lack of water. All this evening's efforts, those jerry cans lost along with Mrs. Greene's basket. She opened the cabinet and the empty rum bottle rolled free. Can't draw blood from a stone, can you? she remembered Enman's favourite saying. Yet Enman could have been on the far side of the moon, their date at the Magnet a distant dream.

And what sorts of noises would be pouring, she wondered, through the walls of the Grove's dingy rooms? Its guests enjoying more than the daytime fishing, no doubt. If she had stayed over too, she and Enman could have at least *tried*. The strange surroundings might have fanned romance into their doing it. She might have talked him into calling in sick next morning and taking a taxi or a bus with her downtown.

She didn't like drinking, had no desire for it, but a sip or two might have helped summon sleep. Why, oh why, would he keep an empty? She opened one drawer after another, looking for liquor: nothing. All she stumbled across was Mrs. Greene's figurine, its chipped, beheaded body and noggin cocooned in a doily. The spirit of good taste had intervened! Pity help *her* if she had been the one who'd broken it.

There was nothing for her sleeplessness but to try and read for a while. *The Hygiene of Marriage* fell open to a page headed "Venereal Diseases." Good grief. Her face warmed, the movie screen in her head featuring the scene with Rick Gregory, his cameo appearance in her apartment. She had let nothing slip about him or the sordid little affair. As far as she knew about Enman's past, it was a blackboard with barely a smudge of chalkdust. Its highlights were puppy love, a childish crush on Win, once, a couple of brief, juvenile flings with tellers, fairly platonic, he said. By his own admission, there was no one in a skirt worth chasing in Barrein, except perhaps Isla.

So there you go, she told herself. Nothing to worry about, certainly not in matters of hygiene. She tried not to wonder about Gregory's philandering, the chances of a man who appeared decent being infected. But, oh God, the language the writer of this stuff used: the word *carrier* made it sound like newspaper delivery.

She stifled a laugh at the thought of Mrs. Greene holding forth about Shag Cove's glory days—who begot whom, a homespun Sodom and Gomorrah—while the Sunday roast withered in the oven.

Lighting a fresh candle, she skipped ahead to "Childbirth." A few lines in, she could have used a large drink of anything, for courage. The pages brimmed with warnings about "quality" people shirking their duty to supplement, strengthen, "the stock" of future generations. "Possessing an automobile carries more prestige than having a baby," the author lamented, and noted that "We have been more concerned about preventing sexual experience to the time when certain magical words are said over a couple than we have been about preventing feeble-minded or syphilitic children from being born."

True enough, Una thought.

"When one stops to consider what a childless old age may mean," the chapter continued, "one will see that there are not only eugenic and other social reasons for rearing a family but that parenthood has no small value from the standpoint of self-interest as well."

Una imagined Enman reading this. Had it helped sway and bring him around to the idea of being a father?

Then the author asked, "Who are the persons that society would select as parents for the next generation if it had the power and a reasonable amount of eugenic enlightenment to enable it to make such a selection? What tests would be applied? One may imagine a eugenic test as something fantastic that might eliminate even some good people like ourselves." Then Professor Millard Spencer Everett posited seven questions to determine who was qualified for parenthood, questions about a couple's desire for children, their demonstrated ability to provide a happy home, their economic, educational, and moral qualifications, their ability to provide "a reasonably good mental and physical heredity." The remaining questions made Una pause. One asked whether the husband or wife had "any disease which could be acquired by the child congenitally." The other was even more sobering: "Will childbirth injure the health of the mother?"

The rest of the questions made Una think of Hannah. It took an educated, kind person such as herself, Una thought, to see the merits of a Hannah. For no reason, she remembered a photo she had seen in the paper, showing the mannequins the ARP used in teaching recruits first aid. Boy Scouts wearing armbands were administering mouth-to-mouth resuscitation to the inert rubber figures laid out upon the Common's grass. Smiling life-size substitutes for wounded, suffering people.

Of course it was callow, even a little cruel to think of Hannah as a practice pupil. But then Una imagined some of the children she had taught during her practicum, in which teaching felt like no more than babysitting, with the homeroom teacher casually observing. Maintaining and improving your skills meant practising them. Practising them on Hannah would keep her occupied until things changed.

Una heard a noise from outside. It was very late. A rap on the window, someone tapping on the pane. The paleness of a face loomed there—enough to nearly send her out of her skin. The ARP? Didn't they know to come to the door?

But it was no ARP man. It was Clinton Goodrow, never mind it was nearly one o'clock. He was shouting in, "We seen the light and Win said, 'that poor Una, all alone with no Enman and no water. Whyn't you see if she'd like to come and stay here?'"

"Thanks, but it's all right—I'm fine." She felt a fleeting sense of obligation to invite him in, a courtesy in exchange for his concern. Minus that gait of his and his hint of an underbite, Clint was not a bad guy. Not a bad guy at all. A person like Win could do worse, or a woman whose husband cheated on her.

Had Mrs. Gregory been made the wiser? she wondered. Perhaps, more likely than not. As swiftly as the thought occurred to her, Clint's face bobbed away from the window. By the time Una peeked out the door he was gone.

Of course, the more people who knew about her lapse in judgment, the harder it would be to ensure it stayed behind her. People never blamed the man. She hoped, fervently, that Gregory's wife had been kept in the dark, exactly where she resolved to keep Enman. The past was past. But there was no fury like that of a wronged woman, Una knew from her own feelings. Without a job, she could not possibly return to life on her own. And since she was married, the thought struck her anew, the letter to the superintendent was, for now, a futile move.

"You're in a right piddle," Kit would say. "Might as well get cracking, start breeding, unless you want to float along forever idle." Teach, have a baby, or fritter her days away being a trinket hanging off Enman's arm, amusing herself tutoring someone who would never do algebra, or thrive past grade four.

13

SMOKING ONE CIGARETTE AFTER ANOTHER DID NOTHING TO QUELL THE shakes. The evening ending up as it had, he would have killed for a drink—though he had begun to think being relieved of a burden was not a bad thing. Beulah couldn't bring his friend back, or the proper feeling in his legs. But if ever he had faced a test of will, this was it, because Clinton's boy could not be too hard to track down; the gal at the desk might even have directions. Enman had seen the truck himself once, at Hubley Hill's springtime gig when Hubley had him run home for his violin then coaxed him up on stage. The Goodrow kid had handled any thirst the dancers worked up. Everyone on their feet, except for Una.

It wasn't hard to imagine the truck nearby, in a clearing by the Run that wound through O'Leery. Bottles tucked to cool amongst the stream's mossy rocks. He could easily walk; losing a car that was a money pit was more than a mixed blessing. Maybe Beulah's going missing was Fate's odd seal of approval on his return to Barrein, where plenty of people got along without owning a car.

And this was a test, all right. It must be. There was a higher reason for Beulah's disappearing into thin air. Borrowed? If that was the case, she would have been returned by now, so much for Enman's being unburdened. So, stolen: it really didn't matter by whom. A test of his mettle, Ma would say, of his resolve to quit drinking. The ability to let useless things go.

But why?

Why not, my son? It isn't for you to ask, she might say. The inscrutability of things rested as grimly as the room around him, with its grimy sink wedged between the bed and the window, which was jammed shut.

After splashing his face, Enman trudged reluctantly along the narrow upstairs corridor to the bathroom. The smell of vomit greeted him, and a spattering of blood in the toilet and along the edge of the yellowed tub.

Thank heavens Una wasn't here to savour this taste of the city spilling past its bounds into O'Leery. People's bodily functions on public display. He did what he had to, then hurried back to the room, shoving a chair against the door with its busted lock. The Grove had seen better days; just ask Hill, who had entertained in its dining room a thousand years ago.

He wished he could call Una, but the hour was much too late. He hoped she wasn't nervous being alone, and that she had locked up. He stripped to his shorts. His getting into bed set the springs jangling. At least the sheets were clean, stiff from the clothesline. A surprise, like the surprise relief that had come to him that Beulah was, or might no longer be, his to maintain. A goner. The relief hit him afresh, finding its spot again, a lightness between his ears. The writing had been on the wall for months, that the car was a goner. All the better that some unsuspecting loser had taken her off his hands.

The hard part was how he would get home—hitch a ride with someone who just happened to be driving? No more than two or three cars a day passed on either route, and with tomorrow being Saturday, not even the mail truck would be running. Home to Una. Once he got there, he would just have to swallow his loathing of the sea and get Inkpens' to fix him up with a boat—or never leave Barrein again in this life or the next. This would be troubling for Una, and trouble for Una could mean trouble for him, but they would adapt. He liked that she wasn't a pushover; he didn't mind her petulance so much, it kept him on his toes. It signalled some small vulnerability of hers, he guessed. Whatever it was, it kept her at a slight distance from him, which was curious. Enticing. It only made him want her more.

The thought made him smile, despite his craving for a drink. Smiling was infinitely better than putting a fist through the wall.

Una, Una—the narrow, noisy bed was much too wide without her. And what if, what *if*, just say for some reason he never made it home again? A foolish notion. But life threw such sucker punches, oh yes, it did. The thought of not seeing Barrein's headlands or the cape house at the top of the lane filled him with an ache, a regret for how easily he had left them behind once, believing life was better lived in a hive of streets, among strangers.

That's what I like about you, Enman Greene, the way you fear the worst, Una liked to tease. But say he stepped out right now, into the hall, out onto the porch, or by the road, and met the eye, let's imagine, of some good-for-nothing drunk, only the wary, violent type spoiling for a fight, spoiling for some kind of action? O'Leery was crawling with these, certainly by its reputation. What if he ended up going home in a box? Death would be the end of the same road he had started out on, and there was something acceptable about this, death being death. But where would his passing into oblivion leave Una? Alone, virtually friendless. But maybe she would fare all right, who knows, once she let herself get acclimatized. Found her sea legs, so to speak. People did. Give her another month and she would thank him for rescuing her from the morass of town.

Noise erupted out in the hallway. Fearing someone might burst in, he didn't dare get completely naked. The steamy, squalid air made it impossible to sleep. His shins itched as if his scars had fleas. But this was not the worst of it. The urge for a good belt of alcohol burned clear to his eyes and ears and down into his gut. And into the night's belly the noises piercing the walls were like cats in heat—couplings so vivid you wondered if it was something the Grove put in the water, some sort of drug driving things.

Well, it gave him time to think, though this was not wholly a blessing. He thought of his friend. He imagined the car smashed up or lying at the foot of the dam dividing O'Leery Lake from the Run. People joked about the junk on the bottom: a baby carriage, an outhouse on its side, bodies, for all anyone knew. In his mind's eye eels wove in and out of Ma's picnic basket. Worse was the thought of those jerry cans of water sitting there, while Una made do without a drop. Although, from what he heard, the water supply in town was gone to rat shit, so to speak, gallon upon gallon fed into ships making the ocean crossing—so much so that a church had burnt down when the firemen's hoses collapsed for want of pressure.

Twice he got up, cupped his hands under the tap, and drank, guiltily, to slake a fierce, galling thirst. She would be beside herself, his poor darling. Or making the best of it, which was more like her, Una being resourceful. It was brash, unkind, of him to underestimate her. Possibly, Hubley Hill wasn't the only fella with his head up his arse, considering her to be ever so slightly inept, a bit of a prima donna perhaps, Enman thought. And what would Hill know?

So there you go, he comforted himself. It's not like the inconvenience will be forever. Una will make out just fine.

It wasn't till dawn seeped through the blind that he slept—or, alerted by sounds of life below realized that, in fits and starts, he had dozed. But nothing opened till eight at the earliest, and who knew if and when there would be someone around to help. There was nowhere to get something to eat, and cabs didn't run out here. He waited till seven-thirty to pull on his clothes and creep downstairs to the phone. He hesitated, but knowing it was the responsible thing to do, dialled.

"A car stolen in O'Leery? You don't say." The police dispatcher might have asked why he was calling. "You're in luck, though, apparently." A party heading south this morning had their fishing trip sidelined by a vehicle blocking the road. A blue Chev less a fender, found with its hood up, suggesting the driver had done some tinkering before abandoning her. "Not even the decency to push her into the bushes so's others could get by," the cop said. She was blocking "a major artery" and in the event of an air raid or evacuation, "putting lives at risk."

"Dumping's illegal," Enman heard, and that he would be ticketed.

So he wasn't going to get off so easily, being freed of the car. "But what about those responsible?"

"No need to get stroppy with me, mack. Get her towed. Right away. Hop to it."

Busily eavesdropping, the desk clerk filled in details of the discovery. The party of guests had turned around and come back disgruntled, setting lesser sights on O'Leery Lake, where they might hook a boot or bicycle wheel if they were lucky. This was supposed to cheer him up? She asked if he wanted to wait around for breakfast.

Bleary-eyed, he went out and strolled up and down the main drag's dusty shoulder till the garage opened. Maybe someone could run him out the inland route, give him a tow, or the car troubles would be ones he could fix himself, enough to get him home? "Keep your shirt on," said the mechanic, who also agreed they would take a look.

By now, of course, Isaac would be shitting bricks wondering where he was, forget it was Saturday. This in itself was no big deal, Enman was used to working six days a week, having done so at the bank. Luckily he had change and the phone outside the Magnet was working. "Serves you right for driving that heap. Don't worry, take the time. We'll settle your pay later."

Dialling Una, he couldn't help but think of Ma's amusement at Isaac's name, which someone said meant "God's little joke," Isaac defying anybody's urge to laugh.

Una sounded sleepier than he felt. "When will I see you?" The ache for a drink stirred again but he swallowed it back: a pill no less bitter, it occurred to him, than what Ma must have gulped down whenever Hannah Twomey had crossed her path. Now Una knew all about Pa and Twomey's sister, she had reason to look down on Barrein, on him. He should have kept it to himself, since Ma had acted as if the old man had never taken a shine to that tease, Cecelia. "See what happens when drink dictates?" Ma had said. Though the old man's lapse had followed a broader dictum: the flesh wants what the flesh wants.

"I'll see you when I see you, sweetie—could be this morning or this afternoon, hard to say."

"Later, alligator." Her sigh sounded resigned but miffed. Anxious.

There was barely time to hang up the phone as the mechanic bar-relled up in the truck. Though less macabre, this was like going to claim a body. Climbing in, without a moment's hesitation, Enman accepted the mickey the grease monkey dredged from under the seat. It was early to be tippling. He really didn't want the stuff, but neither had he fully expected this errand.

He and the mechanic drove in silence. So it mightn't be the end of Beulah, after all. Then he thought, What *about* trips to town? What about seeing the doctor? O'Leery's doctor didn't count. Without a car, how would they manage Una's restlessness, that restlessness her reason for bringing Hannah around in the first place. Or was it simply to show other people up? The idea lodged like a pill in his gullet. Surely she hadn't meant to rub his nose in his laxness, his ignoring Hannah. Not his sweet Una. Rub your nose in *what*? she would have said, had he framed it so.

"You okay, buddy?" The mechanic nudged the mickey at him again.

Enman preferred to let sleeping dogs lie, especially when he saw Cleary's eyes in Hannah's, watching him. The old man's cravings, the kind that fed Bart Twomey's dealings, staring back from his own eyes whenever he looked long in the mirror.

"Can't be too much farther, is it, man? When didja say she went missing?"

Enman shrugged. Perfecting a playing technique meant more carefully observing the position of his wrist, hand, and fingers, best accomplished by further scrutinizing himself in the mirror. One reason to hang up the violin, the *fiddle*. Let single-minded Steady Hill and his steadier strumming score a radio hit, if that's what Hubley wanted. Avoiding liquor-soaked dancehalls was another way to free himself from Cleary's ball-and-chain.

"Hey. 'Nother drink, bud?"

Enman reached for the bottle, sipped. "It runs in families, you know," Ma once whispered, "the love of drink." Except giving up violin, the pastime that kept his hands busy, that is, literally off the bottle, would only allow for more time to drink *and* mean never playing Dvořák's largo. But no sane person wished to see the eyes of a drunk or the feeble-minded staring back from the looking glass.

Taking a last swig, the driver grimaced, then fired the bottle out the window. "Not saying much, are you?" It sounded funny coming from a fellow half his age.

"Don't suppose you've got another of those tucked away?"

The mechanic made a bored sort of noise, shook his head.

Could say the same for you, kid, you're not exactly talkative, Enman wanted to say. But it was nice riding up front, higher than usual. Around them the dry woods resembled tinder. Only the tenacious trees thrived, spruce a damn sight tougher than his marigolds.

Tougher than the thirst that rode him.

Then, after a while, there she was: Beulah, jammed like a cork in the road.

Slamming into reverse, the grease monkey jackknifed and backed up.

Nothing to be done but jump out and direct the guy. Dizzy on his feet—oh, that smidge of whiskey on an empty stomach, the sun beating down—he could barely look at her, Beulah like a friend after a falling out. A falling out with George. A day's falling out with Una would have been a thousand times worse, a permanent falling out unbearable. He would have sooner fallen out with Ma at times.

Blame cheap whiskey for allowing him to even imagine the notion of being separated from Una: another damn good reason for quitting, he knew. Which he had done, was doing now—yes, definitely. No question, no going back on it—now that the mechanic's offering left no more than a headache and an opening for groundless worries to pour in.

The dispatcher had been right about Beulah. Her raised hood was an invitation for critters to nest there. He imagined Ma's voice—"rust and moths, my son"—while peering at the engine's crumbling parts crisscrossed with electrical tape. *Store not things of earth but of heaven. None of it lasts, life or its disappointments, though one thing that persists is this: We're our brother's keepers.* No mention of sisters or wives.

Those itchy, crawling hours at the Grove had offered time, too much time, to mull over plenty of things. Not just things about him and Una, but Ma's death, his holding her hand. The horrified flash of something in her eyes right before she stopped breathing: had she glimpsed the old man waiting across some gauzy divide? Yet Una had found Ma peaceful—"Finally," she had whispered, tidying the bedside, with the doctor on his way, too late. "Guess she got tired of waiting," Una had told the man. Would she speak that way to Snow? Una's disappointment with Dr. Brunt was not as strong as Enman's was with her at the time, though he'd soon gotten over his. He knew she was disappointed about living in Ma's house and staying on in Barrein, and he hoped her disappointment would not grow bigger than her, bigger than them. But you accepted things. And no, Ma hadn't looked peaceful at all but plagued, panicky—if not fighting death, then unwilling to succumb. For all he knew her Blessed Mother had appeared at Ma's window, a broken figurine.

And he heard Ma's voice again in his head: "Never mind how others behave. You're to act properly. Any son of mine—" she would say, an eye cocked at the Meade kids traipsing by, dragging with them Sylvester's reputation for being no good.

"Buddy? First things first—them tires," the mechanic was yelling. He had brought replacement ones, but Enman didn't want to think what they cost. Gad, the cost of things as basic as food and gas, especially when Una demanded, deserved, a certain style of upkeep, beyond having nice clothes. Dinners out, movies. *Peter Peter pumpkin eater*, leapt into his head while the guy cranked the jack: the nursery rhyme Ma had recited—*Had a wife and couldn't keep her*—those last weeks when her mind wandered—*Put her in a pumpkin shell*—and barely knew what she was saying: *There he kept her very well.*

For Una, living in Barrein might feel like living in a pumpkin. In the Grove's dingy light this had come to him, and the unthinkable—entering and exiting his brain faster than a bullet would have—that the decent thing might just be to let Una go.

Let her find someone more equipped to give her what she needed, what he seemed unable to, given whatever it was he lacked. Whatever might make her happy, given whatever her disappointment spoke of, beyond the city things she missed, since doing a lot of the things most wives did didn't seem to. There was more to her dislike of cooking than fear of the stove.

The "new" tires were as bald as Hubley Hill's head. After getting the mechanic to come all this way, Enman could hardly balk. At least they held air, and already it was practically noon. "You in a rush, bud?" The kid waved his wrench. "Good news. Like I tells you, there's nutting here that can't be fixed." Yet, at first, no amount of tinkering would get Beulah to start. He gave the shiniest tire a kick.

"Ain't she like a woman," the kid mechanic piped. Like a woman? Had he let Beulah's name slip? "Cars, man—can't live without 'em. Can't live with 'em unless you're rolling in dough." The guy hitched and winched her up. She was bucked so high in front her taillights scraped the dirt.

The entire ride back to O'Leery, a chokeweed of cares twisted around his conscience, frustration and guilt over Hannah and Una. He was a little afraid of his failings further catching up with him. His old salary had been enough that he could have helped pay for someone to take Hannah in, if someone had been willing to. Helping Twomey with Hannah's keep would have been a waste of money; Twomey would've squandered it on himself. Enman's earnings at Inkpens' were half what he'd made at the bank. Una's goodness to the girl was like compound interest on his debt to both of them, for putting up with him.

He remembered Ma saying, "Una's a nice enough gal. But lofty, don't you find?"

Call it loftiness, call it Una's airy determination, it was what he liked, loved most, never mind that sometimes it set them apart. Una was like the wind personified depicted on a nautical chart at Inkpens', a face shown blowing from one top corner.

A more primal navigational aid than a compass.

Where would he be without her?

"New brakes for sure, carburetor needs looking at, plus body work. Could take a few days," was the garage's verdict. Up on the jack, Beulah looked even worse from underneath. His gut's emptiness caved to a rocky feeling. He had to get home, couldn't hack a second night at the Grove, let alone a third. He needed to see his wife, needed to make up with her—though make up for what, precisely, he felt queasily unsure: maybe whatever it was was bigger than anything you could put into words?

And probably it was foolish, downright superstitious, but as soon as he had a second he would find glue and mend Ma's statuette.

He hated asking, but there was this urgency: "Any chance bumming a lift?"

"Slim to none—unless someone's going that way?" the kid yelled out to the owner manning the cash, then turned to him again. "More good news, though. Got the parts, and things're a bit slow, so, you never know. Might getcha on the road a bit sooner, anyways."

"Get yourself a bite, meantime." The owner dug inside his coveralls for a pen. "They got the panfried haddock over the Grove there, not bad.

But before you head over, just need your John Henry, okay pal? In lieu of a deposit, just say." A grimy thumbnail indicated where to sign the guarantee that Enman would return. "Take your time, eh. Have a beer. Heck, have one for me too."

"Sure," he said, then hurried to the grocery up the hill. If it was half as good as Finck's it would have what he needed. When he walked in, heads turned and eyes narrowed—not surprising, him being a stranger. But then the clerk sang out, "No big deal, folks. Buddy's from Barrein, seen him with the Goodrows, can't be all bad, then. What can I do you for? It's just, well, we've had some trouble with foreigners."

"Suspected ones—Jerries." Tucking her hands in her apron, the fat girl at the cash breathed the words slowly from rosebud lips.

"Last thing we need's the RCMP on our case too, you catch me?"

14

THE PHONE WOKE HER, CLAMOURING BELOW, IN THE MIDST OF A DREAM impossible to shake off. Una had been washing dishes in the vast, bright kitchen of the house she'd grown up in, a house in which she'd often felt lost. But she was the mistress, the master, of it, with its bay windows and balustrade, chandeliers, and carved cornices and lintels—the house exactly, vividly, as it had been when she was a child.

Except, Una remembered as she leapt from the bed, the rooms were empty, the walls a uniform khaki green, the smell of mothballs everywhere. Even as she flew downstairs the smell lingered, and the dream's trenchant sunlight, pouring through hallways, leading her to the draughty tiled bathroom where her mother was being sick.

As she grabbed the receiver, breathed "Hello," the dream's chilly aura was a shawl around her shoulders. Too late she remembered the thermometer.

"So Clint didn't land you in the ditch?" Enman's voice was smooth and easy and frustratingly calm. He, after all, had spent the night somewhere with hot running water.

"Great," she replied to his news, disappointment clouding the picture in her mind of a shiny new car, herself at the wheel, wearing sunglasses and a chiffon kerchief like Kit's.

He babbled about rides, taxis, and getting home as soon as he could but not to hold her breath.

Hold her breath—for what?

Through the window she caught the sea's tight glint: another beach day in five or six weeks of such days that had gone beyond being monotonous. She pictured herself knocking on Isla's door again, flailing her bucket, and Isla's daughter burping her baby, its legs curling like a kitten's. And Hannah, she pictured Hannah too, the girl's eyes lighting up at practically nothing.

The futility of life here sank in with the heft of a knife cutting softened lard. The day ahead loomed like all the rest, as prescribed as paint-by-numbers canvases Kit deemed art for those lacking imagination. Una saw Kit's point but tended to disagree. Because wouldn't it be grand to be Kit—just a moment's pettiness crept in before she banished it—making such judgements, coming and going as she pleased.

Hormones.

This feeling of hers, a slow whirlpool of ennui, had to be more than the effects of a dream to be dismissed. Progesterone was Dr. Snow's name for the culprit. She thought again of Isla's granddaughter: infant fingers soft as the chamois Enman used to polish his car. But how long before tiny fingers turned grasping? Picking and pointing. The nastiness of children, who could deny it, even if you loved their imaginations? Peed pants, snotty noses, hectoring voices, and that way kids had of never questioning that the world revolved around *them*. Perhaps Kit was right: minimizing exposure to them spared you becoming cynical.

Kit said the same thing about some men.

But this was sour grapes! Because there *was* so much more about a baby to long for. A peach fuzz scalp, rosebud lips, the delicate sponge that was an infant's brain. It was one thing to guide someone else's child through the wonders of a curriculum, another to guide your own offspring through lessons you designed out of love. A world handpicked for it, a world with butter, not margarine coloured with orange dye, a world of lawns with grass, not rocks and weeds, of water from reservoirs, not wells, she had said to Enman.

"Dunno where you'd find a world like that, dear," Enman had said, and drawn her close.

Lying on its bed of cotton-wool, at its base the thermometer contained what looked like a tiny silver cake decoration. As she picked it up, its glass cool and as slippery as if greased, it slid—*shit!*—from her fingers. It was an icicle shattering everywhere. The floor's slope nudged the mercury ball, pretty as a bead but poisonous, under the bed.

Goddamnit. When Enman got home, he would have to dispose of it.

Pulling on her bathing suit, she pushed out her stomach and her breasts. The thought of Enman was jarring. For all his fumbling goodness, he seemed, suddenly, to have fallen away somewhere, to have retreated a lot farther than from sight and more distant than O'Leery.

THE TIDE WAS IN AND, DESPITE BEING LATE MORNING, the beach was deserted. Her loneliness only added to her day's irritation. She let seafoam scrub her toes while lines from movies washed wantonly in and out of mind—*Casablanca* especially. Bergman's Yvonne asking Bogart's Rick where he'd been the night before, his hedging, "It was so long ago I don't remember." Her "Will I see you tonight?" and his "I never make plans that far ahead." As far as she recalled, Yvonne hadn't been trying to conceive. No one in movies wanted to get pregnant, babies being where romance ended.

As she ducked under a wave, a gull nearby picked at a fish. She had read, of course, how a bad seed got passed along in families, though certain traits, aberrations, might skip a generation—or not. Take Enman and his weakness for liquor, his fondness for Barrein, and his alcoholic father, who, despite his wandering eye, had never strayed from this place. Did Barrein apply brakes to everyone's ambitions?

Oh yes, brakes. Something else Enman had mentioned on the phone.

She stepped from the surf, moved onto dry sand. The sun razored down, the sea a dazzle so sharp it hurt to view it. Everything was lost to the glare, hidden, as mysterious somehow as her emptiness, the feeling of a void as deep as the seashore at night.

Bracketed by rocks, this stretch of beach could not have been more lonesome. The perfect spot, really, for anyone who was up to no good, like Win's bootlegging son. Or for someone desperate enough to do something rash, a person inclined to walk in over their head, for instance—too far, too deep—and keep going.

No one around but gulls to see any lines she might have drawn for herself in the sand before waves washed them away. Lines about leaving Barrein, or staying, which boiled down, she knew, to leaving Enman or remaining married.

It was then she spotted driftwood at a distance, freshly deposited by the tide. Dark against the sand's dazzle, it had a shape interesting enough that she imagined lugging it home, if she could have, and using it to decorate the end of the lane, as Kit would do, or the big rock behind Enman's garden.

But no, it wasn't driftwood at all but a person, the last thing she expected to see. A bather stretched out on the sand, just above the tide-mark. He lay on his back, hand shielding his eyes.

Her heart still raced from her dip, the thud of her pulse in her ears. Before she could veer off to her spot in the dunes, clothes and towel dropped there aimlessly, the man sat up. He gazed her way. He appeared to be frowning. His wet hair looked the colour of rockweed. His hand moved and he waved and even smiled. He was shirtless, wearing only pants. His face and his build were familiar—it was him, her Gary Cooper, the fellow who had seen her bathing, seen her climb naked to the rock. God.

What time was it, anyway? It must be noon, the way her shadow pooled underfoot as though she had melted into it.

He *must* be camping, then, somewhere in the vicinity, spending several nights sleeping under the stars.

Curiosity lightened her step. The fellow, still smiling, beckoned. The gesture was chummy and sweet as Clint Goodrow's nod could be. Except he was younger, so much younger, and much better looking. Enman might know who he was, Enman who wouldn't be home for hours and then some. Who knew when she would have company again? Company to save her from herself.

She left her shadow behind and marched over to him. He didn't speak. He grinned up at her. The muscles of his chest were traced with sweat. His burn had turned to tan. The man patted a place on the sand beside him.

His callused brown hand was ringless, she noticed.

Everything in his smile was an invitation.

It felt a bit like being in a movie, playing Judy Garland, dropping to the sand, arranging herself beside him—fetchingly or not. He was so much younger than she was—even younger, possibly, than she had first thought.

She could have been his older sister, though not, thank God, his mother. His eyes were like a starling's, watching her every movement. His own movements were small, careful—economical, Enman might say—as if to conserve his energy. She had the feeling that she herself had somehow rehearsed this scenario, experienced it in a dream only slightly less unsettling than this morning's. A dream she'd had after visiting Dr. Snow's office in February, that she was auditioning for some sort of part.

Quite possibly this *was* a dream, or a mirage, the man reaching over, his hand moving to hers. A mirage, she told herself. Or a symptom of heat stroke.

She did notice, couldn't help but, how quickly he rose to the occasion, as Rick Gregory would say. When his fingers brushed the crook of her arm she closed her eyes, almost expected to catch a whiff of Old Spice—Enman's—or no, not aftershave but that cool-as-cucumber secretive man-smell of warm skin, sweat. The scent was mixed with that of oiled leather as her fingers, still a bit numb from the sea, moved to his belt buckle.

There wasn't another soul around. She would have spotted someone if there were. The only ones to watch were the birds, the beach, and the moment itself, which lay somehow outside everything.

She squeezed her eyes shut—the sun cast black and red shapes through her lids—as she tugged down the top of her suit. It was already low-slung and gritty inside; was it such a brazen, unnatural thing to do? She felt his tongue circle each nipple. She could hardly believe this was happening. She was lying in a blitz of sun, on a surface where everything seemed to be gritty yet melting, while her mind floated on a watery surface of its own. His lips—his tongue briefly grazing hers—tasted salty and metallic. Lake water? His smell had a deeper note of petroleum and unwashed clothes. She wanted to speak then, to say *something*—but what, and more to the point, why?

Lying flat, lifting her bum to squirm free of the suit, she thought not of Rick Gregory but of Enman. Getting out of the suit took long enough that she might have stopped, stood up, walked away. The suit's dankness twisted around her knees—enough to make her laugh, jarring enough that he stopped helping. His teeth were crooked, she saw, and his chin, in need of a shave, had a sparse prickle of beard. Still, with its fine bones his face was handsome. A son in his likeness was bound to be handsome too. But his clear blue eyes looked suddenly wary, afraid? "Oh my God, you're not a virg—," the words escaped before she could swallow them.

He grinned, oblivious of his teeth, and slid his hand over her and down, moving his fingers, pressing, probing, poking.

It was so simple, the simplest thing in the world. Is that why the world used that word to describe some women?

Easy.

When she felt him push inside—his body's taut, surprising weight on hers—whatever friend or foe, Kit *or* Win might say hardly mattered. It was a respite from loneliness, and possibly even a means to an end: justifiable. A silly concern about her nudity being indecent flared, then fizzled: except for one shoulder, where the sun seemed fixed, the man's body covered her as squarely as a beach coat.

This little vacation from herself was as fleeting as the flicker of sun on her brow. The man groaned with what sounded like relief, as if he had waited a very long time for this. The name he breathed into her ear was, naturally, someone else's. Then he was kissing her all over, trying to pull her on top of him. Her turn to shield him from the sun?

Gregory had only wanted to smoke afterwards, then play cards. And Enman, poor Enman, well, he generally went right to sleep....Never look a gift horse in the mouth, or was it in the eye? she thought, slipping back into herself, resisting the tug of the man's arms. She reached for her bathing suit, covered herself with it as much as she could, lying on her back.

"If you don't mind..." She didn't know what to call him. Except for the name he had uttered, he still hadn't spoken. She moved her hand as if to clear a space. He obliged by edging over so she could lie there, flatten her back to the sand, press herself to it. The ridges of his ribs brushed

hers. She shut her eyes to avoid his, staying so still she felt like a manne-
quin, one of those laid out on the Commons for youths learning first aid.

As if to rub life into them, he rolled her fingers between his palms,
squeezing them almost painfully: bone on bone. A gesture of forced sympathy? Regret? Kindness?

When he spoke, finally, his voice was surprisingly proper, English-
teacher precise, more so than Carmel Rooney's or Mrs. Greene's. She
thought of the young men she had attended high school with, her mother's idea of healthy prospects. Unlike her mother's tone, its undercur-
rent of judgement carefully contained by social niceties, his tone lacked
such snobbery. His properness was nothing like the properness of their
neighbours on Waegwoltic Avenue. "You're a very pretty lady," he said
shyly, touchingly so. Kneeling, he touched his cheek to her collarbone.
Ridiculous, she suddenly felt, her lying there in her altogether, the sun
basting her all over.

"It's, this is…look, it's not what you think," she managed to spit out.
But already he was standing and buttoning his pants, brushing away sand.
She stayed frozen.

He looked baffled, then alarmed. He was married, his wife not far
away, like Enman perhaps, putting in time in O'Leery.

"What is your name, please?"

The squawking of a gull just then mimicked Mrs. Greene's pesky
warning: Don't you hurt my son! Wheeling off—thankfully—the bird
was gone.

She really didn't want to say. But how to avoid telling him while
lying there already so exposed, everything laid bare but the scandalous
flutter of hope she felt inside her. The hope of conceiving was gutting now
that she realized she had acted out of a cold agency *and* her desolation.
Repeating her name, he pronounced it correctly. "Charming. A beautiful
name for a beautiful lady." His name, uttered as a honking flock of shags
flew by, sounded like Phil or "fill-em," the way Clint Goodrow said "film."

"Greene," he said, "like the colour?"

But now he was putting on his boots—heavy black ones, odd for a
summer day—tying the laces, slinging a greyish shirt over his shoulder.
"I'm—sorry. Oonah. If you need—I cannot stay. But, could I see you
again?"

It sounded so sweet, so formal, so high school. How crushed he would be to hear no, so she zipped her lips. He kissed her, a friendly smack, the way Clint might kiss Win or, once upon a time, Enman might have kissed Win. Would Enman still kiss Win if the chance arose? she wondered. Then the man was scooting away, little puffs of sand at his heels. She managed to get back into her suit.

The grit of sand pricked her, at the same instant her stomach rose. The man's speech, with its stiffness, seemed to echo in her ears, left a sickening burn. A foulness pooled in her mouth as the man's strangeness swept over her.

It was like expecting the sky to fall, like leaving the audition hall in her dream to find thunderheads massed overhead. Something, the darker the better, to remind her of her rashness—her transgression. Yet nothing but blue winked down, the sky the same colour as the sea, until a few wisps of cloud knit together and gently unravelled. Watching their swirling helped calm her. Being calm helped her stay still enough to let the truth of what she had just done—something that made her date with Gregory as innocent as *Merry Melodies*—nudge itself beyond agency and the strange possibility of conception to the vague, wild hope that a baby would redeem everything she committed.

After a while the wisps became batts which formed a gallery of faces, none of which looked familiar.

A gull passed over, carrying a mussel in its bill, circling then smashing it open on the rocks, a late lunch.

She imagined other kinds of bills. The kind Enman knew *all* about, monetary transactions. Transaction. As she spoke the word aloud, it rolled easily from her tongue, resonated in her ears, then roosted in the airy space between them. An exchange. What she had done was no different, really, from a bank trading currencies, or Enman swapping cash for liquor wherever he bought it. And hardly different at all, when you thought it through, from Enman sending Dr. Snow a cheque after her appointment.

The surf's soft rumble pushed away her own harshest objections to all of this, objections based on sentiment. Sentiment could be dangerous, she knew. She thought of the hygiene book, how its author would say that, at its worst, sentiment was a smallness of mind that hobbled human progress. Hadn't Snow said that someday results would be achieved using turkey basters and humans could be grown in petri dishes?

Having acted in the interests of biology, let biology work its wonders. If she lay still long enough for her body to cooperate, she could even convince herself that it had been Enman taking the bull by the horns in this fair trade, this exchange of services on a beach.

Eyes shut, she clenched every muscle fibre, asking the sun's blessing on every wondrous loop and sac inside her. She would let the sun's heat seal whatever activity might be going on inside, while burning away a secret nobody needed to know. Still she grew cold pressing her tailbone down, the suit's clamminess raising goosebumps. The trouble with having her eyes closed was that it played the man's face across an inner screen. A silent film. Matted dark blond hair falling across one eye. Chapped maroon lips against unpleasant teeth, and a gauntness that did not mesh with his youth. A nose that was slightly hawkish, but preferable to a snub one, and the rest of him attractive, appealing, even bamboozling. It was best not to forget that he had been good-looking, although she knew the sound of his grunts was something to be pushed firmly from her memory.

People acted pragmatically all the time, without letting emotions, love, enter into things. Love belonged to marriage, just as the hygiene book said. Love is patient, love is kind, said Mrs. Greene's Bible. Love is also in the eye of the beholder, Una thought, and judgement belongs to those who exist outside love, on its periphery. Watching the man hurry off, she had longed for him to be Enman, not leaving, of course, but, by some trick of sunlight, approaching.

Finally rising, snugging up her suit, she padded carefully back to where her belongings lay. Every blade of marram, whiskers in the dune's wrinkled face, glinted as the sun slid from behind a cloud. A married woman! it seemed to gloat. A teacher to boot!

Then it struck her again, the way he had smelled.

Like diesel, to rhyme with the other name he had uttered.

She had just put on her clothes when a voice called out, a familiar, haranguing one ringing over the dune.

"Wouldja look at this! Never thought I'd be so jeezly lucky!"

Win came struggling towards her, a string bag bulging with good-ies swaying from each shoulder. She jerked her chin toward the horizon, matted now, vaguely, with a yellowy grey like the cat hair Una swept from under the bed.

Not a figment at all, it was a fog bank. It hung there, waiting.

"Hell's bells, Una—don't look at me like that. I'm not a ghost. If anything, girl, I'm someone that seen one, or just about."

One of the bags full of tins, most missing labels, clanked to the sand. "Don't suppose you seen this." Win yanked something the colour of smoke from the other bag, carefully unrolled it.

Even before Una recognized it, the odour hit her. The smell was like that of spoiled meat—no, blood.

A jacket—leather, with a gored pocket, a single row of buttons, each embossed with a little anchor. Her stomach knotted. It was just like the one she had seen hanging on a branch. Its ragged lining was a crusty red. As if that wasn't enough to make her gag, Win pulled out something grey: a serviceman's cap, woollen, wedge-style, but not like those the Canadians wore. It had a red badge with an eagle on it and a swastika—the symbol splashed across the *Enlist!* and *Smash Hitler!* posters plastered everywhere.

"Don't suppose you'd know anything about it?" Win's chippiness made her chest tighten. Queasy, Una stuffed the jacket back into Win's bag, managed to mumble about getting back in time for Enman.

"Whoever's jacket it was, they mustn't be in too good a shape." Win gave a frightened laugh, watching her. Una's heart kicked inside her.

"Well. Maybe it's a trophy—washed up like the rest of your loot." Una spoke hastily, not meaning any criticism.

"Right." Win stared at her, offended.

In scrambling to apologize, Una ended up sounding glib. "Pity it didn't come with a body."

"Well, you'd know about bodies, you poor dear. Helping with Mrs. Greene's arrangements and that."

Una couldn't tell whether or not Win aimed to be conciliatory, but was not interested in lingering to find out. Clutching her towel, she turned quickly, making for the path.

"Where's the fire? Keep me company. You wouldn't help me with these cans, never know what's inside 'em. You're welcome to half. Beat Iris

Finck at her trade—might be something nice here. Last time was tinned pears in their own juice."

If it hadn't been Win making the offer, it might have seemed a friendly one.

"Alrighty then. Hubby approve of you parading around in your birthday suit? I thought not. Give me a hand and I won't breathe a word." Win laughed more loudly than usual.

A gaff hook of a comment, it jerked Una to attention, stopped her in her tracks.

"Oh my, the weight of these tins'd cause tennis elbow, a double case. I'd be much obliged, Una. Stuff's too good to leave—heck," Win's chuckle rang out, nervous yet light, "we could set up shop, you and me, go head to head with Iris. But for now, isn't it nice, seeing as we're headed the same way, to watch each other's backs?"

15

THE HOUSE WAS DESERTED WHEN HE GOT THERE WELL AFTER LUNCHTIME, LOCKED up tight and no sign of Una anywhere. It felt like he had been gone for weeks, although, wouldn't you know, the car had run like a top all the way home. As good as new, less that front fender, negotiating the turns with barely a hiccup. He had hoped to find Una watching for him from the window or running out to the yard. But in the house, dust waltzing in the sunlight was the only thing stirring. She had gone off on some day-long jaunt? Not even Tippy was there for a cuddle. A cup of tea or a waiting sandwich would've been nice. Then he remembered the jerry cans and tramped outside to free them from the trunk.

Amazingly, or not, they seemed untouched, the water piss-warm when he ran some into the basin to wash off the worst of O'Leery. Then he fished the tube of glue from his pocket. It was something to do while he waited for Una. It was still a Saturday after all, and some of it, like Ma's ornament, could yet be salvaged.

But when he checked the parlour drawer, the figurine wasn't there. The doily was, but not so much as a shard of porcelain. He went back out into the kitchen. Ah! There it was beside the trash, ready to be dumped. Una was nothing if not a neat nut, a tidy housekeeper—sometimes a bit too tidy. Aside from her severed head, all of the Mother but a portion of the base was intact. He pried the lid off the glue, applied the stuff with his finger. *For best results, let dry for twenty-four hours before use.* He had to smile. For use as what, a golden calf, an idol to pray to? Were that the case, he and Una might have launched prayers for the peaceful resolution of their small differences through its intercession.

When the figurine was more or less repaired—barely a chip in her base, a near-invisible seam through her beneficent smile—he placed her back in her spot. He felt a pang that Ma had lived so small a life that such an object could have meaning—but then look at him, saddled once again with the car.

He lifted the Dvořák record from its sleeve, placed the needle. No, with time on his side he would not skip to the second track but enjoy the first with all its bombast. Its triumphant noise pretty much summed up the better parts of the day. Freeing the violin from its case, he prepared to bow along to the gorgeous adagio, its gentle conjuring of a fine day's beginning, a fresh start.

Life isn't all cherries, my darling, nor should you expect it to be, from wherever she was, Ma seemed to remind him. *We all have to do things we don't like. Enjoy those things you do.*

He had played through the record twice when the clock's ticking caught him up.

Where *was* she? Should he start rustling up supper? She would be ravenous after swimming and tramping all over God's green acre. It was important that she be properly nourished. Who needed a doctor to tell them that?

He opened some beans, sliced bread for toast and what was left of a tomato, filled the kettle—then thought better of it. Who knows what might be in the water. Anyone craven enough to steal a car, any car, might have easily tampered with it; you couldn't put it past them. He tipped the beans into a pot, ready to heat up.

Still no Una, and nearly five o'clock. Something must have happened; she had slipped and twisted an ankle—worse, fallen and broken something, hit her head, gotten lost? It was ridiculous letting his imagination charge ahead of itself. But at a quarter past he strolled out by the road, leaving the door open in case she'd lost her key.

No sign of her on the road, so he kept going. His feet carried him as if they knew something he did not. *Now don't borrow trouble*, Ma's voice pursued him. *A penny for your thoughts*: Ma used to say that too, and so had Win, when they were kids. No doubt Win had upped it to a nickel after landing Clint—because didn't marriage do that at times, force a fellow inside of himself?

He was almost upon the beach before he spied her by the water— yes, it was Una, he could tell by the silhouette of her slender body—and the neighbours, Clint and Win. They were huddled over something lying at the surf's edge. A bedroll or an extra-large ditty bag, something lumpen and dark lolling there like a washed-up seal.

Except, it was too big to be a seal.

As Enman got closer, he saw Clint was dandling a gaff hook and hauling whatever it was ashore. Only then did he spy two men, strangers, stumbling from the dunes, wielding what looked like a sheet of plywood. As he approached, upon them now, they heave-ho'ed the object onto it. Then, suddenly, the sight was a punch to the gut. Terrible things ran through his head as his feet dragged him closer.

Una looked up then and her face was pinched, and Win was crying. "Found 'im, the gals did—some poor bastard, Christ only knows who," Clint was yelling up at him. Una looked past Enman with numb, fixed eyes.

The fellows with the makeshift stretcher were ARP, it quickly dawned, with their armbands and bright vests. They were both young. One of them puked into the shallows.

He felt something inside him freeze as he pictured George Archibald. This body had not been in the water for long; he could see where the canvas it had been wrapped in had fallen away. If it had been, the face would have been black and bloated. But it was blue around the mouth and a gash at its throat was blackish purple, the skin at the edges a deepening grey. Then he realized that part of its head was missing.

Good Christ.

"Oh, my darling girl." He reached to comfort Una. She pressed herself to him, sparrow-boned, trembling. The way he had pressed himself to her, telling her about that blazing, tar-streaked night at sea. All he could think of was a bird in a bad wind. One of Father Heaney's maxims echoed back oddly: *Better to give comfort than receive it. Be for the troubled a channel of peace.*

Una was babbling, "We were coming along, minding our own business, and saw this...."

"Shhh now, it's all right," he kept saying. Though of course it wasn't— not for this poor bugger anyway.

He suspected that somehow, someday, Una and Win might become friends. An evening out, the drive home together, that was all it had taken for Una to look somewhat more kindly on Win.

The ability to look more kindly on most things usually helped. But all the sympathy and pity in the world could not enhance the look of that bluish face or prevent the sight of it from reaching deeper into his gut—what in the name of?—It loosed in his mind the flares of other dead faces, eyes seeing nothing or what passed for hell.

Or purgatory, which Ma—in moments less influenced by Father Heaney's speculations, such as after the old man's passing—had considered a lingerer's stopgap. *You feel them hanging around*, she used to say. Like they've got unfinished business, so they're not quite happy, not just yet, leaving the rest of us to fix their messes. Fix their messes so that someday somewhere they'll be free to rollick about.

"It's as if your father's still waiting for me to say, 'I forgive you, Cleary, so go away, would you?'"

Now Clint was clapping him on the shoulder, drawing him and Una towards himself and Win into a silly group hug. "Hey, buddy—this is the last frigging thing you need to see," he was saying. "Look, these fellas are here. Take Una home. Win and me'll see what's what. They'll want a statement, I'magine. Who knows but the *Herald*'ll send a raft of reporters to grill us. Win and me, we'll handle it."

Clint gave Una a funny look—no pretending to himself Enman didn't see it—a look staking a claim that the find was Win's. That Win's being from here made her a more credible witness. Which made some sense, but lent credence to Una's complaints of feeling snubbed, excluded.

"It *was* both gals who found him?" Enman asked just to be sure.

"Yeah. Now, gwan—get Una out of here. Her delicate nature and all." Clint's eyebrows tented. "These ARP guys got everything under control." Though this was questionable, the way the one kept gagging as they hefted the body on their plywood.

Now Una was weeping, and no wonder. He stole a quick, final glance at the men's burden. The longish dark hair, the shadowy beard. The stretcher-bearer stumbled and the wrapping slipped. Enman glimpsed clothing, sodden trousers and a sweater.

Win let out a strange little moan. Speechless, they gaped at the badge sewn to one sleeve: an eagle insignia against red and the black of a swastika.

"Good Christ." Enman caught his breath. "He wasn't swimming out there, was he?"

"How far offshore do you think the bastards are?" Clint gripped Win's hand.

"Closer than you think." Enman pulled Una close. He would have to prod the ARP boys into quicker action. "Sure you fellas can manage?"

"Got the fire truck up back of the pond," one of them said.

Una hardly uttered two words, stumbling away.

When they got home, he sat her down and got supper and put some in front of her. Only then she warmed up enough to ask about Beulah and the Grove.

She sighed and said how nice it would be to have a *new* car. Then she stood, saying the excitement had worn her out and it was time for bed. "Coming up?" he expected her to say, but after visiting the privy she slipped upstairs without a word.

Una was more delicate than he had thought. Her delicacy proved how little Ma had known her, once pointing out to him Una's toughness. "You have to be tough to be a dervish." Of course, Una had appeared tough, tending Ma's needs.

Watching from the front room, seeing Win and Clint coming up the hill, Enman grabbed the bucket, a pretext for popping over. Clint was by himself on their porch, and licked his finger tersely, held it to the breeze. "Thought we were in for a bit of relief, earlier. But no go."

When he asked after Win, Clint seemed disgusted. "Well—as you might imagine, she's beside herself. Beside herself that no one's been listening. All these months, she's been saying we ought to be vigilant"—this was the word Clint used; he and Win had wasted no time speaking with the paper?—"with the Jerries so near." He sounded suddenly accusing, as if it was Enman's fault, or Una's, that the dead man had come ashore. "How many more, you figure, are out there, alive?"

The bucketful of water Clint gave Enman went a long way in cleaning up the kitchen, a chore that kept his mind off the worst of this treacherous business, his memories of his ship being hit. But every time he thought of the body, the need for a drink surged with such a fierce heat it made him clammy.

The mahogany chest was empty of liquor, of course—it wasn't as though Una would replenish it. He rooted around inside it anyway, Ma's figurine looking down all the while. From its place high on the shelf you couldn't see the damage to it. Then he crept upstairs in the twilight to peek in on Una.

She was curled on her side, her back to him, and by the sound of her breathing, in a dead sleep. That gruesome business at the beach had taken more of a toll than he had guessed. Una wasn't as tough or as practical as Win. He hoped Win's practicality would rub off on Una and that being practical would remedy the flightiness that contributed to her being lonely.

With nothing to drink and no light—he hesitated even to burn a candle, having now such proof that the enemy hovered—he could either listen to music at whisper-volume or go to bed. With tomorrow aimed at making up lost hours, by dawn he would be writing up invoices, balancing payments and expenditures, forget it was the Lord's Day—a meaningful thing to Ma and Ma alone.

Careful not to disturb her, he crawled in next to Una. When she shifted he spooned against her and held her close. The warmth of her, her slip of a body inside that cotton nightie, was all a fellow could want. How was it that such an awkward, solitary sort as he had found himself so lucky?

For the first time in weeks, months, he wanted, really wanted, to do the thing she was usually so greedy for. But she moved away, sighing in her sleep.

At first light he woke. Sunday was the best day of the week to get caught up at work without Isaac peering over your shoulder.

Una stirred. He brushed her hair from her cheek. He stroked her arm the way she liked, moved his hand to a shin tucked up under the nightie. Usually such a move made her respond. But now she flung her arm out and reached for something, swore.

"Can you see it? My thermometer," she mumbled, pointing vaguely to the floor, and then, "Is that the cat I hear, wanting in?" She asked when Tippy had last been fed.

"This worries you?" He laughed, expecting her to laugh too, though she didn't.

He held out his arms. "I can saunter in when I like—it's not like Isaac's got his time clock ticking."

It was a simple statement which she somehow took umbrage to. "Oh, but we all must do things we *don't* feel like." Una spouted Ma's expression. Perhaps she didn't intend to be sarcastic, but her mimicry made him suddenly defensive.

"If not for my poor ma, God knows where I'd have ended up. Living with the Twomeys? How about your mother, what kind of a mother was she?" He said it kindly, he was curious, since Una seldom mentioned either of her parents.

She smiled glumly. "I've told you about her problem. That's about all there is to know, I'm afraid." She spoke pointedly, and he regretted bringing it up, determined not to rise to the accusation in her voice.

"Okay, easy. Forget I asked. Look, I know it was rough, what you and Win saw. Gave you a fright. It's a dire thing—"

He told her how, once, he'd helped the Meades comb the shore for a relative who had fallen overboard, and he and another kid had found something wedged in the rocks—wedged like food between molars, he almost said—before Sylvester Meade could yank them away.

"Yes—well, we can't be Pollyannas for ever, can we."

She sounded disinterested. Disinterested *and* cross, if you could be both.

"I only wish Clint or I'd seen it first and headed you off, you and Win, spared you both the—"

"Ugly details?" She licked her lips, touched her fingers to them. They were likely parched, another thing somehow his fault?

"Una. What have I done now? What *is* it?"

Her laugh was almost cruel. "You have no intention of ever leaving, do you. You love it here, being back."

She chewed her lip, but then leaned over the bed to give him a kiss, a tight peck on the lips. "My next appointment's supposed to be in September. Guess I'll be driving myself there, if you won't set foot back in town." Her voice sounded light now, and was full of a strange but welcome resignation. "I really can't imagine the need to see Snow then anyway, unless something changes. So—are you going to lie here all day till Inkpen comes knocking?" She moved to flick aside the blind. "The sounds in the night—sure it wasn't rain? If you run next door and fill up the kettle, I'll see what's to fry up. While you're at it, maybe Clint'll let you haul back enough to fill the tub. I'll go out of my head if I don't have a proper bath."

What could he do but oblige, and oblige with a wink? "If he says it's a loan, I'll be sure to say we'll pay him back."

At least she smiled then, sort of, on her way out back.

16

SAME AS WITH FACING A ROWDY CLASS, UNA DECIDED, SHE WOULD FACE her misgivings, her fears, about the beach. She would not avoid it just because of what had happened there, her deed and her and Win's discovery. The beach was her refuge, her solace. Overcoming apprehension meant diving back in to whatever made you afraid, the next day and the next and the next after that. It was foolish to think you could avoid some things, good or bad.

Despite the morning's being overcast, the instant Enman was safely out of sight she set off. She would skirt the first beach where, by now, the curious would likely be gathered. Let them be. Their presence might ward off interlopers. The breeze would clear her head.

Attempting to flee Win's company the day before, she had looped towards the water. There she had spied it. Fabric—a thick bolt of fabric, a bedroll maybe?—being dragged back and forth by the waves then pushed toward shore, never mind the surf's reluctance to let go. Canvas draped with wrackweed, had it fallen from a vessel? Her newly hatched fear, second only to that of being caught out by Win, was stumbling upon something awful. You heard about grisly discoveries, people like Enman's shipmates after having been hit, human vultures—Win and her ilk—swooping in after a sinking to snatch anything useful.

It couldn't be. She had stepped into the water to get a better look.

Something raw poked from one end of the bundle. A seepage tinged the backwash pink. Not quickly enough to back away, she had discerned the shape. A face under wraps, a torso. Cloth. *A man of the cloth*: the phrase blazed through her as she'd backed up, leapt away, heels dredging sand. A fanciful notion, a trick of her overwhelmed brain.

Una let out a shriek, she must have, because Win had come running. By now the thing had beached itself. Dropping her stash of cans, enough to do the rest of the summer and then some, Win had crouched and peeled back the canvas. What Una saw made her gag. Turning, she spat into the seafoam. "Don't you be upsetting yourself," Win had said, or something just as inane. Win had held her hand. Una had let her.

She could barely remember the rest, the two of them running to fetch Clint. "He'll know what to do." She had sat there in Win's kitchen while Clint phoned the ARP. Then she'd hurried back with both him and Win to keep it company.

The bedroll, the bundle. The corpse.

So much for the Clint who had pressed his thigh to hers. This Clint, the one who stepped in, was bossy and gruff, cracking a joke—a joke!—about what she and Win might have done to land some poor nameless bugger in the drink.

A crude, pathetic attempt at comic relief, even if a person were forgiving of Clint, which Una felt forced to be.

"Don't look at me," Win had said.

A small mercy, at least, that none of them knew the fellow. "Imagine—*recognizing* someone" was all Una could manage. Eyeing her a little askance, Win nodded.

"No chance recognizing this bastard," a voice had piped, descending out of nowhere. Seeing the fellow's ARP badge and armband, she and Win had stumbled into one another, stepping aside. Win clung to her arm. "I'll say," Win had snivelled in a decidedly superior way.

Win's tone was a sharp instrument. What, exactly, had Win seen beforehand? Before they had come upon each other in the dunes, before all of *this*.

But why should she second-guess the sequence of things, the way her encounter with the man had obviously gone unseen? Was she punishing herself for what she had let happen? As the sun burned through cloud, brightening then bleaching everything, so would yesterday's doings sharpen in her memory then just as quickly fade. Alone, level-headed, she walked herself through the previous afternoon's encounter, as it had unfolded, all but invisibly.

Dropping her things where *it* had happened—the nameless act, little more than a fantasy—she spread the blanket and stretched out on it, still in her clothes. Once again she was completely alone, not a gawker in view. Overhead the clouds clotted and churned. An offshore breeze crinkled the sea, a deep blue at the horizon. As true a blue as some wild irises Enman had pointed out once by the pond, as some bluets he'd noted in the grass.

What was to be done with such a husband, so guileless, so *good*— keep on pleasing him? Mrs. Greene had likened marriage to knitting: knit purl knit purl, just keep going like that. But say you dropped a stitch. Did you keep going, letting it mar the rest of the work, or rip it out straight away and start over?

One good reason right there for not being a knitter, Kit would say. Una closed her eyes against the mackerel sky, didn't dare let herself remember the man's touch.

She was thinking, grimly, about what to make for supper when something jostled her. A warmth nudged hers. An arm, a hand. There was no chance to stand or even sit up and tell him to disappear, that his company was not wanted. He was kneeling there—"We meet again!"— all muscle and sunburnt skin.

He was no figment of the imagination, offering a twitch of a smile as he picked up her towel and shoes, then dropped them, calmly pulling her to her feet. Before she could pull free, he ran rough fingers over her palm, gripping her hand more tightly, kissed the tips of her fingers. She felt her breath seize, disgust trapped inside her. He gestured towards the marram, the trees behind it, spruce barely a screen against the brewing wind.

"I am glad to see you again."

"You have no right to—"

He paid no attention to her objections, tugging her along. The stubbled marram driving splinters between her toes. "What is the matter?" His voice was a jeer.

"I'm going to report you." She knew what he was. Her voice was pathetic, tiny and frail.

"You did not already?" His laugh, for all its boyishness, was bitter. Cruel. "Do you have a husband?" Contemptuous. "But we so enjoyed each other, Oona. Why not again? What is to fear?"

His grip on her wrist was a vise as they reached a break in the evergreens.

"If you let me go I'll keep quiet. I'll say nothing. I promise."

"A promise." He laughed. Limbs had been freshly cut from the trees, the smell of spruce overtaking that of sand and salted grass.

"You don't want to keep a man company? Bring him some comfort?"

Her blood pounded in her ears. "I'm old enough to—please."

They had reached a tiny clearing, with the remains of a campfire and a shelter made of tarps rigged to the branches. A charred metal pot lay on the peat, and some tin mugs and plates. Hanging from a nail sunk into a trunk was a rabbit, red dripped from its mouth. She glimpsed a blanket spread on the ground beneath the tarps, bundled clothing.

She struggled to sound calm. "I am old enough to be your mother."

"It is not the finest hotel, I am sorry. I suppose you would like fine sheets, champagne."

"If you let me go, I won't breathe a word."

"What, Oona, do you know of mothers? Shall I tell you of mine?" The oddness of his question and the bitterness in his voice frightened her more, if this was possible. "When I was a boy she would take me to Luna Park. I would watch the women like you at the waterslide, parading themselves. Their wares."

The glint of a gold filling in his stained teeth.

As he spoke the slow patter of rain began. He had let go of her now and glanced up, his eyes hooded, their lids bared to the moisture. He wore a tight smile. Just when she felt her nerves would snap and her heart beat its way out of her chest, she managed to lurch from his reach. He looked stunned.

"I did not mean to frighten you. I am not that desperate a man, believe me." He laughed again. "You have a husband? A home where a friend could lay his head, enjoy a meal?"

As suddenly as the raindrops had begun to fall, they stopped, and the wind shifted. Who knew he didn't have a gun tucked somewhere and if she turned and ran, he would shoot?

"A friend in such times is a friend indeed." His smile had weakened to a grimace, his eyes narrowed. Abruptly he squatted, folding his arms and burying his face. He was laughing or crying. She could not tell which, or whether it was simply a gesture, a ploy, meant to ensnare her. "My family is no longer alive. Kreuzberg," she heard. Berlin, Hamburg. Firebombings.

Through the branches cracks appeared in the clouds. The sun peeked through them.

"You expect me to feel for you?"

His blue eyes were shallow and cool, surprised. He wasn't much more than a schoolboy. Beads of moisture on his face were rhinestones, the cheapest.

"*Nein.* There is no feeling bad."

In spite of her disgust, a cold terror froze her there.

"Not even over lost ones—?"

He shrugged, gazing at her. His eyes glistened, the strange hint of tears. "The spoils of war." He lifted his hand, moved as if to rise and strike her, instead, rocked back on his heels. "Go home to your husband. Tell him what you have done." He reached for her ankle, and it was this gesture that snapped whatever strange, momentary hold he had on her.

"Goodbye, pretty Una. If you change your mind, it might be too late."

His eyes were the same leaden colour as the horizon melding with the sky.

As she ran, tripping and stumbling over the dune, the sun was a muzzy glow through the clouds sorting themselves into skeins of grey. Fog. A glittery drizzle sprinkled down. Her feet were bleeding, her things left on the beach soaked by the tide, which had crept up and all but claimed them.

Una trembled as she pushed her feet into her wet shoes, wrung water and sand from Mrs. Greene's blanket. "Forgive us our trespasses," she imagined Marge Greene whispering, as she had from her sickbed. "Deliver us from evil," the priest had prayed over her open grave, as Enman threw in a handful of thin soil. "Keep us free from sin and safe from all distress, as we await the coming of our Lord."

She wished she could do as Enman did with his record albums, lift and reposition the needle from one track to a softer, lighter melody. The kind of melody that might have the power to hold you in its thrall forever, and chase away demons and the disorder of having far too much undisciplined time.

17

THIS TIME UNA CAME RIGHT OUT INTO THE YARD, ATTACHING HERSELF TO him as if he had been overseas fighting, was just returned from France or Holland. She was in her bare feet, her towel and blanket hung on the line, though not her bathing suit. He noticed Cleary's beads were gone.

"Oh, my darling—put that poor Jerry beggar out of your head, the unlucky sod. Who knows but he got what he had coming? Though you hate to think it. No word yet how he ended up here?"

He could feel her flinch. Now she too had a grisly memory to live with, a memory like a permanent lodger who occupied a bed but paid no rent. As he entered the kitchen, he saw her shoes drying by the stove. "Got caught unawares, did you, fell asleep in the sun?" He felt like a bit of an intruder in his own house, because the spot where he had done *his* homework, all those years ago, was laid with a scribbler, writing supplies and a smattering of opened schoolbooks.

She wanted things all set for the lesson, she said. Her voice sounded a little like the sap had been drained from it. The water bucket by the counter was filled to the brim, and the sink too. With any luck, hope against hope, this patchy fog preceded a downpour long and hard enough to fill the well.

"So she's teachable, our Hannah," he said lightly.

"Nothing some patience and coaxing can't fix."

He didn't quite trust the pluckiness in her voice; it didn't convince him.

For supper she had gone all out. Ritz cracker pie and scallops perfectly seared. She had picked some daisies and put them in a glass on the table. They had just sat down to eat when Clinton phoned. A meeting had been called, Clint said. Eight o'clock at Finck's. The ARP and some navy brass were coming out. "Be there or don't bother showing your ugly mug again, bud." Enman laughed. But it must be serious, serious enough to keep Iris Finck up past her bedtime.

The pie was tasty and worth lingering over. His "That tastes like having more" a genuine compliment.

Una only took a tiny sliver for herself. "If we were in town we could go to Please You Bakery or Diana Sweet's for dessert."

"Who could tell those crackers aren't apples? My, you've worked wonders, Una." In the city the ingredients would be no better, though it struck him, for the umpteenth time, that things with her would be simpler there.

Una jumped up, barely finished, and rushed to get the dishes done. "Well, you said we were going. I need to get out."

"What about your pupil?"

"If Hannah was coming she'd be here by now."

Picturing Finck's and a swarm of curious, frightened faces, he would have rather stayed in. She ran upstairs to find shoes. Her ropy ones had fallen apart at the soles, he noticed, inspecting them.

He was happy to leave the car parked. With Una's arm looped through his, they set out. The fog was heavy with moisture, pregnant with it. Its strange chill was a shock to the skin. Savouring it, they took their time. Una slowed to a snail's pace. Suddenly balky, was she too wishing that they'd stayed in?

Hubley Hill would be there and have everyone asking what Enman had against fiddle. Now there was talk the Labour Day dance was going ahead after all, though it was still more than a month away, square sets and other "down home" stuff he decided he wanted little part of. He guessed Una was coming this evening to back him up, see that he didn't succumb to Hill's strange waffling.

"Listen, sweetpea, I know how it feels."

"What?" Her voice was sharp.

"People. The things they say. They mean well, mostly."

"Right. What's the road to hell paved with?" Her face looked piqued, suddenly, her expression weary. "And 'good things come to those that wait,' I've heard that too."

"The road would be worse with bad intentions."

"Bad ones? Well, yes. Hardly a need to point that out, is there."

PRETTY MUCH ALL OF BARREIN was packed into Finck's—Meades, Inkpens, and not just Hubley but Hills Enman hadn't seen in a dog's age, even a few O'Leery-ites, as Iris called them, including Flood from the Magnet. Mrs. Finck herself was holding court, wearing her best stained cardigan, flyaway hair in a topknot. Bart Twomey leered in all his odiferous glory, arse-crack on display as he leaned over the counter, blocking everyone's view of the ARP man and navy fellow tucked safely behind it.

The man in uniform doffed his officer's cap, peering around at everybody. Ainsley, the fellow in ARP overalls, also from O'Leery, puffed out his cheeks, sighing like there was a jackpot in store and he for one could not wait to claim it.

"Attention—we need your attention, fellas. Ladies too," Ainsley corrected himself. "It's come to our attention that—"

Clint could not contain himself. "Come to your attention? Maybe you should listen to my wife here. She and Una Greene here, these gals, they're the ones that found—"

Win grimaced, then glanced over at Una and gave her a determined smile. The smile was sympathetic, and as Enman saw it, could not have been kinder.

"Yes, sure. Of course," Ainsley said. "But can anyone tell us what they saw, if they noticed anything suspicious, unusual, leading up to—"

Win looked sharply away then, avoiding Una, it seemed. Was it possible that Win did not want her sharing the limelight? Win glanced back, her expression pleasant. Looking around, Enman couldn't help feeling that all of Barrein, past and present, was represented. Hints, echoes, of lost parents and grandparents in people's faces, the voices of the dead and their speech steeped in their descendants' genes. It made growing old easier somehow, Enman thought, being surrounded by others whose youthful experiences had been much as his had been. He didn't need to explain himself or his past. Shared experience equalled oxygen breathed in a place where everyone knew everyone else, from whence they had come and whence they were very likely headed. The details were just colouring within the lines, comfort to be taken in the lines themselves, the mix of happenstance *and* coincidence they contained. Their lives were as layered as the sea, he imagined, a sea whose bottom was immune to tides, its surface bobs and swells only mildly affecting what went on below it. Day to day worries, and such niggling annoyances as Twomey's presence and the way it piqued Enman's guilt at neglecting Hannah.

Twomey's presence now was hardly less troublesome than it had been at the old man's wake, he decided. Cleary laid out in his dark suit, Ma sitting beside the casket in her drab woollen dress. Whiskey making its rounds through the church hall.

"We have every reason to believe," Brass was saying, "the deceased was enemy forces—"

In Twomey's half-cut stance, that attitude of his, was something of his sister's—before Cecelia had run off and disappeared or died, however the story went. The rumours around Hannah's begetting a mystery to Enman until Ma had sat him down and trotted out a few sparse details. "Everyone makes mistakes," she had said, as much to excuse her choice of a husband as to forgive the old man. Win, God love her, had recently filled in more, wondering how Hannah could be the offspring of a woman with "boobs like fried eggs—easy over," as she'd bluntly put it.

"—Met with foul play...nature of wounds," Brass's voice, his fake English accent, wove in and out, rising above people's murmurs. "At the hands of some vigilant citizen...or one of his own company—?"

Cecelia had been ahead of him and Win in school. The most he remembered of her was how her hips moved in sync with her jaws chewing on spruce gum, which she rolled on the tip of her tongue. Not that he had been looking. Ma would have put his head in a chokehold. Somehow he'd thought the gum kept away scurvy—all the kids chewed it back then, playing Robinson Crusoe or Long John Silver.

"—A member of the Kriegsmarine—"

Rolling off Brass's tongue, the foreign name was like a smell that wafted sharply then drifted away, not so different from the way tales of Cleary and the Twomey one drifted. Familiar, outdated, these stories, to most of the village—especially now that the principals were long gone. Bart Twomey had been decent enough to raise Hannah, Enman struggled to convince himself, if being raised by a deadbeat could be considered better than being raised by nobody at all.

"The *issue*, folks, is that we fear someone—locals—fraternizing, mixing with, aiding and abetting—" the navy man was saying.

Fraternizing: the word sank a hook into him, and he thought—though he'd been trying not to—of his coffee breaks spent chatting with Archibald. At the same moment, Win's eyes grazed him and Una, looking to them both to bolster her objection. "God. What do you take us for? Who in their right mind would—"

The officer cut Win off. "If coerced, madam."

Pressed against him, her face a bit pale, Una squeezed Enman's hand.

He pushed away the image of George the night of the sinking, of George in the chilly room by the vault, polishing his shoes. Pushed away the thought of him dead, because it no longer bore thinking of.

"We want reports, anything unusual," repeated the uniform's ARP sidekick.

Excited, hopped up like nobody's business, Iris Finck slapped the countertop. "I've been saying for months—haven't I, Lester—you can hear those Jerries up to the devil's business charging their batteries or bombs or whatever. When I'm trying to sleep and Lester says, Hear that?"

Una blushed, staring downwards at her shoes, dressy for the occasion. They were ones she seldom wore, not the best for walking in. Isla Inkpen stifled a smile. Pounding the counter, Twomey made the candies jump in their grubby jars. "I seen them myself, come to think of it—fellas up the lake, not from around here, acting like they owned it."

"We all see things while in our cups," a Meade snorted, prompting Twomey to take a swing. His beefy fist grazed a stack of matchboxes. Amazingly, it didn't topple. Greeley stepped up, ready to restrain him.

"Order! *Someone* must have specifics? Times, dates," shouted the navy brass.

"I just gave 'em to you," Iris Finck spoke again. "What more d'you want?"

Drawing Una close, he whispered, "I've never seen old Iris so lively," When his lips grazed her ear, it felt warm, too warm. Was she coming down with a cold?

Una's eyes shone unnaturally. "I'm perfectly fine."

Well, it *was* warm with so many packed in, and Twomey's little display had made people move back, further crowding him and Una. Greeley stayed put. The heat of Mrs. Finck's enthusiasm was certainly contagious.

The brass fixed on Win. "Mrs. Goodrow, is it? Can you describe what you saw?"

At this point Enman felt the need to interrupt, was forced to shout over several heads, "How long was buddy in the water, if you don't mind us asking?"

The official ignored him, eyeing Win. "Madam, were you able to identify the body you saw?"

Win glanced back at Una and rolled her eyes, then faced him. "As if! Wasn't a pretty sight, Una can also tell you. Though he could've been worse, I guess." Win shook her head. "Of course not. How would I know who he was?"

The officer glowered, clearly irked by Win's tone. Meanwhile, the officer had pulled something from a briefcase and laid it out between the sweets and some cakes of Sunlight soap. It made Enman think of a gutted halibut, that same grey. A jacket.

"Our friend, the deceased,"—the fellow arched his eyebrows— "wasn't wearing this. But you discovered it, correct, Mrs. Goodrow? Earlier in the week. We can confirm it's—"

Part of a uniform, you didn't have to be a mucky-muck to recognize it. It was the attire the enemy wore in newsreels. Without matching trousers, it made him think of a body missing legs.

Enman cleared his throat. "Good, good—but, as I was asking, sir," he spoke up, ignoring Twomey's scowl, "by your estimation, how long do you figure the body was—"

Una cut Enman off to aim her own question at the officer. "Isn't that why we have experts? Pathologists." It was almost as if she was lumping Enman in with the ARP. Her voice was loud but tremulous. Isla smiled into her hand, patted Una's arm. Una did not brook fools being in charge, which Enman suspected stemmed from her having to bow to the odd incompetent principal who hadn't deserved the authority he wielded.

"Might I remind you, Mrs—? It's wartime."

Before he could stop himself, Enman raised his hand. "I would ask that you don't speak to my wife that way. If you don't mind. Sir." Clint snickered at Enman's audacity, and so did Isaac, perched on a wingchair dragged from Iris's front room, the chair in which Lester had "dozed off."

"You're leaving us at the Jerries' mercy, is what you're saying," Isaac croaked, then hawked. Silence fell before the old fellow swallowed; heads turned as he set his jaw. You could barely breathe for his cigar smoke and the smells of hair tonic and the odour rising from the baby in Isla's arms.

Suddenly Una was no longer gripping his arm or holding his hand, or even standing there. She was slipping through a gap opening in this mob of folks he'd known since forever. He caught a quick glimpse of some rust-coloured stains on the jacket's lining before he could angle himself towards the door. It was the perfect moment to exit. She *was* ill, that was it. Ill, as in pregnant? Forget what she had said. It was no cold: it was a sign, unbeknownst to her, that their bodies and their maneuverings had cooperated? Twomey thundered behind him about "motherfuckers havin' at each other" and how, if *he'd* "got hold of them bastards *then* you'd see blood."

"Not around the ladies, Bart," Enman managed to shout back, then felt sanctimonious.

Sylvester Meade, ever the contrarian, corralled him with his rheumy eyes. "Enman Greene, defender of women."

"Suffering God!" someone muttered. "Bunch of numbnuts, all of youse." Then Timmy Flood was waving something—a ticket stub—yelling, "I've got proof Jerry's been among us. You could've sat in the same seats."

"I just needed air," Una explained once he'd squeezed outside and caught up. He tightened his fingers around her clammy ones, but she wrenched her hand away. A fine drizzle was falling. Without warning it thickened, mist enveloping them in its chill.

They hadn't made it ten yards from the store when a torrent ripped through the fog, rain lashing down in sheets. A car crept up alongside them, then sped past. The navy fellow and the ARP man barely turned their heads, rubber tires hissing in the downpour. The taillights were two red squiggles.

In the slashing wet it was impossible to read her expression. She was imagining the bath she would draw? The mascara she had put on for their outing streaked down her cheeks, a blackish ruin. "There's something I need to tell you," she said.

His spirits leapt, in spite of his apprehension. It was selfish to bring a child into a world of war. But after being around Isaac, seeing how the man loved his sons, Enman had warmed to and welcomed the thought of childen. He hardly felt his clothes pasted to his body or the sting of hair tonic in his eyes. *This* was going to be it, what he hoped for almost more than life, news to set everything right.

"Enman. I can't lie. I've—"

It didn't matter that he hadn't considered a baby the be-all and the end-all, hadn't warmed to the prospect as fast as she had. His moment of hope was supplanted, and the feeling of letdown that replaced it allowed the strangest thought to take hold. In the city these days there were a hundred men to every gal, so people said. What was keeping her here with him in Barrein, with what he feared might be a snowball's chance in hell of getting pregnant?

"I've applied for a position. I'm still waiting to hear." Her voice wobbled, begging his patience?

"That's grand, dear. Grand." He meant it too, sort of. So the school board had relaxed its rules about hiring hitched women? But she had planned all along to move back without broaching it. Thank Christ for his banker's voice and the never-failing ability to summon it. A drink would have fixed him right up, no question. Just a shot.

"I'm glad to hear it, Una," he said after a minute or two. "Sometimes, if you don't mind me saying, your gifts seem wasted, staying home."

Then, Lord knows why, he thought of Cecelia Twomey, how before she'd taken off—even before the fling with his father—people had said she was like the village bike left outside Finck's store. Just about everybody had ridden it from time to time.

"There, now. Don't worry. We'll make out fine. We have so far," he said, because she'd gone silent again.

Once in the house they shook off what they could of the rain. Una ran upstairs to change into something dry. Remembering some extra work—some ledgers in the cubby under the eaves, he told her—wet to the skin, he fled to his old room. It felt odd shutting out her humming as she puttered in the bathroom, odder still when he peeled off and stretched out alone on the narrow, lumpy mattress.

But he needed to gather his thoughts. The first thing his mind reached for was a drink: the imagined taste of rum swirling down his throat, warming his eardrums, warming him from the top of his head to his baby toes. From there his brain lurched back to the first time he had got drunk, a vague recollection of swaying up the stairs, shutting the door on Ma's voice.

He'd been fifteen years old. Ma must have known; how could she not? If Archibald's example hadn't set him straight, who knows but he would have ended up a drunken Peter Pan living under her roof.

At his head the pillow smelled musty, and the spool bedstead of old polish. Otherwise, the room bespoke what he could only think of as a female fussiness. It was graven into Ma's embroidered runner and the picture Una had hung of a boy and his collie in its fancy frame—a long-ago present from the old man atoning for one absence or another. Cleary had occasionally ventured to the States, supposedly on business, selling the Meades' catches of lobster when people in Barrein would as soon fertilize gardens with the stuff than eat it. "'Avoid Pa's example'—of making a living to the south, or drinking and womanizing?" he had asked, the distinction between them somewhat hazy.

After a while he got up, dragged the wooden salt-fish crate of ledgers from its spot, and rifled through them noisily, opening one on the bedspread in case Una peeked in. Much as he wished she would, she didn't. But he stayed put, lying there in his shorts, listening to the foghorn out on the island making up for lost time. It was a sound that, along with the scent of finnan haddie and pie wafting upstairs, had soothed his boyish heart. It had instilled the feeling that being ashore, no matter what happened, he and Ma would be all right, safe and comfortable enough.

The fog itself had always felt like a blanket, insulating them from the Meades and the Twomeys and any others whose dissolute ways seemed threatening.

The cosy little room had been his shelter, inviolable. But now it felt draughty and unsound, as if the wind might drive the rain in between the shims. He heard the toilet flush and Una's cry of relief at having water. After a while she padded in. Her bare soles made a sticky sound on the varnished fir. She brushed her hand over the pages lying opened there with all his dogged entries. "The job was in the paper. I should've let you know before jumping at it. It's a bit complicated, it seems. I'm awfully sorry."

"For what exactly?" Must they always speak at cross purposes? He took her hand, ran his thumb over her narrow palm. For goodness sake, she was making a lot more of this job than was necessary, building a drumlin out of an anthill, he thought, mildly pleased with himself at the analogy. She mightn't even get the job. But if she did, he would have to demand a raise to cover the cost of a decent car or her room and board in town. He tried to imagine them living apart.

"A tiny bit of warning would've allowed me a head start on adjusting, cobbling together some funds," he teased, though he was thinking again of statistics: that ratio of men to women. And who wanted a weekends-only marriage? The loneliness would heighten his need. She shut the book on his hand, pulled him to his feet and to the other room and their bed.

The weather battering the window reminded him of being at sea: just what the Jerries would have ordered. They operated most efficiently on nights like this, under cover of storms. He pictured a depth charge spooling down the side of an Allied destroyer, hitting nothing. He longed even more for a stiff wallop of rum—the sad truth.

She snuggled closer in the sag, but when he pulled her to him she rolled away. "There's something else. I was let go. Last year. Fired, for a mistake on my part. I should have said."

He laughed a little uncertainly. "You're not the first to lose a job."

"It wasn't quite…as I let on. It involved another teacher." She watched him for his reaction.

"So your eye wandered from the kids." Enman smiled, a bit confused. "I guess that mightn't be the first time that's happened to someone." Her look was almost sullen, until he realized she had tears in her eyes. "Can't be as bad as all that, now. Are there other things you haven't told me?"

"Of course, there aren't. But, I was out of a job and—"

"That's when you saw me." He waited, patted her hand, pressed it to the sheet, away from him.

"Don't worry. I'd have told you about the job I've applied for before dragging you back to town."

"So what was it, then, that singled me out, that you seemed to like?"

"You needn't ask that. But if I'd known we'd end up here, I wouldn't have given up my flat. I wouldn't have been so quick to—"

"Our flat. Come now, and you and I would never have bunked in together?"

"Lovely way of putting it."

He flapped the sheet. "Oh my dear—you know as well as I do what a hellhole it's become. People crammed into places not fit for rodents. Dodging vomit every time you hit the sidewalk."

"It's war. We won't be at war forever." Perching on her edge of the bed, Una wiped her eyes.

"The Allies and the Jerries, maybe."

What was going on behind those eyes? Despite the tears, they seemed dulled. Weary—of him?

"Oh, things change, Una. They won't always be like this. You'll have a child. You've got Hannah to work on. Things are looking up."

"Looking up?" She laughed bitterly. "I've made a mistake. Thinking I could do *this*, playing house, helping with your mother and—"

"Marrying me? If you think so. Sorry you feel that way."

She flinched at this, curling on her side, curling into herself.

"Come on now. Tell me it's only been since Ma passed, your unhappiness—"

"You tricked me into coming here, staying."

"Tricked you? What state were you in to be so, so…bamboozled? I suppose next you'll say the cocoa was spiked."

"What?"

"At the Egg Pond. When you said you'd never met a nicer guy and wouldn't mind spending time—"

"Please. Maybe I'm not solely responsible for feeling *this*." She waved at the walls as if she were imprisoned, then she smiled weakly. "But I married you to save my hide."

When she turned to him again, saying nothing, he rose in silence and found the stack of bills and receipts from the spike he had brought from the office and stashed in the other room, and started downstairs. "If you don't *mind*, I've got figuring to do."

This was a stretch, since the past week business at Inkpens had waned slightly, and the week before, despite what Enman had told the bank. Neither he nor the Inkpens had raised it, and the bank hadn't asked for a closer look at his figures, but the previous month things had lagged as well. Fewer ships had been hit. But it was jumping the gun to think that Jerry wasn't the worry he had been.

Now he *needed* a drink. But in lieu of liquor, he had debits and credits to balance and to steady him. To hell with rum. To hell with blackouts. With both the parlour light and his banker's lamp blazing, the rain streaking the windowpanes turned shadows into ripples of light. They fell across the flimsy papers, the carbons with his signature. His fingers, too clumsy to go near the record player, let alone his violin, fumbled with the pen, totting up sums and subtractions, entering the final figures on crisp lined pages. An invoice to the navy for repairs to a dinghy, its duplicate receipt stamped *Paid*. Another from a boatyard in Pictou that was doing joint repair work to a corvette, the Pictou yard reaping more than the lion's share. Allotments over rivets and screws.

He doodled. Doodling wasn't serious—its absence of purpose, its lack of intention allowed his marks to remain just that, marks. But aimlessness gave way to rumination. What had she done to merit getting sacked? Una had seemed so charmed, so in love, yet she had tricked *him*? He struggled to believe it, her affections had been calculated. He was a milk ticket, a supplier of rent. He pictured the flat, a coal fire behind the grate, the noisy neighbours. Children crying, a couple's arguing coming through the ceiling at all hours. "That will never be us," Una had said. Who knew she wouldn't pick up where she had left off with her first mistake, her misdemeanour? Yet, he had the strange idea that if he continued to move the pen it might strike out her cold calculations, her opportunism, at least draw the pair of them back to where he'd thought they had been.

Into the small hours, the rain drummed its message about equality in love: what's mine is yours and what's yours is mine. But his doodling led to ruling two distinct columns on a fresh sheet of foolscap. One was headed with Una's name, the other with his. He knew he probably wasn't obliged to split things down the middle, but felt the need to. Stagnant savings, Beulah, the house. He jotted words, dollar values. But how on earth did you divide disappointment, dismay?

Through a break in the rain a long, low boom sounded—an explosion out at sea? Even as he dwelt on it, a voice inside coaxed, Now don't go jumping the gun. It's nothing really, it's not so bad. Unusually playful, Tippy leapt to the desktop and batted at the page, knocking over his pencils. Freshly sharpened, the leads pointing upwards was how he liked them arranged in their mug: such order was the antidote to disorder *and* sobriety's reward.

Moving to the cabinet, he reached blindly inside. He would drink to himself and Una—no, solely to Una, for having given him what she had of herself, however falsely but freely, he thought bitterly. And then, why not, he'd toast his lifetime's worth of sums and subtractions, problems easily solved.

The empty bottle slid free—Una had tucked it behind that bloody book, the book that seemed almost to blame, at least partly, for this turn in their marriage. Tumbling from his grasp, the bottle connected with the floor and lost its neck. A speck of rum darkened the mat. *Hygiene*, he mused, as if the conjugal state were armpits to be bathed, a scalp to be de-loused.

Too late he heard the stairs creak. He pressed his arm across the foolscap sheet.

In the lamplight Una's face was ghostly. He slipped the paper into a ledger, turned the page. Was it possible her paleness had a certain glow? She hesitated and when she finally spoke, her voice had a rasp. "That was a wasted evening. Do you suppose they'll come around asking more questions? People do love a fuss." She spoke as if the matter, any imminent threat it might speak of, was well past.

"They do." He didn't bother mentioning Flood's theatre ticket or the bloodied jacket. But then, just for now, the enemy threat rated a certified molehill measured against the mountain facing him. Facing *them*. He murmured about her getting the job. A done deal? he guessed.

"Not really. But if I do get it, it'll mean dropping Hannah. Like with everything else, I got ahead of myself, taking her on. There'd be no time left to tutor her."

"Oh? You couldn't do it on weekends?"

Silence weighed as if a rock from the backyard had rolled between them, taking up so much space neither could squeeze around it. As a child, he had imagined Mi'kmaw giants tossing erratics from the barrens.

"After the fuss you made over her, Una."

"I didn't say I would abandon her. Or you."

Wasn't it said that having a youngster in the house kept couples together?

Mentally he added a third column headed with Hannah's name to his sheet, dismissed the thought as Una slumped on the sofa. The pragmatism behind her choosing him was perhaps a small matter in the bigger scheme of things. What heart did not have secrets?

"However we got together, you're my wife. It's not that big a deal. I forgive you."

The strange idea flared of Hannah living under the same roof as them, then just as quickly fizzled as curiosity snared him. "What exactly did you and your teacher friend do?"

She picked at her cuticles, told him.

"How long did it last?"

She pulled at the embroidery on a cushion as she spoke—Ma's busy-work when she should have been minding his underage drinking with Hubley and some other teens behind Finck's store. Una hugged herself, arms stubbornly crossed like a little kid acting out an embrace.

His stomach unknotted. "Well. Why not write to them both, the principal and the super? Apologize, say you're different now."

"What, and put the kibosh on any chance of coming back?"

He approached her like the rare bird she was. "Oh now, it can't be as bad as that." Una wasn't alone in having flaws, being prone to making mistakes. He was just as culpable. Dumb as dirt, he had been, falling into, committing *his* biggest mistake, the error of his ways, imbibing. Moving to town at eighteen, getting his teller's job, making after-hours drinking an obligatory lark. Slowly feeling the burden of it—hangovers, lost Sundays, how it was a kind of tether, a teat—then receiving George's advice, given in the echoey room with its shoeshine bench and urinals.

Reaching up, she touched the stubbly cleft in his chin. A gesture that brought back Father Heaney's joke about Saint Peter leaving a dent, turning the sinful away from the Pearly Gates. Her cheek, when Enman kissed it, felt cool and dry, in contrast to the dampness in the air, the weather giving the windowpanes a beating.

"As far as I'm concerned, the sun—my sun—rises *and* sets on you."

She glanced away. "I might've guessed marriage was a strange state."

"Like a sharp, mostly comfy pair of old shoes you've slid your feet into then can't throw out or replace."

Una laughed at his joke, rather uneasily. She pointed to the red-covered book, the colour of beef liver under his lamp's greenish light. "And a recipe for furthering the race. Making babies like making perfect desserts."

"Sure. And 'matrimonial' squares are a fancy name for date squares. Ah, but I wish you'd been straighter with me." He paused. "What's to stop you from seeing this teacher again?" Once more she looked as if she was about to turn on the waterworks. "Oh, forget I said it—go on up now and get some sleep." She clung to him, but he gently pried her arms away. "I'll stay where I am. Won't be sleeping much anyway, with Jerry on the prowl." It was meant more as humour to smoothe things over, but her face kind of crumpled, and she looked more than half as old as Ma slipping upstairs.

HE MIGHT HAVE BEEN NAÏVE at Christmas, but one thing he *wasn't* was a drinker. Not anymore. He'd stopped, yes he had—or he could stop, any time he liked. This just wasn't the right time, not after having his wife admit that she'd done it with someone else, married him, more or less, he guessed, on the rebound. But even if Beulah could be trusted to get him to O'Leery and back, by this hour even the Goodrow kid would have shut down.

The rain had let up when he set out. Win's adage as good as a hand cuffing his ear. *What sensible fella buys the cow when free milk is up for grabs?*

Cuckold was the word, if you could be cuckholded before being married, he was a cuckold. Its very sound was ridiculous. Like a rooster getting its comb cut off and losing its strut. The only thing worse was being a pansy or getting called one. She had kept the teacher's name from him—it hardly mattered—but was it possible they were still in touch, that the teacher had pursued her? Of course, if he came from town, any-one would have noticed the car. Was it a friend of Kit's? Or not a man at all but Kit herself? Now his thoughts blazed out of control. There'd always been something funny about Kit; he had often wondered—he liked her well enough, had nothing against her, just wasn't sure these feelings were mutual.

Then it struck him: the science teacher Una had mentioned once. Though who precisely the fellow was mattered far less than the thought of her naked with him. Enman's stomach heaved. It was humiliating, especially when he thought of how she asked him to perform. The only way to deal with such hurt was to blot it out.

The hope of doing that drove him past Goodrows' and Mrs. Finck's and on past the graveyard. Fog socked in the shore, the first lights of dawn tinging it yellow; the sky was the colour of an old smoker's beard. He fought off a kind of nausea. God strike him dead if he didn't half expect Ma to reach out from her plot to stop him going farther. Sea and sky shrouded, gone was the horizon he had imagined walking like a tightrope when he was small. Now he worked to straddle the puddles, the earth so starved for moisture the ground was glutted with wet.

In the dingy light Twomey's place looked stripped of paint, where elsewhere fog favoured bursts of colour, the other houses' dark greens, reds, dull yellows, and blues. Once upon a time Twomey's had been green and yellow like a dorey, back when Bart and Cecelia's old man was alive. A scrap of curtain covered the door's cracked windowpane. The girl would be asleep, God willing. Twomey himself would be just getting started, his trade hitting full swing hours after the Goodrow kid ran out.

He thought for several long, hard minutes before knocking. How bad was it that he couldn't wait the couple of hours till Robart was up, and cadge a drink off him? But he thought of Una and the need wormed through him, its chafing growing worse. A disease, Ma had called the old man's drinking. But how could an illness be a craving—so tempting, so comforting, and so quickly and easily sated?

That's what raised its fist, though—an illness—and that's what thumped the door jamb's splintery wood. Forgetting himself, he laid all the blame on the illness keening through his veins. Illness promised that things would be fine, they'd be all right, sure they would, with just a little help. But then whose face appeared in the window but the girl's?

Sliding the bolt, barely covered up in a ragged nightgown, she muttered about "Missus" and her own "behaving" and not "bothering Mister," meaning him or Twomey? Hesitating, she shrank back to let him in, muttering Mister this, Mister that. Regardless who she meant, he was no better than Bart for being here, he knew. He knew and hated himself for it. Hated how his eyes felt bleary and tight, his face and body too, weary and cramped, as if he hadn't slept in a year, and how, on top of everything, his heart was in a vise because he really didn't want to ask. And he hated how he'd hated the thought of the girl being at Ma's table that first time, hunched over Una's books. Because of what such smallness said about him.

"I'm here on business." He cleared his throat, speaking as if he'd waltzed into the bank. "Is your uncle handy?"

The sight of her pudgy feet on the ruined linoleum tightened the vise around his heart.

She waved him ahead, which was too bad. Better he'd waited outside, because the mess took his breath away—the table buried under bottles, plates and tobacco tins, the stink of cat pee and boiled turnip permeating everything. Of all things, Hannah held out a little dish of something: green and yellow gumdrops, lint-covered from the lining of someone's pocket? His eyes might well have been full of sand, they twitched so. Her look—scared, hopeful, and surly all at once—made him rub them. Before he could accept a candy, Twomey came reeling into the room. He was wearing only longjohns, the top part buttoned wrong.

"Well, well, if fish don't stink. It's Pussy Greene." Then Twomey turned on the girl. "Wha'd I tell you, Idjit? You're not to let in any old son-of-a-whore."

"I think, Bart,"—he cleared his throat again and wanted to spit—"her name's Hannah."

"Aww. So you've come to tell me somefin I don't know. Enman Greene. Aren't you the king of arse-lickers, the big brudder!" Twomey slapped his shoulder, clearly enjoying this. A blemish on his ruddy, stubbled neck glared red. "Oughta call the Mounties on you, busting in where you're not welcome. No respect for a fella's home."

Slumped over the table, the girl shifted things from pile to pile. Enman couldn't see her face, only her back, which looked soft and broad through the ragged nightie. That she was shivering took a second or two to sink in.

"My wife"—his voice felt reedy and thin, yet he was determined that Twomey hear it—"tells me Hannah's quite the pupil."

Twomey smirked. "Well there's an authority, that one, isn't she just." Smashing his fist down, Twomey sent a plate wobbling to the floor, where it clipped the bottom of the stove, shattering. Tacked to the wall above, like something glimpsed through mist, a list caught his eye, and the glint there of a tiny gold star.

"Only pupils I care about, Greene, are these—see 'em?" Twomey pointed two fingers at himself as if to poke out his own eyes. "What they're looking at they don't much like."

Hannah hunkered there picking up smashed china. The room was just light enough that he could read the chunky printing below the star. *Precipice. Antique. Piebald.* Where in God's acre would a girl like this have need of such words? He pictured Una poring over Cleary's tattered dictionary. Something inside him slackened, went shammy-soft.

"Easy now, Bart. All I want's a pint. Hun'erd proof stuff, as you say. I'll pay what you ask. To tide us over, bud, till Robart sorts me out."

"Us? The missus got a thirst too, does she. No wonder. No grass grows under that one's feet, eh?" Twomey sniggered, rocking backwards. Only then was it obvious how tanked he was. "Or under her back, wha'? Butting in where she ain't wanted. 'Ooh ooh ooh, mind the lady, Bart, her virgin ears.'" Twomey's voice rose, shrill and obscene. "Telling me to watch *my* tongue. And you, you little sleveen—" Narrowly avoiding a tower of pots, he staggered over, ripped the girl's handiwork from the wall, and balled it up. Hannah started to cry then; the sound was like a cat choking. "And *you*, you arse-kissing hamster-balled son of a bitch, stuck up just like your old man, thinking he could shag Cece and not pay a price—" Twomey waved his fist. "You can get the fuck out of here."

Was it the illness speaking, or what? Speaking and unleashing something. The instant Enman's fist—the bones of all five knuckles—connected with Twomey's nose was a spongy, gristly jolt. The snap of cartilage, its give, sent a tsunami through his muscles. It exploded up through his arm and down his spine.

Eyes rolling in their sockets, Twomey's head snapped back with a crunch. The blow's force echoed as Twomey stumbled towards him, stunned. Something like lightning striking a freshly driven nail bounced around in Enman's head. The girl was screeching now, "Stop it, Mister, stop it!"

The red decorating Twomey's nose was bright, almost festive. Yet vomit climbed Enman's throat as Twomey reeled closer. Enman managed to grab the nearest thing, a frying pan with food crusted to it, to fend off Twomey's fist before it could land. The punch merely glanced off of the pan, which hit Twomey's jaw.

"Get out of here before I fucken kill you," the man spat through blood and bits of tooth.

Momentarily frozen, Enman recalled a time in the schoolyard, a couple of Meades cornering Twomey and yelling about Cecelia, *Did he get some too?* and Twomey singlehandedly beating the shit out of both of Sylvester's sons.

Behind him, Hannah was whimpering, scrabbling for cover. His brain would barely turn over. But as it did he uttered, mortified, as if from some lofty distance, "You'd be half entitled to."

Because what sort of loser would turn his back on a half-sister, then stroll into her uncle's house at dawn to punch out the fellow's lights? He'd been spoiling to do so since they were kids, of course, ever since the day the old man had tossed him in, trying to make him swim. Twomey, hateful even then, had laughed his head off, his own father nowhere in sight.

"You arsehole." Twomey's voice was a hiss. But by some stroke of luck the guy stayed where he was.

The birds were just awake, a sparrow singing from the big old boulder outside. Escaping ahead of him, the girl had vanished like a salamander scooting for cover. Next to some oil drums and the ruins of a shed lay the axle-less hulk of a car and beyond it, an outhouse. Was it too much to hope that Twomey wouldn't stagger outside with his shotgun?

Enman hovered behind the shed, waited. A mewling sound was coming from the privy. Hannah was huddled inside. The reek! It did nothing to settle his guts as he put his arm around her.

Drawing her out of there was as slow as removing a splinter. "He'll kill me, Mister." Tears and snot and the fleshy warmth of her seeping through his shirt. But it drained away any guilt he might have felt over Twomey, a prickly courage welling up in its stead.

"Don't you worry about him."

Whatever Una had done, he had fussed more over marigolds than over his own kin, when he could have, should have, tried harder to help the girl.

The gunshot shattered the stillness, the bullet ricocheting off the dead chassis. The sound rolled from the dripping spruces and hung there in the air. Enman seized Hannah by the arm and pulled her, finally, running up behind the boulder and on to the road. Another shot cracked a tree limb. Eyes round as burls, Hannah had quit crying but was whingeing now about shoes.

Only then—half dragging, half carrying her—he remembered she wasn't wearing any. He'd put her and Una in a boat and row them both to town to buy some before he would go back.

18

IT TOOK KIT A BLOODY DOG'S AGE TO ANSWER. WAKING TO AN EMPTY house—not so much as a snore rising from downstairs, and no sign that Enman had even dozed on the couch—Una had gone straight to the phone. Shying from calling Isla's, lest the ringing woke the baby or Isla's daughter answered, she had no one else to turn to.

"Who is this?" Kit's voice was fuzzy with sleep.

"It's—it's me. Enman's gone."

"Enman—?" An uncomfortable pause. Some hasty throat-clearing. "Gone? Gone where?"

"He's left, Kit. He's left, and I don't know—"

"I'm sure he'll be back." Now Kit sounded miffed, breathless. A pillowy sigh ensued.

"Well, yes. But he's got a fondness for the booze—and he means to stay here. Here in this village. He meant to all along."

There was a breezy silence. Kit sniffed. "Oh, dear. Why am I not surprised?"

Una thought of what her mother had been fond of saying: *Marry in haste; repent at leisure*. Over the line came a rustling, the lazy squeak of bedsprings: a voice, a whispered question, "What is it?" The voice a man's or a woman's, too fleeting to tell.

"Oh Una, dear. Things will sort themselves out."

The ease in Kit's voice encouraged her. "Look, I'm hoping—I wonder—*could* I stay with you? For a few—just for a little while, till Enman, till things—till I figure out what to do."

"To do?" Now Kit's voice was wary. "About what?"

"The job, well, for starters—and, you know, I just need a roof over my—just until I get set up and—"

"So you've heard?"

"Well, no. But I hope to, before too long. In the meantime, I wouldn't impose. No more than a week or two, until—"

"Enman's a lovely man." Kit paused. "And they don't hire divorcees either, darling, only widows." She gave a sharp little laugh. "Well, the war's a widow-maker. Gregory's a loose cannon, but he's not *that* bad. Kidding. I'm sorry. Listen, it's just not doable, having you stay, not with company here right now."

Hearing Kit speak that name made her seem farther away than Quinpool Road could ever be. Saying a quick goodbye, Kit promised to call, then the line clicked dead.

So this is how it goes, Una marvelled, sitting on a kitchen chair, catching her breath. A burning moved from the pit of her stomach to the base of her throat. She made herself pick up the phone again, asked the operator for the number. It didn't matter what hour it was. The principal had boasted about being an early bird. And what was pride but a faulty sense of self, she thought. She would explain her predicament, this time she would plead her case. But when the principal's wife picked up, Una lost her nerve, saying the operator had made a mistake.

Enman's stubbornness and Kit's long memory were bad enough, why risk further injury, a hat trick? She tried to fathom Kit's distaste for men, which was understandable but still puzzling, ever since the staff room joke about someone clipping his nails. "Who needs them?" Kit had hooted, they all had, when the secretary said, "Men or toenails?"

There wasn't a thing to be done but go and crawl back under the covers, pretend it was someone else's bed, someone else's life. Never mind there was water for a good tub-soak. This mattered "less than a hill of beans," as Mrs. Greene would say, the old lady's tut-tuts so loud in Una's head that even dragging the quilt over it failed to drown them out.

WHO KNEW HOW LONG IT was before voices roused her, Enman downstairs talking to someone. The shy, halting replies made it plain who it was. Clutching her stomach, sick with remorse for her own stupidity, she managed to get up and pull on some clothes. Stymied by guilt, she flopped down again. She heard footsteps on the stairs. Voices swelled in the next room, the clang of hangers, the sound of something being dragged across the floor. What in the name of God was Enman doing, having Hannah come and help herself to his mother's things? Or worse, Una's teaching materials?

Far less tidy than pride, shame wasn't nearly as tough a lifeline as anger, she decided. What did shame do but hold you hostage? She had the words rehearsed, the ones that had formed themselves last evening, during that godawful sideshow in the store. Win had been nicer than she had imagined possible. Well, some people were full of surprises. The thought bolstered her. She stalked into the little bedroom.

There was Hannah, looking as if she'd been sleepwalking all night. Enman himself was kneeling at an old tea chest full of his mother's shoes. He held up a pair of oxfords Una had politely refused.

"These should do the trick," he was saying, "for now." He'd already laid one of his mother's shapeless shifts on the bed and some embarrassingly elastic-less bloomers.

"Maybe Missus has a braz tucked away somewhere that'll work." He pronounced it the way his mother had, to rhyme with jazz. Then he looked up. "Hello, Una." He spoke as if it were the most normal thing in the world to be outfitting Hannah in his mother's glad rags.

IN THE KITCHEN WERE A cold pot of tea and the remains of some buttered toast. Una's backbone was the consistency of jellied chicken as she sat down. From overhead came the burble of water filling the tub. Enman ambled in but didn't so much as glance over. He fiddled with something in the sink. A glimpse of his hand wrapped around a mug was another little kick to the stomach. His knuckles were purple.

"Don't ask," he said.

"Are you going to tell me what's happened?"

"Happening." His voice was begrudging. "I thought you'd be happy."

"I had her here for tutoring, not to *live*." Before she could grab at his wrist he made for the mudroom and went outdoors. And then Hannah was standing there, filthy feet peeping out from under her mud-splattered nightie. Upstairs, the tap burbled away.

"What, pray *tell*, is going on?" Una might as well have asked the stove. Hannah snivelled that she couldn't go home again, and what would happen to Uncle? Who'd make his lunch, who'd mop up the blood? Who would tidy up after him?

"The blood?" Only then remembering the tub, she galloped upstairs. Hannah tailed her like a stray cat.

"Hush now, hush," Una whispered. Through the window she watched Enman striding down the hill, late for work. *Work.* The word itself was so ordinary as to be unhinging. "Have your bath. Then you can tell me what's going on. I guess you know as much as anybody." She managed to put on a smile. Hannah looked as if she'd come through a hurricane, one that had swept away her every possession.

Stuffed among more of Mrs. Greene's things was a quilted house-coat. A gift the old woman had saved for some occasion or other that never materialized. Hanging the robe on the hook, Una shut the bath-room door behind her. Containing the problem, one miniscule, temporary part of it, calmed her enough to pause and listen from the landing. But then a fresh worry arose: Suppose the girl's never had a tub bath before. Whatever had happened, whatever Enman had or hadn't done, he wasn't thinking straight, he couldn't be. Surely Isaac would see this much and send him home.

Because she needed him to come home.

If Enman was out of sorts, whose fault was it? Hannah's muffled bursts of humming held Una's attention as she watched for him from the window. It wasn't hard to put two and two together: the empty bottle, a run-in with Barton Twomey. But she shuddered to think of Hannah sucked into it—worse, of herself as culprit for intiating all of this, and, by association, Twomey's victim-to-be. Because now she would have to look out for the girl, which had not been part of the plan, showing Hannah her ABCs. Robart Inkpen kept liquor in the safe, it was a well known fact; why hadn't Enman gone to Inkpens' instead of Twomey's, chosen their more respectable, less incriminating business as his source? Or maybe he had but was so upset he'd forgotten the combination. If he was upset, who was to blame for *that*? Now look whose lap it had all fallen into.

She gave a sharp rap on the bathroom door. "Feeling better in there? Nothing like a hot bath, is there? No one, they didn't…hurt you, when whatever happened happened—between your uncle and Mister, was it?" How sordid, how seedy to implicate Enman, who, despite his shortcomings, was so decent. As soon as she said it she stepped away, stationing herself again at the window. Through the salt-streaked pane she glimpsed a movement in the yard below, Enman returning—please, *please*—or some animal, a foraging deer maybe, now out of view but stealing towards his garden?

"No, Missus. En-oh." Cheerier than was sensible, Hannah emerged, beaming pinkly in Mrs. Greene's housecoat. She rubbed her hands over its stiff satin. "Mister never laid a finger onto me. I guar-an-tee youse." Marge would be spinning in her grave, virtually tilling the turf. "It wasn't nothing much, I mean you didn't miss nothing. Mister wanted likker, Uncle said some stuff, Mister almost kilt him, that's all. Cross my heart, hope to die. 'Cept I don't. Hope to. But sometimes Uncle might. Hope. For me to. But it's okay. Mister said I ain't going back."

What *had* Enman told her?

"I guess not. If that's what Mister says. I've never known him to lie," she barely managed to whisper. Suddenly her heart was halfway up her throat, the burning replaced by her pulse. Because a creaking sound had broken the stillness downstairs—the screen door opening?

Oblivious, breezing into the spare room, Hannah admired herself in its spotted mirror.

"Pinky pinky pinky p-i-n-k! This ain't a pig colour, is it Missus. If I can spell it can I keep it?"

"Of course—I don't mind if you do." Una's stomach buckled even as her lips smiled. "Now do me a favour, will you, and stay put. Do you understand? Not a peep—promise?"

"A promise is a promise is a promise. Cross your heart and hope to die. That's a promise. Except the dying part. I don't want to. Do you, Missus?"

"Not just yet."

But there was no one downstairs. The kitchen was just as Enman had left it.

She hurried back up to retrieve the disgusting nightie and lay out more clothes, leaving Hannah to pick from them while she hastened to fill the washing machine. Then she dug out some simple arithmetic to occupy the girl. The washer's churning and thrashing calmed her enough to root through the upstairs closet for other amusements, a tangle of Marge's abandoned sewing projects. Maybe Enman would interest Hannah in finishing them? Beside a box stuffed to overflowing with scraps of fabric was Una's suitcase.

Inside it lay her school clothes, her little navy jacket missing its shoulder pads, donated to Enman to use as gardening knee pads. Underneath the jacket, each blouse and skirt seemed a talisman of some serviceable, sensible life. Tucked inside the case's musty pocket was Kit's wedding gift, a little framed picture of Gainsborough's *Blue Boy*. The boy in his wrinkled satiny garb looked too twee hung against the wallpaper, Enman had decreed. "Who wants a fussy little prince presiding over their every move?"

"Over yours." Una had said it jokingly, referring to their furtive lovemaking in his boyhood bed. She had been all too aware of his mother in the next room. Had he even guessed that her tone masked frustration?

Was this the first of the cracks that had widened into a chasm between them? It didn't help seeing Kit's Xs and Os on the picture's backing, or the pencilled inscription: *For Una and Enman, January 2ⁿᵈ, 1943. Here's to a happy life.* "Long" and "together" were conspicuously absent, any sentimentality conveyed by the boy himself: his rosy cheeks, his innocent pose, his luxurious figure swathed in chilly, satiny blue.

While Hannah figured and fussed at the kitchen table, Una busied herself, begrudgingly, putting fresh sheets on the little bed, setting aside for Hannah the clothes of Mrs. Greene's that would fit. A blouse and undies still in tissue paper, grey socks, and a boxy grey skirt. Imagine adopting a child, she told herself, an orphan, say. Would you dress it in the same drabness it had arrived in, or in gay, jubilant colours? A lot of people were most comfortable in what they were used to.

Downstairs, she drew a chair up to the table where Hannah worked. The girl's wet hair curtained her face, dripping onto and puckering the scribbler's pages. What was there to say? Una saw that she was trembling.

"I'm scared, Missus. Uncle's my uncle. He's all I got. I should go back. But I don't wanna—not yet. Don't make me, Missus. Not yet."

"Of course you don't."

Feeling almost sick, she dug out the grade-five reader, paged to a story the kids had liked, and, in a haze, read aloud about a boy named Sam and his dog in Muskoka.

"Musko-ka-ko-la!" Hannah gave a quaky cheer. But then her face paled. "Oh my wordy durd, Missus. What if Uncle comes lookin' for me?"

Hadn't it occurred to Enman that Twomey might do just that? A chill ran up Una's arms as she imagined a lurking presence—a flash of movement, a greyish-brown blur—ducking under the clothesline, loitering by the step. Not Twomey's though, she told herself; he couldn't move that fast if he tried. Whose, then?

A deeper chill prickled at the nape of her neck. Her body had its own memory, of the way the young man on the beach had placed his elbows on the sand, his palms bracketing her head, and the way his lips had curled, pronouncing, enunciating, his words.

A sailor, of course, she knew, because of his salty, diesel smell. Even as she put words into his imagined mouth—"You're a pretty woman, a very pretty woman. Why no husband? Una Greene-like-the-colour. Why so alone and available?"—she wished she could erase them, wished she could rub out all memory of him. Like re-doing a child's composition, replacing mistakes with corrections to produce a proper, clean version. But she didn't want to rewrite pages, she wanted to tear them up. Because no amount of tinkering could erase what she had done.

"Missus? Maybe I should go now. Go and tell Uncle where I am. Maybe you could come with me."

And now, was she being punished?

"No, Hannah. Not a good idea. Wait till Mister comes home, and see what he says."

19

A FELLOW COULD DO MUCH, MUCH WORSE IN A BOSS, IT DAWNED ON ENMAN. Isaac didn't bat an eye at him or at the bottle he cradled, despite his being caught red-handed removing Robart's finest from the safe. Furthermore, Isaac could have knocked Enman over with a feather, saying to go home and stay there "till you're more yourself, man."

He leaned into the backyard boulder, sucking back the whiskey's burn. No way they could see him from the house, though why it should matter, he no longer knew. The "little Twomey one" had seen his true colours, witnessed his spoiling for alcohol *and* a brawl. Hannah knowing his weakness was worse than having Una know, somehow. A slobbering alcoholic, a dithering drunk was what he was.

Sitting on the ground, he flexed his legs. Wet soaked through his pants and shoes, but who cared? Not him. Not only had he followed in Cleary's footsteps, but he had turned into his father. If Una had used him, it was no one's fault but his own. Along with the liquor, the sad truth stung his gullet, trickling down.

Their combined burn was only sharpened by the sight of his mari-golds become, overnight, an orange mush. "Okay you little beggars…." Yanking them out, roots and all, he fired them one by one at the fence, to join the Javexed knotweed. Chubby, off his rope for once, made his way through a gap to come and paw for a treat.

"Sorry, buddy, don't even have a stick for you, do I." If he had his damn fiddle he could've tossed that.

Lying down on the sodden grass, he took a deep, scalding swallow. Chubby nudged his wrist. Never mind who might be watching. Win would be one of them—she had known all along he was a loser, a chicken-hearted, lily-livered loser, and didn't he and his wife, foolish as a character from *Looney Tunes*, deserve each other?

For better or for worse, maybe they did.

Chubby slobbered over his hand, then gave his chin a lick. It was just enough to coax him to his feet. Swinging the bottle, he swayed a little, fell. Finding himself engulfed in goutweed grown suddenly rampant, he knelt to tackle the stuff—"you goddamn little buggers"—its slimy stems adding green to his bruises. "You goddamn little bugger," he cursed with each tug. "I guess we're all in a fine pickle, Chub." The dog cocked its ears.

Downing the dregs, he ran his good hand over Chubby's snout.

This cursed summer. Where was September, that month with its whiskey-golden glow? He clasped the empty bottle to his chest—oh, like a light, like a burning candle next to his heart!—then fired it as hard as he could towards the privy. A tune started up in the back of his mind—the Vera Lynn one they played every waking minute on the radio: "We'll Meet Again." Maybe Steady Hill should try a rendition of that? He smirked at the thought as Chubby rolled around belly-up at his feet, scratching his mangy back.

He tried humming Dvořák, the humble, gently hopeful part, but the melody eluded him. A tune from Prokofiev kept cutting in, the Russian's happy ending to Romeo and Juliet.

When August ended, so would life as he knew it. What would he do? How would he cope, especially now, having the girl under his wing and, God knows, Twomey out for blood? Maybe teaching would make Una "more herself" again. But the prospect of this only made it harder to imagine her gone.

In the fuzzy distance a patch of blue appeared above the barrens, and the timid glimmer of sunshine. Rubbing Chubby's chest, he imagined a full bottle, whiskey the same steeped amber as bog water. The dog panted and smiled its doggy smile, sitting on its haunches. Then Tippy reared from under a rose bush and Chubby was off—the way that cat moved, you'd never guess it had three legs. Or maybe it was just that his own legs felt thick as the jam Ma had once overboiled, engrossed in praying the Divine Mercy Chaplet. His head felt that way too, the whiskey's heat having flared up through his ears and under the roof of his skull. Such a slow fuzzy burr that it didn't register, not at first, the shout coming from the house: his name being yelped.

Forcing his weight onto his elbows, from behind a kind of veil he watched Hannah waving and hollering from the stoop. His arm, log-heavy, felt asleep the way his legs did, but he managed to wave back. The thought crept up with a mortifying clarity—I'm no better than a Barton Twomey—then struck as hard and mercilessly as if Hannah had marched out and slugged him. *For God's sake, Cleary, if you must go boozing, don't let people see you at it, especially not that poor girl*: Ma's pained salvo blazed its way through his head, too late, of course. Hannah disappeared inside. The only thing for it was to get up and onto his pins, and see what Hannah was yelling about.

He managed to get behind the boulder in time to bring up. As he hunched and gagged, a cantata filled his head, a slurry of voices living and dead—Una's, Ma's, the old man's and even Hubley Hill's—all singing the same line: let it go, fella, get over it, whatever *it* is. In his imagination, he raised the full bottle that existed only in his mind, and biffed it after the very real empty he had pitched toward the outhouse. He imagined the tinkle of glass shattering over rock. *It's never too late, my boy*, he heard Ma say. And then he imagined pure gold liquor seeping into the chokeweed, reaching down through the pitifully thin soil to water the graves of Dinky toys, anointing weeds and rust and the beaten paths of all and any who had passed this way—such ordinary, unforgiving ground, it was, fairly worthless and, in its inscrutable way, heartless. Why care about it, why let himself be tied to it as his forebearers had been? They had had little choice but to be. He had a choice, sort of. But having a choice made him feel even more tied to the spot, solid ground set against human fickleness.

The waffling of people's minds and hearts, he thought, as Vera Lynn—songbird of the Forces—crooned from somewhere, wispy strains of "We'll Meet Again." It was coming from the house, the song that had played on the radio New Year's Eve. It wasn't Ma singing. For the briefest flash, swaying towards it, he imagined the voice was his dear, confounding Una's.

SEIZING HIS WRIST, HANNAH DRAGGED him into the front room. For the strangest gut-wrenching second it was Ma he saw sitting on the sofa. "I see you're being well taken care of, Enman." It was not Ma, of course, not Ma at all, but Mrs. Finck. The woman made an effort to stand, holding out a veiny, speckled hand. "Two ladies looking after you—a bloody harem. Your ma'd be some pleased."

A queer look passed over Iris's face. Was her poor old husband reminding her of ancient jealousies? Maybe Lester, Cleary, and Ma were on the other side of the veil, all being friends.

Backing up, the old doll sat and arranged herself awkwardly on the upholstery. Her lumpen feet in oversize shoes dangled above the floor—a sight she was, even in his state he noticed, and had to stifle a laugh. It was kind of amazing that Una had—he supposed Una had—invited her in.

"Ahem," Iris Finck cleared her throat and the fog in his head thinned, making itself as scarce as the girl. Una was nowhere in sight, and Hannah had wasted no time clearing out.

"Shy, are they—your ladies. Anyways. Enough pussyfooting around, see, before I collapse of nerves. All right, like Lester says, it's usually best to just spit things out, isn't it." Iris fixed him with eyes as rheumy as they'd seemed eyeing Lester's accordion that time in the snow.

He hadn't a jeezly clue what she could possibly be here for, unless it was to express, very belatedly, condolences about Ma.

"You want to, um, fill me in, Iris?"

"It's 'Mrs' to you. You kids. Back in my day it was Missus and Mister. When I was your age—"

He worked to stifle a burp. He wanted nothing more now than to go upstairs, rinse out his mouth, and go to sleep. "If you've got something to tell us…?" He took a deep breath, focusing his gaze on her nose. It was oddly delicate for the rest of her face.

"Then I'll be blunt. See here. You don't need to be looking after *two* gals." Her voice was grudging. "Word gets out, Enman Greene. You and your wife don't owe nobody a thing." Only then did he notice the mail in her lap. It must for Una? "What I mean to say is—oh, dammit, Lester says…well, here you go." The envelope was yellowed and had a bit of peppermint or mothball stuck to it, which she plucked away before she pushed it at him. Her face was unusually pink; maybe it was simply the change of scene, the first time in years he had seen her anywhere but in the shop.

"Look. You've no good reason to feel beholden, man." Her breath was uneven and seemed to come a little too fast, as if the act of speaking might strangle her.

"I'm sorry—?"

"I don't need to explain the *volume* of personal news"—"noose," she called it—"that passes regular through my place. Now and then the odd item goes astray, hardly *my* fault. Better late than never, I guess." She shrugged, then gave a shiver and a nasty little laugh. He could almost feel Lester's bony finger pressing into the centre of his back, the time he'd pinched a humbug—four years old and thinking how clever he was flirting with danger, defying the law, getting away with it. A single stale candy. Not worth a lick of sugar when the old man found out and told Ma, and Ma took the wooden spoon to him, and supper was mustard on bread.

"Lester had a soft spot for you kids. On account of not having his own." Iris stared at Ma's mat where Tippy had picked at the roses hooked into it. Despite his wooziness, and realizing how his breath must reek, he bit back a smile. God only knew what else Lester told her, kept on telling her.

"I guess it comes with age, does it? Having youngsters ignore you. Worse, them thinking you've nothing intelligent to say. I'm old but I'm not stupid.

"Go on, open the letter," she urged. "I have reason to believe, uh, that the one your pa knew, *that* other Twomey,"—she picked something from her sleeve, the petrified crumbs of an earlier meal—"well, let's make it crystal clear: got herself pregnant down the States, then came home to have it. Her baby, I mean."

Iris's throat-clearing was the kind usually saved for what she called tire-kickers, people who wanted to look but not buy her merchandise, loath to spend their money. But now she'd got talking she could not stop. "Listen to me," she said loudly enough to rule out any hint of glee. "You have it from the horse's mouth. Sue me if you want. But I swear it was just, well, interest in my fellow man that prompted—*made* me peek."

She gulped to catch her breath. He wondered if she needed a glass of water.

"Seventeen, eighteen years, that's a long time ago," Iris continued, "at least it is for you young ones. Water under the wharf. But the upshot is, you don't owe Hannah Twomey a thing; her uncle neither, you don't owe either of them a proper rat's ass." With that, she struggled to her feet.

"But…the old man travelled down to Boston. He's the father. But that's not the point. The point is—" His voice was thick and he felt faint. "Makes no difference who the father was, she deserves better than what she's got." The whiskey hadn't finished with him. If he didn't race upstairs he might be sick right here.

"Well you're nothing but your ma's son—a sucker for punishment. If you don't want to read it, hand it back. You won't be holding a grudge, I hope, taking matters to the Post Office."

A shaky smile flitted over her face and he glimpsed, perhaps, the enterprising girl whom Cleary had supposedly been keen on before Ma got him to the altar. Long before he himself was a glint of possibility in the old man's eye.

What could he do but shake his head, throat clenched, and say of course he wouldn't?

"Well, you might be foolish as the birds, but you're decent. She did a good job raising you, your ma. But if you don't mind me saying, you'd be smart to cut out the sauce. Look at the grief it caused your dad, treating liquor like his best friend. The kind of friend that tricks you into thinking shit is chocolate." She looked to be sweating now, her cardigan as bulky as a sheep. Sweating with relief, maybe. "Well that's it then. What they say about him knocking up Cecelia Twomey is a load. You heard it here and I've got Lester to vouch for me." She eyed him with a look of expectation, as if a reward of tea and cake might be in order, or an extra-celebratory cup of Ovaltine.

"Lester always said you and your ma would be better off knowing the truth. He and your dad grew to be buds, but why your ma never took a shine to me, who knows. Her and I were polite enough, just never quite hit it off. I'd of taken up with Cleary myself if not for his fondness for… Marge knew it too, maybe she was jealous? Water under the *bridge*," she sniffed, gathering herself. "But then along came that prime piece of merchandise, my Lester, all the swagger a gal could want and—"

"Lester was a good fellow," he managed.

"Cleary too, in his own way. Don't you forget it. Now you're taking your time opening that damn letter. So I'll tell you plain and simple, it was a Meade that did it." Enman gawped at her and she gawped back, as if he was dim. "Lester seen him and Cecelia going at it out back of Twomey's shed. Sylvester moving like he was sawing—"

"Sylvester Meade? You're saying…." His gorge pooled with spit; at least he could breathe through it, scared to swallow it back. "Least I can do is run you home," he said helplessly, though she was looking lighter on her feet. A decided swing to her arms as she shuffled to the door. "Sylvester Meade," he marvelled, shaking his head.

"Land, is it true your car got drove by Nazis? Riff-raff joyriders. Imagine."

He swallowed, holding back the taste of bile. "I guess, if that's what they're saying. Iris,"—she'd reached the doormat, was headed for the steps— "is there other mail I should know about?" She was keen to make a getaway, clearly, freed of whatever if any guilt she had hauled around. Guilt, perhaps, for whatever injury her silence all these years might have caused Ma. "Anything for my wife?"

"You'd be the first I'd tell, Enman Greene. Abysinnia—I'll be seeing ya—like Lester says."

As he shut the door, the nausea lifted sufficiently for him to slouch back in and flop down on the couch. He was too beat to lift a finger, even to turn off the radio. He never did make it up to bed, staying put to sleep it off.

"YOU *FLATTENED* BARTON TWOMEY? ENMAN Greene, what in the name of God's got into you? You can't just move *her* in here." It was Una standing there in the dimness—late afternoon or early evening, who could tell? She reached for something, the note he had let slip to the mat. Coming to, he felt his heart beating. It was as though he'd never thought to listen to it before.

Cradling his head, he lay as still as possible. "I could ask the same of you."

The weak, staticky jags of someone's singing reeled in and out from the station in Boston. By some fluke it had come in loud and clear earlier, when he'd staggered in to meet his visitor. Still, music was the best medicine besides drink for calming him, even if the record sounded like it was being played at sea, the airwaves catching every roller.

"One minute you're defending the girl, Una. The next you want Hannah gone."

Wiping her hands on her skirt, Una unfolded Mrs. Finck's offering and read it. He gazed at the water stain overhead. Its fern-like fronds mimicked frost, their lushness heralding a leaky pipe, either from some past plumbing disaster he could not account for, or an imminent one. "Oh my," she kept saying, reading Cecelia Twomey's fawning apology for lying, for keeping his father in the dark about "Sly." She knelt to take Enman's hand. Hers felt sticky-warm and damp. "I'm sure whatever you did, Twomey had it coming." Her voice trailed off, then gathered steam. "But Hannah's not our responsibility."

The singing switched to piano music—choppy, crackling chords that substituted for anything he might have uttered in response. A mercy to his throbbing head that it wasn't one of the Russian's swaying, crashing symphonies, their dissonance and strange harmonies.

"Enman!" Una's eyes were bluer than blue, angry. Her whole appearance had sharpened. Every line, every wrinkle in her face that the sun hadn't tinted appeared more deeply etched; even her wiry hair fought to resist the wallpaper's faded look.

"If there's no returning her, since you moved her in, Enman, you'll be the one tending her." Una spoke like a principal. "Imagine, the three of us crammed in here." She made it sound as if the place were no bigger than a fish store and derelict, and cast her gaze around the room. Now that the drought was over, he imagined her fretting about the damp suddenly eating plaster and wood, and mould taking over. From the kitchen came a jubilant voice, Hannah reciting times tables. Ten times ten times ten equals a thousand. The easiest thing in the world, of course, adding zeroes.

"Mrs. Finck should hire her." Una's voice was impatient.

"The world's got enough grief, why add to it?" It had enough grief to blow itself to kingdom come. What was the point, he wondered, of lighting fuses? "Una, we can't go back on something we started. It's like burning a ledger when you don't like what's written inside. You start a fresh page, hope for the best. In the red or in the black, you carry on." And you keep carrying on until you arrive at the last set of figures, while only guessing at what they will reveal, he thought. The trick was staying level, maintaining calm despite whatever downturns loomed there. To be glad of the pages themselves. "I guess we all have to find our own happiness." It wasn't quite what he wanted to say.

"God. You would find it under a rock or a black-spotted weed."

"Weeds, rocks—they all count." Reaching for her hand, he thought of the naming of objects, how words were even more inadequate than numbers in describing the completeness of any one thing. All they gave was its approximation.

Her eyes had a pleading look. She traced his knuckles with her finger. "Look at you. Sure you didn't slug a wall?"

"My one regret is that I didn't belt him harder."

She might have laughed, it would have helped if she'd laughed, but instead she smiled wanly. "Takes two to tangle, doesn't it."

There was a burr behind his eyes—"Don't we know it"—a scratchy irritation which he blinked back. Tears brightened Una's. She tried to fan them away with the letter. Grabbing the letter, he made a paper airplane of it and aimed it at the desk.

"Hannah's not going anywhere, she's staying. If Twomey comes to lay me out, he lays me out. I won't be surprised."

"Enough of surprises."

He just shrugged. It might have been the Lindy hop executed by one partner with two left feet, the way they danced around everything. Neither seemed able to take the lead or step out, until finally Una spoke. "I've been stupid, okay?" She said it almost too quietly to hear. "Enman. Can we *not* be strangers to each other?"

EVEN IN CRACKLY SNATCHES THE music riding the airwaves from Boston offered its assurances of harmony. Sober at last, Enman lay there long after she had escaped upstairs. A sonata—smoother and more even-keeled than a ballet, with its wild mood swings and elevated hopes. Then a symphony. Chaos, catastrophe, and swirling bombast, melodies not working out as they ought—to his ear, at least. Hubley Hill would have hated it. His poor old violin was propped in its case against the desk, all but forgotten—as forgotten as after Cleary had given it to him a few months before he died. An atonement, maybe, for the 'cordine, as Lester had called it. While giving up drinking, Enman had taken lessons from a fellow in town. Now the thing might well sit there and rot.

Given his lack of practice time, he would never be able to play as he hoped to, Hubley's music as hard to execute as classical. What made a piece pleasing was all in the hands of the player. The chops to start and stop on a dime, to tease out sounds as pure as they sounded on records—it demanded a child's willingness to struggle along, delighted simply at the wonder of ekeing out notes, never mind rhythm and melody. And yes, discordant as it was, the blaring symphony had an order.

In the midst of its final movement Hannah tiptoed in. Through slitted eyes he watched her fingering everything in sight: Ma's lace runner, the doodads on the shelf, though she avoided the damaged one. Then she went for the radio's knobs, and things strewn across the desktop. Someone else might have told her to stop. But her curiosity cheered him, and the pains she took picking up and straightening his pencils. Unearthing something from under his books, she laid it aside to pet then chase out the cat. He heard her moving about the kitchen, heard Una shifting something overhead.

When the station cut out completely he rose to tune in another. "Bewitched, Bothered and Bewildered" floated in on the airwaves, then "White Cliffs of Dover." Vera Lynn's crooning offered a chipper, melancholy peace until Hannah went thumping upstairs. Her lilting voice and Una's travelled down, weaving in and out of the song, such a sad one about parting. He strained to hear what they were saying: it was like introducing a new cat to an old one, the newcomer had to stake its territory. Hannah's humming filtered down. He couldn't tell if they were arguing, but if they were he owed it to both to play referee.

Reluctantly he ventured upstairs, hovered on the landing. The lyrics drifted up, then "Lily Marlene" came on. Funny you never heard songs about divorce, the word pressed between his thoughts like a dried leaf. They were transforming his old room into one for Hannah. Una looked up from the carton she was dragging into their bedroom. "Let's make sure you're comfortable." Her voice was full of mock cheer.

He patted Hannah's shoulder, lifted another of Una's boxes from his old bed.

"It's not as though we need the room for guests. Unless your friend comes to visit, in which case Hannah won't mind taking the couch—will you?"

The chances of needing it for a nursery didn't seem too pressing as Una kept slightly aloof, busily hanging up things of Ma's on hangers she'd pulled from their closet. He didn't suppose Hannah would mind her closet lacking the height to properly hang a coat or dress. He did not need to say "Make yourself at home" as Hannah flounced upon the bed, arms flung wide to gauge its width. He thought at first she was grinning. Her cheeks blazed, her bottom lip quaked, and she shook her head.

"Maybe I'm dead, Mister. Maybe this is that place Missus Goodroad says we goes, after."

"The pearly place." Una shot him a glance, one of amusement. He didn't know what to say.

"Thank you, Mister."

"Don't thank me, thank Una, I mean, Mrs. Greene." Because already Una was coming around, her flash-freeze having melted, thank God. Her moods were more changeable than weather. He wondered if in other marriages moodiness could become grounds for divorce.

DOWNSTAIRS, ATOP INKPENS' LEDGERS, LAY this year's seed catalogue, dropped there by Hannah. Easier to contemplate than any couples he knew divorcing was the idea of a hard, sudden frost. Even a freakishly early one carried spring's hope of revival, at least.

Was it the wisdom of plants people lacked, the gift plants possessed for striving towards light?

All silent upstairs, as night fell he pored over the catalogue. Ignoring Ma's selections, he circled new ones, foolproof things like crocuses— crocuses for cuckolds—which he'd plant for whomever was around come spring. He wanted something to look forward to. He would not be sorry to see the tail end of this summer, barely a seed pod to redeem it. *But the past is past and tomorrow looks after itself,* he recalled the old man saying, whether while in his cups or not, it didn't matter. Unless the winter brought exceptionally bitter cold and no snow, plants generally came back. Brown-eyed Susans, for instance, hoarding the heat of a drought to bloom by the ditch when others failed. Phlox, too, the mauve stuff whose leaves mildewed white in a summer of rain but bloomed till November. Planted a lifetime ago, Ma's still came up by the lane.

"We'll Meet Again" lofted him into the wee hours. Finally, switching off the radio, he listened hard for the sounds of Una and Hannah sleeping upstairs, and burrowed into the cushions. The sofa's springs were like a web of cysts, their mothball smell as engrained in the upholstery as his and Ma's past.

In his mind's eye, dim balls of light—her face and Cleary's—threw off shadowy sparks, then retreated along separate vacant pathways—Ma's into the furthest, deepest crannies of the house, the old man's through and beyond the barrens—until Enman could no longer picture either one. Their loss was sadder to him than Una's ever could be, actually. But it was a cold comfort, realizing this.

THE DOOR TO THE LITTLE room was ajar, the burble of Hannah's snore as regular as a metronome. Above his childhood bed loomed a dark little picture—that girly one of a boy in blue. Maybe Hannah had wanted it, amused by the boy's princely getup? She was too old for dolls, too old to be treated like a kid. Yet, tucked in, despite Ma's nightgown showing where the covers dipped, she looked like one. A strange and strangely beautiful half-child, she looked eerily at home—as much at home, he decided, as any of us can be.

In the other room Una lay so still it stopped his heart, her face in a greyish band of moonlight. He paused at the threshold—better me than Gainsborough's little prince watching over you, he thought, as he slid carefully between the sheets.

Moving next to his wife, he took pains not to let his skin touch hers. Every part of him ached for it, though, ached for the feel of her, for things to be all right, if not as they had been.

To his amazement she moved closer, and pressed herself against him.

He wanted to speak but could not. Her breath was in his ear, warm and soft and a little sour. Astonishingly, their breathing seemed to fill the room and it wasn't so bad, not so bad at all, not nearly as impossible as he had imagined it to be.

Out there in the boundless dark, from the island a foghorn sounded, and as he and Una shifted, the bedsprings yielded to their cautious weight. Una stifled a nervous giggle.

"What if Hannah hears? I wouldn't want her to be frightened."

"Frightened?" He felt his face burn, glad of the moon's dimness. "Of people making up?" His hand lounged on the strange territory of her shoulder, which felt oddly new and unexplored. "I imagine she's heard worse. A lot worse."

"Granted."

Sink or swim, fish or cut bait. The only way to overcome an aversion is to jump back in. So the old man's voice returned from years back, and with it the chill of water below the wharf, its iciness up his nose and in his eyes—and how his thrashing had kept him from sinking like a stone, arms flailing towards making the strokes that had later saved his life but not George's.

It was too late to undo the snarls in their marriage. But in choosing to stick it out, with time and patience and gentle tugging, the knot at its centre would tighten. Following something through, you and it could be saved.

Perhaps.

"Enman? *En?* Are you with me?" Una was breathing in his ear, reaching for him. And quite possibly Hannah did hear. The bedsprings complained till they were close to giving out, and still he couldn't quite grasp or believe the relief that flooded him, that joined—or seemed to join—the both of them.

For him, at least, it was the sheer cooling relief of letting go of thinking how and in whatever small or large way Una had used her wiles to hook him, hoodwinking herself into believing marriage was what she wanted, not simply a smoother ride through a troubled patch in life. Letting go enough to forgive *her* if not her wiliness.

When they were done, they listened to Hannah's snore become a soft whistle that could have been a spring peeper singing.

"'Here we are,'" he heard himself whisper tunelessly into Una's ear, "'out of cigarettes.'" He interlaced the fingers of one of her hands with his, and held tight. Clapping her other hand over his mouth, she moved his knuckles to her lips.

She lay half on her side, half on her belly, as relaxed as could be.

"*Une.* My *numéro une.* Shouldn't you be—? Here. I'll shove over, let you get on your back. There, now. Keep still."

She laughed then, regretful, he hoped, for her deceit. "It takes a bigger person than me to forgive the one who knowingly causes hurt. Maybe it's easier to forget their cruelty itself."

He guessed this was Una's oblique way of apologizing, appealing to his kindness? After her waffling over Hannah's staying, he thought the apology might be better directed at the girl. "Hannah's the bigger of us, you mean?" He felt a prick of guilt. "You're afraid she'll remember your about-face, *your* odd welcome, and hold it against you? Hannah hold a grudge? I doubt it. She's already forgiven you. What's the cruelty *you'd* like to forget?" He squeezed her hand, teasing. "Sometimes you baffle me. Forgive *me* for saying it, but I wonder at times if you know your own mind." He pulled her close again, felt her hair's softness at his ear. "I guess we all have our little blackouts, don't we." The wrong word. "Our whims." Yet Una's whims seemed more capricious than other people's, and the thought of this burrowed like a tick.

"So it was more than marrying on the rebound? I would like to know. And what if you meet someone better?" He felt the silkiness of her arm touching his. "Tell me, then I'll blow it off into the ether."

"Oh, Enman. Can we just let it go?" Then, after a moment or two, she thanked him for being patient.

HE DREAMED VIVIDLY THAT NIGHT, for the first time in months. The dream was all about water. At first he was walking on it. Next he was wading past the dropoff where the undertow clawed the sand away—well beyond the point of safety. Someone onshore, a woman, was hollering: "Don't, please don't—come back, Mister!" But then he realized it wasn't him but Barton Twomey, an off-camera Barton Twomey, she was yelling to: "You've done some crazy things, but don't go all to pot on us and do another."

The woman was Win. Win Goodrow. It was her standing there shouting, and she was holding a bundle: a wee swaddled baby—his.

"Bart! Enman! He'll be lost without a dad."

Then the dream shifted to winter, the water to ice. He was scrambling across the frozen harbour, leaping from one ice pan to another, across gaping black crevasses, a shortcut. Because Iris Finck had died and the store was closing for good, and if he made it in time he would have his pick, his heart's desire, of all remaining stock. But there was a greater urgency. He was in a mad, crazed rush to buy Crown corn syrup and Carnation milk, fixings for baby formula. For he'd been caught short, and even as he leapt he could hear its wailing. Win's bundle was abandoned now on his stoop, come to call Hannah its sister.

He woke in a sweat, yet washed in a damp, sombre calm. A quiet jubilation filled him. Una was curled there next to him.

"I do love you, Enman," she whispered, "You know it, right?"

Of course he was already late, and wouldn't blame Isaac if he docked him more than a day's pay for truancy. Una had his breakfast waiting when he practically tumbled down the stairs. He was guzzling down his tea when the radio spilled the news. Overnight a corvette had hit a U-boat and captured the crew, the handful of Jerries, it was assumed, that hadn't gone to the bottom with it.

The strike had happened inside the harbour approaches, it seemed, southwest of the Neverfail light buoy—this following reports of recent alien sightings, a possible enemy landing in the general vicinity of Barrein and Shag's Cove, or perhaps even closer to the East Coast Port, near Bear or Herring Cove. The prisoners, suffering hypothermia and treated according to convention, had been taken to the East Coast Port "for processing."

As if they were meat, he thought.

"More work for Inkpen's?" Una wondered, turning her back as Hannah came thumping downstairs. Una shook her head. "And double the fodder for Win."

20

EARLY SEPTEMBER, 1943

"GOT SOMETHING FOR YOU," MRS. FINCK'S CROAK CAME OVER THE PHONE.
"Might wanna haul yourself over, Missus, and collect it." The old woman
made no bones about watching Una open it, though every so often she
pretended to swat a fly. Hannah had the sense, at least, to busy herself
picking through the grubby yard goods that constituted Finck's "fabric
section."

Well, that superintendent had taken his time drafting his reply—
though when she hadn't heard before Labour Day she pretty much knew.
Still, reading it was crushing. They had wanted high school experience, he
wrote. An upstanding person with sound moral judgement and a background in chemistry. Married women need not apply.

Una wasn't surprised. She had resigned herself to the reality that
the principal would forward her file, and the hope that the reason she
was available might be fudged, had faded. The hateful rule about married women stood unchanged, which added insult to the super's veiled

threat that teachers not meeting the code of conduct were liable to have licenses revoked.

If the letdown was stamped all over Una's face, Iris Finck hardly noticed.

"Hey! Girl! Hands off! Nobody wants material tha' looks like it's been drug through mud—unless Missus plans on paying? Lester's right, saying 'get out of yard goods.' The young ones these days, too flippin' lazy to sew." Iris's raspy voice wavered theatrically. "Too much maaaysuring and cutting for them, I guess."

But then the old woman's eyes came to rest on Una, a glimmer lighting them.

"And what's up with you, Missus? You're looking a little…oh my, Enman's righteous shine has rubbed off on you? Next you'll be sporting haloes, you two."

A particularly snide remark, given how piqued Una felt. Making matters worse, Hannah dove right in. "Looks like that all the time, Missus does. Felt so sick she had to lay down while I did my morning's reaaadin'."

Grin and bear it, Kit would have preached, the main reason Una put off calling her.

"Well, well. Last time I saw that look on someone, antidotally speaking, it was Isla's girl."

What was more obvious than Una had hoped flew right over Hannah's head. "Missus is gonna learn me how to sew," the girl crowed, beaming. The nausea was not just in the morning but lingered all day.

Una gathered her wits enough to correct her. "Teach. Someday. First things first, then maybe we'll see."

But to save face and take her mind off the sudden queasiness that overtook her, she did the nice thing, the decent thing, and took five yards of greyish flannelette off Mrs. Finck's penny-pinching hands. It was on Enman's nickel and what price, an excuse for a few minutes' peace while Hannah sewed?

Back home, Hannah helped set up Mrs. Greene's ancient Singer in the little bedroom and Una started in with a lesson, as best she could, a basic one on hemming.

"There—in and out, see? You push the treadle, make the needle go—"

"Like a pecker. A bird, I mean, pecking."

Una took a deep breath, gazed at the window. Despite the rockiness in her gut, the deepening shock that her body had a will of its own, she had to bite down hard not to laugh. With Kit present she would have laughed, Kit would have said a sense of humour saved you. The lesson, like so many others, was futile. The girl ended up sewing two flannelette squares back to front, then accidentally snipping them in two.

"*God*, Hannah! What were you thinking?"

"You're not gonna send me home, are you, Missus? I mean, Uncle would, he'd—"

"Oh, dear. We haven't yet, have we?" The poor kid. But it would wear on anyone's nerves, Una thought, having Hannah underfoot. The house wasn't big enough for two these days. "Why not take a little hike, go for a swim?" she hinted repeatedly, taking every opportunity to shut the door and stretch out on the bed. Though beach days were history, long past. At any rate, Hannah seemed not to hear.

The sewing fiasco forgotten, Hannah dashed off to unearth the grade-four reader. She wasn't gone but a second before she hollered up, all in a flap, "Better get your arse down here, Missus."

What did a person have to do for a moment's rest? Then Una's stomach buckled. Oh please don't let it be Twomey, please, not just now. She let her mind roam back to Enman's book—that blunt instrument of a book on marriage hygiene that dictated who should and shouldn't have babies—and tried to recall what it said about the havoc all of this played with your body. She'd have looked it up. Except the book had disappeared, oddly, along with the liquor and any obvious signs of his drinking.

Maybe a drink, a tiny one, would have fixed her up. A thimblefull of dry sherry, maybe.

Downstairs, God in heaven, it wasn't Twomey but her neighbour who filled the mudroom door. It was the first time in weeks and weeks, the first since that nerve-wracking night in the store, Una found herself face to face with Win. Standing there, Win's face puckered into a wincing smile. Oh, but Win didn't speak. She was too busy darting her eyes around. Yellow, so much yellow.

"So?"

At the table Hannah toyed with a scrap of cloth. She whispered to herself that it would make a "dipe" for a baby that didn't grow—like Isla Inkpen's granddaughter who, for whatever reason, failed to thrive.

Win didn't say a word. She had a paper bag in her hand and she held it out. Nodding slowly, "Nice," she finally said to Hannah. Hannah glanced up then, clearly baffled when Win handed her the bag.

"Did you hear? Finck's is closing—for good. Iris, well, she told me just now, wanted me to be the first to know. Can't imagine us with no store, can you? 'Let someone else run it, someone with time on their hands,' Iris says. 'Got places to go, Win, folks to see.'

"Thought maybe, what with his figuring and your...you and Enman might try giving it a go. You've got a head on your shoulders, Una. Now the opportunity's here." Win laughed lightly, eyeing her. "'Hell's bells, Lester, gimme time to pack,' Iris was going, 'Hurry up, man, and wait!'" Win spoke to the floor. Ill as she felt, Una couldn't hold back a snicker.

Hannah, meanwhile, had opened the bag. A blush spread over the girl's face.

"Figured it was something you'd like. Said to Clinton, I said, 'The Twomey girl might like that, seeing how she enjoys humming.' 'And Enman,' I said, 'wouldn't he be tickled pink having his sister play an instrument.'"

Win's face took on a funny look, wistful with a tiny hint, perhaps, of apology.

Hannah pulled out the gift inside the bag and waved it. Her face was as full of the devil as it was with glee.

Una definitely needed something then, besides the soda crackers she had scarfed down earlier. "Be a help, Hannah—put on the kettle, would you? Tea, Win?"

Tea is calming, cooling too, in moments of duress, even the principal had said.

The thing looked rusty and even at that distance smelled fishy. Hannah held it to her ear, the way you would a seashell. Grains of sand fell from it when the girl put it to her lips. A smile tightened Win's mouth. A gloating, superior smile. Then Hannah blew into the instrument and a gritty wheeze of notes whistled out.

Was it a sailor's jig on a summer's day that the notes brought back?

Who knows but Win wasn't thinking the same, or of something darker.

"A mouth organ, go figure. Never know what the tide'll drag in, do we ladies?" Win cackled.

The kettle shrieked—thank God for small mercies—and Win went silent. She gazed around again, casing the place, sure, fixing on some other paper bags lying by the cellar door. Each bag was labelled with a colour written in pencil. Enman's precious order from East Coast Seed ensured that Hannah would have her very own bed of flowering bulbs to moon over come spring.

Una had taken him to task over it. "Really. You don't think that's a bit much? So she'll be with us this spring, then summer, and then fall." She's here for the duration, Una had thought, working to hide her dismay. She need not have bothered.

Enman was oblivious anyway. "Why not, sweetpea?"

Win's eyes swept from the bags to the cellar-door calendar and lit on Enman's jottings about waxings and wanings and prospects for an early frost.

There were no more red Xs.

"Enman's ma would approve." Win gave a stiff, choppy nod, watching Una snatch up the kettle. Then she breathed in loudly, obviously revving up for more.

"One more thing. I've come to apologize—for before, I mean. If I was ever short with you. Maybe I was, a bit. What I might've said that time, about you parading around buck naked."

Hannah sniggered into the harmonica, spewing a blather of notes.

"What exactly *did* you see, Win?" She held Win's gaze.

"Nutting I haven't seen a thousand times myself," Win laughed, "gawking in the bedroom mirror. Except, except—you looked kind of sad, pitiful I mean, lying there on the beach, you know, in your altogether, more's the pity, all by your lonesome like that."

The place inside that Una assumed would be her uterus tightened.

"That's what you saw?"

Win shrugged, slack-jawed. "Guess I felt kind of sorry for you." Win eyed her suspiciously, those eyes the eyes of a shrew. "What do you take me for? You expected me to take a pit-chure? Live and let live, I always say. To be honest, I was kind of scared that day *you* were day-ud, the way you were lying there. Before we found that Jerry."

Hannah butchered "Twinkle Twinkle Little Star." Una felt her face burn. In spite of herself, covering her mouth, she couldn't suppress a giggle as she felt, then recognized, a flutter. The instant she lit upon it, the sensation stopped. When she tried to summon back whatever had sparked it, she couldn't. There was only its blur inside her, a soft, faint twitch as indefinite as a leaf unfurling. The perfectly ordinary feeling of her stomach against her lungs.

Win peered at her then. Hannah spat sand into her palm, wiped it on her shirt. The grin spread across Win's face like a house materializing through fog.

"Oh. My. Jesus. Does Enman know?"

Win bustled over and hugged her so fiercely that Una almost didn't hear the scuff of soles on the mat, or the satchel's thud as it landed on a chair.

The satchel containing the checks and balances of Enman's other world, the sum total of Inkpens' enterprise.

"Does Enman know what?" Doffing his cap, he was smiling—looking puzzled but smiling with his silly, strange expectation that surprises could be—were, more often than not—good. He nodded to their visitor. "How are you, Win?"

"Better than Iris Finck." Win beamed slyly. "And how are *you*? Isn't it the truth, hon, we all pay for our fun."

"Exactly right," Hannah piped up. "You should hear them two goin' at it, Missus Goodroad. When I'm—and you wanna know something else? Babies poop. Put that in your pipe and smoke it, Missus Goodroad." Then all at once the girl's smile sagged, an anguished look storming in to replace it. "Does it mean, Mister, that with a baby there woon't be room no more for me?"

Any, *any* more. But Enman wasn't hearing. He was looking completely idiotic, baffled, gobsmacked, shaken.

"Jumpin jumpin jumpins," he started crowing, the most foolish grin imaginable overtaking his features. Then his arms were around her in a hug, a smothering one. "You're joking, aren't you? Just yanking an old fella's chain."

She hadn't really believed she would get pregnant, still did not fully believe she was. She had held off mentioning it, expecting Enman to be almost as confounded, as stunned, as she was. But he kept his hands on her waist like he might get down on his knees and talk to her belly, shed tears of joy. But he stayed put, and she could feel his soft chest fill and his arms tighten then loosen. She felt his words hum in his throat before she heard them. Words that should have made her blush with happiness, or at least relief, but instead made her feel cornered. Some earnest talk about knocking down walls, adding room, managing.

"Get over yourselves, would you? All of you." She pulled herself free, feeling nauseous again. "Land's sake—I haven't even seen the doctor yet. It's probably something else, I mightn't even be. So can you drop it? Can you just? If there's one thing I can't stand, it's people getting ahead of themselves."

Enman Greene turned three shades of red. "Win, my darling,"—how Una disliked hearing the term of endearment speciously applied—"Clint'll be wondering where you're at, won't he. Maybe you should run along now." And in a voice as gentle and cosy and grey as summer fog, "What's that you've got there, Hannah?"

"Just a little something I brought her," Win murmured. "It's been in the sea for a while, I'm guessing, so it should be free of germs."

"Well you're a piece of work and a half, Win." He said it admiringly.

And bending low—giving his old girlfriend something-and-a-half to take home with her, proper thing, as Win would say—drawing Una close again, he put his ear there, to her belly. Neither Enman nor Una moved as Win slipped out through the mudroom.

"When, dear? How soon? So that's why you've been feeling rotten—but why didn't you say?"

"I don't know, I really don't. I was afraid to. In case you wouldn't be pleased. I wanted to be certain first, I guess."

Disentangling herself, smoothing her skirt, she went and got the letter, handed it to him. He whistled through his teeth, rubbing her back. "Well. They say when the boss in the sky closes a door, he opens a window. There you go! Don't give the school board another thought."

"What window, Mister? Can Uncle see out of it? I hopes not."

As a fresh wave of nausea hit her, Una hurried to the pail in the mudroom.

"Poor, poor Missus, coughing up her cookies all the livelong day." In any other circumstance, Hannah's singsong would have made her laugh. Hannah patted her shoulder, passed her a remnant of grimy flannelette, went to fetch saltines.

"Thanks, dear. Where would I be without you?" Una tried her solemn best to smile.

23

COMING A WEEK OR TWO LATER, SNOW'S NEWS WAS EXACTLY AS THEY'D
longed for and delivered as expected, with smugness and a kindly pat on
Una's shoulder. "Well done, Mrs." And for the father-to-be, a handshake:
"You too, Greene. And, you'll be happy to hear that by Halloween or so
the morning sickness should lift." Una beamed with relief at that.

What Enman didn't expect was afterwards, in the car, the gap that
spread between the two of them. There was a gap, too, between this
moment and how he had envisioned having the news confirmed: relief,
Vs for marital victory! Hallelujahs! Jubilation! The world opening, finally,
like a dinner-plate dahlia, all radiance and bursts of colour, all promise and
rejoicing. Their marriage receiving the blessing that was due, a blessing
that would be like a starter shot from a pistol. At last, their lives together
would truly begin, lives guaranteed to proceed entwined! Having a baby
would silence once and for all any notions of Una's leaving.

After seeing Snow, they drove around for something to do. No, it
wasn't at all how he had pictured the news becoming official. He had
imagined something delicious, cosy, celebratory. A candlelit supper, a

fancy cake, glasses filled with punch. Foolishly, he realized, he had also imagined Una going to the doctor by herself. Her surprising him with Snow's verdict, their clinking glasses then holding hands, gazing out the kitchen window at a magnificent blood moon.

Instead, he felt just now like he had run straight up Citadel Hill. Driving around the foot of it, watching the signal flags at its summit recede in Beulah's rear-view, he clamped a sweaty hand over hers. "Whoa, baby," he muttered like a fool at an old lady, braking just in time to let the woman hobble across Summer Street. The spitting image of Ma, she was, until the woman waved her fist, shouting, "Slow down, you bloody moron!" The rest of the way to the Gardens, two full blocks, he drove as an octogenarian would. Dogs could've pissed on the tires, indeed.

"I'm sorry," was the most Una seemed able to muster in the car.

"Sorry?" He mopped his face with a hankie—the mid-September day was warm and had a burnished feel, a soft, cidery glow lighting the treetops in the Gardens. He stopped and parked on Spring Garden Road and they got out. He held her arm gently—almost the way he would have held Ma's, though Ma had never been keen on being treated like that, like a child. They should take a gander at the dahlias, he said, while the dahlias were in their prime. Another couple of weeks and they'd be ruined by frost, though this seemed unlikely given the Indian summer that had replaced late August's run of cool, rainy weather.

They were almost to the Gardens' tall, fancy gates when a raucous gang of sailors forced them to cross the street to the opposite corner, by the Lord Nelson Hotel. If things between him and Una had been friendlier, he'd have steered her into its dining room for a late lunch—an extravagant, joyous meal to toast this next happy phase of married life. Instead, they stood in silence. A man beside them happened to say, "Did you hear the big man himself is here in town? Winston Churchill. Kid you not. Top secret. Swear to God, hurry and you'll see him. Up on the Hill. He's got some ladies with him, taking in the view."

Una perked up. Enman laughed. "How come you're not up there? Didn't hear a thing on the radio."

"Don't be a stick in the mud. We can see flowers any old time." Una pulled him back to the car.

Outside the Citadel's gate, overlooking the Old Town Clock, a handful of naval officers gathered around a stout, stolid oldster who looked for all the world like a large, baldheaded baby in a yachtsman's cap. Two nicely dressed women, one young, one older, stayed by his side as the man called out about "sacrifices," pointing his walking stick at the harbour below, at the ships crowded into Bedford Basin. Despite his leisurely gait, Churchill smiled a bit testily at a man who looked like he could have been from the newspaper, doodling on a notepad. He flashed back the "V for Victory" sign at some sailors on a grassy rampart flashing the sign at him.

A handful of passersby had gathered and, joining them, Enman and Una obeyed as a police constable directed them to a spot some fifteen feet away.

A woman walking a dog stopped and gaped. "What's he doing here?"

"It can't really be him." Una craned closer. Enman gripped her hand. It felt a little warm and clammy. She wasn't going to be sick again?

"If not, he's a good actor."

An officer raised a trumpet. "There'll always be an Ennng-lund," the tiny smattering of people sang along, "and Ennng-lund shall be free."

"If Ennng-lund means as much to youu—" Una joined in.

Reining in her dog, the woman shook her head. "So the Brits are gonna save us. Sure. Wipe out every Jerry till not one of them's left?"

"—As Eng-lund means to meee."

Chewing a cigar, Mr. Churchill and the women were hustled into an unmarked car, and none too soon as a complement of men came through the fort's gate, past its sentries, yelling as they cut downhill. Enman could already imagine them drunk.

He hadn't had a drop since Mrs. Finck's odd visit. A drink to toast the prospective baby would have helped wash the news down, let him celebrate by raving about it. But the sharp, clear light of sobriety had taught him to chew over, swallow, and practically digest each word before spitting it out.

"So there you go, Una. Your brush with fame. Something to tell Junior about."

"My last brush with things beyond Barrein, you mean."

THEY DROVE BACK DOWN THE Hill to the Gardens and parked near the lofty wrought iron gates that, as a kid, Enman had pictured whenever the "Pearly Gates" were mentioned. He led Una through a smaller, swinging gate into the Gardens' oasis. The hum of bees ousted the noise of people and traffic.

Looking pale, Una sank to a bench, closed her eyes.

"I'm not sure why you're so keen to be a dad. You never really wanted to be, did you?"

Something her friend Kit had said once came back to him: "Not me. None of that baby stuff for me. Not in this life." Was Una now thinking the same? Or perhaps she just wanted to put her head down, figure out how to get through the next month and a half.

"A comfort in our old age." Una's look was whimsical, then she seemed resigned. "I don't know what having a baby in the house will do to your practising. Maybe you'd be happier devoting your time to something easier, like violin. God, the things we do to avoid being alone. Sabotaging ourselves *and* others."

"I never thought I wouldn't be a father," he lied, and patted her arm. "This is my party too, dear—*our* child." The words *were* a little like sand on his tongue, he had to admit. The world was so full of grimness, it struck him anew. Not things you wanted to subject a child to, even if, as the Churchills of the world would say, living in hope you could expect a certain goodness to prevail.

Una watched a bee disappear into the spiny yellow heart of a bloom. "You don't have to...I won't blame you if you change your mind, if you can't be—"

Her trying to let him off the hook was insulting. But he didn't let it show, or let his smile flag. "A name—it'll need a name, Una."

"*He.* A he will find it easier to get along. It's a man's world." Una gave a long, determined sigh. "I suppose we'll cross that bridge when—"

"I'm sorry about the job, you know."

She had left the letter in the hall until Hannah finally used the back of it to print a list: "suplys Ill nede for schul."

"Look, let's get out of here." Una leapt up. "I can't stand the smell of these things, can you?"

There was no fanfare in the street, nothing to suggest that a dignitary was in town. Churchill's visit was an alien landing that had nothing to do with them. "What *was* that, anyways?" he joked, nursing the hope that the afternoon could still be savoured. Since he had taken it off to bring her to the doctor, they might as well enjoy some sights. Una peered dully out the window.

"How would I know?"

He had an idea that seeing the waterfront might lift her out of her funk.

The last time he'd been anywhere near Pier 22 had been that frigid night in February, after being brought ashore by the corvette men who had saved his skin. Before the war, while working downtown he'd enjoyed lunch breaks strolling through the cargo sheds, taking in the sounds and smells of goods being unloaded. Crates of oranges and tea from exotic places, bales of rubber, sacks of rice and tapioca flour spilling over concrete floors, to the rats' delight.

As he took the turn onto Marginal Road he slowed. A gang of men were being marched from the port's little brick immigration office and across the tracks to a waiting train. Una gasped, seeing the circles painted on the backs of their jackets and knees of their trousers.

They were prisoners of war. Though their uniforms were shabby there was no disguising the fact they were Jerries. The sight of a blue officer's cap sent an icy current along Enman's spine, its charge moving to his legs. The last time he'd laid eyes on someone wearing such a cap had been amidst the blazing black of that February night, beyond the harbour approaches. The U-boat had surfaced long enough to inspect the carnage it wrought, cruising by close enough that Enman and his mates in the lifeboat had glimpsed the captain waving from atop its conning tower.

"I'm sure they'll get what's coming," he heard himself say, "the poor bastards."

UNA SAID NOTHING. SHE JUST stared out at the chain gang, such as it was, and a tear wormed down her cheek. That solitary tear finally made him lose his composure.

"Good grief, Una! You should be happy—what the heck's the

matter now, like everyone and their dog's raining on your parade? I thought this was what you wanted. Starting a family. Having a baby."

When she turned to him her look was pure disbelief.

"Enman. Am I not allowed to feel what I feel?"

Whatever that might be, he thought, since her moods changed like the weather.

22

ONE EVENING A FEW WEEKS LATER, ENMAN AND HANNAH WERE BUSY IN THE
kitchen and Una was resting on the sofa when Win burst in on them.
Win barely stopped to knock at the back door. Without hesitation,
undeterred, she bustled from the kitchen to the front room and paused
in the doorway, newspaper in hand. "Beat this!" The cartoonist's drawing was of Winston Churchill and two ladies on the Hill, the statesman
shaking an officer's hand. In the picture two fighter planes flew overhead
and the harbour below was chockablock with battleships. "See? There's
the Clock in the background,"—Win pointed it out to Enman at her
heels—"so it's got to be Hellifax. How'd they slip this one past us?"

Enman smiled as he explained that he and Una had been there.

"Get out!" Win slapped her cheeks, amazed. "How come you never
told Clint and me? Oh, but you two have had other things on your
minds, Enman tells me." Win eyed Una knowingly.

Now Enman was speaking for her, as if she couldn't speak for
herself?

Win had also brought a mackerel, freshly caught. It was in a paper
bag by the sink, Hannah could clean it, she said. "My word, Missus,

you'd better start thinking about putting meat on those bones. That baby needs—well, as soon as you can keep food down again, I mean."

Enman's eyes brightened. "Hannah's going great guns, stepping in with the cooking. Poor Una can't stomach the smell of food."

Una turned her face to the wallpaper. Not when food was warmed-over Spam and peas straight from the tin, and the forks had egg yolk between their tines. Though she didn't mean to be so picky.

"Well, isn't that something. Isla's looking for help minding her grandchild. Hannah could go down and pick up some tips on babies. It wouldn't hurt. You're going to need help. Must be some excited, though."

Enman gave a little clap, then clasped his hands in a knot and flexed them. "True enough, aren't we Una?"

Win nodded happily. "Good. Then I'll arrange it. Now, listen. The best thing for your ailment? Fresh air. Come take a walk some day out the shore. Pickings are slim, but you never know what we might find."

Una drew a thoughtful breath. "No, thank you."

THE HUCKLEBERRIES ON THE HILLSIDE blazed red that October, and the fish blood in the sink and on the knife was the same colour. Hannah tugged away the gleaming purple innards and Enman remarked on the marvel of their functions: "A beautiful mystery." Hannah wrinkled her nose, shook guts from her fingers. "Not anymore, Mister." Gagging, Una ran upstairs.

She was appalled at what was happening to her, the way her breasts, no longer small and pert, felt heavy and hard, as if they and the rest of her body had developed minds of their own.

That night in bed, Enman spoke quietly into her ear. "If you don't want to have it, maybe something can be figured out? Snow might know of someone who could help you."

"Get rid of it? How could you suggest it?" The thought of some dreadful hack, a hundred times worse than the doctor in O'Leery, was even more appalling, unthinkable. "It's too late." Besides, she hoped she would soon feel better.

When Win paid her next visit, just before Halloween, she said Isla was happy to take Hannah now and then. "No need to thank me. Tippy got your tongue, dear? By Christmas, trust me, you'll be out of the woods—you'll feel like a whole new person." And Win waxed on (and on) about the small life inside Una, and how by the fourth month pregnancy did wonderful things to your hair.

As the days shortened, the nausea eased. But it was replaced by the feeling that her body had been usurped by the being growing inside it. She could no longer button the tops of her skirts, her waist thickening in a manner that suggested overeating and not the neat, rounded bulge she had imagined. She craved beets—not the beets themselves but their taste of dirt. She craved strawberries while the huckleberries lost their leaves, the bushes turning grey on grey. She spent most of her time upstairs lying down, listening to Hannah banging pots below. Win and sometimes Isla came to the door with plates of cookies and war cake, just what everyone wanted, Una thought cynically. Enman would creep in after supper and leave slices of it on the dresser. Its seedy raisins were like having sand in her teeth.

"Eat up," he kept saying. "You've got the baby to think of."

One day after work he mentioned having called Snow. "I spoke to him myself, since you won't. 'Baby blues' can happen before the birth, he says, not just after. It's not unusual."

"Thank goodness for that." Una wished she could erase the doubt, the cynicism, from her voice.

"You will snap out of it, he assures me."

She tried to speak brightly. "He would know."

"Win would like to come up and see you."

She brushed off some crumbs, picked away a seed.

"Sweetie. Can't you try and cheer up? For Hannah's sake. For me."

Hannah, at least, had learned to keep to her room when she wasn't downstairs or at Isla's. She "read," having figured out the grade-three reader enough to recite its simple, repetitive sentences.

"Why not teach her a little grammar? It wouldn't hurt."

And what had he done for Hannah lately? He had talked Carmel Rooney into parting with a spare desk, wedging it into the little bedroom. But he hadn't done a thing about fitting a crib in there, let alone adding a nursery. Not that Una particularly cared.

Enman lost patience. "Some of us don't have the luxury to lie about. Take a walk, like you used to."

And some didn't have the luxury to listen to records uninterrupted, while someone else pestered for help stitching together patches of fabric Mrs. Greene had cut out years ago to make a quilt.

Una threw her hands up. "You know as much as I do about quilting, Hannah." All Una wanted was quiet.

And then Isla paid a visit. Her smiling face was a jarring but welcome brightness until her eyes went to Una's stomach. At last, her granddaughter was almost walking, Isla said. "I'll bring her over to show you."

Una grinned weakly. "Don't trouble yourself. I can imagine what a toddler looks like. How cute she must be, I mean."

When Una showed Isla downstairs, Isla smiled in at Hannah reading in the front room, Hannah's tongue between her teeth, forefinger pressed to the page.

"It looks bigger without a casket in here. Listen. You and Hannah should come for tea."

"Looking like *this*?" Una forced a laugh.

"But you hardly even show yet."

The last time Una had ventured out was to Finck's, and only because Enman was at work and she needed Epsom salts to soak her feet in. She couldn't rely on Hannah not to return with jars of old candy, dried-up shoe polish, or other ancient merchandise Iris sought to unload before closing shop forever. Never again would she set foot in the store, pregnant, Una had told herself. She had been swarmed by two Meade women she barely knew, the pair cooing over her as if she were a laying hen. It was disgusting to be treated like public property, strangers eyeing your stomach, wanting to touch it, asking when you were due. And then Sylvester had appeared, ogling her.

"Didn't know Enman had it in him."

"Have what in him? The ability to impregnate someone?" Una had put the box of salts right back on the bare shelf, feeling their cruel eyes on her as she hurried out, empty-handed. Iris calling, "Now, Missus. No need to get in a flap. The man was just teasing. Best to calm yourself. Don't want that baby coming out all high-strung."

"That's just plain stupidity," Una snarled back.

IF HER BREASTS HAD ONCE been small and pert as barnacles—and if only she could have leaned forever into such fanciful, magical, thinking—they were now as curved and veiny as moonsnails' shells, the creature inside her a hermit crab. The only good thing was that "B for butter" had all but stopped coming over the airwaves.

On the shortest day of the year, the start of winter, wrapped in the evening's darkness, Enman sat on the sofa with her, her feet in his lap, massaging them. In the kitchen, Hannah dropped something. "Hell's bells shit frig. Missus is gonna take my head off. She already hates my guts, Mister." Shouting from the other room, Hannah still hadn't learned to lower her voice.

"No, Missus does not," Una yelled back, the blood thumping in her chest, the feeling of something strange and shapeless moving beneath her stomach. Not only was it causing her to lose her figure, but soon it would press on her bladder, add heartburn to heartache. "If you don't want to have it," Enman's words came back to her. To abort a helpless foetus and rid herself of its burden would have only closed the gap in a circle of trouble, Una thought—the circle of trouble she had let herself in for, the gap a tiny, already shrinking one where any hope of light might creep in. It no longer mattered to her that the being's existence was partly owed, she felt sure, to a boy-man not just capable but guilty of terrible things, a boy-man who was likely dead by now, or jailed.

"Guilt wears you down faster than the worst punishment," Kit had said, in a tone Una now considered unctuous. Did Kit feel guilty for letting her down, ignoring her friend in need? Kit would know about this "wearing down," Una thought, if Kit had a conscience.

Isla called up just then to invite Hannah down on the pretext of baking sugar cookies and, more importantly, for a lesson on sterilizing bottles. Isla's granddaughter had been weaned from the breast, and her daughter needed help making formula.

Enman packed Hannah off with a cup of sugar in hand.

The night was cold, a wintry draft coming in around the windows. Una went upstairs and ran a bath, the best way she could think of to keep warm. The running water drowned out the sounds of Enman's record, his violin straining over top of it. Steam coated the pane where the blind moved in the draft. There was no blackout, but she wanted only candlelight, and the flame quivered. She made the bath as hot as she could stand it and climbed in. She was glad of the dimness, how it softened the sight of her body. She hoped that the bath would soothe away its tenderness. Its heat barely took her mind off the air's chill. Sliding down under the surface, she shut her eyes to avoid seeing her navel. It had begun to smoothe out, as round and blank as a statue's eye. She thought of her mother carrying her, the cord so briefly connecting them. It was hard to imagine her mother's slight, brittle body swollen like this. Had she dreaded the changes to it? Una felt the butterfly's flutters that had grown more frequent, the child flexing its limbs?

A person could drown in less water. As the bath cooled, she could have slid under its surface completely, and held herself there. It would have been easy. But she imagined the child. It would have eyes, a nose, and a mouth. Snow had told her she was doing "famously" earlier in December, listening for its heartbeat. She had turned her face away to avoid the raptness of his eyes above the stethoscope pressed to her abdomen.

A creak outside the door startled her. Enman poked his head in. The chill roused her. "Just wanted to make sure you're all right. Enjoying the quiet? It's going to work out. You'll have this one, and forget all the discomfort ever happened."

Leaving, he gently shut the door behind him. She heard the latch click, could hear him breathing there.

"I wonder if it's even yours," she called through the door. "Back in the summer—"

"What? You're talking foolishness. Look. Why are you doing this?" He had stepped back into the room, was peering down at her. She crossed her arms over herself, and even that hurt. She groped for the towel.

"Don't look. I can't stand you looking."

"Oh, for goodness sake. You're lovely no matter what. Now quit that crazy talk. Get into bed and I'll rub your back. Then I'll run down and get Hannah, shall I?"

So she had tried to tell him, tried to warn and let him down as gently as she knew how to. But like a balky student, back when she had cared about having students, he could be told but could not be made to listen.

23

DECEMBER 1943

THE SATURDAY BEFORE CHRISTMAS, A BRIGHT, SNOWLESS DAY, ENMAN took his chances and drove to town. Una opted to stay in bed. He didn't like to leave her alone, so Hannah stayed behind making paper chains for the tree he had brought home from the barrens and put in the front room.

The downtown streets thrummed with an odd festivity, their shabbiness and the restlessness of wandering servicemen relieved somewhat by the holidays' anticipation. Perhaps the season and its cheer offered a brief if illusory feeling of respite from the war. He headed straight for Phinney's music store, its black tile facade only a little the worse for wear these days, a boy washing some dried splatters from it. Inside, people perused display cases, a sailor tested guitars—none as handsome as Hill's Les Paul—and a girl and her father tried out an accordion. Sitting at a shiny apartment-size piano, a boy played "Chopsticks."

Moving to the display of harmonicas, Enman resisted the urge to have the clerk take a violin from the wall and let him try it. He picked the best mid-priced Hohner to replace the rusty one Win had brought over. He stopped to browse the record albums, then crossed the street, hurrying the block or two down to The Book Room. It was across from the provincial legislature building, whose entrance boasted a big fir wreath and garland around the fanlight above the door—reminders that the war couldn't fully overtake Christmas.

He was greeted by the smell of books, the busy cheer of browsers. The lady at the desk nodded and smiled at his request, *An English Galaxy of Shorter Poems*. He wasn't even sure if Una liked poetry or not, she'd never said. But he had heard a carol on the radio, "There is No Rose of Such Virtue," composed by Britten, based on something the composer had read in this very book while marooned here the year before, on his way home to England from New York.

"I'm sure your wife won't be disappointed." The clerk wrapped it for him, the same woman who had sold him *The Hygiene of Marriage*. He hoped she didn't remember.

After that, he went down the block to Wood Brothers and bought Una a cosy, quilted robe like Hannah's, but in an emerald green. Avoiding the lingerie—bullet bras, girdles, and playsuits—he chose a navy-blue cardigan for Hannah. The clerk remembered Una. She was the clerk who was very good at getting him to spend his money. "What size is she, again?"

"Oh, no. It's for my sister."

Finished shopping, he went back up to the Green Lantern, managed to find a spot at the soda fountain, and treated himself to a coffee. While he drank it he thumbed through the poetry book. It happened to have a little poem attributed to Anne Boleyn, of all people, that bemoaned the queen's entrapment. For a moment he regretted his choice of a gift, and hoped Una wouldn't see herself in the poem and its complaint. With any luck she would flip right past it.

On Christmas Day, Una watched Hannah open her present. Enman handed Una her gifts, which Una opened without undue interest and thanked him for. Hannah had made a drawing, which she'd put under the tree, a picture of a stickman waving a frying pan.

"Oh, Mister. It's your fiddle!"

Una opened the poetry book, listened politely while he squeaked out the melody to Britten's carol printed there, after pointing out its lyrics:

There is no rose of such vertu/As is the rose that bare Jesu. He spoke to her silence: "It's medieval."

"Gibberish, too." Una smiled a bit mischievously. Through a gap in the tree's branches and their dangling links of paper coloured with crayon, she pointed to Ma's figurine. "Impregnated by God. Imagine that." Then she looked away. There was nothing under the tree from her, for him or for Hannah. He helped Hannah with the roast chicken and the cranberry sauce Isla made with berries from the bog, and the carrot pudding Win sent over. For the first time in months, Una ate like there was no tomorrow, then excused herself and went upstairs, leaving the poetry book and the robe on the sofa.

Enman taught Hannah how to blow "Silent Night," and when she mastered that, a bar or two of Beethoven's "Ode to Joy." She was still wearing the new sweater when she went to bed, and perhaps slept in it, because she had it on over her nightgown when she came down next morning.

Boxing Day was a Sunday and though he had resisted calls to come down to Isaac's for some Christmas cheer, his old thirst came back with a vengeance, with Una resting above and Hannah on the Hohner every living second. He couldn't wait for Monday and to go back to work. Though business had slowed to a trickle and Isaac said Enman could extend his holidays if he wanted. But no, he was saving up his days off for when the baby arrived.

By mid-afternoon he thought if he couldn't beat Hannah's tooting he would just have join it, and took out his violin. Then Hannah went to Isla's to model her sweater. He was about to head down to Isaac's when Hubley appeared at the door, his "Left Paw" over his shoulder. Hill had been imbibing, it was obvious. Had he noticed the snow blowing down off the barrens he wouldn't have taken his guitar outside without its case. Hubley didn't wait for an invite into the front room with its tidy coal fire behind the grate.

Enman heard the door open upstairs, heard Una skulking there.

"Got a bunch of new tunes worked up." Hubley had grown a bit balder since the summer, his stubbled beard a chalky white. If Hill had let it grow out, Hannah might have called him Santa. Except the thinner on top he became, the more his bones shrank, as bones did with age.

How was it Hill was only a few years his elder? Five foot two, eyes of blue, Enman thought of the song. Hubley always had been sawed-off, though he talked the talk of a big man, clearing his throat then piping up. "How's your wife, anyway?" As Hubley spoke his eyes dragged the ceiling as if any second Una would swoop down. "Listen. I've been an ass. If you'll be the S to my H-I-L-L, I'm willing to try some new stuff. Mozart and that. And split the door in your favour." There was a New Year's dance at the fire hall in O'Leery and Hubley needed a fiddler; now that Enman was here to stay, was he interested?

"Do you good to get out—do Una good too, having you outta the house."

"Give me a day or two. I'll let you know."

"And have no time to rehearse?"

"Not under the gun like this, I might say yes."

"You can't leave her alone, even with the Twomey one here?"

"Sorry, it's just not in the cards right now."

Enman meant it, being sorry, watching Hubley disappear into the twilight, looking like Gene Autry the Singing Cowboy with his guitar on his back. Never mind that Enman hated songs like "Back in the Saddle Again." Still, he kicked himself for being so wedded to his musical tastes, and other things, that he had forgone the Labour Day dance, the kitchen parties, and other shindigs he could have played if he had been more forthright, agreeing to be one half of their duo. He realized he would have enjoyed these events, in the same way Hubley had made up his mind to reach beyond his likes and dislikes.

Lurking there, Una called down, "So, are you going?"

"Not on the eve of our anniversary."

Silence.

"The island. You never did take me there." She meant the one he hadn't visited since he was a teenager, even though it was right there. "The dance. Don't let me stop you." Then she crept back up to bed.

THIS EXCHANGE PUSHED ENMAN TO O'Leery after work the next evening, bugger the dark, the cold, that excuse for a road—at least there wasn't snow—and bugger Beulah. If she died, good riddance, he'd push her into the woods and be done with her. But first he asked Clint for directions, to avoid any dilly-dallying.

"Thought you were on the wagon, bud."

"It's for a friend. I owe Robart. He's been breathing down my neck for it, see."

A quarter-mile or so before the Magnet he hung a hard right. A beagle yapped from behind a picket fence before the frozen lane petered to a bald patch of granite surrounded by woods. True to Clint's word the truck was there, his tow-headed son—Joey? Grayson? Jimmy? he never could keep track of them—lolling from the tailgate with another young fellow nursing a brown quart bottle. Their breath hung in the frosty air.

Joey-Grayson-Jimmy greeted him with a grin, eyes like Win's, taking Beulah in. "Twomey doesn't give a shit who buys his liquor, so what gives?" The kid sounded wary, nineteen years old if he was a day. "Lookin' for a six or a two-four? Alls we got is brew." His mother through and through, he uncapped a bottle, handed it over. Watched Enman take a first sip. "You don't give the rest of us freebies," the friend groused.

The homebrew was yeasty and had a sweet, boggy flavour. Tipping it back, Enman fought the urge to gag. But it was wet and it was alcoholic, and nobody else need know. "How much?" Peeling off a glove, Enman felt around for his little roll of cash.

"Any friend of my old man's a friend of mine. It's on the house. More chillin' in the run—he'p yourself if they ain't frozen. Then we'll talk."

The friend smirked. Joey, or whatever his name was, grinned, a chipped tooth visible in the dusky light. His smudge of a mustache lent him a certain charm; Enman imagined Win getting after him to shave.

"Best beer money can buy, Mr. Greene."

The fact was it made Enman think of murky, peaty urine. "How much you charge for a six?"

"Like I said, the cooler's thataway." The kid pointed to an opening in the naked trees. The slow, faint burble of water drifted through the darkness and Enman followed it, swinging the bottle. It was worse than swill. All this way—he had come all this way, fighting with himself for weeks, months, then finally giving in—to drink bootlegged rot in the woods like some rabid teenager. He wondered what Clint and Win really thought about their son's business.

As soon as he was out of sight, he emptied the bottle into the frozen moss. On a desperately hot day, it might have been drinkable. A little farther in, edged by ice, the stream snaked through a glade with boulders for chairs. The trees creaked in the wind, their thatched branches blocking out what little starlight fell. Shards of glass glinted in the black water, frozen foam scudded over rocks. The air was already sharp with January's bite. In this outdoor barroom with only rocks for company, who knew what critters hibernated? Under the ice the stream sluiced through its peaty bed, having recovered from last summer's dryness, making its way, he guessed, to a chain of stony lakes that emptied, eventually, into the sea. A brace of bottles leaned in a sort of bowl formed by ice-encrusted tree roots and the ruined forks of a bicycle.

He hurried back up the path, handed over his empty. "Got something at home I need to take care of, how could I have forgot?" Shaking his head, he tapped his brow. "Happens, fellas, when you get older. Brain like a sieve. I'll say hi to your parents, Joey—sure they'll be asking." He got into the car as fast as he could and yes there was a God because she started first crack. The reflection in the rear-view much too dark to see what he knew would be youthful disgust.

The next morning snow covered his tracks.

THAT WINTER, THE WINTER OF 1944, two years after the sinking that had cost Enman his good friend, business at Inkpens' ground to a halt. By then the Allies had turned things around to all but reclaim the Atlantic, so the news went, and all around the province work at the little yards was drying up. With fewer ships getting hit and needing repair, there was nothing the big yards couldn't handle as they gobbled up business— the way Una's condition gobbled her up, consumed the person Enman thought she had been.

"Be patient. Wait till the baby comes, she'll snap out of it," Snow insisted on the phone. "She'll be so delighted she won't even remember this phase. Neither will you. You'd be surprised how many mothers—"

Win's visits were the one uplifting thing. Through January and February she popped over regularly, bringing casseroles and other goodies, she herself bubbling over with a determined glee. It seemed she couldn't contain herself: "A baby in the house—just wait!" Funny, given Una's trepidations and how these might characterize their anticipation. But maybe Win was trying, nicely, to prepare him, to prepare all of them, while unloading foodstuffs Clinton could no longer bear to look at—enough creamed corn and tinned peas to feed all of Barrein *and* O'Leery, gleaned from her summer's beachcombing.

"You're not leaving yourselves short?" he would say. With fewer sinkings, far less flotsam, useful and otherwise, beached itself these days. People turned their attention to Una's well-being. The most standoffish Meades asked after her. "She certainly is making herself a stranger," even Isla, who was so friendly towards Una, said. At least Una was eating, while not, as Win said, "at risk of becoming a lard-arse." The way people talked in the store, they would have come up to the house just to have a feel of her belly. Enman wasn't sure how he should react, grin like a cat, or step into the shadows the way some men did, letting women hold sway. He knew Una would appreciate their attention about as much as she'd have enjoyed being told she was fat.

"She's a study in human nature," Enman said, as was he, he thought.

He resolved to dedicate more time to practising. Consistency was everything, ten minutes every day better than thirty every now and then. Chords: two note, three note, four note. More bow, less bow. Arpeggios, major and minor. Hubley's style of music favoured down-bow fiddlers, but the key to a sweeter sound than a Cape Breton fiddler's edge, created by a hard back-and-forth sawing across the strings, was letting a figure-eight motion of the bow soften the tone. Steady speed. The pulse from the bow's angle, not its pressure, setting rhythm and tone. The trick was keeping the hand relaxed, all the movement in the wrist. The muscles remembering.

But then Una would appear, massaging the mound of her belly. "Can't you stop now? Can't you do that someplace else?"

"Fine, then. You're overdue for your checkup. I'll quit if you'll agree to see Snow." He put the violin in its case, propped it behind the radio. Out of sight, out of mind, he thought, and not such a terrible sacrifice, he had decided. For Hill's down-home tunes did have a sameness, a tiresome repetition of rhythms and chords.

"What will he tell me, that I'm pregnant?"

Enman booked the appointment anyway. He drove her, fingers crossed that the car would get them there. Waiting with her in the reception area he was an interloper, the only man in the place besides the doctor. They were surrounded by people only remarkable for bellies pushing out ugly flowered smocks. Those with the largest shifted awkwardly in their chairs, responding with a certain weariness to the receptionist's perky questions. "When are you due? Have you dropped yet? My, you're carrying low, must be a boy?" Una dodged them all, avoiding empathetic glances.

"I won't look like a beach ball, will I?" Una had asked Snow that balmy day in September. It was odd to think of it. "It won't be forever. Patience," the doctor had said, and he repeated it now. "Baby will come like a thief in the night, be prepared."

Patience, Win also said. Isaac had no choice but to cut Enman's hours to a couple of days a week. The Lord opened a window every time he closed a door, or was it the other way around? Or did he just shut them both tight?

March, the Maritimes' cruellest month, amounted to waiting and more waiting. Enman could hardly afford to pay a carpenter to build on a room, which scuttled his plans to move Hannah downstairs and make her bedroom a nursery. On the dreariest night, the first day of spring, forgetting his bargain with Una he rosined his bow and placed it and the violin in Hannah's eager, clumsy hands. Better this than presiding over her efforts at sums and spelling. He tried to get her to bow something, anything, while he reached around her to form notes, pressing strings to the fingerboard. He tried getting her to bow a steady single note on an open string to train her ear. It was a largely fruitless exercise made more fruitless by Una's sighs or her cursing.

He thought of the human brain as flypaper, the way things did or didn't stick. He thought of Hannah's as being especially un-sticky, the way she stumbled over things.

Oddly enough, Tippy the cat became Enman's most reliable companion, a chummy comfort in the early evenings, curled on the back of the sofa and purring in Enman's ear. But just before bedtime the cat would yowl to go out, then make himself scarce until morning. And then Tippy disappeared altogether, a result of his tomcatting, Enman guessed. No one could have credited the grief Tippy's vanishing brought him and Hannah, fearing as both did that the cat had been carried off by a coyote or fox, feeling guilty at the thought. "That's just the way it goes," Una said. Told to stay off her back, by then she was having trouble sleeping. At least Enman's acknowledgement of her discomfort made her a bit more talkative, enough to complain of the baby booting her in the ribs each time she turned.

"Booting or mooning her, take your pick." Win gave a wink when he told her. "Oh, now, paying for your fun, that's being a mom."

As March's snow and sleet gave way to April's mud, he liked to think Tippy was up there somewhere with Ma, having Ma rub his chin.

"You know, I don't see too much wrong with Hubley's guitar-picking," Clint said, around Eastertime. There was talk of Robart and Greely throwing a dance party in honour of Isaac's birthday near the end of May, and Hill had volunteered to play.

Giving up on teaching Hannah much of anything, Enman had put the violin away for good. "Maybe music's not in everyone's genes," he told the girl as kindly as possible. "Never mind. We can't all luck out in that department."

He gave her a wink, mostly for Una's benefit. If she was watching.

Who knew what she saw or didn't see any more.

You heard about marriages landing on the rocks, a couple's future getting swept away in the lightest gale. But having a baby made for rock-solid ground and an anchor both, wasn't it so? A baby was bound to save a foundering marriage, he had heard it said.

This baby would save theirs. He lived out the last, most sullen weeks of Una's pregnancy believing it.

SUCH AN ANGRY, BAWLING THING she was when she came near the end of April, a little over a year after Ma took ill, a tiny, squalling, red-faced infant. Perfectly formed limbs, hands and feet, nose and mouth, and perfect little seashells for ears, and eyes—the world's oldest soul was in those eyes that had no idea, yet, what colour they ought to be. Something of Ma was in them, he was sure, taking his first glimpse of her. Smears of white on her bloodied skin, white like zinc oxide, before someone bathed then wrapped her up tight as a bug in a rug, in the crooked little blanket Hannah had proudly sewn.

He had no idea who bathed her, or who if anyone besides Isla and the doctor were in the room. Something he will not forget, though—as long as he's this side of the sod—was the doctor slipping her into his arms, not Snow but the one from O'Leery who did house calls. The sound of her cries made his lungs seize, truly.

One glimpse of her, that's all it took, and the child grabbed hold of his heart and would not let go.

Things had happened too fast to get Una to the hospital, miles away in town. The most he'd managed was to run to Isla, thank the good Christ for Isla, who came to assist the doctor and was there to hold the newborn while he himself went outdoors to gulp fresh air.

God knows where on earth Win was.

She had arrived with the gloaming, the little girl. So he liked to think of her, descending like that. The crocuses were just up in the yard and it was still light enough to see them standing their ground after how many freezing rainstorms? Poor man's fertilizer, rain following sleet following snow.

Catching his breath, he stood listening to the first cries of peepers waking up in the bogs.

"Holy jeez. Holy Hannah—I have a daughter!" he called back to the clamouring peepers and the sharp, salty dampness. He hadn't guessed he would have a daughter. If he'd had a son, he might have named him Isaac: God's little trick, a trick played on parents who probably were not up to the task of childrearing.

If Ma had had a nicer name, anything but Marge, he would have plugged for that. But "Penelope" came and lodged in his head while he stood getting used to the idea—a baby, a *baby!*—and lingered when, after a little while, Clinton crossed the yard and handed him a lit cigar.

"Guess I can't give you a drink, buddy."

Hating how the cigar pushed away the smell—traces of the mother's body turned inside out, of blood and a more primal scent than those of bone or skin—he'd stubbed it out.

The name stuck with him. Penelope, the faithful wife of Odysseus. Never mind its archness, he liked its elevated, classy, classical sound.

Win—who, as it turned out, had stayed holed up next door the entire time Una laboured, figuring she'd best stay out of Una's way—thought the name was all right.

"Penny," he proposed.

"Call her whatever you like," Una said.

WIN SPOKE SHARPLY–"I DON'T SEE a thing wrong with giving formula"— when he went over there after the third day, seeking advice. "If the kid won't suck she won't suck."

In a funny way Win seemed to side more with Una and her needs than he had expected she would.

"Feed her whatever you want," was what Una said. "I'm sure you'll figure it out."

When her friend Kit came bearing a pink sweater set and booties, Una barely looked at them. She thanked Kit, though, and promised to call, before asking Hannah to take the child away and change her diaper.

Una seemed in despair. "Why must she cry so much?"

Enman wondered the same, rising repeatedly at night to help her rock the infant. "Babies cry." He said it in the kindest way possible, given Isla's reassurance that crying was normal. "We're all she has to comfort her."

Una closed her eyes. "Comfort only goes so far. And when we're no longer around to hold her hand, what then? When she's old, when she's sick. But that's neither here nor there, you think. That's just life, isn't it."

"YOU'RE JUST LUCKY SHE'S NOT colicky," Win was quick to point out, on a mission delivering tinned milk. "My second boy? You remember Garson? Clint and me, we suffered something fierce, let me tell you. Kid wouldn't sleep unless he was on me. Cried for a year without stopping."

That winter, realizing that Una could not run a business, Win had taken over from Iris Finck and by the spring was firmly in charge of the store, despite Iris overseeing it—pretending to—from the room behind the store where she stayed and wasted away with dementia.

"I appreciate your help." Enman repeated it more than once, hurrying Win out the door. They needed quiet, after all, so the baby would let her mother sleep, didn't Win realize? May had barely arrived and Una was exhausted.

"Like mother, like daughter. Tiptoe around and she'll never learn to settle, what with listening for every pin that falls."

"If we need your advice, we'll call." He spoke as gently as he could. Then Win did a funny thing. She rolled up onto her toes, patted away his hair where sweat pasted it to his forehead, and wiped spit-up from his shirt.

"I feel for you, Enman Greene. Always have, always will. There are *some* things that don't change—much. It's not my fault you're hard to reach. Once a pushover, always one."

"How do you mean?"

"You're going to spoil her, holding her all the time."

Less than a month into this and he already felt like the infant was a second skin or a shirt not to be removed. He didn't want to put her down, couldn't bear listening to her crying in her crib in Hannah's room when Hannah was at Isla's or off on her aimless jaunts. Following Una's former habit, Hannah seemed more bent on wandering than on buckling down. Win said maybe she was looking for another home.

Una grew more despondent, lay in their bed watching the ceiling. She seemed immune to his efforts, his confusion, seemed not to register his exasperation.

"You can't blame her for being born. I thought you longed for a baby." He asked point-blank, "Is it something *I've* done?"

"You? Of course not." Her face scrunched into a horrified look, even as she laughed, sort of. "Enman Greene, you are good to a fault."

IT'S NOT THAT HE BLAMED Win—why would he?—or in any way construed Win's stepping in and helping out in ways she didn't have to, as any kind of harbinger of what happened. There was absolutely nothing in *The Hygiene of Marriage* to fill him in on whatever plagued Una.

He tried to get her to see Snow. She refused.

Finally, towards the end of May, he went to see Snow himself.

a Circle on the Surface ◉ 239

The doctor showed him into his examining room, the inner sanctum where previously Enman hadn't set foot. The examining table had lobster-shaped oven mitts covering the stirrups, and, dangling over it, a baby's mobile with tiny pink and blue teddy bears. A floppy cloth rabbit wore an apron like one of Ma's, and wooden blocks sported the alphabet. They were arranged in a row to read *Love is Patient*.

One would have been forgiven for thinking the patients were four-year-olds.

Offering a strained laugh, nodding to him, Snow perhaps misread the weariness on his face. "It takes the ladies' minds off *la divina commedia*—the decor does. You know what I mean. When I'm in there, poking and prodding." The doctor sounded half apologetic. His light brown eyes looked tired but seemed kinder than Enman remembered them being.

"The baby blues? As I've said, these hormonal upheavals happen, far more often than we—"

But Enman hadn't come here to be brushed off so easily, or to beat around any bushes.

"When will she snap out of it?" He matched Snow's gaze with his.

Postpartum depression? Might last a week or two, or even a couple of months, he heard. "Having a child takes adjustment." As if Enman didn't know. Snow spoke impatiently but not without sympathy. Seeing the doctor's instruments—shiny stainless steel objects laid out on a pristine-looking towel—brought back things Enman couldn't imagine bearing, if *The Hygiene of Marriage* was in any way accurate. Una's lengthy labour. The animal grunts and screams he had tried to block out then banish from memory, noises accompanied by Isla's honeyed pleas to breathe, just breathe. He had tried his best to forget all this, especially Una's cursing: *Fuck* the man who'd done this to her, how she'd take the kitchen knife to *it* should a man, any man, come near her again.

"Now, now, Una. That's it. That's it," he had heard from behind closed doors, Isla working to calm her till the doctor arrived, the same one who'd come from O'Leery more or less just to sign Ma's death certificate.

These women, he thought. His beautiful mother. Penelope's beautiful mother. The two who mattered more to him than anyone in the world.

Dr. Snow was a taller man, a more imposing man than that other doctor. He looked bemused rather than shocked, hearing about all this.

"Oh?" he said. "A lot of them say things like that, ladies in labour. The thing about pain? Trust me, they always forget. So I wouldn't be too worried, Greene."

24

THE WORLD WAS A CHILD'S CRYING, IT WAS UNWANTED CLUTTER AND cares, it was knowing that Penelope, like everyone, would grow up, suffer, and die. The world spared no one. It was noise and chaos, smells and colours, too many colours, complications, when all Una wanted was sleep. A smooth, silent, uniform grey she longed to sink deeper into, not silvery, not speckled like a mackerel sky, but a soft unending grey which would be easier on the self, more restful than any blackness. A place where granite met cloud, a place without shadows was her hope. In this hope she saw that she had choices, choices in how to reach this place. The island would be a stepping stone, she could take a boat or swim.

Enman's Christmas gift was a blessing, a beacon that flared through the darkness that closed around her. Anne Boleyn's poem shone through the darkness, it possessed a sense all its own, a deep, gleaming sense, surrounded by the gift's bright, tinny lyrics about Christ the perfect baby, his perfect virgin mother, his hallowed, mysterious birth. Anne's lines were rolling waves, her words were colourless birds floating on the waves' crests.

Anne's words had a sanctity that whispered their encouraging approval, gave Una their glowing permission.

For Una, there would be no steely flash, as Anne's fate dictated, no huckleberries, no red besides the lighthouse's stripes, if, swimming like a fish, cold-blooded, she reached the island's rocks. She would slip under the lightkeeper's eye, beneath his beam. Meet a perfect stranger, dance with him over whalebacks, down the perfect black staircase and into the sea, to wash, perhaps, against Mad Rock. Her sorrows, her faults, her confusions and contradictions dashed away by surf. Bones dissolved in a nothingness that would absolve her of her failings and the world of its failings, and bring such peace. Rest. An end.

25

ONE FINE EVENING EARLY IN JUNE—THE LEAVES IN THE BARRENS' SCRAPPY birch and poplar trees a soft green haze visible from upstairs—Hannah bellowed up that Hill was there to see him. Enman left Una lying in bed with the baby. Hubley was in the kitchen. Hannah had a rack of bottles boiling on the stove. They were jiggling away, a half-dozen rubber nipples and a cooling pot of formula ready and waiting. Offering a bottle of a different sort, Hill was the only one in Barrein who still didn't appreciate that Enman fully intended to stay on the wagon.

"How's Missus? I hear she's not doing so good." Hubley passed the rum. Enman ignored it. Hill watched Hannah fit nipples onto the bottles, screw on lids. He looked incredulous, even a bit astonished. "She's a good kid, is she? You know, at the time I thought you were out of line, pounding Twomey like you did. He's not all bad, he never did nothing to me. Some say he deserved it, though." Hill took a swig, nudged Enman with the bottle. "Why deprive yourself of something that takes the edge off, makes things bearable?"

"Sure, and I've got a new car to sell you."

Enman knew why Hubley was here, Isaac's party almost upon them. Win and Isla had been busy for weeks organizing the dance, convincing Father Heaney to rent the hall. "So much fuss, you'd think Isaac was the Second Coming himself." Up to her eyeballs making lemon squares, fretting that no one would dance to one old guitar, Win kept dropping off samples. Bribes for Una, to coax her to get dressed and to manage the baby, even to get her to smile. "You could help yourself, Enman," Win said, "by helping us out."

Simply to appease Hill, Enman took a quick sip. The burn felt medicinal, strange yet familiar, its temptation a line being jigged down inside him, sharp as a fish hook. Hannah had the baby now, cuddling her. Penny could almost hold her head up on her tiny stalk of a neck, round eyes fixing on him. He couldn't stop searching for the old Una in them, the Una who had liked children and wanted a child. Handing the bottle back, he clipped Hill's shoulder. "Got nowhere to practice, with Una in the house."

"All that Isaac's done for you? Won't look too good, you refusing to play."

"YOU'RE SHITTING ME. I'LL BE a monkey's uncle. You're serious?" That was Hill's reaction later on the phone. "Well. Get off the horn and warm up the axe!" Greeley Inkpen said Isaac nearly fell off his chair when he got wind of Enman's willingness to play, though next evening's dance was supposed to be a surprise. Win was relieved. "Do you good to get out and make people laugh. Kidding! I mean, you've still got a life, it's a shame staying home because Una—"

The only hitch was that Hannah had been enlisted to babysit at Isla's. But Una insisted she would be fine at home with Penny.

"If you're absolutely sure," he said.

Enman stopped at Goodrows' on his way to the hall. "I'm rustier than an old rooster," he confided to Clint. "Guess it's too late now to say I've got cold feet."

"Oh, shut it, if nerves is a problem someone'll fix you up. Get in the truck, I'll run you there myself." Maybe Clint, maybe everyone, was afraid he would change his mind and chicken out.

Really, Enman felt chuffed to be out of the house, freed from the feeling of continually walking on shell ice. He was more afraid of making an ass of himself than he was of the sweet sting of temptation.

Sure enough, the Goodrow boy was parked out back with his truck, Father Heaney willing just this once to turn a blind eye. Maybe that was how you managed in this world, turning a blind eye. "Wouldn't be a party without something to wet your whistle." Clint clapped him on the back, leaving to find Win with the other ladies making tea and doing up plates of sandwiches and sweets in the hall's big kitchen. Last year's calendar, showing Christ and his glowing heart, hung on the wall.

"Don't worry about a thing. Our days of playing for free are o-ver, buddy boy." Hubley waved a forty-ouncer as Enman stepped onto the stage. "I promise you, next time it'll be cash money. Never mind. Have a drink."

"And play a decent note? Don't think so." His gut was a pot of squirming eels as he rosined his bow, the first time he'd taken it out since March. He should have practiced, could have stolen a bit of time at Inkpens', after-hours.

"You'll be fine," Hubley kept saying, as people trickled in. "I mean, you'll never be Don Messer."

The thing was, Enman didn't care about not being Don Messer, why would he? If he could choose to play like anyone, he imagined, it would be Yehudi Menuhin. "And if they don't boo me off the stage I'll be lucky."

"No, I'll be lucky. Just joshing you, En. It's a frigging party. No one's gonna care if *you* mess up, flying the coop for one night. Getting out of the house, I mean."

All of a sudden, he looked up and the hall was packed. He'd have looked even stupider fleeing than staying put, sticking things out. It was more than stage fright he felt. Maybe paralysis was recompense for a few hours' freedom?

"You know 'Little Burnt Potato'?" Hubley whispered sharply. "That's a good opener."

Enman didn't—he had heard it on the radio, sure, the latest hit by Messer and his Islanders. "Give me the lead and I'll see what I can do."

"D major, bud—F and C sharp," Hubley rasped, grinning at the crowd. "They're here for a good time, Enman. Who's here to party?" Hill boomed, then yelled, "Let's hear it for Isaac, our man, and them lovely ladies in the kitchen—" Then Hubley started strumming—plunka plunka plunk—and there was no time to worry about eels or fingering or flubbing notes or any of it. Hubley ripped through "Potato" before Enman had barely found the key, launching from there into "Levantine's Barrel" and "Flanagan's Polka" so fast that already everything sounded the same. Not a pair of feet were still, though, most people loosened up with drinks. By the time Hubley was onto "Maple Sugar" it didn't matter too much about the squawks and bleats he managed to draw out to accompany Hubley's picking.

A string of lights shone blue on Hubley's forehead, accentuating the sweat. Enman supposed he looked the same under this blue that made him think of Una's gloom. But then he peered down at the dancers having the time of their lives, frolicking in some interesting pairings, too—Sylvester Meade and Edgar Lohnes's young wife, for instance, and Isaac, God help them all, dressed to the nines and step-dancing with the priest swishing around in his cassock.

Jesus turns our sorrow into dancing, Ma might well have said. Indeed, he thought, and for a second it was as if Ma were out there too, twirling gamely on the old man's arm. His parents, the two of them just young things, and Lester Finck somewhere glowering off to the side but placing designs on Iris—poor old Iris, the only Barreiner who wasn't there, besides Twomey, Una, Hannah, and the babies. Good thing they weren't; Enman wouldn't need to be reminded tomorrow what a fool he'd made of himself.

Eyes on his fingering, he caught the roughest glimpse of Win waltzing with Clint. Her shimmery pink dress showed off her bony hips and the life ring of fat at her waist and breasts that looked higher and pointier than usual. He noted this the way he did the outline of the cemetery through the darkened windows as Hubley shifted into a medley of "Twilight" and "That Man of Mine." At the corner of his eye a pale face bobbed amidst the hail of swaying and jerking bodies and limbs, and he imagined Una. He wished it was Una, the woman in a greeny-blue dress weaving in and out among the couples. As the woman slipped forward, clapping her hands in time to Hubley's strumming, Enman recognized her as Lester Finck's niece. A woman who stood out like that would always be different from the way she appeared to be, Enman thought. Her appearance merely echoing some illusory version of herself, the way Una's appearance had. He remembered Una the skater, whirling in circles on the Egg Pond's glossy surface. She had been an illusion he had wanted to grasp and embrace and never let go of.

Unspooling herself from Clint, Win shimmied closer, beaming up at him. For a second she was the same skinny, freckled thing he'd kissed below the government wharf once at low tide, in between pulling the legs off starfish to see if they would grow back. Then Win receded and she and Clint seemed to vanish. Next the hall was emptying, like someone— Father Heaney? the ARP?—had just pulled the plug on the festivities.

"We're done already?" Finally warmed up, no longer caring at all if he hit the right notes or not, Enman felt a rush of disappointment.

"It's a fight," someone shouted. "That goddamn Twomey."

He knew then, or had a pretty good idea of, what was happening. Win and Clint were nowhere to be seen. Something made him want to sit tight and keep playing—he'd master "The Little Burnt Potato" if it killed him—but Hubley had set down his guitar and, alongside some stragglers, made for the door.

It would've been wiser to stay put. But curiosity got the better of him.

The Mounties were outside with their cruiser. Father Heaney was begging them not to press charges. Consider it a one-time error in judgement, the boy didn't mean any harm providing refreshments, think of the young fella's parents. Clint was stooped over the boy himself, Joey or Grayson or was it Garson, holding a hankie to his son's nose. Robart and Greeley had Twomey in a half nelson and a chokehold, one on either side of the guy. "Never a dull moment," Sylvester Meade jeered. "Raw justice, fellas. What happens when youse oversteps yourself. What about poor Bart here? It's his territory."

Win fled back into the hall, Enman right behind her, loosening his tie. Despite gulps of fresh air, he was still in a sweat. Win was crying, her shoulders shaking through that flimsy dress of hers. He put his arms around her. Hugging her tight to his chest, forget how sweaty he was, he felt her beery breath through his shirt. Nestled there, she was like a rocking buoy. "That's it, girl. Don't you worry. It'll come out fine," he was saying—not quite believing a word of it, but still—when Clint strode up and peeled his hands from her back. Never mind he was patting her the way he patted the baby, getting her to burp.

"Enman Greene, you smug-assed bastard." Pulling Win away, Clint marched her outside. Meanwhile, Father Heaney had come back in with Hubley. "Guess we'd better pack it in now, fellas." His dog collar looked whiter than white, never mind his hair slicked to his scalp. Isaac kept shaking his head, saying he would kill Twomey himself for wrecking a good time. "Cops'll handle him, so you won't have to," the priest said.

"So that's it?" Enman reluctantly put away his bow, eyeing Hubley. "Steady on, Steady Hills? Next time I'll be in better form."

"That's right, sir. Good enough. Come up the house for a nightcap? Tea?" Having no wife to disturb, Hubley could invite company at any hour.

"Can't."

ENMAN WALKED HOME FEELING MORE pleased than he had in ages, despite the little misunderstanding with Clint. But the instant he entered the kitchen he sensed something was off. The light was on and Penny was crying in her makeshift cradle by the stove. An empty bottle of formula rested on the table, its glass cool to the touch. Hannah was still at Isla's; they'd wanted her to stay late, settling their baby in.

Una wasn't in the front room or upstairs, nor was she in the cellar, where he'd rigged a line for drying diapers. She wasn't on the front step, or in the yard. In a panic, carrying the baby, he checked the privy. She was nowhere to be seen.

He called down to Isla's. Una wasn't there either. A few minutes later Hannah burst in, out of breath.

"Where is she?" His whisper was a hiss as he tried to avoid making Penny cry.

Una's purse was gone and her pretty winter coat too, of all things, though it was warm enough, finally, to do without one.

Aside from herself, her coat, and her purse, nothing else was missing. Aside from the baby being left alone—surely not for more than a few minutes?—nothing in the house seemed amiss.

"Hannah. Be a pet, run next door. Ask Mrs. Goodrow to come over."

It was odd how Win avoided looking at the baby, avoided looking at him as she bustled in, bustled around. It was as if she feared pitying them.

"Good thing she's on the bottle, that's all I can say—there's one way she's not missing her mum." The one way she won't, Win's tone hinted. She seemed edgy, anxious to leave, but stayed to rock Penny while Hannah ran over to Meades' and he got on the phone. Despite the hour, almost midnight, he started calling around. Robart's wife hadn't seen her nor had Iris Finck, whom he roused from a very deep sleep.

As if moving about under water, hitting on the obvious, fighting disbelief, he dialled Kit's number. Kit had come to visit and Una, somehow, had gone back with her to enjoy what she could of a change of scenery, some brief entertainment.

"She said she'd be here, with me?" Kit sounded dodgy, then distressed.

Enough bloody runaround, he almost said. "Look, put her on the phone. If she won't come on the phone, put her in the car, bring her home."

"You're barking up the wrong tree." But Kit seemed more afraid than peeved. "Enman. She's not here."

The baby had fallen asleep. Win put her upstairs in her crib and went to get Clint. A little while later the Goodrows came over together, Clint acting as if his outburst earlier hadn't happened. One o'clock arrived and, fearing a mishap—Una had taken herself out for a breather, a stroll in the dark, had fallen, twisted an ankle, and, befuddled, disoriented, become lost—Enman had Clint help rally a search party.

Despite the hour, despite the dark, all the men in the village, including the priest, the Inkpens, Hubley, Sylvester Meade, and his son—pretty much everyone but Bart Twomey—combed the barrens and the shoreline in both directions, east and to the west past the third beach at Shag's.

When by daybreak they turned up nothing, others came from O'Leery to join in the search, Timmy Flood and all three Goodrow boys including Joey, and even Twomey, begrudgingly, parties fanning out into the woods. They found nothing, no trace.

IN THE DAYS THAT FOLLOWED, the police helped check the East Coast Port's hospitals, the bus and train stations, even the docks and harbourmaster's office for ships' departures and manifests, and, eventually, the city morgue. Out of desperation Enman called the superintendent of schools, and the cousin of a cousin of Una's who'd died in a torpedoed convoy, and even her former principal who offered the name and number of a fellow named Gregory. But nobody could say or would even hazard a guess about where Una might have disappeared to.

There was no note—he turned the house upside down, looking for one—nothing with her writing but the poetry book with her name penned inside, and a grocery list with items jotted down. Canned salmon, cornstarch, Brillo pads. On the back, in Hannah's printing, was a bit of gibberish, the words "kan n e 1 b to god?"

Puzzling it out, he whispered into the baby's downy scalp, "I don't know, do you? Can a father be that way, too good?"

"I'M SORRY FOR YOUR TROUBLES," Hill said over the phone, which was better to hear than "for your loss." Because as far as Enman was concerned, Una was gone on a vacation, that was all. A dastardly, heartbreakingly selfish one, granted, but her smell was still in the house, her old smile hovering in those yellow walls, lingering in their gaudy paint whenever he noticed it. "Get out your axe. Play some tunes. Keep busy." Hubley's advice, as if his days of noodling on violin weren't finally over.

If he hadn't gone off to play, she would not have been alone.

WIN WAS AN ANGEL DOING what she could to help, short of becoming a wet nurse or doormat, though careful to leave diapering to him and Hannah. "Been there, done that." Understandable, he supposed.

Without Win, Hannah could not have managed on her own. And he could not have managed half as well as Hannah did. It was a good thing Hannah liked babies. Not knowing what exactly had happened to Una threatened to bury him alive.

A couple of weeks after Una disappeared, on a run to town, Robart spotted something floating in the waters near the Sisters bell buoy: something blue, Robart reported.

Hearing this, Enman got Clinton to take him out in his boat and they circled around and around, looking and looking, motoring slowly toward the vast, rocking harbour. It was barely summer and threatening rain, and the sea had a steely roll to it. Yet suddenly, strangely, Enman had no fear. He had no fear of the water or the sea at all, he realized.

He and Clinton hugged the shoreline and scouted it as closely as they could. Seeing nothing, nothing at all, they veered out deeper again, and not far from the Neverfail can buoy, Clinton spied a piece of clothing hugging the swells.

Clothing, that's all it was when Enman managed to snag and gaff it aboard. Foolish, *foolish*, the strange leap of something, a flare, not exactly of hope, in his chest. It was just an old rag left to float, cast adrift, lost by someone off some longliner, perhaps. A ragged old coat, its wool was streaked with salt and gnawed by fish and propellers, battered by waves. A bearded mussel clung to one cuff—you couldn't even tell what shade of blue the coat might have been, though something about it suggested a bright cornflower hue.

As he turned it over in the bottom of the boat, peering down, he looked and looked again. And he recognized a button.

There was just the one that the sea hadn't stolen. It was a scratched, faded blue that once might have been almost black, inset with a tiny circle of mother-of-pearl that had somehow survived the surf. Seeing that mother-of-pearl, he hung his head over the side and vomited, aware of Clint stepping past him to the wheelhouse.

Neither of them spoke as they steamed homewards with their find. What was there to say? Enman knew then with certainty that Una was not coming back.

HE BURIED THE COAT IN the garden, unsure about what else to do with it. It felt like some observance of church ritual. He kept the button, though, in a little wooden box Una had given him to keep his cufflinks in. She'd bought it when he bought her the coat for her birthday, at Wood's department store.

It was hard not to picture her admiring herself in Wood's three-way mirrors, tucking in her chin to admire its single-breasted row of buttons. "Gosh, I've never seen anything like these, have you? Oh, En. Hon." She had pressed close, watching him pay, a little in awe of him, perhaps, and spared making her usual joke, "Buy it for me and I'll be your best friend." One day he would give the button to Penny, he decided, not that it would mean an awful lot.

Though he asked anyone with a boat to continue keeping an eye out, nothing further was found. Una had left nothing to suggest she meant to leave them forever, to do such a thing as walk deliberately into the sea. Who knows but leaving home to get some air she hadn't slipped from a rock, and before she could scramble back up and gain her footing, a wave hadn't caught her and pulled her out. In that heavy coat she would not have had half a chance.

Then, not long after burying the coat, opening the *English Galaxy* book, Enman stumbled upon and re-read that poem of Anne Boleyn's.

Oh Death, rock me asleep
    Bring me to quiet rest.
Let pass my weary guiltless ghost
    Out of my careful breast.

If not for Una's beautiful signature inside the book, penned in her schoolteacher's hand, he might have buried it, too.

He struggled not to imagine her last breaths as she entered the ocean's airless vault. For months, night after night, this image floated then beached itself in his dreams: his wife's greyish face, still lovely though lost-looking and thin, a little choker of eelgrass around her neck and her blue eyes cold. A beachstone, perhaps, in each filmy pocket of the green dress he'd helped her pick out before he ever entertained the notion of moving them to Barrein and into Ma's house. The dress's bodice was girlishly modest and maybe this was a good thing, as the tides and the currents did their best to twist and tear it away.

When Penny was older, much older, he decided, he might tell her about the dress, and even about the coat, though probably not. When she was ready, though, he would tell her, one day, how it was the worst thing to find and fall for someone who only pretended that you were their heart's desire. Remember never to hide your true feelings, he would say, he promised himself. Don't hide your true thoughts, especially from yourself. Remember, my duck. It's what he would always call her. Because at four or five months of age, that's what she reminded him of, a duck, the noises she made blowing spit bubbles. Those eyes, resolutely blue, gazing up at him. Tiny fingers wrapped around the bottle, tiny mouth sucking away on its kelp-coloured nipple like her life depended on it, which it did. One solid thing she had to hold onto.

While she fed, that trusting infant gaze of hers had steadily warmed to him as she gave herself over completely to his care and to Hannah's. Poor Hannah, who, unbeknownst to herself, kept them going. Even the day, not sixth months after Penny's birth, when Win phoned while he was at work—Inkpens' busy enough with repairing and an interest in building small, inshore craft—to say a letter had come. A letter for Una. From someplace in Ontario. It was odd for Win to call like that, since she preferred to avoid using the phone with Mrs. Finck there. By then, of course, the rumours were flying, because of Una's disappearance. That she'd been a spy! And other rumours wilder than anything a dozen Wins and Iris Fincks could have concocted. But enough, sometimes, to make him wonder how he could have taken up with such a woman, and think he might've been better off had he chosen not to marry but to remain single, like some old priest, like Father Heaney in his big draughty glebe.

That blustery autumn day, Hannah had bundled up the baby and gone to collect the letter. He found her at the kitchen table, scrutinizing the postmark through a magnifying glass, the one he used for reading extra-fine figures.

"Es-pan-o—?"

Then she looked at him palely, the colour draining from her face. "Who could be writin' to Missus? Jesus—is it Jesus writin' her, you think?"

Enman drew in a breath. "What kind of a joke is that, now—?" He might've risen to it too, as arch as it was playful. He might've laughed. Instead, "Espanola," he read out, as calm as could be, bouncing Penny, then depositing her into the girl's arms. The name rang a bell. There had been mention of the place in the paper, maybe: a prisoner-of-war camp set up in an old pulp mill or factory, up there somewhere in Northern Ontario? Not a place you'd want to visit let alone stay—and he remembered that day in the car with Una, seeing those prisoners being marched across the railway tracks. The day the Prime Minister of Britain had promised everybody victory, victory for either side in any war a pyrrhic victory, Enman thought.

The letter, written in pencil, had no date and no salutation besides "Hello."

I hope this finds you. You might not remember me, in Freundschaft I thank you that some Canadians are decent. My mother, father, and sister as you remember are no longer living. I did not mean to frighten you, what I said about whores in Berlin I ask you to forget. Here, is too much forest, more trees. In your countryside my men and I walked many miles through Gottverlassenen wilderness in search of Unterhaltung, amusement. We found Sehr schlecht alcohol. Violence broke out between my men, ein kampf. One became defunct, he would not have died had I commanded better. In war, far from home, this happens.

It was signed, simply, *Wilhelm Mohr*, and on the back was drawn a map. It showed all the continents laid out crudely—rolled flat like pie dough, Hannah remarked—with dots marking, roughly, two distant points. One was the East Coast Port, it appeared, and the other was some place above the northern shoreline of a Great Lake, Lake Huron. "Weltkarte" had been pencilled below in the same hand.

Map of the World, he guessed it meant, balling the letter up. Lifting a burner, he went to stuff it into the stove.

"Shouldn't do that, Mister. What if Missus comes back?"

So he put the letter inside a ledger, one the bank had no need of seeing any time soon. Then he took the baby back into his arms and pressed his nose to her scalp, the triangular spot where the bones of her skull hadn't yet fused. He hugged her as fiercely as you can hug a baby.

"I'm sorry, Hannah. But I wouldn't hold my breath for something that's not going to happen."

Nodding, she slouched over to the bottom drawer, the one for cake pans and muffin tins, which he avoided because these things reminded him so sharply of Una's attempts at baking, and said, "I'm sorry too, Mister." She dug out a clean diaper, wrapped around something.

Ma's figurine, the head snapped off in precisely the place he'd glued it last time

"I didn't mean to bust it. Cross my heart and hope—"

"Oh, now. I've got just the stuff to fix 'er up—don't worry."

IT WAS WIN WHO SAID he couldn't and mustn't keep things from Penny. Win who insisted that when Penny was old enough to get her period she should be old enough to know about her mother. This might have been Win simply breaking the ice before catching him off guard:

"It was my mistake, see, taking up with Clinton. I don't suppose, Enman, you and I are too old to reconsider?"

Win had brought over a tall loaf of porridge bread fresh from the oven, and he'll never forget how good it smelled cooling in his kitchen. Laying a dishtowel over it, she'd looked at him, suddenly all a-flush.

Taken utterly by surprise, knocked off his pins, aghast, he had felt robbed of speech.

"Let's pretend you never said that." He flung the loaf back into her empty pan. "Edwina. You go home now and tell Clinton to make you some toast and a pot of tea. Go on home and be good to him."

Enough charity, he almost said, we'll make out on our own just fine, thanks. But watching Win flee with her offering, he guessed there was no need to.

For charity began at home, everyone knew. Only after that, proper thing, should it be spread around. So when at last he could bring himself to go through Una's clothes—dresses still on their hangers, all but the green one she must have been wearing when she disappeared, tops, slacks, and undies stuffed into their drawers—he gave them to Isla's daughter, who was about Una's size. Once he got started, it wasn't so hard unloading the rest: all Ma's glad rags, which he fobbed off on poor old Iris Finck, not that she noticed.

And dutifully he found the glue and reattached the Beautiful Mother's head, broken off at the familiar faultline. Some day he'd see if they could mend it at Birks, have it professionally fixed, or else toss it. But at what point was a trinket worthless enough to throw out? When it no longer made him think of Ma, Una, and carols like "Silent Night" and Britten's "There is No Rose of Such Virtue," with their lyrics about a blessed virgin mother?

26

HE HASN'T SEEN THE GOODROWS IN YEARS NOW, NEITHER HIDE NOR HAIR of either one, not since he and the girls left—seven years this summer, to be exact. Sometimes he misses having such close neighbours. He doesn't suppose they've changed much, Win and Clinton, the way the food at Camille's, this joint by the bridge, hasn't.

Sitting across from him, Penny waves her fork like a baton, like she's conducting a symphony for the waitress's benefit. Why is lunch taking so long?

Enman gives her the eye. She's always been a little impatient, precocious.

"What, Dad—they had to go catch the fish? Go all the way out to sea?"

All the way to sea, all the way to Barrein, he thinks. After the war, he'd been keen to get both girls moved and settled before Penny started school. Edgar Lohnes was looking for a house, his wife having a baby, so it was a no-brainer, in a way, selling off the old place to a ready buyer.

It was just a house after all, just a building, just some wood, bricks, and fieldstones—though no amount of money could cover its worth. He still feels that way. But he doesn't suppose, given how things have turned out, Ma would mind so much having the neighbours eating off her Royal Albert plates. Still, it wasn't easy getting rid of everything—everything but a few keepsakes packed into a box placed on Beulah's back seat for the drive, Ma's figurine among them. It wasn't easy leaving Barrein, even harder, maybe, for Hannah. But she's made out all right since getting hired as a packer at Moir's chocolate factory. The Beautiful Mother—he could almost laugh, and barely stifles a smile—hasn't done nearly as well, having not made it as far as O'Leery, intact. It could survive a shipwreck, but not that road. One of these days he'll get around to taking it to Birks, he will. Maybe.

Penny's fish arrives. Steam rises from the battered halibut as she squirts on ketchup, vinegar, pours on salt.

"Whoa, there—that's plenty, duck." He says it just to bug her. Still, that much salt can't be good for you. Is there a point with a child when you can quit repeating yourself, repeating things like a broken record?

"Don't forget your tartar sauce."

She pushes the tiny cup of it his way.

"You're as bad as your grandmother, salt on everything. She used to put it on salt cod, for Pete's—"

"Sheesh. That's one of my favourite stories." She doesn't roll her eyes, the way he imagines a teenager would. He's already said, too often, that for the longest time she reminded him of his mother.

Watching Pen stripe each fry with ketchup, he searches for Ma's reluctance in her smile. Of course it's not there. It never has been. No matter what, though, he loves watching Pen eat, he can almost feel the fish flake between his molars. Her smile is as reserved and mysterious and, exactly in these ways, as resilient *and* half-cracked as the Beautiful Mother's—the thought of which makes him smile. Again.

"If it could survive a shipwreck, so can you," he used to tell her as a baby, and he says it now.

Her uncomprehending eyes are pools, reserves, of what happened before she came into the world and, perhaps—who knows?—what might go on happening after she leaves it. After they all leave it.

It gives him pleasure watching her do almost anything, even certain activities that he expects she will complain about, with justification or not. Get ready, he's heard, teenagers do a lot of this. But Pen's thoughtful. Unhooking itself from the chair, his cane clatters to the linoleum. Penny retrieves and hooks it over the table's edge. She's always been good like this, a good kid, kind, even-tempered, except when she was three or four and would throw a fit if her socks didn't match her skirt.

"Like mother, like daughter," Win once sniped.

"Don't give me that," was all he had said.

She's always been good with Hannah, Pen has. Patient. Sometimes too patient. As a tiny thing she'd take Hannah by the wrist and lead her around the yard. "This, Hannah, is larkspur—*that* is a delphinium."

"Well I seen it's got a flower on it!"

He still keeps a garden, though there's not the time to give it the attention it needs. Arthritis in his knees now and the old damage to his shins means that for every day spent digging, the price is two days' hobbling. But the soil's better here in town, even if the neighbouring houses are so close they block the sun and limit his beds' exposure. Too much shade is a small price for the advantages both girls would have missed, otherwise. It hasn't been all bad, his accountant's position at the bank, the best they could offer him—not too shabby a move, after Isaac Inkpen died and the boatyard closed. A little more luck and he'll be done there before too much longer. Retirement, what a concept.

"Remember to remember," he hears himself say. "When something's right, you just know, duck."

She has a slight sprinkling of acne, a few tiny pimples, probably from eating the seconds that Hannah brings home from her job. All three of them, him, Pen, and Hannah, are idjits for chocolate, just ask Hannah.

Patting her stomach, his girl pushes her plate towards him. "Going once, going twice, Dad?"

He allows himself a fry. Just one. Greasy stuff doesn't agree with him, if it ever did.

At the counter, customers who've been here all along—both of whom, he noticed when they arrived, have had too much to drink—argue over the bill. The waitress argues back, fed up, you can tell. Did he get this stroppy when he used to hit the bottle? He hopes not. Steering clear of the sauce hasn't been easy. But doing so is the thing that relegates his worst sins to the past and keeps them there.

"Aren't you gonna have your drink, Pen?"

On cue, she takes a big pink slurp of cream soda. It moves like mercury inside the straw. God, he thinks, Una and her temperature-taking, which he had happened upon a couple of times. The rigamarole, the performance. But it led to this, didn't it, more or less? To this perfect girl. Once she gets her period, wait till then to tell her? Or that was Win Goodrow's advice. So he may be jumping the gun, a little?

Her round, bright eyes search his. "So what's the big secret? You've got something to tell me?"

Teenagers. They have the attention span of grasshoppers, he's read—but maybe that's a good thing? Or she could be like Ma, poor Ma, with her superstitions and practicality. But maybe we're all like that, it strikes him. Silly and stalwart, impulsive and wise.

There are so many ways to avoid being broken.

There are so many ways to be. In Penny's eyes he sees life's possibilities. In her eyes, so straightforward and blue, are the world's currents pooling as effortlessly as the ocean's, swirls and stripes, striations, moving past the off-ing at each tide's turn. Whether ebbing or flowing, it hardly matters. What matters are their ripples and ceaseless, shifting hues.

Who knows but someday—while watching herself in the mirror, brushing her hair or putting on lipstick—she'll glimpse all of this too and be reminded, somehow. That before she or anyone was born, something of herself and of everyone—though nothing you might put a finger on—was known to the world:

The way we love, in spite of everything. The way nothing is fair in love or in war, and yet we keep breathing.

Ignoring the part about breathing, not having faith in it, *shiza*, we're kitty litter, Hannah would say.

"Okay, Dad. Didn't you say there's cake? And presents? And since you're taking for-flipping-ever and not going to tell me this big scary thing—"

Catching his eye, rid at last of those gnarly drunks, the waitress brings the bill. She's set two pink Chicken Bones on top of it, which happen to be Hannah's favourite candy.

Presents, yes—lots of presents, he's thinking. These include a bracelet similar to Penny's for Hannah, hardly expensive but a token to even things out, not that this trinket with *its* tiny charms—a miniature book, sewing machine, and harmonica—begins to.

He fingers the thing left wrapped in his hankie, the button as thin as a dime, best forgotten. Just wait till Pen sees the piano: the brand new, walnut-finished, apartment-size Heintzman, which, with any luck, Phinney's has delivered in plenty of time to swap out the rental. Yet even as he thinks this he imagines her reaction, preparing for what might be a letdown, his.

"My darling girl. If that's what I said, that's what I said. Sweetpea," he calls her. Except for her eyes, she looks nothing like her mother. She looks nothing like *his* mother, nor does she look anything like him. It's taken a long time to reconcile himself to this. Now he feels for the envelope in his jacket's inner pocket, the envelope with its crumpled, one-page letter. The strange, solemn respect for Una it had imparted, eventually, once its chill and his numbness subsided. The respect of distance.

Otherwise, he might've taken a cue from Iris Finck, poor dead Iris, steaming open envelopes, but gone further, held the letter in the steam from the kettle not to smooth but obliterate it, turn its paper and pencilled words to grey mush.

Over the years he has grown more and more certain that its writer must be, is, her father. But whoever her father is or was no longer matters—if, in fact, it ever truly did. Pen looks like herself.

"I love you, and not just because I raised you," he imagines Ma saying.

So he begins, stalling for time, a little:

"Let me tell you what I can about the person who gave birth to you. Let me tell you what I know about her."

Then he hesitates. Changing tack, he tells her how much, in fact, she was wanted. Wanted with everything he and that person were made of. How much she is loved. How much she has taught him about love and something of the need not to cling to your ideas of what love means but to be willing at times to let these ideas go.

"Guess what? You're stuck with me. And not just because I've put up with, um, raised you, Pen."

One of her favourite jokes.

She wrinkles her nose, scowls. Is there anything known to nature that'll match a teenager's disgust? "That's it? That's all?" No longer a child, she is not old enough, or wise enough, or woman enough—yet—to be made weary by the things that wear you down, that wear you out.

"I didn't really know your mum, not very well. Not the way I wish I had. Not the way I should have," he apologizes. Reaching inside his jacket, he takes out the letter. He slides it gently across the tabletop and into her hands. Smooth, nimble hands that are warm, and still small enough to be a child's. The way they have always fit into his.

His own beautiful child's.

"Perhaps," he tells her, "perhaps this person knew her a little bit better."

AUTHOR'S NOTE

RUMOURS ABOUNDED ABOUT U-BOAT CREWS COMING ASHORE IN ATLANTIC Canada during the Second World War, rumours largely based on hearsay and dismissed as fable. Enman and Una's tale is exactly this, a fable. Barrein and O'Leery are imaginary places, though they share a few geographical features with communities in Halifax's Mainland South. Mad Rock, though, is as "real" as real can be, a shoal charted at 44° 25′ 52″ N, 063° 33′ 37″ W near Sambro Island, and part of the treacherous Sambro Ledges, the site of countless shipwrecks. Neverfail is a shoal in Halifax Harbour, first documented in 1826, named in 1853 by Royal Navy surveyer Captain Bayfield, and ever since 1893, marked by a succession of can, light, and bell buoys. One of dozens of navigational aids in the world's second-largest natural harbour, as it operates today the Neverfail Shoal Light and Bell Buoy is marked H8 on the Canadian Coast Guard's List of Lights, Buoys and Fog Signals, its List of Lights number 518. Its position is 44°33′15.5″N, a location off Bear Cove, between Chebucto Head and Tribune Head near Herring Cove. In 1943, the year this story takes place, a black can buoy with "Neverfail" painted on it was laid to mark "a 4½ fathom patch" while its corresponding light and bell buoy was moved "about one cable to the south," according to the late Rear Admiral Hugh F. Pullen. This is the marker Enman and his friends kept an eye out for. Just so you know.

ACKNOWLEDGEMENTS

THANKS BEYOND MEASURE TO THE WONDER WOMEN AT NIMBUS/VAGRANT, the amazing Whitney Moran, Terrilee Bulger, Elaine McCluskey, Heather Bryan, Emily MacKinnon, and Karen McMullin, as well as to Matthew McNeill. Thanks to my brilliant editor, Bethany Gibson, who asked the many tough questions that helped to anchor fable with realism and make the novel what it needed to be. Thanks to my writers' group, Lorri Neilsen Glenn, Binnie Brennan, and Ramona Lumpkin, for their encouragement and grit. Thanks to the National Museum of War in Ottawa, Maritime Command, the Maritime Museum of the Atlantic, Veronica Stevenson at the Canadian Coast Guard Marine Communications and Traffic Services (MCTS), and the Mainland South Heritage Society, all in Halifax. Thanks to Cindy Handren, Shawn Brown, and Dawn Rae Downton for all our laughter. Thanks to Dan Conlin for his tour of Sambro Island and sharing the tale of the Devil's Staircase. Thanks to the late William Naftel and to Stephen Kimber for their books on Second World War–era Halifax, and to the late Rear Admiral Hugh F. Pullen, RCN, for *The Sea Road to Halifax: Being an Account of the Lights and Buoys of Halifax Harbour* (1980), which contains L. B. Jenson's 1976 drawing of the Neverfail Shoal light and bell buoy. Thanks to William Hall's 1912 *Navigation* in The People's Books series, for elucidating, sort of, why someone might call a ship a *she*. The passages on eugenics and child-bearing which appear in the novel are borrowed from Millard Spencer Everett's *The Hygiene of Marriage*, 1942 edition, pages 132 to 135. My deepest thanks go, as always, to my sons, Andrew, Angus, and Seamus Erskine, who drew me to Alex Colville's 1995 serigraph,

Navigation, an image which helped clarify my vision of Una. Most of all my thanks go to Bruce Erskine, for riding my writerly waves and being my patient, life-saving buoy during the intensive rewriting and revising of this book. Without your love and support, I would be a dustball under my desk, seriously.

OTHER BOOKS BY
CAROL BRUNEAU

After the Angel Mill

Depth Rapture

Purple for Sky

Berth

Glass Voices

These Good Hands

A Bird on Every Tree